D0193787

High Tide at Noon

High Tide at Noon
by Elisabeth Ogilvie

DOWN EAST BOOKS / CAMDEN, MAINE

Copyright 1944, 1971 by Elisabeth Ogilvie
Reprinted by arrangement with the author
ISBN 0-89272-216-9
Cover design by Michael McCurdy
Composition by The Sant Bani Press, Tilton, N.H.
Printed in the United States of America

5   4

Down East Books / Camden, Maine

To Donald MacCampbell

Although the characters represented in this book
are entirely fictitious,
Bennett's Island actually exists — under another name.

Other novels by Elisabeth Ogilvie
reprinted by Down East Books:

Storm Tide
The Ebbing Tide

1

THE ISLAND LAY VERY STILL under the clear golden light of a midsummer noon. The whole world was bathed in a windless silence, steeped in warmth. Yet the air, alive with a peculiar clarity, had a sparkling edge.

Here in the great bay the sea held a blue that shook the heart, but the sky laid hold on you in a different way. The islands rose from one blueness and touched another, and in the glowing light they shone white and creamy and tawny and red, crested darkly with spruce. On the farthest northern horizon the mountains billowed along the sky in richly tender curves, grape-blue with distance. It was a day to drink like wine, and feel its intoxication seep through your heart and soul.

The dragger was incongruously dingy and loud in all this brilliant silence. Bound for the fertile grounds far to the east of the Island, it had swerved from its course to enter the harbor. It was such a quiet harbor that when the engine stopped, and the boat slid noiselessly toward the wharf, the silence beat hard against the woman's eardrums. Or was it her heart that hammered so? She didn't know; she only knew she was taut with the effort of sitting still on the bow while the man made a line fast to the wharf. She sat Indian fashion, hands gripping her ankles, and her eyes tried to see everything at once. There lay the Island; entering the harbor, you were in its arms. She'd always thought that, ever since she could first remember.

How strange the harbor was now, like a blue bowl filled to brimming, the water hardly murmuring as it moved against the rocks. Strange, and dreamlike . . . There were no boats at the moorings, that was it. Not even a punt or a dory left behind, not even a forgotten mooring buoy. There were no slim white boats lying above their tranquil reflections, no faint click of oarlocks across the harbor as a dory came out from the beach. Even the gulls were hushed in this hushed place, where the buildings stood locked and boarded-up along the shore, knee-deep in beach peas and evening primrose. The houses stood desolate against the woods, their gardens gone wild and full of birdsong now that there was no one to frighten the singers. The windows looked down at the harbor and the dragger, and the woman there on the bow, and they were blank and unseeing; yet, curiously, they stared.

"Wharf never was much good," one of the men grumbled, and she turned to look at him, eyes wide and dark in the pallor of her face. She spoke as if she were in a dream. "What did you say?"

"I said the damn wharf never was much good, and it's sure gone to pieces since nobody's been usin' it. It'll come down for fair in the next williewaw. Don't look as if 'twould hold you, Jo."

"Oh, she ain't so hefty," the younger man said, as she stood up and stretched her cramped body. There was a wing of too-early whiteness in her black hair, but she had kept a young girl's slenderness, and her bones were strong and long under smooth, healthy brown skin.

"I guess I'll be leaving you boys," she said. "It was grand of you to go out of your way to drop me here, Larry."

The older man looked dourly at the Island. "What I don't like is leavin' you here, a woman alone in this godforsaken place twenty-five miles from nowhere. It gives me the creeps just to look at it. Too quiet."

"It's waiting," said the woman in a low voice, and her lips curved in a small secret smile. Then it widened and flashed across her face, full of an inner vitality that made her dark eyes wonderfully alive in spite of their weariness. "What is there to be afraid of? It's safer here than it's ever been. And the house is still there." She began to climb the ladder to the wharf, her hands and feet swift and familiar on the rungs. "Toss up my stuff, Larry, and thanks again."

"You're sure you ain't scared?"

"*Scared?*" She was scornful. "Go catch your fish. I'll see you when you come back tonight."

Larry scowled and shrugged, plainly disavowing responsibility.

The younger man, casting off, looked up at her with an unmistakable glint that said *She's a fine woman, easy on the eyes.* Then the dragger was on its way again, its engine echoing back and forth between the red and tawny-yellow ledges with an ear-shattering clamor. The woman stood alone on the wharf without an atom of uncertainty in her bearing; her hands were thrust into the pockets of her shabby suit jacket, her neck rose slim and strong and brown from the open collar of her blouse. Her black head was high, and her chin had unconsciously squared. She was listening. She was watching. . . .

There were no boats in the harbor now, no lobsters in the lobster car that floated, an empty and rotting box, beside the empty and rotting wharf. There was no sound of saw and hammer from the workshops, no freshly painted buoys hung against weathered shingles, no new traps of yellow wood piled high on the beach rocks. Bennett's Island was a desert island now, forgotten and scorned save by the woman whose footsteps sounded so strange in the emptiness.

Joanna Bennett had come home.

It was queer how the smell of fish clung to the old shed on the wharf. At the far end of its gloom there was daylight, sun and spruce trees, and a blue sky. She walked among the old hogsheads that had been such a torment to her curiosity in the days when her head barely reached the tops, and she couldn't see what fascinating and pungent treasures they contained. Now, though she knew they were empty, she couldn't resist stopping to look, and then went on, grinning a small grin at herself. It felt good. Her face had been quiet and unsmiling for so long.

She came out by the store, with its cobwebbed windows — at least the spiders still lived on the Island. The red paint around the door was faded to pink, and the sign, Bennett's Island Post Office, was hardly readable. Now she was in the village, and all at once its silence swept down and entered into her so that she walked along like a creature in a dream, herself no more real than that dream.

The old path was choked with Queen Anne's lace, evening primrose, the delicate blue chicory, and tansy; it smelled hot and aromatic in the windless sunshine, and it was full of small contented buzzings. When she passed the dun-colored shabbiness of the house called the Binnacle, she could look up toward the well. The grass had grown tall around it, in its central place in a field that was a silvery-green sea. She went toward it along an overgrown path and put the cover back; below, she saw her own face darkly, with blue sky behind her head.

When she looked up she saw Gunnar Sorensen's windbreak of spruces. The big house behind them had always been dazzlingly white and exquisitely neat, its shrubs groomed with Scandinavian tidiness. Now the clapboards were grayed with wind and weather, the seven-sisters bush that crawled over the door was rosy and white with unpruned bloom, and the hollyhocks hid the windows in tropical flamboyance. The lilac plumes had faded on their bush.

Joanna turned away from the well and went down the road. She went past the fish houses built on the shore, with their spindle-shanked wharves high above the rocks. Here was the long bait house where the men had kept their hogsheads of herring, across the road from the old wharf where the boats were hauled up for repairs. If she looked hard at the ruins, she thought, she would see herself squatting there in overalls and tattered sneakers, black pigtails down her back, peering with intent and pretended understanding down into the cockpit of her father's boat and listening to the intricate and sometimes profane diagnosis of the engine's ailments. But somehow it always happened that he looked up, his squarish brown face absorbed, and saw her there.

"Run home now, and help your mother," he said patiently, day after day. "The shore's no place for a girl." She would go, her heart seething because the boys could stay, even the ones who were younger than she. Men had all the privileges in the small but complete universe that was the Island.

Beyond the beach, where a great anchor had been sunk in the pebbles and sharp-edged grass since long before she could remember, the road turned off. One might go around the curve of the beach, on a plank wall over the stones, and reach the handful of houses built there above the water's reach; they had the high bulk of eastern Harbor Point beyond them to cut off the wind, and the fields behind them. Or one followed the proper road through the tawny, sweet-smelling marsh that was so starred with the heart-shaking blue of wild flag.

Joanna turned into the road, lingered by the old boats on their sides at the edge of the marsh. The battered and disreputable sloop was there, the one she used to play in; one mast had fallen at a crazy angle, but the other one still tilted gallantly at the sky. And here was another boat, not so old. . . . Unbelievingly her finger traced the faded name, and something wept soundlessly within her for this boat, hauled up into the marsh, the once trim and glistening whiteness of her, because her skipper thought he'd be coming back. . . . The boat was named *Donna*.

She hung back, looking at the harbor and the little dilapidated camps near the anchor, and the way by which she had come through the sunlit emptiness of the village. She looked everywhere but before her as she followed the road into the marsh. But finally, in spite of herself, her eyes were tugged upward and she saw the house.

It was built on a high place between two coves, at the top of a sloping meadow; the road went to the foot of the meadow and turned off to border Schoolhouse Cove, which was the shape of placidly shining loveliness in the noon sunshine, and wander off through the daisy-spattered fields to end where a cluster of white buildings gleamed against the Eastern End woods.

But Joanna had no concern with those houses and the woods. She left the road and went on soft sand among the sprawling, gray-green beach peas and stiff primrose, and walked through gate posts bleached to silver. Grass muffled her feet now. As she went up the slope, Schoolhouse Cove lay below her left hand, and at her right lay the whole meadow, a veritable pool of sunlight lying against the massive darkness of spruce woods. And before her there was the house against the sky.

Joanna stopped, and the scent of the Island was all around her, red clover and white, sun-warmed juniper, bayberry leaves, and the sea. Her hands were tight in her pockets and her heart was swelling until it was too big, until it was stopping her breath, and making her throat ache. She was no more an unreal creature walking in a dream. She was flesh and blood, and she stood in an emptiness worse than she had ever dreamed. At this moment she knew the full stature of her loneliness. She wanted to storm at the silent trees, the unmoving rocks, the great, placid, unthinking ocean; she wanted to fling herself into the grass, and dig her nails into the warm moist earth, and stifle her mouth against it.

In an instant that was like eternity, the storm passed. Reality was upon her. . . . They're all gone, she said to herself. You know where they are, why they're not here. You know which are dead, and why the others will never come back. You knew before you came. But you came, didn't you? *You're home.*

But this wasn't home, a deserted island taken captive by the grass, an empty house against a hard blue sky. Somehow she forced her feet onward through the tangled grass, dreading to come to the house and its irrevocable solitude, yet driven. She looked around her with strained and desperate eyes, as if seeking a sign. There was no sign.

She reached the front doorstep. The grass was high around the stone, and the rose bush sprawled its long suckers across the door. She thought, you could pick roses from the sitting room window, little spicy white ones . . . and she saw her mother standing on the stone slab, pruning back the branches, her face serene and absorbed and all the great wide sun-washed world of sea and sky around her.

Her breath quivered in her throat. She was sharply grateful for the raucous shriek of crows flying toward the woods. With a swift thrust she put the key in the lock, and the door swung open, almost as if it had been waiting for her touch. The smell of a closed and empty house came to her nostrils. Closed and empty for a long time. . . . She went in, and shut the door behind her.

The silence of an empty house, from which all voices and the sound of feet have gone away, is different from the sunlit silence of out-of-doors. At least there you can feel the wind on your face and see the grass stir. But the door was shut behind the woman, Joanna, and this inside quiet was a heavy and tangible thing. It sent a tautness through her body; she found herself straining her ears for a sound somewhere — no matter how faint — and she walked on tiptoe, as if she must preserve the stillness, as if some doom would fall on her if she marred this perfect hush.

But it was strange to be quiet where there had been so much noise. Almost she could hear feet running on the stairs that rose before her into the gloom. Her breath caught sharply. Oh, God, she thought, and folded her arms tightly across her breast to stifle the pain that burned like a physical thing. She moved like one entranced toward the kitchen.

Sunlight lay in pale rectangles on a floor coated thinly with dust. The silence held; there was not even a fly to drone through the warmth. She walked across the room, forgetting to tiptoe, and her light step seemed brazenly loud. With brown hands that wanted to tremble, she took a key from a nail and wound the old-fashioned clock · on the shelf. She would make a sound, she thought, and take away this terrible emptiness.

Suddenly, with a mad whirring of wheels, the clock began to strike. She stood staring at it, her hand to her mouth, crying silently to it to stop. But it went on and on, and memory sprang into being in her brain, vivid and cruel.

There was another time when the clock had gone mad like that. Without volition her feet carried her toward the sink: her hands moved out to touch the cold edge and her eyes lifted to the old mirror hanging there. She saw her face in the greenish depths, hollowed and pale, her hair very black above that pallor, her eyes very wide. She dropped her lids and behind her she felt the sunlit emptiness of the kitchen, and she heard the clock whirring and striking over and over.

The crazy thing, she thought on the verge of panic. It's loud enough to wake the dead. Her hands tightened on the sink until they were white. *Wake the dead . . .*

And all the ghosts who walked in the house came alive.

2

THE YOUNG GIRL JOANNA stood looking at her face in the mirror, and the dishwater was warm around her thin, bony wrists. She tilted her head with its heavy black mane and said seriously to herself: Am I pretty?

Her eyes glinted at their reflection from a sooty curl of lash, and her brows were wide black brush strokes on a brown forehead, clear and spacious and marked sharply with the widow's peak that belonged to the Bennetts. Am I pretty? she thought, and smiled so that a dimple came into one cheek, to match the cleft in her chin. Well, not bad, she decided impersonally, and dismissed the question.

"I could swear those pots of mine to the south'ard have been bothered," her brother Charles was saying, and she stopped dreaming over the dishpan. In the mirror she saw them standing around the stove, tobacco smoke wreathing their heads; Stephen Bennett, her father, filling his pipe with leisurely fingers as Charles talked to him. It was to his father that Charles always spoke first; he was the oldest son, and some day he would be standing in his father's place with his own boys around him. This seemed to draw them together, so that Joanna always thought of them in later years as she saw them now in the mirror over the sink: side by side at the end of the stove. Philip and Owen, who were younger, stood a little apart from them.

Charles Bennett never forgot he was the oldest, nor did he ever let anyone else forget it. He looked like Stephen, having the gypsy darkness that marked most of the Bennetts, the black eyes, the big nose, the stubborn strength of chin, and the big, long-legged frame. But he had a quick arrogance that was not his father's, or perhaps Stephen had lost it with the years.

"Yes, by God, they've been hauling that string to the south'ard," Charles said crisply. "It's happened once too often. I know who's set his pots right around me—some of 'em damn near on top of me."

"I was on the wharf," said Philip, "when George Bird came in this morning. He'd been out before anybody else was stirring. Pretty near three hundred pounds. That's good fishing when the bugs are tapering off."

Philip was twenty and tall, and broad of shoulder, but there was a mildness in his speech and looks, taken from his mother. His eyes were quiet and gray-blue in his tanned face. His hair was not the Bennett black, his smile not so flashing, nor his scowl so dark. His thin-lipped mouth held a gentle humor.

"Yes, my boys, Georgie did himself proud this morning."

"By God, we ought to haul with a gun on the washboards!" Charles cried out.

"Don't talk like a fool, man," his father said. "What good would that do? Even if you could prove they'd hauled you, shooting wouldn't help."

"It would show 'em we know what's going on and we don't intend to take it sitting down." He leaned forward, and the arrogant jut of nose and chin came into a shaft of sunlight. "There's plenty others on here that feel like carrying a gun. But they're all like you, Father—they stand around and say it wouldn't help. They won't take a gun with 'em and find out. Put a bullet hole in the Birds' waterline a couple times when they're helping themselves to somebody's pots, and they'd take the hint. Most of us are too damned easygoing around here!"

"Meaning me?" Stephen's rare smile flickered, and Charles had the grace to redden.

"It's time we ran those bastards off the Island!" Owen leaped explosively into the conversation. Keeping silent was always an unbearable strain for him. At seventeen he was cock o' the walk—or of the beach—but sometimes he couldn't make his father and older brothers believe it. They turned toward him now, Stephen and Charles with lifted black eyebrows, Philip smiling a little.

"We could get rid of them easy. What if none of the Birds ever got a lobster day after day? What if they didn't even find their traps, next time one of 'em went to haul? Man, would *that* gowel 'em!"

"Golly, our rooster's learning how to crow pretty good," said Philip, and Owen flung up his stubborn chin. A lock of black hair danced on his forehead.

"You'd sit still and let them bug your pots right off the beach and be too lazy to do anything," he accused. "We've had those sons o' bitches bleeding the Island for too long! Maybe it wouldn't be so bad if lobstering was poor and they didn't have enough to eat. But Simon had him a new boat this year, six months after he came home from that freighter without a nickel in his pocket. And young Ash has money to burn—*plenty*. But he's not enough of a fisherman to make all that out of his little string."

The scrawny young Ash had been Joanna's bitterest enemy when they went to grade school on the Island. She spun around in a whirl of dishwater and excitement. "Well, why don't we do something right away?" she demanded. "Why don't we do what Grandpa Bennett used to do—order 'em out, the whole damn—*darned* shootin' match?"

"Because Grandpa owned everything then, darlin' mine," said Philip. "But Father and Uncle Nate weren't like Grandpa. When they got the Island, they sold hunks of it to the men who looked like good workers."

"And George Bird was one. So when his crew starts raising hell, there isn't one damn thing we can do about it—legally." Charles crushed out his cigarette with a vehement gesture. "Can't even keep 'em off the shore. George's got a shore privilege."

Stephen took his pipe out of his mouth and his quiet dark gaze took them all in, from the oldest son to the thin and glowing girl. "Well, have you all said what you've a mind to?"

They looked at him in quick, uncertain silence, and then his slow smile was reflected in Charles' eyes. "Sure, I guess we've all said over five cents' worth. We're listening, Father."

"Thanks,' said Stephen dryly. "As far as the Birds go, Owen's got the soundest idea." Owen glowed and his father added, *"Sound—* if I held with robbing another man's pots and cutting them off. I don't. So I'll have no more talk of it, Owen."

He turned to Charles. "Somebody's been bothering you, and I don't like it any more than you do. You say you can swear it's the Birds. Can you?"

Charles said with uneasy anger, "It wouldn't be anybody else."

"Why not?" Philip put in. "There's more than one on the Island who'd like to gowel the Bennetts, Cap'n Charles."

Stephen nodded. "It's been known to happen, a man thieving from somebody else, and all the blame being laid to another with a bad name. You can't go off half-cocked after the Birds without proof, Charles."

"Proof!" Charles' nostrils were rimmed with white. "What more proof do I need, by the Jesus, when I find my pots with the doors open and bait bags stolen, and George Bird bringing in three hundred pounds?"

"His traps are all to the west'ard," murmured Stephen. "If anybody saw him to the south'ard, you'd hear about it."

"But young Ash is set right on top of me, the little rat!" Charles rapped back at him. His Bennett temper was out in the open now. "And there's more than one's told me about seeing George come up alongside of Ash, outside the harbor! I'm telling you, Father, I'm damn sick of this stinking mess. A bullet in the waterline is the only kind of talk they understand!"

"I'll have no more of this talk about guns!" For an instant black eyes locked and fought with black eyes. It was Charles who gave way first, and Stephen went on in a milder voice, "It's proof I want. *Proof.* I know it's hard to get, but you'll get it in time, if you try hard enough. You can't come up behind them on the water, but you can follow them along the shore. It'll take a while, but in the end it's worth it. Take a gun out, and the first thing you know you've got a shooting feud like what's been going on at Brigport for the last year! That's your stinking mess, Charles! The state ought to get out there and clean it up, they'll never stop it themselves." He put his hand on his son's shoulder. "That's the Brigport way of doing things, but not the Bennett's Island way. And there'll be no Bennetts mixed up in it."

His fingers tightened on the obstinate shoulder as he watched Charles' locked face. "Seems to me we're a little too good for that, Cap'n Charles. Oh, I know they call us too damn high-minded over at Brigport, and around the shore; too big for our boots. But that's what keeps us able to live with ourselves. And you'd find yourself poor company if you'd been trimming up another man's gear, or if a bullet went wrong and hit a man instead of his boat."

He looked around at the rest of them. "Bring me proof, and I'll be with you all the way. Until then — well, this goes for all of you. The Bennetts have always upheld the law, instead of taking it into their own hands."

Charles turned suddenly and walked away from him. "Honestly, Father!" Joanna burst out. "You're too *decent* for this place!"

Charles was putting on his rubber boots. He looked up at her with the swift and charming Bennett smile. "That's right, Jo, talk right up to him. The rest of us can talk from hell to breakfast, and he'll still tell us to remember the Golden Rule."

"Charles," said Donna Bennett from the doorway. They all looked toward her as she stood there with two of the bedroom lamps in her hands. She was slender and tall, her light brown hair smooth and silky under the neat braids she had worn from young girlhood. There might be fine lines in her face, worn with the bearing and raising of Bennetts, and there was certainly white in the braids. But her eyes could be as wide and gently amazed and contemplative as they'd been when young Stephen Bennett was courting her, the new schoolteacher, and trying to sweep her off her feet when she wouldn't be swept until she'd made up her mind.

"Charles," she said now, and Charles, meeting those eyes, shut his mouth. Owen turned his scowl toward the window, and Joanna felt her mother's cool blue-gray gaze on her own hot cheeks.

It was then, in that instant of silence, that the clock went crazy. For a moment they all stared, stricken with a common amazement. It struck twelve, thirteen, fourteen, and fifteen, before Charles threw a boot at Philip and roared, "Stop the damn thing!"

"I can't," said Philip innocently. "It's a Bennett clock. It won't shut up till it's out of wind."

Laughter burst across the room that had been ominous with storm a moment before. And now it was a good place to be. Joanna, watching them with their big, whole-hearted mirth, father and sons alike, felt love and pride run through her like a warming fire. She met her mother's smiling eyes and a little current of understanding passed between woman and girl. *Men,* it said in loving amusement. *Our men.*

Stephen clapped Charles on the shoulder on his way out to the workshop in the barn. Philip took his cap from its hook. "Going down to the shore, Cap'n?"

"Yep!" said Charles cheerfully. "Say, Sigurd ran ashore on Tuckanuck this morning and bent his wheel—you seen it?" Halfway to the door he slid his arm around his mother's waist and began to waltz, incredibly light-footed in his rubber boots.

" 'Let me call you sweetheart,' " he sang tunefully, " 'I'm in love with you . . .' "

"Charles, the lamps!" Donna cried, but she was laughing at the same time.

Owen came across the room and leaned against the dresser by the water pails, watching Joanna wipe the dishes.

"Jo, want to do something for me today?" The Bennett smile was a little different in Owen. It held at once a sweetness and a reckless charm that was known to work wonders. Not with Joanna however, who gave him a suspicious sidewise glance.

"What is it?"

"Don't look so ugly. You know you like to paint. It's my double-ender. Honest, Jo, you're the only one could do it like I want it."

"Well—"

"You're a damn good fella, Jo!" He went out whistling. The kitchen was abruptly silent except for the rattle of dishes and Donna's soft humming as she filled the lamps and polished the chimneys; but the air still seemed to vibrate with the echoes of strong, deep-chested voices.

Joanna swept the hardwood floor, already scrubbed to whiteness, and gave the bright rag rugs a cursory shake on the back doorstep. She took the orts—table scraps the dog Winnie didn't want—down behind the house and threw them to the gulls in Goose Cove. Now she was her own man till supper time.

The fresh sweetness of early June—the Island's particular June—lay all around her and she felt like a gull who has been caged, and then let free to sail once more on great gray wings across the fathomless blue lakes of the sky. It had been a cage, that school on the mainland twenty-five miles away; her mind winced, and locked itself against the thought of two more years to go. But now she had all summer before her, and the sun was warm on her head as she walked down the road in her good-feeling dungarees and one of Philip's shirts. And there was an especially satisfying smell to be breathed from the marsh, a scent made up of new grass and warm black earth.

She heard the steady thrumming of an engine and hurried her long legs so she could be at the beach by the time the boat came round the point. She recognized the sound—she knew each engine as one knows the voices of friends—and this was one of her favorites. It was Karl Sorensen's *Priscilla,* with his son Nils at the wheel.

It was a sight to make Joanna's heart turn over and send a chill of gooseflesh along her arms, the sweet way the boat skimmed past the harbor ledges with the water curling back in a sun-shot glitter of white and crystal from the high bow. She came swiftly across the smooth blue water, straight as an arrow, like a creature with life and impulse of her own. Then the fish houses hid her from Joanna, who wished for perhaps the nine-thousandth time that she were a boy with some hope of having a boat of her own.

With the *Priscilla's* engine shut off, it was very quiet. A gull mewed lazily overhead, and the beach lay deserted in the sunshine. Joanna sat on Owen's overturned peapod. Presently he would appear with the paint; in the meantime she was content to look through narrow dreamy eyes at the blue shimmer of the harbor beneath the point's tawny height, and think the long, long thoughts of fifteen.

A shout split her reverie to bits, and she lifted her head to see the *Priscilla* at her mooring, and Nils standing on the bow. His fair head glinted against the sky.

"Jo, come and get me!" he yelled between cupped hands.

She slid off the double-ender and her thin brown hands were quick, untying the painter of the nearest skiff. This was what she liked, the feel of a boat under her feet and the oars in her hands, the tug of water against the blades and the effortless rhythm of a perfect stroke, with the tiny whirlpools it left behind. . . . The punt nuzzled gently against the power boat's wet white side.

Nils came aboard with an easy lightness that barely rocked the skiff. "Thanks, Jo. I don't know where my punt is. Sig's idea of a joke, I guess. He's probably lugged it upstairs in the fish house."

"You been to haul?"

"Me, go to haul with the old man's boat?" His slow smile came alive all at once, a good sunny smile without craft. It took away a certain Nordic austerity from his young tanned face. "What do you think Grampa Gunnar would say to that? 'Ya, you make the boy soft — let him row!' Nope, I was over to Brigport."

"Why didn't you tell me you were going?" she demanded.

"I clean forgot. You can go next time."

She rowed hard, eyes stern under black brows. "Can I steer?"

"When we get outside the point."

She nodded, feeling a deep satisfaction. With Nils, a promise was a promise. She glanced over her shoulder at the beach and saw Owen coming down to the water. It swirled and chuckled around his boots as he pulled the bow up on the pebbles.

"Cleopatra on her barge," he drawled. "Pretty good, the way you squareheads get the women to tend on ye." He nodded at the peapod. "Paint's all ready, Jo. And go easy, for God's sake. Don't slap it on too thick. Cripes, I'll be glad when I can haul from a power boat like a human being."

"Stop throwing away your money on sweaters and flannels and white shoes," said Joanna, "and you can buy Tim Gray's old boat. He'll sell her — bare boat — for a hundred fifty."

"How come you know so much about it?" he asked suspiciously.

"Oh, I listen around!"

Nils' Swedish tidiness wouldn't let him drop ashes even on the beach. He deposited them neatly in the cuff of his boot and said without haste, "She's looking right out for you, son, and it's no joke about the *Old Girl*. Look, with the money you make you could buy her in a month, pick up an engine somewhere—"

"I don't want any goddam decked-over dory! I'll have me a thirty-four footer, with lines like a yacht. And she'll be built to go." His dark eyes scanned the harbor, already seeing the boat of his heart, trim and elegant, at her mooring.

"You'll never get her, the way you throw your money around," said Joanna unfeelingly.

"Get to work, brat."

Joanna put her hands in her dungaree pockets and looked across the peapod at him. Two years younger, she was almost as tall, and her black head tilted at just the same arrogant angle.

"How much do I get?"

For a fraction of a moment, Owen looked amazed. But only for a fraction. "You mean you want *money?*" he inquired in gentle distaste. "You never said anything about it when I asked you."

"But I was thinking about it," she said, utterly unmoved by his expression of hurt reproach. "Two bits an hour. That's my price."

Black eyes challenged black eyes, and deep inside of her something was laughing a little, but it was scared too. Never in her life had she asked any of her brothers for pay for the chores they gave her to do. But she was fifteen now, and it was different. "Twenty-five cents an hour," she said briskly.

"Fifteen," said Owen. His smile was sweet.

"Twenty-five. Or do it yourself."

Owen shrugged. "Oh, I guess I can afford to give a kid a little spending money. Come on, Swede."

"I'll have the first two hours now," said Joanna calmly but irrevocably.

Two pairs of Bennett eyes narrowed, two Bennett jaws tightened. And then, before Nils' humorous blue glint, Owen reached into his pocket and tossed her the money. He walked off without another word.

"He'll get it back before sundown," said Nils, starting after him.

"He'd talk you out of your eyeteeth if he could."

"Not me," said Joanna briefly, and picked up the brush.

3

THE SUN WAS WARM on her head and through the back of her blouse, and the gulls drifted and cried in the high radiant reaches of the sky. Sometimes a man came across the beach and the stones rolled under his rubber boots. An engine roared occasionally in the harbor; a child called out, over on the rocks where Marcus Yetton's youngsters played among the tidewater pools, looking for crabs. The whole busy, quiet, self-sufficient life of the Island flowed around Joanna as richly and placidly as the paint flowed from her brush.

She knew without thinking it in words that the Island was a good place. There were work and money and food; there was not a poor man on the Island, unless you counted Marcus Yetton. But Stephen Bennett said Marcus was his own worst enemy, spending his money on foolishness and hobbling along with cheap gear and flimsy pot-warp. But at that the Yettons had plenty to eat. So did Johnny Fernandez and Nathan Parr, who lived in the shabby camps between beach and marsh. She looked up at them now, as they sat in the sun smoking their old pipes and baiting trawls, and she knew that these two, who had come as transients years ago, had stayed on Bennett's Island because it was a good place to be. The Bennetts had made it so.

And all the world wanted lobster to eat, it seemed. Prices were high, and the hauls were big. Only this morning a smack had come out from Friendship, wanting a thousand pounds in a hurry; they had cleaned out Pete Grant's car and bought each man's haul as he came to the wharf, at five cents more than they'd been paid a week ago.

She looked up as a power boat came in close to the beach, and scowled, recognizing George Bird. He had taken up some of his traps, with Closed Season beginning in another ten days, and now he was dropping them overboard in shallow water. When the tide went down, he and his boys would carry them up the beach to be stacked.

But in this sunny peace, she could be philosophical even about the Birds. There always had to be a worm in the apple. That seemed to her to be a very apt thought, and she would tell it to Charles at supper time.

I'll never live anywhere else but here, she thought. None of us will. This is Bennett's Island, and we're the Bennetts. We'll live here forever. . . . When she looked up she saw the road across the marsh, the sloping meadow with its daisies like a new snowfall, and the house high and white against the luminous sky of June. The marsh, the rocks, the meadow, the beach where she worked, the massy woods looming blackly beyond Goose Cove—the Island belonged, almost every foot of it, to the Bennetts, her father and her uncle Nate, herself and her brothers and her cousins. And so it would always be.

"Ahoy the peapod!" Nils hailed her from his brother Sigurd's boat, tied up at the old wharf while her propeller was being fixed. Joanna looked up, squinting against the sun. "You've done your trick. Come aboard and set a while."

Her aching shoulders and knees, and the glistening yellow expanse of fresh paint, told her the two hours were up. Nils was her chum, he'd see that she didn't work overtime. She climbed the old wharf from the wet rocks where the tide was going down, and went aboard.

The boys sprawled on the lockers, smoking and talking, Nils and Owen, and Uncle Nate's second son, Hugo Bennett. He was a slight merry boy with a tumbled curly head and the brilliant Bennett eyes. There was a mischievous sweetness in his look, and though he was older than Owen and Nils, he looked younger. Now he was smiling dreamily at his cigarette.

"Yes sir," he said blissfully. "Pretty damn good, I call it. She's built from the ground up, that one— Hi, Jo."

"Maybe she used to be." Owen was skeptical. "But she's a mite wore off at the corners by now."

"You don't know anything about it," said Hugo earnestly. "The trouble with you guys is you don't have any technique."

"What the hell good is that?" demanded Owen.

Hugo threw him a look of intense pity for his ignorance, and began to enlighten him. Joanna felt a twinge of boredom. Women again. That was all they talked about. She sat cross-legged on a locker beside Nils, who seemed to be balanced on the back of his neck, and smoked one of his cigarettes while she considered his quiet common sense. She was beginning to think most of the Island girls were pretty dumb to run around in the bushes with a pack of gormless idiots who spent most of their spare time bragging. Nils was different. He could have ten women on the string without anyone knowing it.

He caught her look, and winked. "Hey, Hugo," she interrupted her cousin, who was now rather flushed of cheek and bright of eye. "Who is it this time?"

Since Joanna was one of the gang, he told her cheerfully, and she grinned at him, the dimple deep in her brown cheek. "You want to know what Charles said about *her?*"

"Jo, are you aboard?" She heard her father's voice so suddenly that she caught her breath and choked violently on a mouthful of smoke. Owen pounded her back. Nils deftly popped a stick of gum into her mouth. An instant later she came out of the cuddy and climbed on to the wharf where her father stood.

He looked down at her sternly. "Joanna, run along home. The shore's no place for a girl."

"I was just going, Father."

"And spit out that gum."

"Yes, Father."

For a moment his hand rested on her shoulder, and the smile in his eyes came warmly to life across his face. "Too bad you couldn't have been a boy, I guess. But your mother and I like our girl."

She ducked her cheek to touch his fingers. In this moment of rare closeness she dared to say it. "Father, why can't a girl have a boat of her own? Even just a punt?"

"I never thought much about it, Joanna. A boat's a funny plaything for a girl to want. And don't you ever think about new dresses?" He glanced at Philip's faded blue shirt. "Or are you going to wear your brothers' clothes all your life?"

She straightened, flung up her chin. "I'll wear 'em all summer as long as I have to dress up all winter, by God!"

"Watch your tongue, my girl," he warned her, but his mouth twitched. He had always been proud of her spirit.

Sigurd Sorensen, a big, yellow-maned Viking, came across the wharf with Charles.

"Steve, you been down there an' looked at my wheel? Looks shacked to me. Hi, Jo."

"That's Steve's sixth boy," said Charles. "Hello, mutt."

She nodded gravely at them and walked away. If she had to go home and do the dull and senseless tasks allotted to girls in this life, and leave behind her the good solid talk of men, about boats and wheels and engines and the summer fishing, at least she could take the long way home.

In the flood of afternoon sunshine the village lay asleep, the harbor a wide blue mirror at its feet. The season was always late on the Island, so now in June tall old lilacs, purple and white, bloomed fragrantly against silvery shingles or white clapboards. And everywhere the grass was green, crossed and recrossed by narrow paths fringed with chicory and wild caraway's fragile blossom; where the grass grew tall, it was starred with daisies.

Joanna crossed the field by the well, and turned by Gunnar's spruces into the lane that led past the long low clubhouse under the trees, where the suppers and dances were held; then it led her into the big sunshiny space, drifted with daisies and the occasional fire of Indian paintbrush, where the empty Whitcomb place dreamed against a wooded hillside, and swallows swooped toward her with their shrill little cries. The path turned away from the house to trail mysteriously through another bit of woods into the Bennett meadow.

But Grandpa Bennett's apple orchard grew in these woods, and it was here that Joanna stopped at last. For the orchard was in bloom. Here, with the great spruces towering in dark and immobile silence around them, the sunlight streamed across boughs heavy with pink and white blossom; the little trees stood knee-deep in the tall grass. A cuckoo glided without a sound into the shadows.

Joanna stood taut as an arched bow. She might have been completely alone on the Island, in the world. . . . It was with her eyes still rapt, as one who has heard Voices, that she turned her head and saw someone standing at the far end of the orchard, by the cemetery gate. Her return to the thoughts of this earth was rapid. It was Simon Bird.

In five minutes she could be safe in the meadow, in sight of home, she thought, remembering an instant of panic and struggle in the blackness of the schoolhouse entry during the Island's Christmas party. She'd never spoken to Simon Bird since. But she had watched him, sometimes.

She watched him now, standing motionless against a tree trunk while he came toward her through the long alley of sun-splashed bloom. He had a thin tanned face and flat cheeks slanting to a lean chin. His red hair was like copper with the sun on it, and he was slight and narrow-hipped in his snug dungarees.

"Hello, Joanna," he said softly. "Pretty up here, ain't it? Almost as pretty as you are."

"I'm not pretty," she said, her throat roughening. "Don't talk so foolish."

"Sure you are. Oh, not like one of them candy-box covers down in Pete Grant's store. You got something else. Fire." His chuckle was a sound of secret amusement. "I ought to know that!"

"What about those girls down in Cuba, that you told Charles about?"

"Oh, that trash." He shrugged. "They're second hand. everybody's handled them. Me, I like to be first. How old are you, Jo?"

"Going on sixteen." They hadn't said it was Simon who hauled their traps, they'd talked mostly about his father and Ash. The other girls were always giggling about Simon, and she thought they were dumb, but it was true what they said about him—he *was* good-looking. And they all had an eye on him, too. But as far as she knew, he hadn't looked back.

"See here," he said. "Look what you did that night. You're sorry, ain't ye?" His eyes, his slow smile, wheedled her. He came close and she saw the faint little white line in his tanned cheek. She remembered, her heart hammering all over again, the thick darkness and her terror and her fingernails breaking his skin, his muttered, *"Christ!"*

"Well, you wouldn't let me go," she muttered.

"I only wanted to kiss you. Would you fight like that now, Jo?" His voice dropped. "After all . . . what's a kiss between friends?"

She wished he wouldn't stand so near. It did some odd thing

to her breathing. Her eyelids felt heavy, as if her thick lashes weighed them down. This was the time to run away, and she knew it. If she wanted to run away . . .

"Would you fight now, Jo?" he murmured. Her feet wouldn't move, and the tree bark was rough against her cold palms, and deep inside her head a voice mocked her. You don't dare say *no*, it said. You're a coward, wanting to run away. What are you scared of?

I'm not scared of anything, Joanna answered it, and the sense of adventure was warm and sweet in her blood. She was not a child now, and it was time to find out things for herself. And deep down, in some wild, forbidden corner of her brain, she had never really forgotten how Simon's mouth had felt on hers in the brief moment when he'd succeeded.

I want to *know,* she thought defiantly. Was it wrong to want to know? So she tilted her chin at fate and said in a perfectly level voice, "I wouldn't fight . . . again."

"I didn't think you would." Simon stepped back. He lit a cigarette and things became real again. The world broke in. Already the orchard was in shadow. The breeze was freshening, and the robins were singing as they always did when it was almost evening.

Simon looked at her through cigarette smoke. "Take a walk with me, Jo . . . tonight. Only your folks won't let you out. The old man's not lettin' any of this Island trash get near his daughter."

"I can get out when I want to!" she said, her cheeks scarlet.

For a long moment they looked at each other. Then Simon said, "Round 'bout ha-past-eight, I'll be up at the Whitcomb place."

She thrust her hands into her pockets and walked by him without another glance. "Don't disappoint me, Jo," he murmured. He didn't touch her, yet his voice halted her as his hand might have. She turned to look at him, and all at once that sense of adventure was back again, clamoring in her blood, sending a liquid brightness into her eyes, and softening the curve of her young mouth.

Then, with the unpredictable whimsy of a young colt, she began to run, straight down the path to the open meadow beyond.

4

OWEN WAS GOING TO PLAY POOL at the clubhouse after supper, and Joanna went along with him. Hugo was already there when they arrived, knocking balls about the table. The main building was kept locked, to keep the children away from the glossy hardwood dance floor—capital for sliding—but all club members had their keys. Most of the young crowd joined when they were the required sixteen years, and had saved up the fee for a life membership—ten dollars.

Hugo's eyes held a darkling twinkle. "Hello, mates. Look what I got!" With a conjuror's flourish he brought a flat bottle out of his boot.

"Where'd you get it?" said Owen skeptically. "They say you can go blind, drinking that cheap stuff."

"Hell, nothin' cheap about this!" Hugo was affronted. "Forest Merrill's old man got it off a boat yesterday, outside the Rock. It's pure Scotch whiskey."

"I'll tell you about that after I try it."

"You know a lot about it," said Joanna. "You never even tasted pure Scotch whiskey."

"Shut up. You playing?"

"Nope." Her tone was carefully airy. "I'm going over to Gunnar's and see Kristi for a while."

As she reached the door Hugo called after her. "Hey, Jo!" Leaning over the table he grinned like a very good-natured devil. "What *did* Charles say? You know—"

"I'm not letting her tell you and she ought to know better," said Owen with sudden brotherly propriety. "Go on, beat it, Jo."

"Aw, you just want to tell him yourself!" Joanna made a face at him and went out. The cool dark wind blew against her hot face as she went up the lane toward the Whitcomb place. It loomed large and pale against the vast blackness of the woods. How very silent the Island was tonight, she thought; it semed to be listening, holding its breath. . . .

A tiny red glow near the steps was Simon's cigarette. She saw it move, and heard his soft voice.

"Hello, there." He put his arm around her. "What are you shaking for? Cold? Come on." His arm urged her up the steps, he opened a door, and she recoiled from the chill blackness of the house.

"Is it all right?" she whispered huskily.

"Sure it's all right. My dad keeps the key. Nobody'll ever know, sweetheart." He was so near, yet unseen, that his breath was warm against her cheek.

They went through the cold silence of the house into the front room. It was like moving in a dream. Everything was strange and unknown; not the least strange was the nearness of Simon. She could smell the stuff he put on his face after he shaved, the clean dampness of his hair; she could imagine how it looked, its red darkened by the wet comb as it sprang into waves. She could smell his sweater, too, soft and woolly. At last he stopped her and put his arms around her, and she was glad, because he was real and she was so queerly afraid. Not of the dark; she'd never been afraid of the dark. . . .

Simon kissed her. His mouth was gentle and oddly hot against her wind-cooled skin. She stood rigidly still, trying not to tremble, and kept her lips pressed tightly shut.

"Relax, darlin'," he whispered. "I've got a lot to teach you and you're going to like it. . . . Relax, honey."

He kissed her again and again, and gradually she began to feel a sweet drowsiness creep over her. She felt heavy in her eyelids, in her head, in every finger, each muscle; she only wanted to stand there in the tight circle of his arms, leaning against him. Almost without her knowing it, her mouth went soft and willing under his.

His breath quickened. "You're a sweet kid," he said, his voice blurred. "A damn sweet kid. Let's sit down."

There was some furniture left in the almost-empty house, and they sat down on an old cot. Joanna was dreamily glad she'd come. The afternoon in the orchard seemed years ago. She hadn't known then it would be like this. . . . She leaned against Simon and he put his face in her hair, and kissed the back of her neck. It sent little feathers of delight along her skin. Without thinking at all, she put her hand on his face, wondering vaguely at the fiery heat of it, and drew his head down.

"Oh, my God!" he whispered, and his arms tightened.

"Your heart's beating hard," she said with a soft little chuckle.

"How's yours?" His voice thickened as his hand slipped over her breast. Hardly breathing, she lay in the circle of his arm, her mouth trembling and eager for his kiss. It came, hard and urgent, no longer gentle. And with it he moved so that she felt herself leaning backwards against an arm that lowered her very slowly, very gently, very steadily. She yielded with no thought of resistance.

"That's right," he whispered.

It might have been his voice that broke the spell. But all at once the sweet languor was gone; even its memory didn't exist. Joanna was wide awake and trembling with cold and fear in an empty house, a dark house. She put her hands against his chest and pushed.

"What's the matter?" he muttered. "Don't be afraid of me, sweetheart."

"Let me up," she breathed. It was as if she had walked in her sleep and had awakened to terror and struggle in darkness. "Please, I want to go home, I don't want to stay here!"

She fought against the arms that held her while the soft voice cajoled and pleaded. "What are you scared of, Jo? I won't hurt you. I swear you'll be all right, you won't get into trouble or anything!" He talked rapidly, with growing incoherence, words tumbling over words. She knew he was frantic, and her terror grew. "Look, Jo, if you're my girl you'll have everything, all the money I make, silk stockings, candy, a watch, anything—*Jo!*"

He smothered her gasps with his lips and she fought him with all her wild young strength, but it wasn't enough. It wasn't enough until, to her own huge surprise, she burst into tears.

"Oh, Christ," said Simon, and let her go. "So you're goin' to pull the salt-water business on me, are ye?" He was no longer afire, but coldly furious. "I'll give you five minutes to get the hell over it, and then you'll listen to reason. I don't let anybody fool with me, lady. Sooner or later, they pay up."

He sat on the cot, smoking a cigarette. In the dimness his face was a thin devilish mask. Joanna stood shivering in the middle of the room, trying to calm herself. Through the window she saw the light in the clubhouse, a yellow glimmer through the moving spruce branches. It was the loveliest thing in the world, that light. If she were there now, she'd never ask for anything else in her life . . .

Her lightning dash took Simon by surprise, but not for long. When she flung herself across the room, Simon was off the cot; when she reached the bottom step, he was at the top. His voice tore at the darkness. "Come back here, damn you!"

She ran headlong through the uncut grass that was a wet tangle around her feet. Those feet were sure and swift, and they needed to be, with another pair thudding behind them. One misstep, one stumble to bring her to her knees in the uneven path—don't think of that! she warned herself. Escape was the thing.

Somehow she reached the clubhouse porch, and he stopped out in the dark lane. She went into the poolroom, making herself move slowly as if there were no reason for hurry, stifling her aching breath. She was thankful for the shadow outside the boundaries of the table, and for the intentness with which the boys played. Owen was making a shot, and Hugo looked on. It was Nils who looked up at her and nodded. He had come after she left; he knew, then, that she hadn't gone to see his sister. She stood against the door and felt her body burn with shame under his level blue glance.

"Kristi gone to bed?" Owen said over his shoulder. "Time you went home, it's way after nine."

"I'll wait for you," she said.

"You will like hell! I don't want the old man on my neck for keeping you out. He doesn't think much of you being on my coattails all the time, anyway."

He turned back to the table and the game went on. Joanna felt wave after wave of nausea assault her stomach. The shadows in the lane were thick, and it didn't do to madden a man as she'd maddened Simon tonight. *Sooner or later they pay up,* he'd said. She'd heard enough about him around the shore. . . . But I didn't know how it would be! she thought wildly. I didn't know that was the way you felt! She sat down on a bench against the wall, her sweaty fingers clamped on the rough edge.

Nils leaned over the table, his hair silver-blond in the light. His cue moved like a serpent striking, and Hugo whistled softly. "Not bad," Owen conceded. Nils grinned, and put his cue in the rack.

"Come on, Jo, I'll walk you home."

"Cripes almighty, hasn't she gone *yet?*" Owen scowled at her. "What's eating you? Scared of the dark?"

"Look," said Nils in easy good humor. "Everybody's scared of something. My grampa's afraid of the fairies, and I've seen you lay back your ears at three lights in a room. And girls don't like rammin' around alone in the dark. I thought you knew all about women, Cap'n Owen."

They went out, Joanna torn between relief and shame. But the relief won out, for the lane was filled with an almost impenetrable darkness, and there were rustling sounds under the trees. They turned at the end of Gunnar's spruces, and as they passed the well, Nils said casually, "What do you want to fool around with that low-life bastard for?"

"What do you mean?" Something leaped in her with shamed terror.

"Simon Bird. He was there in the trees—lit out for home when he saw me."

"I don't fool around with him!"

"Then what are you scared of? O.K., Jo. I know you don't fool around with him. I'd have heard it around the shore before this. But you thought you'd tinker with a little fire. Is that it?"

"No!" To her horror, tears shook her voice. "I hate him! He's like a devil!"

"Well, don't tell the whole Island, darlin' mine," said Nils mildly. His arm was snug and solid around her shoulders. "I'm damn glad you found out what he is. You know, kid, I'd hate like hell to hear your name come out of that mouth of his down around the shore some day. I'd feel like grinding his face so hard into the beach rocks he'd look like a dead cod the gulls'd been at. Not to mention what your brothers'd do to him." He chuckled. "They'd likely warm your jacket, too."

Disgust made her shaky and sick. She remembered Hugo and Owen and the others and the things they talked about. The words were different sometimes, but they all added up to the same sum. A girl was easy, or she wasn't easy. . . . "She was rarin' to go, and then she froze up on me, the little bitch!" they said. . . . She remembered countless afternoons of talk, the inevitable comment on almost every girl or woman who walked by the beach. But she'd been safe; she was Joanna Bennett, who thought a lot of herself and looked at those others with the fierce intolerant scorn of her youth.

"Nils, he can't say anything about me," she said swiftly.

His arm tightened. "That's good. Look, kid." His words were slow, and endlessly kind, as they always were for her. "It's natural for you to want a man of your own. But you're no slut, like some of 'em around here. My cousin Thea and them . . . You don't have to do everything they do. And at least you can get you a man who knows how to keep his mouth shut."

They had reached the gate now, and the circle of his arm was friendly and warm and comforting, not at all like Simon Bird's arm. "Look, Nils," she said with a little chuckle. "Did you ever think how funny it is? Lots of people on the Island think we go around together. You know — that sweetheart stuff."

"Crazy as hell, aren't they?" said Nils. "Well, I guess you'll be all right now. It's only about three looks and a holler to the house."

"Hauling tomorrow?" She leaned on the gate and looked up at him in the starlight. She saw the glimmer of his teeth when he smiled.

"Sure. Want to come?"

"Oh, *yes!* Golly, Nils — thanks for everything." You were lucky, having a chum like Nils. He was so steady and unsurprised. He was so good. It made you feel warm and very rich just to see him there. But you didn't say things like that to your chums. Joanna said again, "Thanks for everything, Nils."

"Any time," said Nils.

5

In the morning light, the evening before might never have happened. To Joanna, kneeling by her window, the delicately cool, bright air stroking her skin, it was like one of those dreams of vague horror that she used to have when she was small. It was something that had happened to another girl, not in this world where the day was as naive, as smiling, as blue-eyed as a baby. A drift of buttercups spilled across the meadow, each bright and shining head dancing in the wind. The Indian paintbrush blazed with new fire close to the prodigal snow of a half-million daisies. The swallows were sleek blue shadows skimming across the grass, and the more intrepid of them rose high to dart in circles around the gulls that floated over Schoolhouse Cove. The young crows shrieked from the woods.

There were jewels everywhere. There were jewels in the sea, stretching limitlessly to the east and the south, to the Camden mountains and the faint blue line of mainland in the north and west. There was a jewel clinging brilliantly to each twig, to each blade of grass and flower in the meadow. The smoke from Uncle Nate's chimney, far across Schoolhouse Cove, rose straight and blue. Somewhere a dog barked, an engine started up in the harbor, and from over behind Goose Cove Ledge came the drone of hauling gear and the frenzied clamor of startled gulls. The Island was up and at work.

A whistle rose faintly and tunefully to her ears. She saw Stevie coming through the gate, carrying the milk can. He was a thin straight little boy in overalls, with a coppery skin and a black forelock. Winnie, the collie-spaniel, bounded through the tall grass like a swimmer breasting the waves, and her ears flopped merrily over her head, her tail was a gay plume. Joanna smiled and began to dress. The kitchen was empty except for Donna, already fixing the dinner vegetables, and Stevie, eating his breakfast. Stephen and the older boys had gone to the shore. Mark, who came between Joanna and Stevie in age, was weeding the vegetable garden over by the woods.

Donna glanced smilingly at Joanna's dungarees. "No dress this morning?"

"I'm going hauling with Nils." On an impulse she bent to kiss her mother's cheek. Mother, you'll never have to worry about me, she thought, remembering the night before.

She heaped a plate with fish hash and poured milk from the pitcher, feeling as if she could eat the world. Stevie watched her from the other end of the table. His eyelashes were very long, at eleven he was terribly ashamed of them.

"Is Nils your fella?" he asked interestedly.

"Don't talk so foolish!"

"Well, Mark said—"

"Mark says a lot more besides his prayers," said his mother. "Joanna what about your work? Will Nils wait for you?"

"Sure he will!" She leaped toward the stairs like a gazelle. Hers was the chamber work, the beds to make, the rooms to tidy. She did a large part of the washing each week, when she was home from school in the summer; she did most of the ironing. Her arms were as strong as a boy's for splitting kindling or lugging water if none of the brothers happened to be around.

Donna's clear pallor and erect slenderness, that made her so distinctive a figure among her vigorous, dark-eyed family, were the direct signs of her fragility. Sometimes Joanna, in a surge of fierce protective love, wanted to take over the whole burden of the household. But somehow Donna had arranged it so the girl had a part of the freedom that meant so much to her. For to be on the water and around the boats was as necessary to Joanna as the air she breathed.

This morning she raced through her work, her mind leaping ahead to the beach where Nils was probably waiting patiently. She hoped his grandfather hadn't taken it into his tyrannical old head to come down and sniff, and ask him what kind of lobstering was that, to sit on the beach on a fine day and smoke. Gunnar had learned discipline on sailing ships and he never let his sons and grandsons forget it.

Her premonition was right. When she came over the brow of the beach, the old man stood by Nils' double-ender; Nils stood beside him, one foot on the gunwale, his strong-featured face impassive under the broad visor of his cap. Joanna hesitated, seeing Gunnar pound one fist into the other palm; then with a tilt of her chin she went down the beach toward them.

They heard the beach stones rattle under her sneakers and turned. Gunnar was past seventy, but there was not a thread of white in his thick brown hair; he was stalwart and erect in overalls and flannel shirt. His cheeks were like russet apples and his eyes were bright blue, crinkled at the corners; he looked like a jolly Kris Kringle. Joanna hated him.

"Hello, Mr. Sorensen," she said civilly.

"Ha, Yo." His gnarled brown hand took Joanna's chin. "You look more like your grandfadder all the time. Same eyes, same mouth, same chin. He vass hard, yust like steel." He pinched Joanna's chin and beamed at her. "Not much like your fadder, huh?"

Joanna jerked her chin free. "Will you please not say anything about my father?"

"Ha!" Gunnar sniffed, and the twinkle grew. "Impertinence, is it? If you vass mine—"

"You'd hang me up by my thumbs in the barn and take a whip to me," said Joanna swiftly. "But I'm not yours, thank God, and if my grandfather was anything like you—" She bit her lip, suddenly abashed by her bad manners and startled at the current of hate that surged between herself and the old man. "You going now, Nils?"

"Get aboard." His face was still impassive.

The peapod slid across the quiet harbor waters, among the moorings where only punts and dories lay; the power boats were all at work. This was a spell of fine weather and nobody was lazy on Bennett's Island when the Closed Season was so near. Nils rowed standing up, pushing on the oars with long, effortless movements. Joanna looked past him at the shore and saw Gunnar still standing there, a squat black figure against the sun, somehow frightening. . . . She felt gooseflesh on her arms and then laughed at herself.

"I didn't mean to slat around," she said meekly. "I suppose he'll take it out on you."

"He'd been taking it out on me for an hour before you came along." Nils grinned. "Nothing new. He's on the prod, that's all. Drivin' Kris and David and me from hell to breakfast."

"He's always taking a dig at my father. I won't have it." But a little thread of fear ran through her anger. "Nils, you don't think my father's soft, do you?"

"Your father's all right. You know Grampa. He ran away to sea when he was eleven, and seafaring men were hard tickets in those days. So he thinks anybody that doesn't raise his kids with a Bible in one hand and a whip in the other is a fool."

"We had the Bible, but the most we ever got for lickings was a lath across our seat."

"Remember how you used to go out and sit on the woodpile and howl?"

She grinned at him. "And you'd come up to get Owen, and if you came anywhere near me I'd throw kindling at you!"

They were both laughing then, and the peapod was outside the harbor at last, so they couldn't see Gunnar on the beach any more. Now the boat seemed to leap forward over the bright water, and a sort of exultation possessed Joanna, made up of the crystalline sun-washed coolness of the morning, the whole blue and shining world around them, the rhythm of Nils' body as the oars swung the peapod with arrow-swiftness toward the first black and yellow buoy.

Nils shipped his oars and gaffed the buoy with one quick swoop. The boat rocked gently, in the cool dark shadow of the rocky shore, while the warp fell in wet coils at his feet; at last he caught the rope bridle and pulled the trap aboard. Balancing it on the low gunwale, his hands in the thick white cotton gloves scraped off the sea urchins and opened the door. There were innumerable crabs to be thrown overboard, and there were four lobsters. Three of them he tossed into the tub without a second look; the fourth one he measured with the gauge, and tossed it overboard.

"Good start, Jo," he said briefly, as he took out the bait bag and strung a fresh one, bulging with herring, into place with a swift stabbing gesture of the bait needle. "You're no Jonah."

"It doesn't look as if you've been bothered."

He pushed the trap overboard, letting the warp play through his fingers, and gave her a sidewise glance. "Who's been bothered?"

"Charles." The buoy splashed overboard, and Nils began to row again. "He wants to take a gun with him," Joanna added.

"It might come to that yet," Nils said.

The morning went on, brave with luminous skies and the glitter of sunshine across the water, the dazzle of gulls' wings and the sound of them as they came down in a shrieking rush when Joanna shook out the old bait bags. Nils hauled close to the shore, under the shadow of the high wooded places, and over the ledges whose rockweed swayed gently in the water like miniature meadows in the wind.

Their conversation was brief, but entirely satisfactory, the sparse words of two friends who can be as companionable in silence as in talk. When Joanna was thirsty, she drank from the water bottle; toward noon they shipped oars and ate mammoth sandwiches of beef and homemade bread, while the water chuckled and slapped at the sides of the boat, and the great, barren rocks of the lonely west side towered high above them.

Life was good, Joanna thought. It was even better when Nils let her row for a while. The whole blue expanse between the Island and the sun-bright ledge of the Rock was dotted with boats. She could pick out her uncle, and Philip; there was Nils' father, Karl, out by Shag Island, where the grotesque black birds sat on their rocks looking down at him. That cloud of gulls far to the east'ard marked the homeward progress of Jake Trudeau, shaking out the old bait bags as the *Cecile* chugged steadily along.

"Look there!" Nils said suddenly, and she saw Charles' boat come around Sou-West Point toward them, the water flashing back from the bow. The rocks threw back the beating echo, and gulls on the half-submerged Bull Cove Reef took off in a fluttering cloud of white wings. The two in the peapod watched, Joanna with a lifting thrill in her heart, Nils with pure delight caught unconsciously on his face.

"She's an able handsome lady, see her go!" Joanna chanted from the old song. The engine slowed to a muted pulse as the *Sea-Gypsy* slipped toward them across the water. Nils rowed to meet her.

Charles looked at them merrily. "What kind of a haul did you get, you Svenska?"

"Good," said Nils. "How'd you do?"

"They've been hauling hell out of me," said Charles, looking extraordinarily cheerful about it. "Well, I want my sister."

"What for?" said Joanna.

"Orders. My orders. And don't ask the skipper questions or you'll be sorry. Come aboard before I haul you over with a gaff."

"But *why?*" Joanna didn't move, and Charles laughed at her.

"Listen, lady, don't you like surprises? After I came 'round here on purpose to pick you up because I thought you'd kind of hanker to come with me. Just about through for the day, Nils?"

"Just about. You better go with him, Jo. Can't tell what he's up to."

It was true, Charles was up to something. She knew that. Ever since she could remember, Charles was the lordly one, the biggest brother of all, who hardly ever noticed her; but there had always been the amazing instants when he chose her, and no other, to go with him. *One thing, you can keep your mouth shut,* he'd told her.

She watched him now as he lounged on the washboard, old yachting cap on the back of his head, his white shirt dazzling in the sunshine as he smoked and swapped shop talk with Nils. She weighed the respective advantages of going with him, or staying with Nils, who would let her row the peapod. Curiosity won out, and she climbed over into the *Sea-Gypsy's* big cockpit. Charles grinned at her.

"Couldn't risk missing something, could you, darlin' mine?"

She threw a full bait bag at him, but he dodged, laughing, and it went overboard. "That'll cost you a nickel, sweetheart!"

"Wild woman," Nils drawled.

"Some man'll tame that fire out of her some day." Charles unfolded his long legs, then hesitated as Nils took up his oars. "By the way, Nils, maybe I ought to tell you something, if you're on your way home. So you'll know what the hell you've run afoul of, if anybody starts riding you down on the beach. Your grandfather's been talking to my old man."

Nils' eyes narrowed. "What's he been saying?"

Charles sniffed and wagged his head, and suddenly Gunnar was before them. "Your girl—she bad for the boy, she keep him from his vork. Ya, he vass good boy, he vork all vinter till dat Yo come home from school!" Charles smiled at the slow flush in the younger boy's face. "Oh, we know he's a crazy old bastard. But he likes to do his chewing in the face and eyes of the whole Island. The beach wasn't what you'd call empty."

"You wait till I see that old devil!" Joanna felt suffocated by her rage, she wanted to throw things and hear them smash. "I'll tell him something—goddam old fool—" She raged up and down the cockpit until Charles caught her by the shoulder and clapped a hard hand over her mouth.

"Seems like you've said enough to him already," he said dryly.

"What did your father say?" Nils' voice was quiet.

"What do you think he said? Any of the rest of us would've had plenty to say, but not the old man. He wouldn't lower himself to argue with anybody that was so beside himself." There was pride in Charles' tone. "Besides, he don't talk over his business on the beach. He looked Gunnar up and down just once and walked away. Left the old son of a bitch sputtering and fizzing like a fish out of water." He laughed, and started up the engine. "So long, Nils. Think nothing of it."

Nils began to row. The space of glistening blue widened between the two boats, and Joanna stared angrily after the peapod, wishing she hadn't climbed out of it. She'd show Gunnar! So he had to stir up trouble, because the Island was too peaceful at the moment! Oh, she knew all his nasty little tricks. And how long were they going to take it from him, those sons Karl and Eric, with grown families of their own? If there was any chew to be made about her and Nils, why didn't Nils' father make it? Why did there have to be a chew? Why, Nils was another brother to her—only a little better because he didn't try to team her around, and he was generous with his gum and his boat and his cigarettes.

If they tried to keep her out of Nils' boat just to please old Gunnar, she'd show them something. But they wouldn't try; they wouldn't say anything. Her father and mother knew better than to listen to the old devil. The tight knot in her stomach loosened. She went aft to the wheel and confronted Charles, hands in her hip pockets.

"Well, what goes on?"

Charles grinned. "I got a little errand to do—out there to the no'theast point of the Rock." He pointed across the water. "Who's that out there?"

"Ash Bird."

"Yes. Young Ash. Well, when I went to haul this morning there was more'n one place where little Ashly was set right on top of me. Don't know where he gets his courage from. So I went home with my lobsters, and Ash was still out—and now I'm back again."

"If it isn't the father it's the son," said Joanna. "Charles, why do they do it to us?"

"Because we're the Bennetts," said Charles. "Because we own most of the Island, and we got a way of thinking we're somebody."

"Well, we *are* somebody."

"Maybe," said Charles, "but that Bird trash don't think so."

She thought of Simon, pleading with her in the darkness, threatening her. If Charles, or any of them, knew about that . . . Was it because she was Joanna Bennett that Simon was so dead set on having her?

"What are you going to do?" she demanded eagerly.

"Damned if you aren't spoiling for a fight, young Jo!" Charles laughed at her. "But I'm just going to have a word with that boy."

"Well, what are you going to *say?*"

"Just give him a mite of advice," her brother said mildly. "I wouldn't go against the skipper's orders. Wouldn't hurt the boy any. After all, Ash is kind of a little fella."

Ash looked startled when the *Sea-Gypsy* came alongside. He was a thin, sulky youth, with none of the handsome self-assurance of his elder brother, or the mock-meekness of his father. Well he might look startled, with Charles a black young giant in oilskins, whose gaff caught and quivered in the washboards and whose big hand fastened in the front of Ash's shirt and dragged him against the gunwale.

"Hello, Ash!"

"What do you want?" Ash tried to laugh. "Hell, what is this?"

"Just a little neighborly greeting," said Charles genially. "Seems like your pots have moved around some in all this weather we been having. Shoved right up alongside mine, some of 'em are. I thought I'd let you know, so you could move 'em."

"Sure, sure," Ash stammered. "I never noticed—guess I ain't reached that string yet—"

"Round on the east side," said Charles benevolently. "You better take a little sail around there. If I had a suspicious nature I might think you'd been there already—'bout daylight—hauling my traps."

His smile was benign. "But it's a good thing for you I have a Christian mind. Because if I thought you were robbing me I'd haul hell out of you, my boy. And I'd give you the biggest, worst, goddamndest beating you ever had!"

Sweat sprang out on Ash's forehead. "Aw, let go, Charles," he said with a feeble grin. "You know damn well I'd never touch your gear."

"Sure I know it!" Charles let go and clapped him on the shoulder with such robust goodfellowship that Ash fell backwards over the engine box. "Kind of unsteady on your pins, aren't you, fella? Well, I'll be getting back to work."

He lifted his cap with a flourish, and the *Sea-Gypsy* leaped away like a creature glad to be free again. Joanna had one last glimpse of Ash, sitting limply on his engine box and fumbling with a package of cigarettes. She looked at Charles and they began to laugh.

They headed for the eastern end of the Island, passing under the shadow of the great rocky crest called the Head; it was yellow in the brilliant sunshine, and there was always a surge and swell below it, even in the calmest, fairest weather. Around the Head, on the lee side of the Island that looked across at the tawny, sloping fields of Brigport and its white houses, they passed the perfect and tranquil curve of Eastern End Cove. The fish houses huddled on the bank, and above them the Trudeau houses crouched, gray and shabby. Between the Eastern End and the harbor there was a long thick stretch of woods, and then fields; the Trudeaus seemed to live on an isolated little island of their own; and the village said it was a good thing.

Past Long Cove, then, and Uncle Nate's place looked serene and comfortable across the meadow where his cattle stood knee-deep in buttercups. . . . They were almost back to the harbor before it struck Joanna again: Gunnar and his talk. Oh, she'd get even with the old— It was exciting to have something to be good and mad about. She went to stand by the wheel.

"What else did Gunnar say?"

Charles scowled. "That was all he said." She caught the faint emphasis on the *he,* and pounced on it.

"Who else said anything?" she demanded.

"I'll tell you, kid, because I hate to see you walk in there and not know what it's all about." He looked straight ahead at the creaming surf around the harbor ledges. "It's just more wind, like Gunnar's chew, and we all know it, so don't let it bother you. Only Mark brought home a story from the shore and sprang it when we were having a mug-up, and it's got 'em all by the ears up there."

Her lips were very dry. "What is it? Where'd he get it?"

"I don't know. He just said he heard it, here and there . . . about you and Nils rammin' around in the dark last night."

"He walked home with me from the clubhouse." She looked at Charles steadily. "What's that to talk about?"

"Nothing. Hell, you don't think any of 'em at home believed Mark's yarn, do you? Only they—" Charles looked embarrassed. "You know how the Island is. You're a kind of a pretty kid, and they've been waiting to get something on you, something to talk about. It's a way of getting even with the old man, that's what it is, if they can spill a lot of dirty chew about one of his kids."

She felt sick inside. "Tell me all of it," she commanded.

"Well, somebody—Mark couldn't find out who—was hanging around outside the clubhouse last night when you fellas came out. And they started the talk around about seeing something. That damn little scavenger picked it up and brought it right home."

"Seeing *what?*" she said relentlessly.

"Seeing you fool around in the bushes," said Charles, looking straight ahead at the wharf, and then Joanna knew. *Simon.* Strong above the cold furious nausea that gripped her rose the certainty that if she only said his name, by nightfall there wouldn't be much left of Simon Bird. She turned toward Charles, her face ablaze; she opened her mouth, and shut it again.

The tiredness that came was worse than the nausea. She couldn't tell who it was. She couldn't let them know how she knew without telling them of that shameful meeting there in the darkness, and then they would look at her and know her cheapness and her disloyalty.

The *Sea-Gypsy* was slipping across the harbor now, setting the other boats to rolling, and she saw Nils' peapod rocking at her haul-off. Nils couldn't do anything, either, except take Simon over, and she knew, with a weary wisdom, that a beating wouldn't help. They were caught. . . . It's a trap, she thought, and I made it myself.

Charles said, "They don't believe it, kid. At home, and plenty of other places on the Island. They know how you and Nils are, just chums, that's all, ever since you were big enough to tag after him and Owen. But there's a lot of dirty-minded sons o' bitches on this place who can't understand this chum stuff—they go by what they used to do in the bushes."

The *Sea-Gypsy* glided to the car. Two other boats were there; Jud Gray and Jake Trudeau were selling their lobsters to Pete Grant. For a moment she hesitated on the gunwale, dreading to pass them. The world and the Island lay around her, so beautiful as to break her heart, but people were dirty and hateful and cruel.

Jud Gray's amiable face smiled at her, and Jake Trudeau said " 'Ello, Jo," looking, as always, like a very good-tempered pirate. It made it easier for her to cross the car to the ladder, even though she knew they'd been out hauling all morning and hadn't heard the story yet. For she knew that over every Island dinner table Joanna Bennett would be the chief topic of conversation. From her they'd go on to other Bennetts, to her father and mother, to the boys with their arrogant heads. It was a knowledge to make her feel like dying inside.

Charles stayed on the car talking shop with the other men, and Joanna walked up the wharf, and past the group lounging in the sun outside the store. She carried her head with a splendid assurance, though her ears were supersensitive to the sudden pause in voices that would begin again when she had passed.

They'll talk, she thought, but they'll eat every word they say about the Bennetts. And I'll make Gunnar and Simon pay, if I die doing it.

It was a promise. And some day, when the right time came, she'd keep it, as the Bennett boys always kept their promises. She walked through the village with her chin high and her mouth steeled against this new and vicious world, and turned at the road that led to her father's gate.

6

JOANNA CAME INTO THE KITCHEN, a thin straight girl in dungarees and shirt. She knew that a tiny muscle jerked at one corner of her mouth, but she couldn't unclamp her teeth. The rest of the family were at the dinner table. As she dipped cold water into the wash basin, she heard Philip's mild voice.

"Tom Robey at Brigport has a seine he'll sell cheap. The way the dogfish rammed around in the net at the end of seining last fall, we ought to have a new one before we go again."

"Listen," young Stevie piped up. "Why can't I go with the seinin' crew this year?"

"You ain't old enough," said Mark, with the superiority of thirteen over eleven. "What would you do with them little pindlin' arms?"

"What do *you* do?" said Stevie truculently.

"Boys," said Donna, and they subsided.

Stephen said in his moderate way, "I'd want to see any seine Tom Robey's selling, before I bought it."

"He's the lyin'est bastard that ever feet hung on and was called a man," said Owen cheerfully, "but does he make money bootleggin'! *Cripes!*"

"What's bootleggin'?" inquired Stevie.

"Never mind, son," murmured Donna. "Owen, eat your dinner."

"The Robey boys told me they'd make me a partner . . . meet schooners outside the Rock—"

"Owen, you heard your mother." Stephen sounded final. At another time Joanna would have grinned. Owen was trying to stir things up a little, and nobody would be stirred. They only told him to shut up and eat his dinner, as if he were Mark or Stevie. But today she felt as if she would never want to laugh again.

She couldn't keep on drying her hands indefinitely. She must go in there, and when she sat down they would see her, and in spite of their love and their belief in her, a silence would settle heavily upon them.

For one breathless instant she thought of telling them the whole story. But she knew at once that it was impossible, that she couldn't stand there under the searching gaze of all those masculine eyes and her mother's cool and measuring glance. The very thought of it sent color rushing hotly over her neck and face—a wave of heat across her whole body. Now, for them, she was innocent. But not after she told them about Simon Bird. They would never understand it in a thousand years; even she couldn't understand it now. The moment in the orchard seemed a moment in a shameful dream a long time ago.

They could forgive her for being talked about, lied about; but they couldn't forgive her for meeting Simon Bird.

She pulled out her chair and sat down. The younger boys kept arguing, and Philip, beside her, said, "Ahoy, Tiddleywinks!" Owen said, "Hi, brat," and went on eating baked haddock. Her mother smiled, her father nodded pleasantly, and they continued discussing the probability of the mailboat's running every day this summer instead of three times a week. Joanna looked at her heaped plate; baked stuffed haddock and mealy potatoes, swiss chard canned last summer. It was her favorite dinner but she couldn't eat it with that twisting, tightening knot where her stomach was. And she couldn't eat hot gingerbread with whipped cream, either.

Somehow the meal passed. Charles came in, and the eternal shop talk began again. Joanna made herself relax. It would be a good hour before she could escape either to her room or to the woods beyond Goose Cove. A vision rose before her eyes, a vision of a place she had found deep in the woods, where the silence was walled in by great spruces and she could walk in a cool green gloom pierced by thin, infrequent spears of sungold. A place where the soundless flight of hawks through the branches only increased her solitude.

Never, it seemed to her, had the Bennetts been so gay, so talkative, so noisy. Almost as if they were making a special effort to show her nothing bothered them.

At last she could clear the table and wash the dishes; at last the house was emptied, and Donna went to her room to lie down. Joanna worked mechanically, her mind absorbed in putting her thoughts in order. This story that Simon had begun from spite—he'd keep it going until someone stopped him. But here was the wall again, and she was already bruised from crashing against it.

Only Nils could try to stop him. But Simon would make no secret of it, if Nils split his lip or blackened his eye; he'd flaunt the marks around the shore, and she could almost hear his easy, silky voice: "Guilty conscience, that boy. Tryin' his damndest to shut me up. Hell, I bet anybody could take that Jo out, if they played their hand right. . . ."

No, Nils mustn't do anything. She washed and wiped dishes in a fury of speed. They must pretend Simon wasn't real. Those who wanted to believe him would believe him anyway, and the others would only laugh at him. Let it die, if a story about Joanna Bennett could ever die, she thought with the desolate woe of fifteen.

Owen came in with an armful of wood and dropped it in the box. "I guess that'll hold ye for the rest of the day. It's damn hot splitting spruce. Know it?" He drank a big dipperful of water and turned to go out again.

"Wait a minute, Owen!" she said impulsively.

"Hell, sis, I'm in a hurry." He scowled and pulled away as she caught his sleeve.

"Charles told me, out in the boat . . . Owen, aren't they going to say anything?"

"What is there to say? They don't believe any of that trash—no sense getting goweled about it."

"But the whole Island's talking!"

"We can't do anything about it, Jo. They'll always talk about us, and it can't hurt us so long as we know we're all right. Talk's cheap." He broke away. She stood watching him, her eyes wide with imminent tears.

At the door he turned back. "I been thinking, Jo. You didn't chance to see anybody hanging around the clubhouse last night, did you?"

She shook her head dumbly, her hands fumbling with plate and towel. He was already out. Through the screen door she saw him, poised against the glittering afternoon, eager and impatient to be off across the meadow to shore. "Owen, if you see Nils—"

"What about him?"

She turned back to her dishes. "Oh, nothing! You're in an awful pucker for anybody as lazy as you are."

She heard the peculiar crunch of rubber boots going away through the grass. The silence pressed about her, a silence made up of familiar sounds: the old clock on the shelf, the constant gentle rote of the sea on the rocks, the faint far-off clamor of gulls, the sleepy noonday talk of Donna's chickens under the windows. And in this silence the world suddenly righted itself. She would find Nils, talk it out with him, and that would be all. Her heart lifted with a swift buoyancy. Owen was right, talk was cheap, why should she listen to it or worry about it as long as it was lying talk? The family wasn't worrying.

In a sudden joyous reaction from despair she put away the dishes and hung up her apron. *Talk's cheap,* she repeated, as if it were a magic formula, which somehow it was. Of course it was hard, knowing you were being talked about like Thea Sorensen, or Marcus Yetton's wife, who was always making pies for Johnny Fernandez. But she wasn't Thea or Susie. She was Joanna Bennett.

"Joanna," said her father's unhurried voice, and she whirled with a gasp. He stood outside on the doorstep where Owen had just been. "Come out and sit with me a few minutes."

She sat down beside him, cross-legged in Indian fashion. The doorstep was in shadow, but out in the sun the grass was a green sea, while in the distance the ocean matched colors with the sky. Her father's pipe smoke mingled pleasantly with the lilac's dreamy fragrance. He looked thoughtfully at a lone spruce out on the point, his profile dark and somehow austere.

"Your mother tells me I don't know how to talk to a girl," he said wryly. "Maybe so."

"You do all right," said Joanna with an appreciative grin.

"Thanks . . . well, what I want to say doesn't take a lot of words." He turned his head and looked down at her, his smile warm in his eyes. "Jo, I'm asking you to do something—something to help your mother and me."

"Sure, what is it?"

Stephen Bennett sighed, and Joanna's fingers tightened around her ankles. All at once she knew what was coming.

"I'll be short about it," he said. "It's this. We don't want you down around the shore any more. We've let you run with the boys and their crowd all over the Island, in and out of the boats, because we thought it was a child's right to be free. But you're not a child now."

Not a child, but a frantic thing, wild and protesting as the cage doors shut. . . . I didn't know they'd do this! she thought passionately. They can't! . . . And her father's voice went steadily on.

"You're too big to be running around in dungarees and hanging on the boys' coattails. Remember when I sent you home yesterday? Well, a girl of your age always around the shore like that—it makes talk."

"Talk's cheap!" she said violently. But it wasn't magic any more, not against her father's words.

"Maybe, but it's not the way of our family to go about asking talk to be made." He sighed again. "Joanna, this is as hard for me as it is for you. But your mother and I've been thinking about it for quite a while, and this latest mess—do you know about it?"

"Charles told me."

He nodded. "Well, it's foul enough, but it was bound to come, Jo, the way we've let you run free. It's a sign. Sign you're growing up. People seeing you as a girl, not just Steve Bennett's kid."

"But I don't want to grow up!" The passionate words burst from her before she realized. "I wish something could happen to me so I'd stay a kid forever, if growing up means all this chew, and staying at home, and never having fun any more, just so they won't talk about the Bennetts!"

The compassion of his look brought the sting of tears to her eyelids. She was terribly ashamed. He stood up, and his big brown hand rumpled her hair affectionately.

"Joanna, I don't like telling you to stay home. It's like putting a gull in a cage. But it was bound to come sometime. You couldn't go on like that forever."

"I know it." Her lips felt stiff. *In a cage.* Four walls. Already she felt them closing in on her, stealing her very breath. And against them rose the too-vivid picture of the beach in the pale morning sunlight, young gulls fighting over a dead fish, a dory pushing off, the shining light on the sea, the sparkling drops falling from the blades of an oar.

Stephen was saying reasonably, "I don't expect you to sit in the house all day. I'm just asking you to quiet down. Remember, you're growing up, and you're the only girl we have. Your mother worries enough about the boys—"

"But you can keep your girl home," said Joanna, and by some miracle she smiled up at him.

"You're a good girl, Jo," he said, "You're the finest kind." He went by the lilac bushes and into the barn, where the shop was, and Joanna sat motionless on the doorstep. But there was nothing in her face that was unhappy or self-pitying. There were only narrow, dry eyes watching the splendid freedom of a gull's flight, and a curiously level mouth; there was a steely acceptance that was not resignation in Joanna's heart.

I'll stay home, she thought. The boys can ram around and drink, and raise hell, but talk doesn't matter if you're a boy. I'll stay home, and there'll be no cause for worry, or for any talk about Joanna Bennett for them to bring home.

But some day the Island will belong to me again.

Someday I'll be free.

7

JOANNA'S ROOM WAS A SMALL ROOM under the eaves, with a window looking over Schoolhouse Cove and the point, and impertinent little boats with red sails on the wall paper. It was a bare room, with its narrow white-painted bed, the chest with the faded red flowers, and the mirror over it.

Bare it was, but not if you garlanded it with the heartsinging hope or the heavy burden of despair that alternately lived in it along with Joanna, who came home from school across the bay so many times to unpack her suitcase on the narrow bed. . . . Fifteen, sixteen, seventeen. There were plenty of homecomings in three years, until that final June; plenty of times to kneel by the window, her arms on the sill, and breathe rapturously the scent that was the Island's own, or watch the snow slant blindingly across the winter-barren point and hide the gray sea, but never its voice.

But when she stopped in her unpacking, a dress in her hands, to watch a boat cut swiftly through the plunging water outside the cove like a gay and living thing, the rapture of return would be gone; the unspeakable delight of coming home to the Island, of which she had dreamed since the last departure, would disappear with the knowledge that the time was past when she could wriggle hastily into her dungarees and be off to the shore and the boats even before dinner.

With slow fingers she could put on a gingham dress and a starched apron, and go down to set the table, and tell Donna all the important things that were for her ears alone; then the men came in, and if they hadn't seen her at the wharf, she was kissed and hugged, and they were all happy together. But all the time, under the laughter and the eager talk, she remembered how it was when there was something urgent and satisfying to do that first afternoon; buoys to paint, or a sail in somebody's boat to try out a new engine, or a long lazy afternoon in the sun, with the boys painting or whittling, and talking about their latest hell-raising.

Then graduation came, and in her seventeenth summer on the Island, she discovered a new truth; that when boys begin to ask you to go to dances, and walk you home the long way — with a stop under a tree somewhere to tell you how sweet you are and pant passionately down your neck — when all this happens, you have lost forever the fine free comradeship of the shore. Stephen was right when he said it couldn't have gone on forever. She tried them all, but in the end it was Nils who took her to dances in the clubhouse and church in the schoolhouse. Nils alone was the same chum he had always been. The story had died, as as far as Joanna knew, no one even remembered it now. If they talked about her, it was to call her stuck-up and say she thought herself too good for the Island boys. But Joanna tilted her chin at the talk, and made sure they'd never have anything less harmless to say about her.

Donna's health was increasingly bad. Time was beginning to take its toll of the frail but indomitable woman who had brought six lusty Bennetts into the world. While Joanna was at school, Nils' younger sister Kristi worked at the big house as hired girl, with Nate's wife and daughter coming to help with the heavy housecleaning.

By fall of that seventeenth year, Joanna herself had decided her future. It was to be here, on the Island, with the family. No need for cousin Rachel or Aunt Mary to come up and help out any more, she told her parents arrogantly. Kristi could go home and help her grandmother. She, Joanna, already had the reins of the household in slim but very strong hands. All the stern promises she had made to herself that fifteenth summer, all the glowing dreams of a career carved out magnificently by Joanna Bennett, free adult in her own right—all faded away before the realization that she wanted to be with her mother, that she could fill the place of a daughter now as never before.

On her nineteenth birthday she stood in her little room, watching the purple winds of dusk come down across the cove, and thought back to the rebellious summer. She had come a long way since then, and there was still time enough before her in which to attain her heart's desire. Every one had a heart's desire, she knew. She couldn't have put hers into words. But the breath and being of the Island pervaded it. I'll know it when I see it, she thought, and meanwhile she could be patient. She was on the Island; the family was all together, except for the younger boys away at high school. And she was nineteen today.

She looked down at her sheer, fine stockings, the new suede shoes, and at the little silver watch on her slim brown wrist, and smiled. Nineteen was a magic word; as yet she didn't know why, but at intervals during the busy March day, she had thought, I'm nineteen! And it had sent a tingling warmth all through her.

Downstairs the back door was flung open, and voices arose in the kitchen, deep and strong and merry, full of vitality and the hungry delight of coming into a bright warm kitchen and the smell of supper, and Donna's smile. The men were back from hauling. It was time to run downstairs and get back to work, birthday or not.

They were all talking at once in the kitchen, their dark faces stung with red, rimed with frozen spray and flying vapor, their heavy clothes giving off the cold breath of out-of-doors. They had been gone since morning, because it had been the first good hauling day in two weeks. Now, home in the warm lamplit kitchen with money in their pockets and supper on the way, they were boisterous as they kicked off rubber boots and washed up. Winnie made ecstatic sorties at their heels, getting in a lick or a nip where she could.

Stephen put on his moccasins and went over to the dresser, where Donna was busy. Joanna heard his quiet voice, around his pipe. "Donna, where'd this bunch of wild hawks come from?"

The spatula lowered over the birthday cake she was frosting. "I married a wild hawk."

Philip had come out of the turmoil around the sink. "But you tamed him, lady," he said. "Tamed him proper, too."

"I wonder who'll tame them." Her blue-gray eyes rested serenely on Charles and Owen. "I don't wonder about you, Philip. You were born with manners, and a way of thinking first. But those two . . ."

The first son and the third were wrestling now, hard and supple bodies driving one against the other, steel wrist against wrist, broad shoulder against shoulder. "Charles has something to keep him in line," Donna said thoughtfully. "He's got to remember who he'll be some day. But Owen—"

"He's the wildest of the lot," Joanna put in. "Don't shake your head at me, Mother. You know it as well as we all do."

Stephen dropped his hand on his tall girl's shoulder. "Hello, birthday child. Sure, we know about Owen. Wild, maybe, but all Bennett straight through. And Life'll clip his wings."

"If a woman doesn't do it first." Philip lifted a quizzical eyebrow. "Ever think what a flock of strange women we'll bring into the family?"

"Often," said his father.

"I don't worry," Donna said. "But I think you boys will have to go off the Island for your wives—there's not much choice here right now."

"Why, Mother, what's wrong with a nice little Dutch heifer like Thea Sorensen?"

"God help us!" said Donna piously, and they all laughed. Philip's eyes and Donna's were the same clear bright gray-blue, crinkling at the corners and full of tiny sparkles when they laughed. Whoever got Philip would be luckiest of all the Bennett wives, Joanna thought. But all Bennett wives would be fortunate women.

Moving quickly between kitchen and pantry, she thought it would be strange indeed if Life didn't clip her brothers' wings. Hers had been clipped almost before she knew how to spread them. But if it had to be women who did it — and she knew the boys were too full of life and blood to live without women — she hoped with all her heart they would choose women of good stock, intelligent, serene, and clear-eyed, like their mother; women who were fit to carry the Bennett name, and bring strong healthy Bennett children into the world.

There'd been too many compulsory marriages on the Island and on Brigport for her not to realize the risks. There was Marcus Yetton, who'd been studying radio by correspondence, and had been considered a boy of great promise till Susie came into the picture. Susie, daughter of a transient fisherman who'd rented a camp for the summer to go trawling for hake. She'd been slovenly and dullwitted, with a faint gleam of prettiness that died as soon as the baby was on the way. Now all Marcus' promise was forgotten; it was a baby a year (in a vain effort to keep Susie at home, the Island said), a boat forever on the beach for repairs, and Susie an uncouth little slut who was a byword on the Island. And Marcus dragged down, down, till he was as low as she.

Jeff Bennett, Joanna's cousin, had a wife somewhere, living with her people. He sent five dollars a week for the child. And Thordis Sorensen, Nils' cousin and Thea's sister, got into trouble with Forest Merrill. They fought terribly, the whole Island knew it; Forest was always swearing she'd tricked him, that somebody else had been there first. . . .

It was something that could happen so easily, a wretched marriage like this, to anyone who was as fullblooded and vigorous as the Bennett boys. But they're *Bennetts,* she thought now, as their laughter and tomfoolery rang in her ears. They weren't just like anybody else, they weren't even like Jeff and Hugo. They had a pride in their name. It was that which would keep them straight.

Her mother gave her a light spank. "Look at all these starving men, and you lallygagging around with your mouth open like little Annie Yetton!"

"Where's the food?" Owen struck the dresser with a huge brown fist, and the lamps jumped.

"There goes that rooster again!" said Philip. They streamed toward the table, toward the fresh-baked hot yeast rolls and yellow butter churned in Nate Bennett's kitchen, the baked stuffed lobster that was Joanna's choice for her birthday supper, the potatoes in their crisp, shiny brown jackets, the pickles that held the spicy sweetness of last summer, the kale that might have been freshly picked instead of taken from a jar in the cellarway, the strong, good coffee, and the yellow Jersey cream in the squat pitcher.

They all talked at once, and to Joanna it was as if they were all warm and safe against the March wind and dusk outside — and against everything else. Nothing could touch them; her love for them all reached out and encompassed them. Though Mark and Stevie were at school on the mainland, they were all one together, so would always be.

It was while Joanna was cutting the cake that Stephen leaned back in his chair, looking rather pleased with life, and said, "Well, the folks for the Binnacle will be here tonight. Ned Foster called up when I was in the store this afternoon — the mailboat's moving them out."

"I'm glad somebody's going to live in that little house at last," Donna said, smiling faintly. "It's such a nice little house, right on the harbor. I hated to leave it when we came up here to live after Grandpa Bennett died "

"Well, the Fosters are just the people for it. He'll be a credit to the Island — he's quiet and he works hard."

"Swell ice cream, Jo," said Owen indulgently. "Tough on you to have to make it yourself on your birthday. If I'd been home, I'd have froze it for you." His eyes glinted behind his thick lashes as he glanced at his father. "What's Ned Foster's wife like?"

"She's probably fifty and sprung in the knees, Cap'n Owen," said Joanna. "Don't look so interested."

"I've never met her," Stephen said. "But they're plain, sober people. I wish we had more of them, instead of the stuff that's come ashore here like so much driftwood. The Eastern End Crowd — the Trudeaus —"

"What's wrong with them?" asked Charles. His voice seemed suddenly sharp.

"What isn't wrong with them?" Owen said with easy contempt. "The *Cecile* looks like an old hake-boat — grease, old bait, and herring scales. I guess Jake never owned a broom to scrub up with."

"The house hasn't been painted since Adam was a kitten." That was Philip. "I suppose it doesn't matter so damn much, living down there on the Eastern End like some of those Kentucky mountaineers. But one of these days that fish house is going to topple to hell overboard."

Stephen nodded. "The whole place down there is a disgrace to the Island. The Trudeaus are too far below the standard your grandfather tried to keep up. Nate was a fool to let Jake buy the Eastern End, just because Jake had a roll of bills in his pocket. Never even asked him where he got the money or why he left his home town in Canada." Stephen began to fill his pipe. "I know Jake's been rum-running since he came to the Island, too. All those trips of his up and down the bay . . . And that lazy young devil Maurice—does he ever do anything but sit around with a fiddle under his chin?" He smiled as he said it, for everyone, even Stephen, had a half-contemptuous liking for Maurice. "I don't say they're bad people, they're just—"

"Just what?" Charles leaned forward, his coppery cheekbones darkening.

Stephen looked at him in good-natured surprise. Owen grinned, deviltry in his eyes. "He's scared you'll say something about that French filly there, Mateel."

There was all at once a silence in the room. Owen broke it, his light tone forced, trying to wipe out what he'd said. "There's not a man on the Island wouldn't like to take her out. But I guess she's waitin' for one of those ginks on a big white horse."

Stephen looked around the table at his sons, and his dark eyes rested on each one in turn; his voice was slow and pleasant. "It's a good idea to let her wait, then. Maybe he'll come along. You boys—" He glanced at his wife, a little current of understanding seemed to pass between them. "You boys will be in my place some day. I hope you pick out your wives as carefully as I picked mine."

"Is that an order, Father?" Charles' eyes were narrow and brilliant. "You make it sound pretty clear."

"I could make it sound even clearer," said Stephen. "I could tell you I don't ever want to see a Bennett boat anchored in Eastern End Cove."

"Don't worry, Father," Philip said pleasantly. "I guess the rooster's right—Mateel won't look at anybody the Island can provide."

"Same with Jo," said Owen. "She turns up her nose at all of 'em."

"Except Nils. Old Faithful," murmured Philip.

Donna said comfortably, "There's no foolishness between Nils and Joanna."

The taut instant was past. Joanna began to cut more cake, and the sharp intensity in the poise of Charles' head, in his whole bearing, relaxed. He sat back and took out his cigarettes.

8

THE HARBOR WAS A WILDERNESS of tossing black water and a knife-edged wind keen with salt; the *Aurora B.* pulled at her already taut lines, the wharf groaned and creaked, the water gurgled and hissed and surged over the rocks below the planks. Every available man and boy on Bennett's Island was there to help carry the Fosters' goods ashore.

The *Aurora*'s masthead lights, and a lantern hung high on the wharf, illumined the work that was a race against time and tide and the ever-rising wind. Joanna felt excitement run and sing through her veins; the hurry, the voices, the strong sea smell, the water, the swinging lantern, even the groaning timbers—they all made her wildly, almost drunkenly happy. She pressed close to the shed, to be out of the wind. There was haste and laughter and cheerful profanity all around her. She watched Charles run along the bulwark from bow to stern, agile as a tightrope walker. Nils and Sigurd, bare heads yellow in the lantern light, tossed chairs to the wharf with magnificent abandon. Philip and Jeff Bennett caught them with an equal flourish.

"Haven't they got nice furniture?" said Kristi Sorensen, close to her ear. Kristi was plump and fair, with round blue eyes and a wonderful capacity for bewilderment.

"Lovely," said Joanna, "but not when those boys get through with it." A high, irrepressible giggle shrilled from the dense shadows in the shed. "Thea," said Joanna. "Your fascinating cousin. She's been switching her tail at the boys."

Kristi looked shocked. "If Grampa comes down here and catches her —"

Joanna dodged, as Jeff and Philip came past with a table. She peered across the wharf to where her father stood in the dusk at the edge of the lantern light. There were two people with him, slight shadows against his height.

"Have you seen the Fosters?" she asked Kristi. "He's a little gray man. But I can't get a good look at her."

"She prob'ly isn't much. It's awful cold, Jo. Come on up to the house for a while."

"I want to see this Foster woman," sald Jo. "Who's afraid of a little weather? Or is it Gunnar you're scared of?"

The words faded on her lips. Her father and the Fosters were coming toward her across the rough planks where the lantern threw its yellow glow. Owen took this moment to leap from the boat to the wharf, his plaid mackinaw flying, his hair a black crest in the wind. Nils sprang up after him, caught him by the arms, and shouted, "Over you go!" For a moment they swayed, laughing, at the wharf's very edge, teeth a white glitter in their tanned faces, cheeks red with cold, one head so fair and the other so dark.

"Careful, boys," Philip said, and they stopped their horseplay. But their eyes still shone with laughter and excitement, they were breathing hard. Mrs. Foster looked up at them, the lantern light full upon her. Joanna saw a trimly plump woman with a white face; a woman whose slow smile curled her pale mouth oddly at the corners, and slipped upward to the heavy-lidded eyes. A pretty woman, one might call her; pretty in a strange, a quiet, and an exquisitely neat fashion.

"Yes, please don't drown yourselves," she said, and Joanna heard as if in a little bubble of silence the low,. almost throaty quality of her voice. She had never heard tones like these; on the Island, voices were soft and quick, with slurred consonants and broad vowels.

The boys stood looking at her, quickly intent. Joanna saw their eyes grow keen. There was something about her that sharpened one's glance.

"That fur coat is some handsome," Kristi whispered enthusiastically. "Real fur, too."

In the shed there was a panicky squeal from Thea, a scramble among the hogsheads, Hugo's merry salute.

"*Hullo,* Thea darlin'! How's my little Dutch heifer tonight? And who's that with you? Oh, I won't tell on you, my boy!" He came out on the wharf, flashlight in hand, and grinned at Joanna. "More damn fun with this buglight— My God, is *that* what I helped ashore a little while ago? I didn't get a good look." He stared at Mrs. Foster, his eyes narrowed, as she smiled up at Owen and Nils.

"She doesn't look like much to me," said Kristi. "And she's married, Hugo Bennett, so you'd better not have ideas."

"Well, sweetheart, if you won't let me love *you* up, I gotta have something!" His eyes were dancing. "Christ, I'll bet old man Foster has his hands full with that one!"

"You're crazy as a coot," said Kristi, with a sniff.

"Come on, you guys, look alive there!" Link Hall yelled from the hold. "If I stay here much longer my boat'll go to pieces!"

"And my wharf'll be sailing to hell down the bay!" Pete Grant yelled back at him. Hugo took a flying leap aboard, Nils and Owen behind him.

"Keep your shirt on, Link m'boy," said Owen paternally. "We'll get you out of here faster'n you can spit through a knothole."

"Come *on,* Jo," said Kristi between chattering teeth, and at last, acknowledging the cold wind, Joanna left the wharf.

9

MARCH, FULL OF WIND AND STORM, came to a boisterous close. Spring was perceptible in the soft breathing of the wind, a new and tender blueness in the sea, the increasing clamor of the gulls who had been silent for so long. Joanna woke in the morning to hear them harsh and jubilant, rising and falling over the harbor like scraps of white paper blown by the wind.

At noon, now, the sun was very warm, and the ground smelled damp and fresh, and there was green grass in the sheltered places. The men stood around on the beach, talking about the spring crawl when the lobsters came in from deep water. But most of the time they were busy making traps, painting buoys, and many a ball of marlin was carried home to be knit into trapheads by the women.

Joanna knit for her brothers and her father, and they paid her for her work. Her hands were quick and strong, and her knots held. She didn't mind the oiled green twine that was harsh to her fingers. It didn't take long to knit up a ball; she sat by the sitting room window and worked at odd moments, while she was waiting for the men to come down to breakfast or in the few minutes before the dinner potatoes were done. Or she might spend an hour or so in the afternoon while Donna mended, and they would talk.

This is a day to be out, Joanna thought one afternoon, as she watched the patterned circling of gulls high above the harbor. Clouds raced across the northern sky; great white ones shadowed with purple, small soft gray ones. The prospect was forever changing, only the line of trees and rocks below remained the same.

From the room behind her came Donna's quiet voice. "Joanna, you've been working at that long enough. Why don't you get out into the air for a while? Why don't you go down and see Kristi?"

"There's only one thing wrong with that, Mother. Kristi has a grandfather."

"It's wicked to hate that old man, Joanna."

Joanna shook her head. "I like Kris too well to go down there and watch that old devil bully her."

"Gunnar *is* hard. But he's had a hard life," Donna said. "It was too bad Karl's wife died, and he had to take his children to his parents, but Anna is a good woman."

"She's a saint. And Gunnar is a fiend." Joanna pulled a knot tight with a vindictive jerk. "Wish I had his neck right here!" Some day he'll pay for what he did to Nils and me, she thought. Gunnar and Simon. Gunnar for his sarcasm and Simon for his lies.

She looked down at the harbor and saw a boat come around Eastern Harbor Point, a gallant white boat riding the combers like a thoroughbred. It was Nils. He had his own power boat now. Another boat came in behind him, a low-slung green boat. That would be the new man, Ned Foster, whose wife was so quiet and neat. Joanna saw her sometimes in the store on boat days; she always stood at one side, hardly speaking, but smiling her odd smile when anyone greeted her. She seemed to be withdrawn into a world of her own.

"The boys'll be in soon," Donna said. "They'll probably want a mug-up."

"Coffee and pie," said Joanna. She went into the kitchen and moved the teakettle over the fire. Winnie, under the stove, thumped her tail in greeting. "Hello, old lady," Joanna said to her. "Kind of tame around here without those wild Indians, isn't it?" Winnie thumped some more and went back to sleep and a dream of the mice she liked to hunt in the barn.

Owen was the first to come in, with a great stamping of feet and slamming of doors after which he said in concern, "Mother asleep?"

"No, you idiot," said Joanna. "How could she be, with you coming in like the devil in a gale of wind? What's that all over your boots?"

"Bait," said Owen with relish. "Doesn't it smell good?"

"It smells good in the bait house but not in my clean kitchen. Take off your boots, my little man."

"What makes you so ugly? God, what a face to greet a hard-working man with!"

She laughed at him, because his eyes were so merry. "You must've got a good haul."

"Hundred and sixteen pounds, darlin' mine! I'm high man to-day. Where's my mug-up? Set out a couple extra cups, kid. Nils and Hugo are coming up and we're going to cut pot limbs."

"Why don't you go with them, Joanna? You haven't been out all day," said Donna from the doorway. She smiled at her children, her eyes luminously blue, her fair head held with serene dignity.

Owen went to her and laid his hands lightly on her shoulders. "Well, my dear," he said, and there was a sudden tenderness across his bold dark face. "All you need is a crown and a train and you'd look like a queen."

"She looks like one already, even in a housedress," said Joanna. She set out mugs and spoons with a cheerful clatter and cut extra-large wedges of dried-apple pie.

The tide was racing in Goose Cove as they followed the grassy edge of the beach; the three boys with hatchets in their belts, potwarp coiled over their arms. Nils carried a saw. Hugo, whose red plaid shirt set off his dark good looks, was brimming with his own particular sort of deviltry. Owen was still in a glow of triumph from his good haul. Nils alone was silent, almost morose.

Joanna managed to fall behind the others when he stopped to examine an old trap on the rocks. "What's the matter?" she asked bluntly.

Nils' mouth twitched. "Grampa."

"As usual! Honestly, Nils, I pity you kids, having to live with him! It almost makes me glad my grandfather's up in the cemetery. What ails Gunnar — spring in his blood?"

"Yep. Kris and David wanted to come along with me — no reason why they couldn't! We were halfway across the barnyard when he yelled at us. It was just plain damn ugliness, and I told him so. . . . Well, Gramma's crying, Kris is in her room, and David's washing down the henhouse."

His words came hard and tight. "He won't dare touch Kris. But if he lays a hand on that kid — Joanna, before God — if he's touched

David, when I get home I'll string the old bastard up by the thumbs and take his own whip to him."

"I wish you would," said Joanna.

Nils looked out for a moment at the white foam on Goose Cove Ledge. Then he shrugged. "Come on, they'll be yelling at us," he said.

They walked along over the white beach rocks, surf tumbling toward them and retreating with a deep, sucking roar. The water was pale green and gray in the faint sunshine.

"I can't put up with much more of it," Nils said. "When my father comes back from the mainland I'm going to have a talk with him. We could have a place of our own — Kristi could keep house, and we'd all be a damn sight happier."

"Oh, golly, yes," said Joanna with enthusiasm. She had never seen Nils quite so angry; she had certainly never heard him call his grandfather an old bastard. Always he had been silent on family affairs, he had been patient with the old tyrant. Too patient, Joanna thought sometimes. . . . "Do you think Karl will listen?" she asked doubtfully.

Nils laughed, without amusement. "Oh, he'll listen. But he'll listen to Grampa too. And Grampa always comes out on top. Father's so used to letting Gunnar live his life for him I can't figure out how he ever managed to get married. Grampa named Sigurd and Kris and me as it was." His voice softened abruptly. "All but David. My mother had her own way for once — and then she died."

Joanna put her hand on his arm, but she didn't speak. Words were needless between her and Nils. He looked down at her hand; at the same time Owen hailed them over the sound of water and wind.

"Cripes almighty, are you two with us or taking a walk by yourselves?"

Nils' austere face broke suddenly into a youthful grin. "The rooster's sounding off. We'd better drive 'er!" They ran, longlegged and fleet and young, across the cove toward the wet dark woods.

They climbed a wooded slope, over fallen spruces and dead branches, and lichened outcroppings of rock. The young trees were brilliantly green among the old ones; here and there a birch stood alone, slender and very white against the darker trees, its bare branches spread in a delicate tracery tinged with amethyst. Little streams of water ran down the slope, across pads of emerald-green moss, to disappear into the ground before they reached Goose Cove. In the sheltered hollows there was ice, but in open places where the sun could reach, there were patches of new green grass, and tiny leaves that meant violets to come.

They scaled the rocky steepness and came to the cemetery, with the orchard beyond it; the wind-racked apple trees were bare, but there seemed to be a faintly rosy tint along the gray trunks. The buds on the big maple that towered above the cemetery were beginning to show red. In a week they would gleam like so many brilliant candle flames against the dark firs.

"My tree," said Joanna briefly, touching the trunk. Nils nodded. "Pretty," he said.

"Who is?" demanded Hugo, swinging around. "Hey, what are you saying to my cousin, you Svenska?"

Owen was inspecting a clump of well-grown spruces with narrow, speculative eyes. "Not much here," he said. "Five or six limbs out of the whole bunch, maybe. Not worth the time."

"He looks at those trees the way he looks at a bunch of women," said Hugo. "You should've seen him last time we went ashore. Looked down that big Bennett nose at everything in skirts. I don't know what in hell he wants for a woman, anyway."

Owen grinned. "Some day I'll show you, son," he promised lazily.

They attacked the next slope, sodden and dark under trees whose branches matted so closely that no sunshine ever struck through. It was cold and damp here, but suddenly they were on the rise, and overhead the sky had cleared all at once to a sunlit, luminous blue. There was warmth and light all around them, and enough trees of the right size to cut limbs for a hundred pots. Later, in the shop, the limbs would be arched into the bows that were the skeletons for the new traps.

Hugo, the slightest of the boys, went up into the first tree. He was incredibly nimble in his heavy rubber boots.

"Looks natural as hell, don't he?" said Owen.

"Anybody that don't believe we come from monkeys ought to see that," said Nils. "Clear proof, just as sure as you're born."

"All he needs is a tail to swing from," Joanna chimed in, while Hugo shouted from the treetop like an embattled eagle.

"Get that saw up here, goddam it! Laugh, you fools, while I'm stuck in a mess of pitch I'll never get free of!"

"We'll leave you there for a monument to something or other," Joanna consoled him. Nils handed up the saw and Hugo began on the nearest limbs. Nils lopped off the choice boughs that grew close to the ground; Owen trimmed them smooth with his hatchet. They worked well together, with no wasted motion.

Joanna sat on a sun-dried stump, listening to the busy "yank-yank" of the nuthatches, an occasional hawk's sharp cry, the trilling and tuning-up of sparrows in the woods. She felt contented here; if only she too could have had a hatchet to cut limbs, she would have been completely happy. But it was pleasant to look for signs of spring around her, and watch the boys at work. Owen was really handsome, she thought with pride; it was nice to have a good-looking family. His every motion was strong and vigorous, his very pose was suggestive of controlled but endless energy.

Nils, tying up a bundle of limbs with potwarp, lifted his yellow head toward her; his faint smile came and went, and then he was absorbed again. With the smile gone, his thin face was taut-lipped, and Joanna felt a pang of angry sympathy.

Life was no easy business for Nils, who must watch his younger sister and brother grow up in the shadow of a viciously domineering old grandfather. His father was a weak wraith of a man who had escaped from the unkind reality of life by simply ignoring it. He worked from day to day in a waking dream. Sigurd, the oldest son, could laugh at everything, even his grandfather. There was a time when he had laughed once too often, and now he lived alone — and right merrily — in a camp on the beach. Nils could have gone to live with him, but he was not of the stuff that looks for an easy escape. He chose to stay with David and Kristi. Loyalty was not just a word to him; loyalty was the very substance of his being, stubborn, patient, and enduring.

Her mind came back suddenly to the sunny clearing, with the nuthatches' busy voices and the pungence of fresh-cut spruce wood, the mild wind stirring her hair on her neck. It must have been Hugo who broke her train of thought.

"You guys — you don't have any technique," he was saying, leaning precariously out from the tree.

"Look at the trash that fish is throwing down," said Owen. "He's thinking so much about his technique he don't know what he's cutting. He's no more use than a flea."

"And just as big an itch," said Nils dryly.

"Go ahead and chew," Hugo invited them. "My shoulders are broad. Anyway, I feel so goddam good I don't care how much you prod." He looked irrepressibly merry. He waited, saw poised in air, and Joanna wanted to chuckle. Hugo was bragging again, and his audience was extremely unhelpful.

"Of course I understand how it is," he said generously. "When a man knows he just can't get anywhere with a woman, cripes, I'd be the last one to blame him for looking ugly." "Put him out of his misery, boys," said Joanna. "Ask him who it is."

Owen drove his hatchet into a stump and cast a resigned glance heavenward. "All right," he said on a sigh. "Whose leg you been feelin' now?"

Hugo came down the tree, attempted to look nonchalant, and failed. Nils sat back on his heels and lit a cigarette. "I suppose we got to listen to his childish prattle."

"You'll laugh off the other side of your face when I get through telling you." Hugo settled against a warm tree trunk, looking dreamy. "Well, I was drivin' 'er along from the store about sundown one day last week—a Tuesday, it was—or was it Thursday? Well, here I am, and there's a lady going to the well with a bucket. So, being a gentleman like all the Bennetts, I carried the bucket home for her."

"Who was it—Susie Yetton?" said Nils. Owen chuckled. And Hugo, with an elaborate indifference that couldn't possibly hide his triumph, said, "Well, boys, I carried that pail of water into the Binnacle."

Owen said incredulously, "The Binnacle? *Leah Foster?*"

"Surprised, ain't you?" Hugo's mouth twitched with excited laughter. "Well, it's true. You could've knocked me stiffer'n a maggot . . . Old Neddie watches her like a hawk, but he'd gone to Vinalhaven, and I guess the lady was lonely."

Owen was frankly scornful. "My God, you're kind of hard up, aren't you?"

"Lemme tell you, chummy!" Exultant color burned on Hugo's cheekbones. "She's got something you'll never find the like of!"

"You been back since then?" Nils asked.

"Sure. Just last night." Hugo looked dreamily into the cigarette smoke, shook his head, and sighed deeply. It was a blissful sound. "I guess it's no picnic for her, married to that old man, and her still a young woman."

Owen straightened up, lower lip prominent and eyebrows a scowling black bar across his brown face. "Let me get this straight. You mean you just carried a pail of water home for her and that was all there was to it?"

"Sure! Asked me to stop a while, in that nice little voice of hers. Welcomed me right in. And you can't blame a fella for trying to be friendly . . . if she acts like she'd like some friendliness." Hugo twinkled, and Joanna stood up.

"He's getting set to tell you all the details. I'm going for a walk before I get embarrassed."

"As if you never stood around and listened with all ears to his crazy yarns," grunted Owen.

"And believed all he said about his technique and just how he gets his women," added Nils.

Joanna rumpled Hugo's head. "Never mind, darlin', if it wasn't for you and your women, I'd never have learned the facts of life. Give me your knife, Owen. I'll get some spruce gum for Mark and Stevie."

As she walked away, she heard Hugo begin, with a deliberate drawl, "Well, when I went into the kitchen . . ." His voice faded as she entered the cool sun-spattered gloom under the great spruces that abruptly walled her in. The path was black mud underfoot, but the gently swaying treetops touched April's cloud-dappled skies.

It was too early yet for the small song birds that would come in migration time to spend the warm months in the Island woods, but the crossbills, the nuthatches, and an early robin were noisily industrious all around Joanna. From the topmost branches of a dead fir, a crow made hoarse inquiries, challenging Joanna's presence here in his domain.

This was the highest part of the Island. In a little while the path turned steeply downward, there was a scent of salt water edging the breeze, and a deepening roar from not-distant surf. Joanna, whistling under her breath, filled her pockets with spruce gum. She wondered if the younger boys, when they opened the box, would remember how the woods looked in spring, how the mud squished around your feet and small coins of sunlight slipped through the green boughs and were warm on your face.

A freshening wind, a glimmer of light beyond the dark trunks, and she knew she was coming out to the water— Old Man's Cove, on the west side. It was hardly more than a gash in the towering red-brown rock. As Joanna went down on the beach the blown spray fell on her cheeks with a cold light touch. The mouth of the cove was choked with foam; beyond it the whole western sea was a sheet of rippling silver, and the world was full of the vast roar. Tiny and shrill came the cries of the gulls as they floated high on the wind.

It was a moment before Joanna's eyes saw a man knee-deep in the surf. His boots were pulled up to his hips, and the foam swirled about his legs as he watched a plank drive toward him through the creamy green and white froth. He was dark against the sun as he caught the plank and waded shoreward, dragging his catch up over the rolling beach stones. Then Joanna saw the coppery gleam of hair that meant Simon Bird.

Almost at the same moment Simon saw her. It had been three years since she had spoken to him. Meeting him on the road or at the store, she looked past him with remote dark eyes. Even in the rush and laughter of a square dance, she would be silent in his arms, as if he didn't exist, and sometimes he would tighten his fingers around her hand until she bit her lips to keep from crying out; but her silence always held, and when he let her go his mouth would be thinned and hard, his face drained white with fury beneath his red crest.

Now he was coming up the beach toward her in long rapid strides, and he was smiling a little. Because I'm not running away, Joanna thought. Because he knows he could catch up with me if I did run . . . Her hands in her jacket pockets had unconsciously clenched, and her face felt cold, as if the blood had quite left it. Watching him, knowing he would presently be close enough to speak, she wondered if anybody else in the world possessed a hatred like this one. When she met Gunnar Sorensen, her resentment boiled and bubbled inside her, and swift turbulent words fought to come out instead of the civil, "Hello, Mr. Sorensen." But it was different when she saw Simon. It was a cold and soundless thing . . . And deadly.

"Hello, Joanna," he said, and it was as she remembered it, the narrow, smoky-gray eyes looking at her with an odd concentration in spite of the easy smile; the voice that was soft as a cat's tread when it stalked a bird. "You're far from home," the voice said.

She looked at him wordlessly, with a black and insolent stare; her bold cheekbones, whipped red by the wind, her strong Bennett nose, her very chin, expressed her supreme contempt.

So they faced each other.

"Mad, ain't ye?" he said. "You've been mad for a hell of a long time, and I don't know as I blame you." She didn't answer, and he went on, "I've been wanting to tell you for a long time," he said, "I know I didn't do right. But I was crazy wild . . . You're grown-up now, you're smart, you're not one of these narrow ones who don't understand the way a man is when a girl's got him hogtied." It was soft and it was beguiling, the way he looked into her eyes. Once, Joanna had been beguiled. But only once.

Her voice was level and chill. "My father has never forbidden anyone to go on his land. But if I can't walk on it without being annoyed, he'll have to do something about it." She felt a sharp pleasure in seeing his face darken. "We can't keep people off the water, no matter how rotten they are. But we *can* keep them off our property."

He took a step toward her, his lips twisting, and she said tranquilly, "The boys are just up yonder in the woods. And they don't like you, for some reason."

She turned back toward the trees, forcing herself to walk when every nerve and muscle cried out to run. He won't dare touch me, she thought. He won't dare . . . Behind her, Simon spoke.

"I won't forget this in a hurry," he said clearly through the ocean's roar. "I won't forget this, sweetheart. And you won't forget it, either."

10

THE ACCORDION RIPPLED BACK and forth between Sigurd's hands. He kept time with one foot, and his forehead glistened with sweat. *Ha ha ha! you and me!* the accordion laughed, merry and loud and unfaltering over the sound of dancing feet. Maurice Trudeau leaned against the stove with his fiddle under his chin, and its voice was elfin-sweet. Sigurd was a yellow-maned Viking, and Maurice was a French-Canadian faun, and the music they made together was lilting and intoxicating and like no other music in the world. The bright notes cascaded from one tune to another. "Soldiers Joy," "Stack of Barley," "The Girl with the Hole in Her Stocking," "The Devil's Dream," and many a nameless polka and hornpipe they had known forever, yet couldn't say where they had first learned it. But they always came back to "Little Brown Jug." Charles Bennett, leading Mateel Trudeau up the hall in a Lady of the Lake, began to sing, and the others picked it up.

"Ha, ha, ha!" they all sang in a mammoth explosion of laughter, until the hanging lamps seemed to sway, and those who stood outside, smoking in the soft April darkness, looked in at the windows. Everybody sang. Old Gunnar, swinging his rosy little wife with almost as much lionlike strength as he used to have, sang, and bowed to his partner with an Old Country flourish. Sigurd roared over the accordion. Jake Trudeau, whom even a white shirt and a shave couldn't keep from looking like a buccaneer, sang it too, swinging Miss Hollis, the teacher, until her feet came off the floor and she forgot her dignity long enough to shriek. Everybody laughed, and Marcus Yetton's youngest, tucked in its basket, woke up and howled.

This was the first dance since last summer, called up in a hurry because of this April day that was like a breath of June. It had been a day of forget-me-not seas and tranquil skies; and now the moon rode high overhead. It was the moonlight and the lack of wind that had enticed the Brigport crowd across the sound.

A good dance, one part of Joanna's mind said, while another part dreamed a little; a good night to walk, it thought. A good night to walk, if you were in love. You could live in another world on a night like this, if there were someone to help you bear its beauty.

But she wasn't in love, and here in the hall her brother Charles was swinging her faster and faster, his dark face laughing and a little crazy; the music might have been strong wine. He let her go, still spinning, and Tim Gray caught her and swung her again. But Tim, tall and quiet-spoken and sandy, was no devil on the dance floor. He held her gently, and then they went down the hall and back, hand in hand, for the Ladies' Chain.

Her father swung her next. "You're as bad as the boys!" she gasped as the rafters whirled across her vision. He laughed and released her. As she went back to Tim she had a glimpse of her Aunt Mary moving toward Stephen like a ship in full sail. Donna was at the dance, but the contre dances were too much for her.

When Hugo slipped his arm around her waist, she smelled liquor. His dark eyes were blazing. He'd been out on the porch with the Brigport crowd.

"Promenade the hall!" Sigurd shouted, and the dance was over in one final mad whirl. The women sank to the benches, handkerchiefs patting wet faces. Most of the men disappeared outside. Joanna went into the little kitchen and found Nils there. He filled a thick white mug from the water pail.

"Have some Adam's ale."

"Thanks. When did you get here? I thought you were going to bed early."

"I thought I'd come over and keep an eye on you." They grinned at each other and let a companionable silence overtake them. Joanna leaned on the serving shelf, watching the faces that were vague in the soft lamplight, filmed with cigarette smoke. The door to the poolroom was open; she saw her father, Karl Sorensen, and Pete Grant, playing, with an intent gallery of spectators.

"May I have this dance, Miss Bennett?" said Nils in her ear. *Smile the while you bid me sad adieu,* sang Maurice's violin.

"Yes indeed, Mr. Sorensen." She dropped a mock curtsey and they moved out on the floor with the ease that comes of long practice. It had been Nils, at twelve, who taught a pigtailed ten-year-old Joanna to waltz.

There was Kristi, with pink in her cheeks, sitting beside young Peter Gray. Joanna lifted her hand to them in a mischievous salute. Gunnar was unexpectedly genial tonight, letting them sit together like that. . . . Joanna's smile died when she saw Thordis, Kristi's cousin; she sat beside her grandmother, yet she seemed curiously alone. The sleeping two-year-old in her arms didn't hide her swollen and discouraged body. The yellow hair was dull, there was no spark of invitation left in the weary blue eyes that watched Forest Merrill, her husband, joke endlessly with one of the young Brigport girls.

Joanna wondered where it had taken place, the mad instant when the gawky, sullen-mouthed Forest had suddenly become to Thordis the sum of her whole desire, blotting out the family, the dreaded grandfather, the gossip — blotting out the whole world until she wasn't strong enough to fight the sweetly evil tide that drowned her senses.

You fool, Joanna thought with arrogant pity. This is what you've got. Didn't you know you could have had more than this? More than Forest? Or didn't you care who took you and gave you a baby before you were eighteen?

There was Thordis' sister, coming in through the door and leaving someone behind her on the porch. Tonight it was one of the Brigport boys. You'd never guess, as Thea sat down primly beside her mother, smoothing her skirt over her knees, that she'd gone anywhere but out on the piazza for a breath of air. But if Gunnar ever got his eye on the spruce spills in her hair, it would be a different story.

Maurice's bow quickened, and the dance whirled to a rather breathless close. It drew near to midnight and the older people gradually left; only the younger ones danced on. The square dances moved steadily toward a riotous state.

Her brother Philip led Joanna out for a Liberty Waltz, which from the beginning was a hopelessly confused affair. Spring was in the air tonight, and a sort of high-pitched exhilaration — only a small percentage of it alcoholic — spread through the group. They were like young horses turned out to pasture in early spring. They couldn't be serious or decorous on the dance floor to save their lives.

The Liberty Waltz turned into a romp. A few girls dropped out, and Joanna was much in demand. Tim Gray snatched her from a Brigport lad; laughing and out of breath she slipped from his grasp into Nils' arms.

Amiably he moved into step with her. "Slow down, slow down," he admonished her. "If you want to hop, dance with Grampa."

"He's gone. And he made Kristi go home, too." Joanna frowned. "She's eighteen—she doesn't need to mind him."

"Habit," said Nils with a wry grin.

"All join hands!" Sigurd called, trying to restore order. But Joanna held back from the circle. "This is too much of a mess. And I'm scared I'll get Ash Bird again."

"What's the matter with him?"

"He's got a feverish clutch, and he's afraid of me. Makes it awful for both of us . . . I want a drink of water and then a cigarette. If you're my friend, you'll fix it up so my strait-laced cousin Rachel won't see me."

"Come on," Nils said indulgently. For a moment he paused, looking down at her laughter-flushed face and sparkling eyes. She winked impishly and walked ahead of him into the kitchen.

The Robey boys, from Brigport, lounged against the sink. The little room was stifling with the mingled reek of liquor, fishy work clothes, and cigarette smoke. And Simon Bird was there. It seemed to Joanna that his face came suddenly toward her out of the gloom. He stared at her, his nostrils flaring a little, his eyes set in dark hollows. It was only for an instant, and then Tom Robey, an amiable young giant, was booming at her, "Evenin', fair one!"

She smiled at him. "Hi, Tom. Hi, Milt. Any water left in that pail?"

"If there ain't, one of these lubbers can go after some," said Tom.

Nils spoke civilly to Simon, who didn't answer. Joanna felt his eyes on her. Let him stare, she thought, shrugging.

"Any lobsters around your island, Cap'n Tom?" Nils asked.

"Hell, the place is alive with 'em. Never saw the bugs so thick." They were instantly deep in shop talk. Joanna looked out at the happy chaos that was the Liberty Waltz.

"I'm takin' you home," said Simon. He was suddenly very close. If she turned her head, she would be looking directly into his eyes.

She didn't move. She only listened to that soft, whispering voice. "I'm takin' you home. So save the last waltz."

She gazed straight before her at the dancers. "It's taken. And what makes you think I'd let you have it, anyway? You should know how particular I am, by now."

"I don't know as you got any call to be fussy. There's others in your family that don't seem to care what they pick up with."

She turned then and looked at him. She was aware of Nils' voice behind her: "But if you car your lobsters and take 'em ashore yourself, instead of selling out here —"

The cup of water was heavy in her hand. For a moment she looked at Simon, one eyebrow tilted. "You need to cool off," she said, and tossed the water directly into his face.

For an instant he didn't move, then like a cat he came at Joanna, his hands reaching for her. She stepped back and felt a great arm go around her, to hold her tight against a rocklike chest. A hand the size of a lobster-pot reached past her and grasped Simon's sweater.

"Now stay off, son," Tom Robey drawled. "You hadn't ought to get mad because a gal's a mite high-spirited."

Simon was inarticulate and pale with fury. Milt Robey was chuckling, and Nils was saying calmly, "You'd better get out of here, Simon, before we turn the whole bucket over you."

"Let go of me, Robey," said Simon thickly.

"Don't lose your temper, m'boy." Tom was paternal. "You jest rest a bit and let *me* handle the little spitfire. What'll I do with her?"

Simon told him, the ugly words grinding out between his teeth with shocking venom. The Robeys roared. Nils moved forward, but Owen, incredibly, was there first, and they hadn't even seen him come into the doorway. His fist took Simon neatly on the chin, and like a felled tree, Simon went down.

"Good enough," said Nils. "You can let her go now, Tom."

Owen scowled. "Yeah, let go my sister. What goes on here?"

"Run along, blackie boy," said Tom. Joanna felt his laughter rumble in his chest. The reek of whiskey and fish was suffocatingly strong. "We was doin' all right before you showed up. What kind of a fool d'ye think I am, to get hold of a pretty girl and not even kiss her?"

His great voice carried above the hilarious racket in the hall, and the nearest dancers looked curiously toward the kitchen. His chin scraped Joanna's cheek. Furiously she swung her head hard against his jaw.

Robey laughed. "Fight away, darlin'! I like wild cats!"

Nils struck him then. Suddenly Joanna was free, and Tom Robey was staggering back against the sink, swearing. "What's up in here?" Philip Bennett asked mildly from the doorway.

"Yeah, let us in on it," said his cousin Jeff, behind him. The music stopped suddenly, and the dancers streamed across the floor. Someone—probably Nils—pushed Joanna hard through the open door to the porch. She jumped off the doorstep into a thicket of raspberry bushes, and looked back.

In the band of light cast into the kitchen by the lamps in the hall, black shapes moved and reeled and twisted. The night was full of the terrifying and exciting sounds of crashing bone and flesh, of quick grunting breaths, of curses forced from clenched teeth, of yelps of excited laughter. Now and then there was a crash of crockery as an elbow swept a mug or a glass to the floor.

She saw a fist dart out into the light, she glimpsed a split bloody cheek for an instant, and eyes that caught the light and gleamed like fire. She saw Maurice Trudeau charge into the thick of it. She winced when Owen went down out of the light, but he was up again instantly. They were all in it, the Grays, the Trudeaus, the Bennetts, the Sorensens—versus the Brigport crowd. Her eyes caught Sigurd poised for a moment in the kitchen doorway; she heard his affable roar.

"Now boys, can't we settle this all peaceable and lovin' like?" His great fist reached out, caught a thin, embattled Brigport partisan by the shirtfront, and tossed him lightly aside. With imperturbable calm, he moved into the fray.

Joanna stood knee-deep in the raspberry bushes, her heart thudding, her mouth dry. Her attention was diverted by a flurry of girls' excited voices at the front of the building. She recognized her cousin Rachel's authoritative tones. "We'll find Joanna—she'll know how it started. She was out there."

"Damn nuisances," Joanna muttered. She waited for them to give up their search and go back inside. Then she turned toward the lane, wading through a thicket that ruined her stockings.

Lights were out all around the village now, and the moonlight lay on the roofs like snow. There was silence everywhere, as if even the gulls and the sea were asleep; the air was mildly cool on her hot face, and smelled of green growing things. She walked soundlessly in a soundless world.

She found her way to the end of the old wharf and sat down on a lobster crate, her back comfortable against the wall of the long boat shop, her presence there screened from the path by a stack of traps at the corner of the building. She would wait until she heard Philip or Owen coming along. . . .

The boats gleamed whitely on the high tide that made a soft, chuckling murmur under the wharf. The silence was an enormous thing; it lay around her like a cloak, she thought fancifully, the invisible cloak in the fairy stories she used to read and believe, religiously. Suppose that while I'm looking at that spiling, she thought, suppose I should see a little creature standing there, all shimmery white, with silvery wings like a dragon fly, and a little radiance around her, all her own?

She laughed softly at herself, aloud, remembering the small sober Joanna in pigtails and overalls, who had trotted silently after her brothers up and down the west side, never breathing a word about the Little Men she expected to find in every hollow tree trunk and in every fern brake. That was why she had loved to play with Kristi when they were very young. Kristi's grandparents believed implicitly in the Little Men; when you went into the Sorensen house you had a queer, breathless feeling, because this was a place where the Little People really came, at night when the family was asleep. . . .

She started suddenly from her half-dreaming as a dory bumped gently against a spiling. The tide had risen to its flood, making a soft whisper on the stones. And someone was walking along the path by the beach, within the shadows cast by the bait house.

Who's this wandering around? Joanna thought with lively curiosity. Maybe it was Susie Yetton, running out to meet Johnny Fernandez—if she really did meet him. . . .

The footsteps on the beach stones came nearer, and two figures came out of the shadows. One was tall and dark in the moonlight; the other, held close in the curve of his arm, was tiny, scarcely reaching to his shoulder. Joanna leaned forward mischievously to watch, as she recognized the tall figure for a Bennett. But the girl . . . who in heaven's name . . . Her heart gave an odd little flip. The girl was Mateel Trudeau. And then she knew the man was Charles. When she had seen him last it had been the middle of the evening, and he'd been dancing with Mateel in a Lady of the Lake.

Joanna hugged her knees tight against her chest, and she could feel her heart thudding. The traps hid Charles and Mateel now, but she could hear their feet, coming nearer. She shrank back as she saw them come past the traps, glad of the shadows around her.

They stopped in the angle made by the pots against the wall, and she heard Charles' voice, low but distinct in the mild still air. "Don't tell me that, sweetheart. I know better. I want to know what's on your mind."

He sounded urgent, and Joanna strained to hear Mateel's answer. She couldn't see them clearly in their shadowed corner, but she knew how Mateel looked with her small, pale face, the short, curly brown hair with a bronze sheen to it in daylight, the faintly tilted brown eyes with their foolishly thick lashes. She'd always thought Mateel was cunning and pretty, even if she was Jake's daughter, but to see her like this, in Charles' arms, was a rather sickening shock. After all, it had only been a month ago when their father told them very clearly and finally what he thought of the Trudeaus.

"Come on, darling," Charles said now, and suddenly Mateel was crying. It was a tiny sound, but genuine. "Is it your father?" Charles demanded. "If he's been lying around drunk again—"

"No, not 'im," said Mateel on a choking gasp. "It's us, Charles. *Us.* Don't you see? I 'ave to go away."

"What for?" he asked roughly. "What've you got to go away for? We'll be married, come summer."

"Oh, Charles, don't you *see?*" the girl wailed in utter despair. Joanna wanted to escape. She realized her nails were cutting cruelly into her palms.

"What is it?" said Charles. He must have taken hold of the girl then, for she gasped. "Mateel, what is it? Mateel . . ." His voice slowed, full of wonder. And then comprehension. "Mateel, what's the trouble? Is it— *Tell me.*"

But Mateel couldn't stop crying.

11

JOANNA WATCHED THEM GO BACK along the beach and across the marsh to the road; it would take them past Nate Bennett's farm and into the Eastern End woods. She stood up, feeling cramped and cold.

It wasn't a beautiful world now. It was a horrible world, full of ugliness that wouldn't leave you alone or pass you by. Ugliness and shame. Charles getting a girl in trouble, and if that wasn't bad enough, it was Mateel Trudeau. Joanna's mind turned sickly away from the thought of the time when Donna and Stephen must know.

She came into the warm kitchen, where the lamp was turned low, and Winnie, under the stove, thumped her tail in a drowsy greeting. A plate of doughnuts and a pitcher of milk were set out on the dresser. Donna had put them there before she went to bed, for the hungry crew that were the joy of her life. But the thought of food turned Joanna's stomach. She went through the motions of washing her face and brushing her teeth, and went up to her room.

She thought of her mother as she undressed. Charles was the first child, born when Donna was a slender blonde slip of a girl; and though Philip had her own mildness and her gray-blue eyes, Donna held a little place in her heart for Charles. He was more like his father than any of the others.

For Stephen it was very simple. Charles was the oldest. Charles would inherit the Island. Yes, being the oldest set him apart from us, Joanna thought as she climbed into bed. He was supposed to know everything, and never do anything that wasn't fitting for Stephen Bennett's oldest son to do. It was Charles who reminded the others of their name; he'd pounded that and his own importance into the younger boys' heads from the time they could walk.

But it all came to nothing in the end. You had to be just like the others around here, didn't you? she addressed him savagely. Just as crazy after women as any of that Brigport trash you're always talking about. Couldn't leave them alone, couldn't even wait till you were married, if you were so set on marrying Mateel Trudeau! And why couldn't you have picked out someone that was fit to be a Bennett, someone we'll be proud to have in the family?

I guess all men are alike, Joanna thought with anguished contempt, only I hoped these Bennetts were a little different.

She heard Philip and Owen come in. She slipped out of bed and knelt by the register, listening to their soft laughter and amused profanity as they washed away the stains of battle, and had a mug-up of doughnuts and milk. The fight in the clubhouse kitchen seemed a hundred years ago, now. Funny, how those ten minutes on the wharf had pushed that thoughtless, lusty world an eternity away.

Philip and Owen came cautiously upstairs. She went back to bed and waited for Charles. She went over and over the scene on the old wharf. There was no escaping it.

As the moments crawled by, her angry shock changed to worry. Why didn't he come? Had they taken some crazy idea into their heads? Memories of suicide pacts floated through her brain; she imagined the gossip that would be rich meat for the village. Her room became a torture chamber.

At last she heard him in the kitchen, walking back and forth between sink and stove. It was a light, but telling, step. Charles didn't know what to do. . . . Joanna got up and put on her bathrobe.

He stood by the stove, tall in his dark suit, his hair rumpled. He held his hands over the covers with an absent-minded gesture that frightened Joanna, because there was no fire in the stove.

"Charles," she said quickly, and he jerked around. For a moment she glimpsed the dark torment on his face, before he smiled and said, "What are you up for, this time of night?"

"I wanted a drink." She hesitated in the doorway, blinking in the light, black hair tumbled on the shoulders of her old striped robe. How did you begin, anyway? Did you just take a long breath, and plunge?

"Charles, I was on the old wharf tonight."

"Who was with you?" he asked lightly. "Nils? I suppose it

was so romantic you didn't even smell the bait house."

"I was alone. About midnight, Charles." She faltered only slightly. "Remember when you came along—and stopped?"

The pretense of lightness was gone. "You heard," he said.

"I didn't mean to listen, Charles! I was just sitting there, waiting for Philip and Owen to come along. The boys got into a row with the Brigport crew, and I left."

"Never mind that," he said roughly. "You didn't mean to listen, but you listened. So now you know what it's all about."

"I'm sorry, Charles." It was curious, but she was sorry for him, not angry any more. Her heart was wrung for him. The things that lay before Charles were not easy for him to face.

There was a strained whiteness around his mouth. "*Sorry!* What is there to be sorry about? I was going to marry her anyway. We'll just get married sooner, that's all."

"I see." Her voice was small and cool. "Well, I'll go back to bed."

"No, wait a minute, Jo. Don't go—listen." He stopped and she waited, her chin lifted. "Listen, Jo—oh, it's one damn bitchly mess! Old Man Trudeau's going to raise the roof and he's likely to boot her around some if she tells him, and you know what'll happen here. The thing that gets me is how I'm going to tell Father."

"I don't know," she said honestly. "You being the oldest. If it was one of the others, it wouldn't be so bad. . . . Don't tell him yet, Charles. Go ashore and get married. Don't tell either family till you get back. That'll get the worst of it all over at once."

It seemed to her that this was the wisest thing to do. Charles looked bleak and worn-out in the lamplight. "That's what I'll do. Listen, kid, do me a favor?"

"What is it?"

"Walk down to the Eastern End and see Mateel tomorrow morning, will you? She's scared as hell, and—well, I'd be grateful." He watched her eagerly, and she forced a smile.

"All right, Charles. We'd better be off to bed now, before we have the whole house up."

She had to get away quickly, before she said the words that trembled on her tongue. Be nice to Mateel, he'd said. It was a funny world where you had to be nice to someone you wished had never been born.

She was utterly weary, body and soul, as she went back to bed.

But for a few minutes she lay awake, listening to the familiar silence of the house. They all slept soundly except herself and Charles; they didn't know that tonight at supper had been the last time they would all be together without a cloud over them; although even then the cloud had already touched upon Charles.

12

On her way to the Eastern End the next morning, she passed by Uncle Nate's place. Aunt Mary knocked on the sitting room window and beckoned. Feeling vicious, Joanna crossed the lawn. She disliked her uncle's wife intensely, and this morning, not at all refreshed by sleep, she wondered if she could manage to be polite.

Sometimes I wish I could wear a sign around my neck, she thought with dour amusement. A sign saying, "Don't speak to me, I bite." She heard her voice, bleakly civil. "Hello, Aunt Mary."

"Well, Joanna! It's not often I see you up this way!" She was a massive woman in starched percale, whose robust health was a continual affront to Joanna; thinking of Donna, she looked with distaste at the heavy coils of gleaming chestnut hair, the hard red cheeks.

"I was taking a walk," she said.

"Oh, I see. . . . Well, there was quite a touse up at the clubhouse last night, wasn't there?"

"So I heard," said Joanna politely. "I went home early."

"I thought you always stayed till the last gun was fired." Her eyes were very bright, watching the girl. "Well, I thought maybe you knew what it was about. Rachel said they just about shacked the kitchen. There'll be a row about that, now. Rachel said—"

"Where *is* Rachel this morning?" asked Joanna.

"Up doing the chamber work. You know, I had to get up for

a headache pill about one o'clock this morning, and I could almost swear I saw Charles going along the road!" Aunt Mary smiled. "But I s'pose it wasn't. Your father's like Nate, about the Trudeaus; we've always been sorry we ever let 'em in here."

"I don't see how it could have been Charles." Joanna's gaze was unclouded. "The boys all came in right after midnight. . . . Well, good-by, Aunt Mary."

She had the door open, and the crisp, windy April morning came in. "Good gracious, the air sure smells good, don't it?" her aunt said heartily.

"You don't want to catch cold," said Joanna, and shut the door decisively behind her. She walked swiftly across the lawn into the face of the sharp breeze from the cove, and turned into the road again. "Damn her," she said between clenched teeth.

Aunt Mary would receive the news of Charles' marriage with greedy delight; she'd lick her chops over it, she'd come up across the meadow with her mouth watering to talk blandly with Donna about sheets for the bride. And all the time she would be prying, dropping little hints and leaders, and watching, watching, watching. . . .

"Hello, sweetheart!" That was Hugo, coming up from the spring. He set his water pails down in the grass and grinned at her. "What makes you look so ugly, darlin' mine?"

"My thoughts," she said crisply. She glanced at the iodine-painted knuckles of his right hand. "Did you get in on the fun?"

"Yep. Helped clean up Brigport. We stove the kitchen all to hell." His grin broadened. "I almost missed it, though—I went out for a while."

"What'll you do if Neddie ever comes in and catches you?"

"He won't, because we've got that all figured out," he said candidly.

"You're shameless, Hugo."

"But I have fun." He winked, and picked up his pails again.

Joanna, following the path along the top of the high bank, looked out at the glittering sea stretching endlessly toward the east. A boat moved out past a craggy point, and a cloud of gulls dipped down in its wake.

The whole world shone and was fragrant. The path lay before her, streaked with cold shadows and yellow sunlight. On her right hand tall dark trees had their precarious foothold among the rocks. Far below them the water curled itself in flashing eddies, and the seaweed moved languorously with the tide. A bluejay swooped noisily across the path before Joanna, and was lost in the woods on the hillside that rose with its lichened boulders, its spruces, and its little sun-filled glades on the other side of the path. The bird was the color of a jewel, the sea was full of diamonds, the day itself had a gemlike radiance. This is a day to be happy in, she thought, and remembered her mother singing, "Oh, the sunshine, blessed sunshine," in the kitchen at breakfast time. Her serene content had brought a lump into Joanna's throat, and it was difficult for her to swallow her toast.

When she reached the clearing at the Eastern End, she went forward to the old weathered fence. The gray wood was warm under her hands.

The land was smooth here where Joanna stood, rolling down from the woods into a narrow grassy field that touched the water on both sides. Seaward, the shore was a mass of tawny, jumbled rock, fringed by scrub spruces, juniper and bay. Northward, from a tranquil, sheltered cove, one looked across the choppy blue-green sound at Brigport. Joanna paused long at the gate to gaze over the peacock sea. Isle au Haut rose from the horizon like an enchanted mountain, and beyond the white shores of Vinalhaven the blue Camden hills lay drowsing against the sky.

Her glance came back to the cove. Maurice and Jake were out to haul, and with the younger children in school, Mateel would be alone. She opened the gate and went in. An old russet spaniel, whose curls were faded and tangled, waddled fatly up the path toward her. She patted him absently, and went on to the shabby house, as unkempt and desolate as the fish houses huddled on the bank of the cove.

What was there to say to Mateel? It was no good to tell her the family would be pleased, because they wouldn't be. . . . She knocked firmly on the door.

After a moment that seemed an age, Mateel opened it. Two things Joanna noticed at once: the thick lashes were wet and stuck together, and her nose was pink. But she smiled, and there was only the ghost of a quaver in her voice.

" 'Allo, Joanna! Come in!"

"Hello," said Joanna briefly, and lied. "I was just walking across to the Head—I thought you might give me a drink of water." She followed Mateel into the shabby dark kitchen, with its disreputable old stove and Jake's long underwear hanging over the oven door to air. There was a smell of freshly ironed clothes in the warm room; a mammoth ironing hung on lines from wall to wall, and over the backs of the mismated chairs.

"Sit down, Joanna," Mateel said with nervous eagerness. "A drink of water? 'Ow about some milk, maybe? It's nice and cold."

"Water will be all right."

Mateel went into the pantry and Joanna glanced at the stove, blacked and polished with very evident energy. The teakettle was scoured to brightness. It made her feel better. She said aloud, "The last time I was here, Maurice was teaching me how to play the fiddle. Remember?"

Mateel's smile was quick and sweet. As she came forward through a shaft of sunlight, carrying a glass, there were little golden flecks dancing in her eyes. "Oh, yes! You were little then, with pigtails. What a squeak you made! An' Owen came in, an'—what did 'e say, that made you so mad?"

"He said, 'Good God, who's killing that poor cat?' " Their laughter chimed together. Joanna thought: and afterwards Father said he'd trim us up with a lath if we came down here again. Jake was rumrunning then, and drunk when he wasn't doing that.

Suddenly they were silent. Mateel's small, pointed face went white and full of dread, as if she had forgotten herself for an instant and then remembered with renewed terror. Her hands began to twist nervously. She turned back to the ironing board on the table and began to smooth out a boy's shirt.

It was those frightened hands that undid Joanna. They were short and brown and sturdy, like Mateel herself; they'd carried water and split kindling and knit trapheads, and rowed, and cleaned fish. All her life Mateel had been doing things with those hands. And now, like Mateel, they were scared and helpless. . . . Hell, are you getting sorry for people again? Joanna asked herself savagely. Are you getting sorry for them, after the mess they've made of things with their own foolishness?

But it didn't do any good to swear at herself, because for a dreadfully realistic moment she saw the mountain that loomed before

Mateel—a mountain that seemed impossible to climb. She had a crazy impulse to put her arm around the older girl, and tell her she *could* climb that mountain, and not to be afraid.

You were foolish, she said silently to Mateel's back. And I wish Charles hadn't fallen in love with you. I'm afraid of what happens to this kind of marriage. I don't want you for a sister, but I can't bear to see anything terrified.

She stood up and walked over to the table. She was much taller than Mateel, she felt like a giant as the other girl looked up at her with soft and anxious eyes.

"Mateel," she sald gently. "I know what's troubling you. Charles told me."

Light burned up in a quick golden flame in Mateel's eyes at the sound of Charles' name. Then her lashes lowered.

"Will it be easy for you to get away?" Joanna asked doubtfully.

Mateel nodded. "I t'ink so. My aunt, she wrote to me to visit 'er, and my fadder said I could go, any time." There was sudden fiery color in her cheeks. Joanna sighed. She felt old and tired.

"Joanna—"

Those hands were frightened again. Joanna said, "What is it?"

"Joanna, do they 'ate me so much—your family?"

"They don't hate you at all," said Joanna briskly. "Of course, they'll be surprised and a little upset at first, but don't worry." She hesitated, seeing her mother's eyes, her father's locked and inexorable face. "Besides," she added awkwardly, "you love Charles, don't you?"

Again the golden flame, the soft quivering mouth, the sudden radiance that transfigured the small anxious face. And Joanna knew the truth, beyond a doubt. She didn't wait for Mateel's husky reply. She said quickly, "I'd better start for home—it's almost noon."

Mateel followed her to the door. "I'll never forget 'ow good you are, Joanna." Her eyes were shiny with tears.

There was nothing to say, nothing to do but smile and escape. When the door shut behind her, Joanna had to hold her feet from running toward the gate. She welcomed the cool bright air on her face; the past half-hour in the small stuffy kitchen had been worse than she'd anticipated.

As she went through the gate, she looked up at the tall spruces against the blown blue and white sky, and felt a little warm surge of kinship, a desire to lay her hands against their rough bark and feel their comforting solidity.

She knew, with a faint joyful stirring deep in her heart, that no matter what happened in the next week, no matter what befell them all in the coming years, the Island would never fail her.

So it didn't really matter what people did, she thought in a moment of strange impersonality. After everything was said and done, the foolish things, the hateful things — the good ones, too — and you'd almost forgotten how they were said and done, the Island would remain.

13

WHEN CHARLES LEFT for the mainland the next morning, it caused no comment at home or at the harbor. The Island men went often across the bay in their own boats, taking with them the lobsters they had carred, instead of selling to Pete Grant; the dealers on the mainland paid three cents more a pound for carred lobsters, and that mounted up, especially if a man had nine or ten hundred-pound crates.

So no one thought it was strange about Charles, least of all the family. Sudden, perhaps, but not strange. Owen talked about going with him. He talked about it long enough to bring a desperate gleam into Charles' eyes, and abandoned the idea just as Joanna was beginning to wonder if she could get through the next twenty-four hours without screaming.

At last Donna had packed a clean white shirt, his good trousers and sweater, and his shaving things. Charles put on his heavy jacket, picked up his oilskins, and was ready to go.

"See a good movie for me, Charles," his mother said. He put his arm around her and kissed her cheek. His eyes met Joanna's, and she called up a gay young grin.

"Charles, don't hug so hard!" Donna was flushed and laughing. "After all, you'll be back in a day or so—you're not leaving forever!"

Isn't he? thought Joanna. Charles let Donna go, and went quickly toward the door. Scarcely knowing how or why, Joanna was there before him. She put her hand on his arm and lifted her face to him.

"If you're handing those things out—" she began gaily. He bent his dark head and kissed her; for an instant her eyes looked deeply into his, then she stepped back and opened the door for him. "So long, and take care of yourself."

"Cripes almighty, he'll be back tomorrow!" Owen called from the other room. "You act like he was leaving home for good!"

"Oh, dry up!" said Joanna rudely, and then Charles was gone.

In a little while she stood by the kitchen window to watch the *Sea-Gypsy* head through the harbor mouth, driving a straight, unswerving course through the gray-green, foamy surge, and point her glistening white bow toward the invisible mainland beyond the western end of Brigport.

Later she saw the *Aurora B.* come plunging around the point, dipping her nose; it was choppy today, and the sky was a mass of scudding broken cloud. Soon the fish houses hid the mailboat, except for her masts; Joanna's eyes were drawn inevitably to the foot of the meadow, as if they must have known what they would see. It was Mateel, following the road instead of the path through the sodden marsh. There was something about the small figure, struggling with the big suitcase that banged against her knees, that caught at Joanna's heart. What a way to go to your own wedding! she thought with mingled pity and contempt.

Mateel, in her best coat, picked her way among the puddles, and Joanna turned away from the window, her black brows drawn. Donna looked up from her mending.

"Joanna, you could have gone with Charles, just as well as not! Why didn't you say something about it?" Her eyes were affectionate and worried on the girl's face. "It would have made a nice trip for you."

"There's nothing on the mainland I want to see." Joanna threw the words over her shoulder as she left the room. "I'm going up and straighten out my bookcase."

Her bookcase didn't need straightening, but she would take any way of escape, no matter how trivial, from the sight of her mother's unclouded calm.

The day crawled endlessly by, the sea roared into Goose Cove and hammered with a continuous hollow thunder around the point. The wind blew; it blew around the Bennett house when the harbor lay in windless tranquillity, but today there was no escaping from the wind, wherever you went. Perhaps in the deepest heart of the woods there was silence. But in the silence, you could hear your thoughts as well as think them. Joanna didn't want silence.

There was once, in the evening, when she almost told. Supper was over, and the lamplight streamed across Stephen's paper, Donna's book, and on Owen's adventure magazine as he lay on the couch. Philip had gone out to the shop, and Joanna, the dishes wiped and put away, followed him. Crossing the dooryard in the raw windy darkness, she knew the whole story was on the tip of her tongue. Perhaps Philip could make things seem a little better, a little more hopeful. His way was so calm and thoughtful and unhurried.

But on the threshold of the shop, with the lantern's light gleaming on the rows of bright-colored buoys, and the fire crackling, and Philip looking up absently from his notebook, the words failed on her lips. What if Philip didn't know? He *must* know. Philip was closest to Charles, how could he help not knowing? She heard herself saying casually, "Working on your log?"

"Mmm . . . know when we all made the most this winter? That week when Moody from Port George and that buyer from Friendship bucked each other till they ran the price up to seventy-five." Philip's blue eyes held a reminiscent twinkle. "We were all kings for a while around here."

Joanna fingered a snippet of twine and Philip squinted keenly at her through his pipe smoke.

"Something on your mind?"

"Nope," she said lightly. "Just taking a walk around the estate. Is it going to blow tomorrow?"

"Blow like hell till high water," murmured Philip. He was already absorbed again in his mathematics. Joanna went back to the house, with the salt wind tearing at her through the night.

Philip was right. The wind died down after high water. Sunshine broke through the clouds and lighted the gray water with a pale steely gleam. There was still a creamy surge around the ledges, for the deep swell came from the ocean's very heart and not from the wind. But it wasn't too rough for Charles to come home. He was like a gull in his savage kinship with both sea and gale.

There was too much for Joanna to do in the house, and she couldn't get out, she couldn't escape from the too-close walls of the house and walk along the grim west side, between water and woods. She watched for Charles; each time she went by the window she expected to see the boat come past the end of Brigport. But when she looked up suddenly and saw Charles and Mateel coming through the gate, she knew an instant of horrible astonishment. They were here.

It seemed like a year, the time when she stood by the window, watching them come up the path through the meadow whose grasses were still beaten down by the wind. Philip came out from the sitting room and knocked his pipe against the stove. Owen came yawning downstairs in his stocking feet, his black hair tumbled, his brown cheeks flushed with sleep, and she heard him say to Donna, "How about a mug-up? Coffee and stuff."

"Do you ever stop eating, Owen?" his mother asked.

Joanna turned around. She was surprised by her intense calm. "Here's Charles," she said. "With Mateel Trudeau."

Donna, eager as a young girl, said, "Charles, back so soon?"

"With Mateel." Philip said it. His face took on a curious stillness. Owen went quickly to the window, his grin delighted.

"By God, she's pretty! What's she coming up here for?"

"We'll know in a minute," said Joanna with the same detached serenity, and went to open the front door.

Charles' lips smiled when he saw her, but not his eyes, and she knew he had steeled himself. Mateel huddled close against him, trying to hide her terror.

" 'Allo, Jo," she said huskily.

Joanna was brisk. "Come in quick, you must be frozen."

"Got anything hot to drink?" Charles asked. He half-lifted Mateel into the hall. Perhaps to show her defiant courage she had used lipstick with a lavish, and unsteady, hand. It was garish against her pallor. Joanna would have wiped it off if she could, but it was too late now, with Donna on her way through the sitting room and the other boys behind her. Stephen was out in the shop.

Donna never looked more regal than she did at the moment she appeared in the doorway. "Hello, Charles," she said quietly. "And Mateel. How do you do, my dear?"

Charles answered quickly and harshly, "Mother, I'm married. This is my wife."

"Married?" The faint color drained from Donna's face. Behind her, Philip and Owen were motionless. "Your wife," Donna said slowly.

"I know it's a surprise, Mother." Charles seemed to forget the others standing there in the bare, chill hall. His eager smile flashed at Donna. "Mother, I know it's a shock, but you know me — I like to do things without talking about them. And a man has to get married sometime. I'm twenty-six."

"Come into the sitting room where it's warm," Donna said. "Mateel looks cold." She put her hand on the girl's arm and smiled into her bewildered eyes. Joanna applauded silently, knowing the effort behind the gesture. They went into the next room and Charles put his arm tightly around Mateel.

"This is the one I wanted. So I married her."

"Joanna, why don't you make some coffee? Mateel, sit down, child." She herself sat down, and Joanna felt a twinge of fear. Was Charles so stupid as to think his mother wasn't upset, because she was so calm? The grim lines around his mouth had relaxed, he was smiling as he looked at his brothers.

"Well, isn't anybody going to welcome the bride?"

"Sure, me!" said Owen with enthusiasm. He leaned over and kissed Mateel's trembling mouth. "I'm happy as a clam at high water." She smiled at him uncertainly, and then Philip repeated the gesture. Donna sat very still, her hands folded in her lap, and Charles turned toward her swiftly.

"Mateel was scared sick all the way out," he said, his words sharp-edged. "Scared of you, Mother. And Father. I told her she was crazy. As if you'd hurt her!" His laughter was a harsh sound. "I told her you'd be glad to marry me off to a girl like her."

Mateel leaned against his arm, biting her lip, her eyes bright with tears. And Donna said in her composed voice, "Just let me get my breath, Charles."

With a sense of escape, Joanna turned toward the kitchen to make the coffee, and met her father in the doorway. How long he had been standing there, she didn't know. But his face was like dark iron. Almost at the same instant the others saw him, and the silence in the room was a heavy thing.

Stephen came forward into the room and looked at Charles. "So you're married," he said quietly. "Did you have to go off and do it like this? Was there any reason why you couldn't come and tell me what you were going to do?"

"I thought it was best this way," said Charles. His face drew into hard, impassive lines; the eyes that looked back at his father were as locked and shuttered as Stephen's own. Both of them hiding, Joanna thought, and suddenly she remembered who had told Charles not to tell their father. Herself . . . She started forward in her chair, and it was then that Mateel found her voice.

Perhaps she was heartened by Donna's gentleness and the boys' welcome. Perhaps she wanted to make things clear to Charles' father, and there was no way to tell her to be silent. Her words tumbled out, shyly and huskily.

"We didn't want to surprise you like dat. Running away. We wanted to tell you and my fadder, and be engaged—wit' a ring, you know." Her little smile was eager and apologetic. "We wanted a real wedding, but we couldn't do it dat way after all. We—it was better, not to wait."

There was no mistaking the truth. Mateel hadn't meant to tell it; no one could possibly want to tell it. But it had slipped out in her eagerness to please Charles' family; to show this man with the stony dark face that Charles hadn't meant to sneak off and do this thing without telling him. Oh, Charles had told her lots of times what friends he and his father were, that no matter what the trouble was, he could always have a fair show from him. But it hadn't helped at all, for Charles was red from collar to hairline under his brown skin, and she felt the twitching of the muscles in the arm around her shoulders.

Donna's face held a frozen composure. Stephen said softly, "So that's how it is. So that's how my oldest son got himself a wife."

He turned and walked out of the room. Mateel began to cry. "I shouldn't 'ave let you marry me! I knew 'ow it would be!"

Charles laid his big brown hand gently across her mouth, and hugged her close to him. Over her curly head he looked at his mother, his sister, his two younger brothers. His eyes, narrow and black above the red-tinged cheekbones, defied them; he looked as if he would never smile again.

He's chosen his woman, thought Joanna, and to hell with the rest of us! She felt a curious pride in him; he was so thoroughly Bennett.

"We'll go now," he said.

No one went to the window to watch Charles walk down across the meadow with his wife. They stood about the room like awkwardly placed actors in a bad play. The couch in the corner where Charles liked to sprawl, reading, his ashtray on his chest; the model of the *Aurora B.* on the mantel, made by his knife—they were suddenly predominant in the room. With his going, the house seemed all at once full of him.

Owen, who hated silence, moved a chair with a jarring scrape. "Christ, I'm getting out of this morgue!" He strode toward the kitchen. Philip paused for a moment, then went to Donna and gave her arm a little squeeze.

"Buck up, Mother. Things'll iron out." Her blue eyes answered him gallantly.

When Philip had gone out, Joanna sat down on a hassock by her mother's knees, as she had done when she was a small girl.

"Mother," she said with difficulty. "It was my fault Charles didn't tell you and Father. He asked me if he ought to, and I told him to wait."

"Don't feel so bad about it, Joanna. It doesn't make any difference."

"I don't like this any more than you do, Mother. But there's one thing—Mateel's not a bad girl."

"I never heard that she was." Donna looked over Joanna's head at the white line where surf broke on distant ledges. It was more than Joanna could stand, this icy composure. The silence bore heavily down on her. She said, "I'd better go out in the shop and tell Father. About what I told Charles, I mean."

In the shop her father worked methodically on his new traps. She watched him for a few minutes in silence; so many taps with the hammer to drive a nail into place, so many nails to a lath, so many laths to be nailed to the bows; and above them, Stephen's absorbed eyes like black granite, and a white line around his mouth, as there had been around Charles' mouth.

"Hello, Joanna," he said without looking up.

She was suddenly a little girl again, hands clenched in overall pockets, confessing it was she who had let the skiff go adrift. Jaw tight, mouth stiff, eyes unfaltering, take a long breath . . . "Father, Charles would have told you about him and Mateel, only I told him it would be better to wait."

He glanced up swiftly. "Well, don't look so stern about it."

"Don't you see?" she demanded violently. "It wasn't that he didn't *want* to tell you—"

"He was afraid to tell me, Joanna," Stephen said. "What you said doesn't make any difference. If he'd wanted to come to me, you couldn't have kept him away." He swung his pipe. "He was afraid to tell me, because he knew how I felt about the Trudeaus, and he remembered what I told him and the other boys." The white line came again around his mouth.

"But if he *had* come and told me, I might have got riled up because he went against my word, but I'd have respected his honesty and the fact that he'd taken a stand and intended to hold to it."

The match flame flared briefly in the bowl of the pipe, and reflected in Stephen Bennett's eyes. "But he was afraid to come," he repeated, and the word *afraid* was not a pleasant one. "Where's your mother? Is she alone?"

Joanna nodded, and he left her. After a few minutes she went back into the kitchen and took the inevitable potatoes out of the bin, and began to peel them. Her parents were talking in the sitting room, and lost in her own thoughts she didn't notice at first that her mother's voice had risen above its usual level pitch, until she could ignore it no longer.

"Stephen, I've never interfered with you. I've never questioned your authority over the boys. But the way you were today—" She took a long breath. "Stephen, you were *hard.*"

"I wasn't hard. I was just. What was I to say to him, in God's name, Donna? He's disgraced us, as well as himself. You realize that, don't you?"

"Oh, yes, it's a disgrace, but it could be even worse, Stephen." She was almost pleading now. "She doesn't seem like a bad girl. Oh, there was the lipstick, but that doesn't mean anything. Joanna wears it sometimes."

"Don't mention Joanna's name with hers," he said shortly. "The Trudeaus are trash, they'll always be trash. It wasn't enough for Charles to run around with the girl behind our backs, he had to get her into trouble. That does it, Donna. That's the whole thing—you can't get past it."

Donna's voice cooled and steadied. "Stephen, I don't like this marriage any more than you do. I felt like dying inside when I found out he had to marry the girl. Do you think it's going to be easy for me, to remember over and over what's happened? But it doesn't mean that Charles is no good, or that he's ruined himself and forgotten all you ever taught him!"

Stephen's feet paced endlessly back and forth. Joanna peeled potatoes with quick tense motions and listened.

"There's something else, Donna," his tired voice came after a pause. "I never thought I had to do what Gunnar does with Karl's boys, whip them into line with a horsewhip. I was positive our boys had something in them we could trust. Oh, I knew they'd raise a certain amount of hell, but so did I when I was their age. But all the time I knew what I wanted. I wanted something to be proud of, nothing that was second-rate. I raised hell, but I knew where to draw the line."

His pacing stopped, and the old couch springs creaked under his weight. "Well, my dear, I made the mistake of thinking our boys had the same idea—the same thing to keep them straight. But Charles didn't care what he got, and if it was that easy for him to get the girl into trouble, you can see what's before him."

It was more pain than anger with Stephen, Joanna could see it as well as her mother could. There'd been twenty-six years of plans for Charles, and now Charles was tied fast to the Trudeaus; to Stephen it meant the twenty-six years had gone for nothing.

"Stephen, we shouldn't have let him go away. We should have kept him here. Why didn't you tell him they could stay?" Donna asked.

"He's got to work out his own salvation," Stephen said heavily. "If he's weak, he'll go all the way to hell. And it's time we found out. If he's half the man I raised him to be, we'll find that out too. See what he does with this rotten mess he's made for himself." Joanna's knife paused; even in the kitchen she heard his sigh, and knew how he dropped his dark head into his hands. Her eyes burned with tears.

"If Charles could go bad," Stephen said, "God only knows what the others'll turn out to be, what kind of trouble they'll bring home to us next. Donna, I wish to God we'd never had a child!"

"Hush! Don't say that, Stephen!" Donna cried, and for the first time her voice broke. "Charles isn't bad, or weak, either. None of them are! Don't wish them away, Stephen. Some day they'll all be gone, and you'll wish them back again, trouble or not!"

Her quick light steps crossed the room, and Joanna knew Donna was going to her husband, It was a strange thing to listen thus to her parents when they thought they were alone. She had no right to be here; their moments together belonged only to them. But she was glad she had listened, and found how they thought and felt.

Now she wanted to get out. The walls were suddenly too close and thick, but outside the wind was blowing, the sea was loud on the rocks, and the gulls screaming overhead, and she would feel the Island all around her.

She poured water on the potatoes and put them on the stove, took down her trench coat from its hook. Those two in the other room didn't need her now.

But she needed the Island.

14

SOME PERVERSE INSTINCT made her take the road to the harbor, instead of the path toward the woods and solitude. She had dreaded the gossip, but now she was ready to meet it; she would handle it with an easy calm and a head carried high.

As she reached the anchor she saw Johnny Fernandez coming up from his dory, his cat at his heels. He grinned at her cheerfully, if toothlessly, from a face the color of very old, very dirty, brown leather.

"Hi, Juana!" he saluted her. "Well, you brudder bring Mateel back with him, huh?"

"That's right, Johnny."

"Me and Theresa—" He nodded at the lean tiger cat. "We was out haulin' and we see dem come. By God, she's pretty, dat Mateel! You get a new sister some day maybe, huh?" he added slyly.

"Why not?" Joanna countered, smiling. "She's a nice girl. So long, Johnny." She patted the cat and went along the road. She was surprised at her ease in answering him. Now for the next one, she thought defiantly.

The village looked drab and deserted in the raw, somber day. There was only the movement of smoke scudding uneasily from the chimneys, and Ned Foster, gray as the weather, getting a pail of water at the well. Joanna walked past the bait house and the boat shop, her hands in her pockets, the wind from the harbor running boisterous fingers through her hair.

It was redolent of salt and rockweed, and she sniffed with a dim stir of pleasure, and stopped to look out between the fish houses at the water. But the tide was low, and a great ledge, completely submerged at high water, now rose before her, black and shaggy with rockweed. It hid Charles' mooring and boat.

It was like a sign, she thought bitterly, and walked on — to see her uncle's wife coming along the road toward her. Joanna felt her skin tighten and her lips grow stiff.

Aunt Mary sailed when she walked. Joanna felt for a moment the same sensation of futile *littleness* she'd known the day she rowed through the harbor mouth in a punt, drifted close to the rocks to watch two young seagulls, and looked up from her deep contemplation of their speckled plumage to see the mailboat bearing down on her.

Only Aunt Mary didn't look half so handsome as the *Aurora B.* had looked to Joanna, after she'd swung the punt's bow safely into the edge of the wake.

Don't let her swamp you, Joanna, she said briskly to herself. . . . They met between the Binnacle and Karl Sorensen's fish house. In the fish house, someone was hammering vigorously.

"Hello, Aunt Mary," she said, her smile wide and sweet.

"Good heavens, child, what are you doing, out without a hat on? Don't you know this is pneumonia weather?" Aunt Mary's eyes flashed indignantly. "I don't know what your mother's thinking of, letting you run around like that. How *is* your mother today?"

"She's fine, Aunt Mary."

"Charles is back, I see. He picked an awful day to come out, didn't he? I met him right there by the anchor." Her gaze sharpened. "He was walking along with Mateel Trudeau. He must've brought her out. Quite friendly they seemed, too."

"That's not surprising, Aunt Mary," Joanna said politely. "That they're friendly, I mean. You see, they're married."

Aunt Mary's astonishment was a powerful and inarticulate thing. Joanna watched her with a little smile. It was very funny and she wanted to laugh aloud. She wished that someone else was there to see her take the wind out of Aunt Mary's sails.

"Imagine that!" her aunt said at last, with a creditable attempt at unconcern. She shrugged and lifted her eyebrows. "Oh, well, I'm not surprised. I kind of had an idea which way the wind was blowing!"

You liar, Joanna thought.

"I suppose your mother's fit to be tied, having Charles bring home a wife — Mateel, at that."

"Not at all," said Joanna sunnily. "Mateel's a nice girl. We all like her very much. Well, I'd better get to the store before Pete locks up."

"Yes, run along, child," Aunt Mary said absently. "Tell your mother I'll be up tomorrow—I haven't been to see her for a long time." She resumed her course, her head bent thoughtfully; at Mrs. Arey's path she veered sharply towards the steps.

Joanna, who hadn't intended to go to the store, walked around the corner of Karl's fish house, leaned against the wall and began to laugh. The hammering stopped and Nils came out. He looked at Joanna without surprise, and grinned. "What's so funny?"

"Aunt Mary—she's so—" Joanna ached with laughter. Her eyes were streaming. "She looked so queer!" she gasped, and doubled up with mirth.

"Laughing kind of hard, aren't you?" Nils inquired mildly.

"I can't *help* it!" she choked. Now she was frightened. She couldn't shake off this crazy feeling, it was running away with her. There was a pain in her chest and through her sides. It deepened with each gust of laughter. Through her tears she beseeched Nils to make her stop.

At last he took her by the arm and swung the door open. "Enter, madam. And pick up your feet, or you'll land on your face."

That was terribly funny. She laughed at the delicious humor of it, and wobbled toward a nail keg, where she sat down. She looked up at Nils with wet eyes, her nose crinkled, her mouth shaking.

"Stop it," he ordered sharply. He put his hand on her shoulder and shook her hard. "Come on, now, stop this foolishness!"

His stern blue gaze searched out her misty dark one, and held it, and she stared back at him helplessly, while the crazy laughter ebbed away from her body. It left her weak and tired and cold. She was suddenly overcome by her weariness. With a complete surrender to shame, she covered her face with her hands, and began to cry quietly.

Nils walked back to the workbench. Joanna let herself cry a few minutes more. Then she took a long shaky breath, swallowed hard, and mopped at her eyes with her sleeve.

"What a rig," she said unsteadily.

"Hell, yes," said Nils, without turning around. "Laughing and crying like a crazy woman. What grabbed you, anyway?"

"I don't know. I couldn't help it." She found a handkerchief at last, and blew her nose. "But Aunt Mary looked so funny when I told her about Charles. I guess it was the first time anything ever got by her." She talked rapidly, fingering the handkerchief. "And she won't dare say too much about it, either, not with Jeff and his mess."

"Here, have a cigarette," Nils said. She took it gratefully, and moved her nail keg nearer the stove. The fish house was like a quiet harbor after storm; she was suddenly glad of its existence, and of Nils.

He whittled a piece of lath, shaping a button for the door of a new trap, and glanced at her incuriously. "What about Charles?"

"He's married. To Mateel."

Nils grinned. "So that's why he handed her ashore as if she never got out of a boat before!"

"How did Charles look, Nils? Did he say anything?"

"Oh, he said hello, but he was too busy keeping his arm around Mateel. His jaw was stuck out, sort of." The knife paused as Nils glanced up at her quizzically. "Know what he looked like? As if he was saying to the whole damn universe, " 'She's mine, and to hell with what you think about it.' "

"How long do you think he'll feel like that? He had to marry her, Nils. Just like Marcus." The words seemed to clog her throat. "You know Charles, he's always loved his freedom. What if he ever thinks he got cheated out of it?"

"Sure I know Charles, Jo. He liked to take a drink, and play poker, and walk the girls home, but if he's found his woman, she's his for keeps."

"It was hell when they came to the house. You know how my father feels about the Trudeaus."

"Sure. And I know how Grampa feels. Well, they aren't much, that's true." Nils nailed the button to the trap with a series of quick, precise blows. "Jake got run out of his home town in Canada, so they say, and Maurice ain't what you'd call hard-working. But Mateel's all right — she's never run around, anyway. I wouldn't be surprised if Charles knew what he was doing. I'd bet any money nobody's been there before him."

Joanna stared at her cigarette, black brows drawn and underlip caught by her teeth. "You don't like it much, do you?" said Nils.

She sprang up impatiently and began to walk back and forth

between the bench and the stove. "Nils, did you ever see that kind of marriage turn out right, around here where everybody knows about it, and gossips?"

"You're all hawsed up about this, and there's no need of it." He put his hands on her shoulders and held her still. "Jo, how do you think Sigurd came into the world?" Nils' fingers tightened. "My father had to marry my mother, Jo. And he loved her so much that when she died, he died too. Part of him did, anyway. That's why he's the way he is."

"I didn't know about Sigurd," she said.

"Everybody knew about it when it happened. And they talked their damn heads off, but it didn't hurt my mother, or my father either. They made out. They were the two happiest people I ever knew. Jo, listen."

"What?" Her smile flickered at him, small and soft.

"There's a lot of chance for Charles and Mateel. Of course, I wouldn't want us to start that way—"

"*Us?*"

"Jo, I've been thinking about it for a hell of a while. There's nothing to wait for: I'm twenty-one and you're nineteen." His lean cheekbones were suddenly stained with red. "Jo, I want to marry you."

She stood very still under the weight of his hands on her shoulders, the fingers tightening until they hurt through her trench coat. She searched the face before her with urgent and startled eyes; she saw the way it had grown intent and absorbed, the tiny muscle jerking in one flat cheek, the jaw set like steel. This is Nils, she told herself. This is Nils . . . old Nils . . .

"That's what I want," he was saying. "I've always wanted it." His mouth relaxed in a fleeting smile. "Surprised, aren't you? You look white. I didn't mean to scare you."

"I'm not scared." She grinned at him. "Golly, Nils, I—I don't know what to say."

"You don't have to say anything. Just think about it." He let her go, and she leaned unsteadily against the bench. Nils said, "I picked a devilish time to tell you about it, didn't I?"

"No," she said absently. "I'm glad you told me. Got another cigarette?"

Nils wants to marry me, she thought. He's in love with me. . . .

She said it again to herself, trying to make it real. Nils is in love with me. When I used to row his peapod he was in love with me. That night when I met Simon —

All at once she felt confused and sad. He held a lighted match to her cigarette, and as she watched him in the tiny glow, it was as if she had never really looked at him before. Each detail stood out with a new and strange clarity.

His look moved up and caught hers, and for the first time in her life, her eyes avoided his. For an instant his whole face tightened. Then he grinned suddenly, the quick boyish grin she'd always known.

"O.K., Jo. What is it?"

"I'm sorry Nils," she said, seeking painfully for the exact words and not finding them. "But — well, I'm not in love with anybody, don't you see?" She could feel her cheeks fire.

Nils went back to his whittling. "All right, Jo. Don't say anything more."

"But I —" She stopped helplessly. There must be something I can do or say, she thought; but at the same time she knew there was nothing. For once in her life, she was almost glad when Gunnar came in.

His cheeks rosy from the wind, a fine sparkle in his eyes, he surveyed them and sniffed.

"Ha," he said benevolently. "You workin' hard, Nils? I bet you get dem new traps out tomorrow, the way you been drivin' 'er."

"Hello, Grampa," Nils said.

"Hello, Mr. Sorensen," Joanna said in a clear, polite voice. Gunnar twinkled at her.

"Well, Yoanna. You helpin' Nils, huh? He works hard, dat boy. Half a trap a day." Gunnar's tone grew rich with sarcasm. "He works fast. So fast he maybe gets his new traps set out by the time Closed Season begins."

Joanna felt the familiar prickly anger Gunnar always inspired in her. Nils whittled imperturbably. "Got to make the buttons, Grampa."

"David can make the buttons." Gunnar's crinkling glance took in Joanna's cigarette. "Smoking, is it, Yo? First time I ever see a voman smoke, it vass on Wharf Street, and she vass a —"

"Sit down and rest a while, Grampa," said Nils quietly. Joanna fastened her coat and went toward the door.

The old man had opened the stove door and was looking at the fire. Over his shaggy head Nils looked at Joanna, his face dispassionate, and she looked back with a sad and beseeching little smile. Stay friends with me, Nils, she thought.

"So long, Nils," she said aloud.

15

THE RAW GRAY WEATHER held for a week, and the Island seemed to have forgotten that it was April. Waking each day to lowering skies and wailing gulls, to the dark wall of the woods, the pewter-colored harbor and the keening wind, the Islanders talked yearningly of what they would do when the weather turned fine again. It seemed as if April, having given them only an inadequate glimpse of its usual soft blue loveliness, might slip away under this pall of gray cloud. Even the birds were late this year.

In the Bennett house the men were irritable, denied the outlet of work and a chance to get healthily tired. Donna had her household preoccupations, and she and Joanna talked constantly and carefully about everything under the sun—everything but Charles. But Stephen couldn't get out to his traps while there was such a heavy chop, and there wasn't nearly enough work in the shop to keep him occupied.

Once Donna said, "If only the sun would come out," with a little ghost of a sigh, and Joanna echoed her bitterly. It became a symbol. If only the sun would come out, the world would begin to turn again.

The week was the longest the big house had ever known. Late in the afternoon, at the end of the week, Aunt Mary came up. She'd been a very constant visitor of late. Joanna went out for a walk. Her uncle's wife ruffled her much more than she did Donna, whose success as an Island schoolteacher had depended on her ability to remain serene in the face of practically everything.

Joanna had gone out for a long solitary walk every day during that long week. She avoided Kristi's company, for Kristi's blue eyes had suddenly a resemblance to Nils', and each memory of her last talk with him brought an aching sense of loss and loneliness. No, it was better to go alone, to be a remote creature. She had covered almost the entire Island except, of course, the Eastern End, where Charles was.

Today she wandered down across the dun-colored meadow and through the dark woods, past the orchard that looked as if it had forgotten how to blossom, and out across the Whitcomb property. The old white house had been empty as long as she could remember. Once she used to wish that someone mysterious and exciting would move into it.

She met no one as she passed through the lane and came to Pete Grant's store. The women were staying in their warm kitchens, the men were sleeping away the aimless hours. There were one or two in the store, talking politics in half-hearted fashion, when she asked for yeast and sugar; when she went out, she knew they'd talk about Charles. No one knew yet that he'd had to marry Mateel, but they always suspected a hurried marriage.

But she was too tired to care what they talked about. If Charles didn't care, why should she? She walked down through the long covered shed and came out on the empty wharf.

The wind moaned around the spilings and whistled across the wet, green-slimed rocks below. The tide was ebbing from the ledges that showed dreary and black, the cries of the gulls were forlorn. Joanna sat down on a log and leaned back against a hogshead.

She was desperately tired. The last week had taken more of her abundant nervous energy than she realized. But there was one thing she did realize, with a cruel vividness; she had not only lost her brother, but a friend as well. She could never again look at Nils and see him as the chum he had always been. It would all be different now. She couldn't even talk to him without a sense of strangeness, however faint it might become with time.

Her eyes smarted as she looked out across the storm-gray water, at the white surf charging the dripping ledges, sliding back into the foam-flecked swells. Between Brigport and the Island the water had a wintry chop. The whole world was wintry today. Even the gulls, floating with the wind, seemed no kin to the white-winged creatures that could soar so exultantly toward the sun, their harsh voices full of vibrant life. Today their cries drifted down to her, shrill and desolate.

The western end of Brigport was edged with moving white; that the seas were high, out there in the open, she knew when the spar buoy was sometimes hidden from sight by a wash of dark water. Between Brigport and the red spar a boat moved with painful slowness against the power of wind and sea. She watched it idly, not seeing it clearly because it was gray, and so far away; but she knew in her mind and body how the bow was plunging and dripping and how each timber would be straining to move ahead; how sometimes the boat would almost stop for a moment, the engine faltering like an overworked heart, and then would come the quick downward plunge into the trough, the nose going under the white wash of water, then coming up valiantly, to keep on fighting.

Who would be out today? Certainly no one on Brigport was foolish enough to go hauling in a sea like this. Joanna watched the uncertain progress of the small boat. It was a little nearer now, so that sometimes she saw the sprayhood. But it was rolling so that it seemed as if another sea would capsize it. It looked tiny and helpless out there, and rather too near the ledges off Brigport. And suddenly, without knowing how she knew, Joanna realized that the engine had broken down.

Her muscles tightened, and she sat forward to watch. Did anyone see him from Brigport? But no one lived at that end, it was all dark woods. And if someone put out from Bennett's, he'd be on the ledges before they could reach him, the way the wind was blowing.

He's a fool, whoever he is, she thought anxiously. It wasn't any island fisherman, taking chances with a tricky engine in this weather. Some transient fisherman, some old derelict, she thought; ever since she could remember they'd been putting into the harbor for a night or two, battered and weary and dirty, living from hand to mouth, forever wandering. She had wondered what hope kept them alive—

or if there were any hope for them to live for. But still they lived, and wanted to live, and the man out there in his helpless little cockle-shell would be leaning over the engine box now, praying and cursing, sweating in spite of the cold wind, working with numbed and clumsy fingers, while the ever-loudening roar of surf battered at his ears.

Joanna stood up. Hopeless or not, somebody would have to go out there. She took one last look before she turned toward the store, and relief was like a sudden sweet breath of air in constricted lungs. The boat was on its way again, heading past those black ledges, as straight as any small boat could go in this sea. Joanna sat down on the log again. She grasped at the thought of this derelict fisherman; easier to let her mind drift idly on him, than to remember the family, Charles . . . and Nils.

There had been a good many wanderers to tie up at Pete Grant's wharf. When she was small, and believed in fairies and pirates, the sight of many an old sloop cruising into the harbor had struck delicious fear into her heart, and she would manage to be on the wharf—at a safe distance, of course—to watch the stranger swing up the ladder, his creased skin burnt black with weather and dirt, his overalls encrusted with salt and fish scales. Maybe he'd have a patch over one eye, or a long scar on his face; once there'd been a man with one arm, and she had been sure a shark had eaten it, until Owen disillusioned her. At daylight they would be gone again, and she would follow them in her mind, giving them strange adventures and mysterious deaths.

Now when she saw them come in, and go up to the store to ask about mooring for the night, and buy canned milk and beans and tobacco—Black B.L.—she still felt wonder, but there was pity in it. Why had they come to this life, so barren and futile? Had they ever been young and bright-eyed, singing to an accordion, kissing girls, getting drunk on dreams as well as whiskey? What lay behind them—and before them?

Joanna knew that, too. She'd heard the men talking of an old boat found drifting by itself, or of someone who had dropped out of sight in the fog or a storm . . . remember old Johnson? they said reminiscently. Used to come in here all the time. Well, he won't be back again. . . .

It seemed as if they vanished from the face of the waters as silently and completely as they vanished from the harbor at daybreak.

The small boat broke down again between the islands, and Joanna watched anxiously. He was away from the ledges now, but he'd drift down eventually on the reefs of Tenpound, if he didn't get the cursed engine started again. Joanna swore with him in sympathy, held her breath as the boat disappeared in a deep chasm between seas, breathed again as it rolled up into sight.

There, it was started again, plunging gallantly forward. Joanna thought of going home, but the sight and sound of the surf on the harbor ledges held her where she was. A fine mess it would be if the engine broke down in the harbor mouth. The boat would be matchwood in no time, and what if the poor old devil didn't have anything to live for? He still had a right to his wretched existence, and she'd feel guilty for the rest of her life if she didn't stay.

So she waited while the little boat tossed like a chip in the wicked top-chop raised by the wind, and the tide running against the wind. The tiller ropes would be groaning now, the timbers protesting, and the water pummeling brutally against the sides. But suddenly, with a little leap and an air of taking a long breath, the small shabby gray boat came into still water.

"You made it, brother!" said Joanna, and a gull perched on a nearby spiling gave her a startled glance and took off into the wind. Joanna waited, though there was no reason to stay. No reason except to give a friendly greeting to the man, and let him know someone had been watching in case he couldn't start his engine. Maybe it would make his day a little less lonely.

The rocky shoreline threw back the engine's pounding, and then there was silence as the boat reached the car. Joanna walked to the head of the ladder. Her father had always been cordial to transients, making them feel they were welcome to a night's anchorage, and his children were the same.

She looked down at the scarred boat with its peeling paint and mended sprayhood, and waited for the owner to come out of the cabin. He'd be biting off a good chew of tobacco, and his beard would be a week old, his teeth scarce. She saw a man in a battered felt hat bent over the open engine box.

"You had quite a time, didn't you, skipper?" she called down to him. "I thought maybe you weren't going to make port."

"Did you have any bets on it?" he said, and looked up. She stared back at him, feeling her cheeks grow hot. This wasn't any battered derelict with a quid in his cheek, no teeth, and a week's gray stubble on his chin. This man was tall and young, and very straight. And when he looked up, answering, and saw her, he took off his hat. "Hello," he said politely.

"Hello," she said. She had never seen a young man like this among the wanderers, and she felt a quick scorn. Didn't he know how to settle down and make a living for himself? She said curtly, "I was going to tell you I saw you break down. Somebody would've come for you."

"Thanks." His smile was oddly gentle and gay across his lean face. He swung up the ladder toward her. "But I wasn't worried. I can always throw the killick overboard."

"It wouldn't have helped you any in that tide rip." For a transient he was remarkably clean, and his leather jacket was good, though shabby. But that wasn't anything in his favor. "If you want the store," she said, "it's right up there."

"But I don't want the store. Not right away. Maybe you can tell me where the Whitcomb place is."

"The Whitcomb place?" Joanna lifted her eyebrows. "But nobody lives there—they moved away years ago."

Again the faint smile, and now she saw how it lit up his eyes, narrow in the thin face that was whitened by salt. They were a curious color between brown and green. She caught herself watching the play of light in them. Bennett eyes were so dark and deep.

"They moved away," she repeated.

"I know they did. They were my grandparents. Martha was my mother."

"Really?" She forgot to be curt; this was exciting. "Why, they were early settlers here—they came right after my grandfather and Gunnar Sorensen came. Of course Martha—that is, your mother— went away and got married before I was born, but I remember your grandfather just a little bit."

"I hope he left a good record behind him. Did he behave himself?"

Joanna laughed. "I guess so. My father was awfully fond of him. It seemed that once when he was little, Cyrus made him a very special kind of boat out of pine from a wreck. We've still got it."

"Gosh, I'd like to see it . . . I'm Alec Douglass. Alexander Charles-Edward Douglass." His mouth quirked. "My father was a Scot."

"I'm Joanna Bennett. Is the Charles-Edward for Bonnie Prince Charlie?"

"You guessed it. A couple hundred years ago some of us were chasing around with him in the Highlands and my father never forgot it."

"I don't blame him," said Joanna enthusiastically. "The first time I read about Bonnie Prince Charlie I went around for months wishing I was Flora MacDonald. I'd row across the harbor pretending we were escaping to Skye." She stopped suddenly. She hadn't ever told anyone, Kristi or Nils or Owen, about those enchanted dreams. And here she was, rattling along like an idiot to a complete stranger.

Her father would say that Cyrus Whitcomb's grandson couldn't be a complete stranger. She said crisply, "I'll show you where the house is. But I don't know what condition the inside's in. The outside's pretty bad."

They went through the shed and came out past the store. Alec Douglass glanced at it.

"I'll come back and get my supplies after I've seen the place."

"You sound as if you were staying for a while."

"I am," he said easily. "What about my boat? Can I leave her tied up there?"

"When you go to the store, you'll have to talk with Pete Grant about it. He owns the wharf and he's got a mooring he lets people use." She led him up past the Birds' and the Grays', and walked along the lane with him until the Whitcomb house showed up at the far end, white against the blackly wooded hillside, the neglected fields surrounding it a tangle of tall grass and wild berry vines. Before them sagged a rusty gate.

"There you are," she said.

"So that's the house my mother used to tell me about," Alec Douglass murmured, and something in his voice made Joanna glance at him. He caught her look and said, "She's dead. So is my father."

"I'm sorry," Joanna said. The house would be a lonely place to come to, for a man with no one but himself. "The house doesn't look very inviting, does it? This is a bad day . . . I don't even know if there's a stove. How would you cook?"

He smiled at her. "The gods will provide. They always do. Almost always . . . Thanks a lot, Joanna Bennett. Maybe I'll see that boat sometime."

Joanna hesitated. The house looked chill and dismal up there against the woods, with the sea of brown grass before it. Closed for years, it would be as damp as a tomb. And if there were no stove, how was Alec Douglass to fix even a cup of coffee for himself?

She glanced at his thin, clear-cut profile as he looked up the lane, and saw the deep lines of fatigue cut beside his mouth, the faint redness around his eyes from hours in the cold wind. He was very thin, and so were his faded denim trousers. He looked as if he were trying not to shiver; he looked as if he were chilled to the bone. And he looked as if he were trying to be very gay about the whole business.

She knew what her father would have done, if he'd been on the wharf when the boat came. He had brought home more than one new arrival; he said a good hot meal put heart into a man when nothing else would work. And this was Cyrus Whitcomb's grandson. That would have made up Stephen's mind for him. It made up Joanna's.

She said without hesitation, "Come up to our house for supper. My father will want to see you."

He didn't waste time in polite protest. He said simply, "I'd like to see him, too."

"We'll go back this way then," Joanna said. As they went along the path by the well, she didn't regret her impulse. She knew she was taking him into a house still vibrating with the shock of Charles' marriage, a house not in the mood for hospitality. But somehow she knew it would be all right, that they would have wanted her to bring him.

They won't mind him, she thought with a curious assurance. I think they'll even be glad to see him.

16

THE SURF WAS A TUMBLING WHITENESS in the cold April dusk as they went through the gate. From the path, they looked down on the long, glimmering curve.

"Schoolhouse Cove," explained Joanna. "That's because the schoolhouse is right above it. Sometimes in really bad weather the tide comes over the sea wall and floods the marsh, so the kids have to be rowed to school."

"I remember that," Alec Douglass said. "I mean, my mother told me about it. She said that was the best part of school."

The lights from the house streamed down across the meadow from warm yellow rectangles printed against the sea-scented dusk. There was a rattle of water pails at the well, and Joanna hailed the sound.

"Ahoy yourself!" Owen's voice came back on the wind. "What you got with you—Nils?" They heard his boots coming through the long grass and he emerged, a shadow from the shadows, beside them.

"This is my brother Owen," Joanna said. "Alec Douglass. He's coming to supper."

"Hello!" Owen's hand came out. "Glad to know you."

"Thanks. I'll take one of those buckets—"

"Hell, no. Where'd you come from? You a lobsterman?"

"Jonesport way," said Alec Douglass amiably. "I'm not much of a lobsterman. Trawling and handlining."

"Comes in handy in the closed time," said Owen. "Been thinking I'd do a little fishing this summer."

They reached the back door and Joanna opened it. Owen went in first with the sloshing water pails, and the warm light and the smell of supper flowed out past him. Winnie leaped forward with her plumy tail flying, her bark a fanfare.

Donna looked up questioningly, the coffee pot in her hand.

"Company, darlin'!" said Owen, lifting the pails to the dresser. "Jo's lugged something home in the way of salvage. Haven't got a good look at him yet, myself."

His grin was wide and friendly, but his dark eyes were keen. Stephen came out from the sitting room, and Philip turned from his absorbed contemplation of the darkness outside the seaward windows. Donna didn't move. And they all looked at Alec Douglass.

He shut the door behind him and stood looking back at them, his hat at his side. The lamplight caught and glinted in his eyes. In spite of the strong Scots nose and gaunt height, there was something oddly boyish about him, with his tumbled brown hair and his quiet, gentle smile.

"This is Alec Douglass, from Jonesport," said Joanna. "He's Cyrus Whitcomb's grandson, and I thought — "

"Can't you see he's chilled to the bone?" Donna's voice cut in brusquely. "Get over to the stove, lad, and warm yourself. You should be spanked, running around the bay on a day like this!"

"Thank you, ma'am," said Alec Douglass, and Joanna knew a sudden joyous warmth around her heart. It was all right to bring him home, and Donna was wonderful, she thought worshipfully.

Philip opened the oven door and pushed a chair in front of it. Stephen said, "Did you say Cyrus Whitcomb's grandson?"

"Yes, sir," said Alec, and put out his hand.

Stephen took it, a sudden light of interest warm across his face. "Welcome to Bennett's Island. I never knew Cyrus had a grandson, but I'm glad to see him. Come down to look at the old place, have you?"

"Come down to live in it, sir."

"*Live* in it!" Stephen lifted a quizzical eyebrow. "Well, we can always use new blood on the Island. Lobster fisherman, are you?"

Alec's smile was diffident. "When I was a kid, my grandfather used to tell me there were lobster fishermen and lobster catchers. Maybe I'll find out which I am."

"That sounds like Cyrus. How did you happen to pick out the Island, though? Where've you been fishing?"

"Stephen, give the boy a chance to catch his breath," Donna said, but Alec shook his head.

"That's all right, ma'am. Cap'n Bennett has a right to know where I hail from. I've been fishing around Jonesport way, sir. Living with my sister—there's quite a crew of sisters I've got, and I'm the only boy. Grandfather died when I was a tyke, and my dad was drowned—then my mother died when I was sixteen." He shrugged. "I've been living with my oldest sister, but I got tired of it after a while. Grandfather always talked a lot about the Island and the Bennetts. I guess he'd never have left it if Grandma hadn't been sick and had to be near a doctor."

He smiled faintly. "But once when I was small he took me down to Vinalhaven, and from a hill over there he pointed out the Island to me. I never forgot how it looked, way out on the horizon."

"So one day you had to come and find it," said Joanna. She saw in her mind the old man and the little brown-haired boy, looking out across the trackless bay at a magic blue line floating between sea and sky; and the boy, remembering, day after day, year after year.

"A young fellow like you ought to have a lot of chances on the mainland if he gets tired of fishing," said Stephen. "It's not many who'd choose to come out to this little place. What made up your mind for you, son?"

He looked at Alec pleasantly, his voice easy. But his family knew the keen appraisal in his look.

"I was fed up," said Alec frankly. "There wasn't any future."

As usual it was too much for Owen to keep silent very long. "No future here, either, except hauling pots. Cripes, Alec, if I lived on the mainland I'd never come out here, twenty-five miles from nowhere."

"Well, you like it, don't you?" Alec challenged him.

"Yes, but this is home."

Alec smiled. "There you are! It's home for me, now. It's just what I want. So far from everything you might as well be dead." His pleasant young voice made the words sound contented. "No one to pull and haul at you and try to team you around. In a month they don't even remember you."

Stephen said, "In a month maybe you'll be crazy with the quiet and the long nights." His mouth twitched. "I've heard more than one and the long nights." His mouth twitched. "I've heard more than one say it."

"Not me." Alec shook his head. "This island has been on my mind for a long time, sir. The rest of them signed over the house to me, and gave me their blessing."

"There's nothing been done to the house for years," Philip observed.

"I'm not a bad carpenter."

"We'll give you a hand!" said Owen exuberantly. It was easy to see he'd taken a great liking to Alec Douglass. "Say, what about your boat? Is she on Pete Grant's mooring?"

"Gosh, no. I'd better go talk to him."

Owen picked up his jacket. "Come on, I'll go with you. We'll have to drive 'er. Once Pete gets up over the hill and takes his boots off, you can't budge him."

They went out, and Donna said briskly, "Set another place, Joanna . . . well, Stephen?"

"Seems like a good boy." Stephen contemplated his pipe. "Of course you can't tell now. Wait till he's been around a bit, and see how he fits into things. See how the Island likes him." He looked up at Philip. "I still can't see why he came out here, though. There's not many boys like him, smart and well-spoken, who'd strike out in this direction when they want to make a change. They don't usually turn toward lobstering in this day and age. It's almost always the other way around."

Joanna said swiftly, "Why shouldn't he want to come here? It suits us, doesn't it?"

"You heard what Owen said, Jo," Philip reminded her. "He said it was home." He turned back to his father. "Maybe he's had some woman-trouble. The way he talked, it sounded as if he wanted to clear out. Probably a girl."

For some reason Philip's easy conjectures made her cross. "A fine pair of Islanders you are, and Bennetts at that, wondering why anybody wants to come out here! He came because of the Island, that's all. Just as he said!"

Her father looked at her in mild surprise, Philip twinkled, and Donna said, "Take out the baked potatoes, will you, Joanna? I'll finish creaming the fish. Stephen—" She paused and looked at her husband, and a flush came into her pale cheeks.

"Well, Donna?"

"Are we going to let him sleep out aboard his boat on a night like this, or in that musty old vault of a house?"

Across the kitchen they considered each other, a grave question in their eyes. Joanna and Philip watched them. It seemed to Joanna that she forgot to breathe for a moment—the moment in which her mother said, with serene deliberation:

"We can put him in Charles' bed."

"Whatever you say," Stephen answered, and went into the sitting room. Silence fell on the kitchen, and in it the two women worked swiftly, without looking at each other. There was butter to be cut, cream to be poured, a fresh jar of pickles from the cellar, a plate heaped with soft molasses cookies.

Noise came back into the house with Owen and Alec. Their cheeks whipped red by the raw wind, their eyes still glinting from some shared joke, they returned, heralded by Winnie. A hook was cleared for Alec's jacket and hat—Charles' hook, Joanna saw with a brief constriction in her throat.

Alec sat by the stove with Winnie between his knees. Winnie was deeply infatuated; her amber eyes were maudlin as he scratched her ears.

"Look what I found aboard Alec's boat!" Owen held aloft a battered violin case. "I brought it up so he could give us a tune after a while. Nothing like having two fiddlers on the Island, in case that bastard Maurice turns up drunk at the next dance."

"My grandfather used to tell me about the dances down here," Alec said. He got up to take the heavy lamp from Donna's hands and put it on the table. "When I started playing my dad's fiddle I wondered if I'd ever play at a dance on Bennett's Island."

His eyes met Joanna's and smiled, with the curious green-brown lights. "Supper's ready," she said. "Come on, everybody." She hurried, getting out clean towels, moving chairs, pouring coffee. Her father and mother sat in their usual places, Philip and Owen in theirs. The atmosphere was fragrant with good food and open-hearted hospitality. They were bent, each of them, on making Alec Douglass feel completely welcome. Seemingly there was no cloud in their world, no thought of Charles down at the Eastern End.

And they had put Alec Douglass in Charles' chair.

Joanna had help with the dishes that night, in spite of her protests. "I always wiped the dishes for my sister," Alec said.

"But you're company now."

"I'm an Islander." He leaned against the dresser and looked at her intently. "At least I'm aiming to be one. I'm not so damn stuck on myself that I think I'm going to walk right in and be one of the boys."

"You're not really a stranger." Joanna pointed out. "Your grandfather had his home here and his shore privilege. It's not as if you rented a camp on the beach and started lobstering right out of a clear sky."

"Yes, but are they all going to look at it like that?"

"I don't see why not." She felt an illogical desire to push his hair off his forehead. "If you're honest, and you work hard, and you're willing to lend a hand—"

"And take advice," drawled Philip from the doorway. "You'll have everybody and his brother telling what to do and how to do it. And it pays to listen, even if you do as you damn please."

"Thanks! I'm glad to take advice from the Bennetts, and follow it. My grandfather always said they were the salt of the earth."

"You've never done much lobstering, you said. Come out in the shop and we'll show you some of the rigging. You need a lot different gear than what they used around Jonesport—this is deep-sea lobstering."

"Mind if I finish this first?" Alec picked up a handful of wet silver. Owen joined Philip and said in good-natured scorn, "Cripes, you'll ruin the wench, wiping dishes. Spoil her. Come on, Alec."

"When I finish." He grinned as they went out, and turned back to the dishes.

"You might as well go. That's the end of it."

"Let's put them all back in the pan again," he suggested.

"Thank you very much for helping me," said Joanna firmly, hanging up the dish towels by the stove. "Now I'll show you the way to the shop."

Alec stood by the dresser, very tall and very lean, and considered her with bright green-brown eyes. "You are a verra deter-r-r-mined young woman, Miss Bennett."

"This way to the shop, please," she said remotely. After all, he was a stranger.

When she came back to the house, she stood for a moment in the empty kitchen, hearing the murmur of her parents' voices in the next room. She laid her hands against her cheeks and felt the warmth of her skin—windburn, she thought.

Suddenly she remembered Nils again. Poor Nils, she thought dutifully, trying to conjure up a picture of him with his dark sea-blue eyes and his grim mouth, trying to remember his fingers on her shoulders and his voice asking her to marry him. She remembered the shock of it, and the sense of loss and grief afterwards. She knew she would remember it again, with more poignance; but now, at the moment when she stood alone in the dim kitchen, something else came between her and the picture of Nils.

She shook herself impatiently and walked into the other room with her easy, arrogant Bennett carriage, chin a little higher than usual. Her father and mother were deep in a discussion. Joanna sat down on the couch and listened to them with some enjoyment. They sounded so normal, she thought.

"I know there's a perfectly good stove in Nate's barn," said Donna firmly. "Mary mentioned it only a few weeks ago."

"If it's the one I think it is, the boy couldn't boil water on it."

"Stephen, don't be so—so—"

"So what?" said Stephen with a dark twinkle.

"So much like your father. Do *you* know of a stove?"

"It's coming warm weather. We might let him take the one from the shop."

Donna's lips tightened. "And have you catch your death of cold working out there some wretched day."

Stephen sighed and knocked out his pipe. "Well then, all I can say is feed him up here till he gets a stove of his own."

"I'd just as lief," said Donna calmly. "I wouldn't worry then about the kind of meals he was getting. He wants feeding up, that boy. His sister couldn't have been much of a cook."

"You can see what you've brought home, Joanna," murmured Stephen. "Your mother is smitten."

"It must be that Bonnie Prince Charlie influence." Joanna grinned at Stephen, grateful for the softening that had come to his face this evening. Donna looked better too. Joanna turned over on her stomach and began to read.

When the boys came in, Owen brought Alec's fiddle from the kitchen, took it out of the case, and tucked it under his chin with a dashing air.

"What'll it be, folks?" he asked blandly, posing against the mantel.

"You're bound to make a noise with that one way or another, aren't you?" Philip said. "If you don't mind, I'd like to hear sort of a pretty noise. So hand it over to Alec."

Alec looked questioningly at Donna and Stephen. "Do you mind if I play?"

"I'd like to hear you, Alec," said Donna.

"Go ahead," murmured Stephen from behind his paper. Alec took his fiddle affectionately into his hands, put it under his chin, and tuned it. His eyes twinkled around at them all; he looked pleased because they wanted him to play. At Joanna, his glance halted.

"What'll I play?"

"Anything at all," she said. "Please." For an instant their eyes held; then he laid his cheek against the smooth, warm-toned wood and poised the bow. There was a sudden sharp pause in the room; without any other gesture than the placing of the violin, the lifting of the bow, he had become the center. All others watched him. Joanna felt a queer, breathless detachment, as if she were watching from very far away. Lamplight caught in his hair, turning the light brown to ruddy gold, but his face was thrown into shadow; his hair and the instrument were the same color.

"My father taught me this," he said suddenly, and began to play. A little tune crept wailing through the room, a lost and plaintive little tune with a refrain of falling tears; again and again that refrain came back, throbbing through the hushed room and talking to the wind that mounted around the house.

And he had brought Charles back to them. There was not one of them who didn't hear the wind outside, and the thunder of the sea, and remember that tonight they weren't all gathered here safe and warm under one roof. One had gone out from this house; and he would never come back as the boy they had known.

Who was this stranger suddenly among them? When Joanna thought she could bear it no longer, the tune ended on a sobbing minor note. Alec Douglass lifted his head and said, "I don't know why I chose that one to start with."

Donna said very quietly, "What was the name of it?"

" 'The Flowers of the Forest.' It's a lament."

"Let's have some reels," said Owen, leaning forward impatiently. "Something fast."

"How's this, my boy?"

This was a gallant marching tune, with a lilt and a swing and an excitement that made it hard for you to sit still, to keep from tapping your foot. It was a valiant, swaggering song. Joanna loved it at once. She was sorry when it finished.

"What was that?" she demanded eagerly, her long eyes brilliant.

" 'The Road to the Isles,' " he told her. "And you should hear it on the pipes! My father wanted to buy me bagpipes, but my mother wouldn't let him. She said it was bad enough to listen to the fiddle, and us kids being Border raiders, without having pipes to drive her mad. Dad was born a couple hundred years too late. He wasn't meant to be a fisherman. He was born for kilts and a Lost Cause."

"He sounds nice," said Joanna. Stephen put down his paper.

"Now Jo, I don't know how I'd look in kilts, but I've got plenty of Lost Causes. The Island's full of 'em."

Joanna winked at him and he winked back, and retired behind his paper. Alec began to play again and the whimsies of his bow threw a different spell around them — a spell woven, to Joanna's enchanted fancy, of heather and coldly bubbling Highland streams, of wooded glens and stags at eve and Walter Scott's stories, and the old, old ballads in a ragged book she'd found once in the attic. The music lilted in the room, the fingers flew with magic certainty across the strings, the bow danced, and Alec Douglass laughed as he played; his laughter reflected in the quiet shine of Donna's eyes, in Owen's vivid face, in Philip's tilted head, and Stephen's absently tapping foot.

And Joanna, sitting on the couch, felt a sudden wild, exultant happiness sweep through her body until she wanted to jump up or dance or shout.

When, abruptly, he had finished, and taken the fiddle from under his chin, there was a breathless stillness in the room. Joanna felt stranded; left high and dry on a rock until the tide of her fierce excitement should ebb away. It was Owen who let out a long reverent whistle.

"My God, if you ever played like that at a dance, you'd have 'em going right through the roof! Cripes, and I thought Maurice could play!"

Alec's smile was pleased and diffident. "I'm glad you like it. But—" He shrugged, and laid the violin in the case. "Fiddling isn't much. I'd rather be a good lobsterman." Without the music he was only a tall, too-thin young man again, sandy-haired, gaunt, cleanly shabby. A little shy.

Joanna, holding a book in her lap, stared absently at the print and wondered what had come over her to make her feel so queer when he was playing. I'm tired and nervous, she thought. That's all it is. Nerves . . .

Donna closed her workbasket and stood up. "I think it's time we thought about bed. Alec, you're staying here tonight."

"But that's too much, ma'am!" He got up quickly, color rising in his lean cheeks. "I can sleep aboard the boat."

"Philip will show you your room," Donna said definitely, and Joanna knew her mother couldn't bear to look at Charles' bed. But no one would have guessed what lay behind that tranquil smile. "Joanna you get the boys a mug-up. I'll go along to bed."

17

IN MAY THE ISLAND became whole-hearted about spring, and burst into blossom. Bunchberry and cranberry blooms, star-flowers—the Island was afoam with them. A wild pear tree leaned over the ancient, red-rusted Whitcomb gate like a slender young girl in white. Joanna, coming along the lane with the harbor silken and blue behind her, and the robins and song sparrows singing their valiant young hearts out from Gunnar's alder swamp, stopped to look at the little tree with tender and dreaming eyes.

She picked a pale delicate spray and walked on toward the house; there was a path through the tangled field now. Joanna stopped and looked up, to watch Alec and Owen against the sky. They were re-shingling the roof, and the sound of hammers was sharp in the wind-less, sunny afternoon.

Owen saw her and whistled, and Alec waved a shingle. "Hello, down there!" he hailed her. "Come on up and set a while!"

"You're too high-minded for me!" she called back, and sat down in the warm dry grass. Peace flowed through her and she wished this hour might never end, this hour made up of the luminous blue of sea and sky, the soft May wind, the white blossoms like a fragrant snow in the hollows and on the grassy slopes wandering down to the water.

She lay back and watched the tall feathery grasses swaying against the sky; far overhead a gull passed in effortless white-winged flight. The sun was very warm on her face and drowsy lids, already it had laid a faint glow of pink across her cheekbones and the bridge of her nose—where the freckles used to be.

This is heaven, she thought drowsily, and was sublimely unaware of Alec Douglass till his shadow fell coolly on her face. She opened her eyes.

"I thought you two were on the roof."

"We came down," Owen explained.

"So I see. Well, I came up to inspect the job, but I'll take a re-port on it. I'm not in a ridgepole-walking mood today."

"Come on and inspect the house, then." Alec looked down at her, smiling, and put out his hand. "You haven't been in it since the stove came."

Joanna took the offered hand, a long, lean, strong hand, and came lightly to her feet "What a mane," said Owen, tugging ungently at the thick black hair. "Another month, and you'll pass for a Shet-land pony."

"I like long black hair." Alec took the spray of wild pear from her hand and tucked it behind her ear. He stepped back and looked at the effect with narrowed bright eyes. Joanna tilted her head.

"How do I look?" she asked, and under his suddenly intent gaze she felt her cheeks grow warm.

"You look—good," he said softly.

"Cripes, no cigarettes," Owen muttered. Alec offered him a package but he refused it. "I don't like those things, they're stronger'n white lightning. Well, if you fellas are going to stand there and look at each other, I'm going down to the store."

He left them, whistling, his hands in his pockets, his stride long and arrogant and free. Joanna and Alec watched him go through the gate.

"He's a good kid," Alec said. "Maybe some time I'll have a chance to help him out the way he's been helping me."

"Owen's all right," said Joanna somberly. Since Charles' marriage, she had frequent qualms about the other boys; she had thought Charles was invulnerable, but he wasn't, and now there were moments of wondering what would happen to Owen, who was ten times more reckless than Charles, and a hundred times more impatient and hungry for life.

But the moments were brief. She smiled quickly at Alec and said, "Can I see the house?"

They went across the wide porch and into the house, whose doors and windows were flung open to the warm air of May. The big bare rooms were full of sunshine, the floors had been swept, the windows washed.

"It smells clean," she said approvingly.

"It looks pretty good since I got rid of the squatters." Alec propped himself against a door frame. "One hornet's nest, a hundred and three spiders, and a family of moths living in an old blanket. Intelligent, too, those moths. They understood the situation after I explained it to them."

"Didn't they mind being put out?"

"Not at all. I told them they might move down to Mr. Sorensen's attic. That was after Mr. Sorensen came up to see me," he added politely, "to tell me there wasn't room for loafers on the Island."

Joanna chuckled. Alec said, "Laugh like that again. I like it. Did I tell you I found a race of primitive men down cellar? They didn't have eyes or chins, and they were white like mushrooms. When the sun shone on 'em, they melted."

"Like snow?" she asked solemnly.

"No. Like candle grease. They left spots."

They walked into the big front room, empty except for a cot, and Joanna felt a faint coldness across her pleasant mood. Once before she had stood in this room, perhaps in this exact spot, and had known what pure terror meant. Now it seemed unreal, like something she'd read or dreamed a long time ago, except for the old cot. Now it was made up with Alec's bedding.

"What are you thinking?" he asked curiously, watching her.

She said hastily, "Do you ever get homesick?"

"Not on your life! This is pretty near heaven, after what I left."

She wanted to ask him why he left home, wondering if Philip had been right about a girl, but there was a tiny, rushing scamper overhead. Alec looked resigned.

"The mice moved in right after I did."

"You can get a cat from my uncle," Joanna said. Through the front windows she could see Gunnar and young flaxen-haired David furrowing the ground for their garden, and wondered idly if they'd seen Owen going toward the harbor, and herself entering the house with Alec. If Gunnar saw me, he'll talk, she thought impatiently. He'll know how long I stayed and all about it.

Her first impulse was to stay, and let Gunnar wonder, but the sight of him had made its little warning signal in her brain. She didn't want trouble, she didn't want the faintest whisper of it. It would spoil everything, she thought suddenly and inexplicably.

"Let's go out," she said casually. "It's too nice to stay in. You've done a good job of housecleaning."

"Thanks, Jo." He was pleased. "But don't go home yet. Let's go rowing."

"I'd love to," Joanna said honestly, and they went out together into the glowing day.

On sunny afternoons in May, the beach was always well populated. Joanna and Alec had to run a gauntlet that would have fazed a girl unarmed with the superb Bennett self-assurance. Her uncle glanced at her from under thick black brows; Jeff grinned openly. Everybody looked at them with unveiled interest.

"Don't take some people long to get acquainted," Ash Bird observed to the world at large. Jud Gray, who with his sons Tim and Peter was baiting trawls, shifted his plug of tobacco to the other cheek, spat, and winked at Alec.

"You want to look out for them black-eyed Susans, boy."

"Thanks for the advice," said Alec politely. He untied the double-ender and helped Joanna in.

"Cripes, she's gettin' kinda helpless, ain't she?" said Forest Merrill. Joanna saw Alec's mouth tighten, his head turn. She said quickly, "Push off, Alec. The tide's going all the time."

A few long strokes took them well past the old wharf. Joanna smiled at Alec and saw his tight jaw relax.

"Are they always like that?" he demanded.

"Don't pay any attention to them. I don't. They're ignorant, Alec. Forest Merrill's no good, and that nasty little Ash Bird—" she shrugged. "Jud's all right, and my cousin Jeff's just like my brothers. I don't even see the rest."

"So I noticed," he said dryly. "I suppose you'll walk through life with your chin up, and not even see the guys who don't matter."

"Why waste time on them? Life's too short."

He had a gentle, twinkling look. "You seen me yet, Joanna?" She hadn't noticed before how deeply his mouth was cut at the corners. It gave his bony face an oddly sensitive cast.

"I'm out rowing with you," she answered him. His sister must have been a battle-ax, she thought. Driving him away like that. She must have driven him away. He never mentioned her; there was something . . .

The peapod glided swiftly among the moorings. As they went by Alec's boat, he gave it a rueful glance.

"I'd take you for a sail in her, but she's pretty dirty. As soon as I make enough from my trawls to pay Pete Grant for my shingles and stuff, I'm going to fix up the old lady."

"How are you getting along, trawling?"

"Well enough to put a little toward my lobstering gear. I'll do better when the hake start to come. I ought to have a good-sized string of traps, come September, if I work hard all summer."

"You're really going to stay here, then," said Joanna.

"This place is just about the answer to everything, Joanna," he said quietly. "A man could be happy here, forever."

Their glances met, smiling, and Joanna felt contented and pleased with life. They were passing the western point of the harbor now, and the great boulders looming above them gleamed saffron and amber in the sunshine. The water rippled quietly against the ledges, dimpled with light; as the double-ender slipped over the submerged rocks, with their dark sea-grass waving gently just under the surface, Joanna could see the swiftly darting shapes of the little pollack; they were silvery-green when the sun struck down through the water.

Alec Douglass had come to the Island and found it good. *The answer to everything,* he had said. Then I'm not the only one, she thought, and her happiness was a vivid thing, tremulously and exquisitely alive. Because of it the whole day glistened with a new radiance.

I wonder why I never felt like this before, she thought, and stopped wondering. It was enough to sit quietly in the stem of the peapod, watching the little eddies in the wake of the oars, looking up at the great blue arc of sky above her and the Island forest towering against it; watching Alec Douglass row.

They were caught up in a wordless peace as the boat cut across the bright water. There was no need for talk. Alec whistled under his breath. It wasn't until they turned back toward the harbor that the spell was broken.

Nils' boat came down past Tenpound. Joanna, seeing it, felt a sudden sadness; without her knowing it, her face shadowed, and locked itself. She looked down at the bottom of the double-ender, at her feet against the planks; at the blue denim of Alec's dungarees, and his sneakers.

"Nils seems like a nice guy," Alec said. He held the oars out of water and let the boat drift.

"Yes, he's all right," she answered casually.

"Remember that first night I came, when Owen yelled at us from the well? He wanted to know if you had Nils with you. I wanted to ask you who Nils was, but I thought you'd slap me down."

"Why should you care who Nils was, anyway?" she asked, and under his absorbed gaze she felt her face grow warm. For a moment she stared back at him, her eyes brilliant, her lips parted. Then she smiled, shrugged faintly.

"There wouldn't have been anything to say. Nils is Owen's chum. And he's always been good to me, ever since I can remember."

Alec nodded. "I knew that."

"What else did Owen say? He's been telling you things, hasn't he?"

"He gets to talking, when we're up there on the ridgepole. Everybody that comes in sight. For instance, he says the Birds are—"

"That's no lie. What else does he say?"

"Oh, he calls Gunnar names too. Joanna, don't look at me like that," he said piteously, and she laughed in spite of herself. "Owen meanders along like a cow in a pasture. Sits there smoking cigarettes and talking. Of course we see a lot of the Sorensens."

"Don't stall, Alec. What did he say about Nils?"

"Only that Nils thinks a lot of you," said Alec. "Is that anything to be mad about?"

"I'm mad because my brother's a gossip. It would be easier for him to cut off his right arm than to keep his mouth shut." Joanna watched Nils' boat roar into the harbor, caught a glimpse of sunshine on his blond head. "It must be late, Alec. We ought to go back."

Alec squinted at the sun. "Gosh, yes! I've got a date for supper at five-thirty. Jo—" He smiled at her enchantingly. "Say the word and we'll stay out here and see the sunset."

"I won't say it. What'll people say if you don't show up, after they invited you?" She wondered sharply who had invited him. It could be almost anyone; the whole Island had taken a deep and protective interest in Alec.

"They'd say I was fey," he told her, "and leave it at that."

Joanna shook her head and looked severe. They went back across the harbor, weaving among the boats; as they came past the old wharf, Joanna saw Nils tying up his punt on the shore. He was gone before Alec beached the double-ender.

The fish houses and wharves were deserted now. There was no one to wink as Alec pulled up the boat and Joanna waited for him. She watched his long hands as he tied the painter, remembering their certain swiftness with the violin. He was still thin, but less gaunt; a tribute to Donna's feeding, the baked beans or chowder, hot bread and pie that she was forever sending down to him.

He came up the beach toward her, his old hat on the back of his head.

"Thanks for the ride," she said. "I loved it."

"I liked it too. If you weren't such a proper young woman we'd still be out there, and I wouldn't have to go home and shave and put on a clean shirt."

"And somebody'd be *terribly* disappointed!" Joanna's eyes danced.

"You needn't sneer. After all, I'm a very likeable guy, and

you can't blame your Aunt Mary for asking me to supper."

"Aunt Mary," repeated Joanna without enthusiasm, and he nodded pleasantly.

"Nice woman. She's got a nice family, too. Rachel's quite an eyeful."

A sore eyeful, Joanna thought inelegantly. You might know Aunt Mary and little Rachel would be right on deck. She was annoyed. She was so annoyed that she turned sharply away from Alec Douglass and his gay little smile, and said, "Well, I won't keep you. Thanks again for the sail."

"Oh, look here! Wait a minute, Jo!" He sounded oddly anxious.

"I've got to help get supper."

"Listen, Joanna. Can I — can't you — will you go with me to haul my trawls sometime?" His cheeks reddened under the tan.

"Sometime," said Joanna coolly. "So long, Alec." They separated. Alec went toward the village, whistling; Joanna, walking around the anchor, stifled an impulse to kick it hard.

Johnny Fernandez came out of his camp and said, *"Psst!* Juana, wait!"

She glowered at him. "Are you talking to me?"

"Si. You come here just a minute, please?" Johnny screwed up his face and nodded violently. "Come see what I got."

Joanna went back past the anchor, wondering what in the world Johnny wanted to show her. Probably Theresa had kittens, and he wanted her to admire the family. Well, she'd ask him to save one for Alec, unless Rachel gave him one.

At first she could see nothing in the dimness, after the brilliance outside. She could only smell Johnny's fish-scented overalls and the frying pork scraps on the stove. Then she saw Theresa, eyeing her malevolently from the table, where she sat between the coffee pot and a loaf of bread.

Behind her, Johnny said, "I bring him in here so he won't meet his fadder."

And then she saw Hugo, lying on Johnny's cot. His black hair was tumbled, his face was putty-colored and beaded with sweat. "I'm sick, Jo," he said piteously.

"Sick! Drunk, you mean. Drunk as a coot at five o'clock in the afternoon."

"You'd be drunk too," said Hugo in profound melancholy, "if you went to see your woman and she wouldn't let you in."

"Oh, is that it!" Joanna sat down beside him and pushed his hair out of his eyes. "Why wouldn't she let you in?"

"She's scared of her husband."

"That skinny little man?" Poor Hugo, she thought sadly, getting mixed up with a woman like Leah Foster. He was weak enough to be completely ruined before the affair was finished.

"Maybe he's skinny," Hugo mourned, "but some day he's gonna kill her. He said so. Did you know—" he pointed a finger at her— "did you know they got run out of Port George before they came here? A man—a man . . ." His voice trailed off wearily, and Joanna prodded him.

"What about a man?" She shook him.

"A man killed himself. Young guy. Married, three little kids. People said it was Leah's fault. He'd been hangin' around her. So they ran her and Neddie out of town." He looked at Joanna fiercely. "But she didn't have any more to do with it than *you!*"

"Of course not," Joanna soothed him. So that was the truth about the Fosters—run out of Port George, because Leah liked young men too well. And Father hadn't known that when he rented the Binnacle.

Hugo murmured on and on. "Neddie's a skunk—he blames her too. Just 'cause the poor guy went off his head. She couldn't help that! But Neddie holds it against her because he lost his house, an' they cut off all his traps. So he told her he's gonna kill her some day, if he ever catches her playin' around."

"I guess that's just talk, Hugo. Is that why she wouldn't let you in?"

Hugo's eyes opened wide and blazed into hers. "No! She had another guy there this afternoon! Foolin' around with some bastard while Neddie's off sellin' fish."

Oh Lord, thought Joanna. I'm supposed to be home getting supper, and Hugo's howling on my shoulder. "Who do you think it is?" she asked dutifully.

A look of indescribable slyness crept over Hugo's face. "I'm not goin' to tell you. You'd be madder'n hell."

"All right," said Joanna gently. "Don't tell me, then. You'd better stay right here till you feel better."

"Don't you want to know?" he asked incredulously, as she stood up to go. She smiled at him.

"Nope! So long, Hugo. Don't feel bad about Leah. She's not worth it." She turned toward the door. "Look after him a while longer, Johnny, will you?"

"Don't you even care," said Hugo slowly, "if your own brother Owen's runnin' after Leah?"

"*Owen?*"

He dropped back with a groan. "I wasn't gonna tell you, Jo."

She stood looking down at him, feeling a growing nausea. Without volition her mind saw a scene that would never be erased; she saw Owen swinging toward the Whitcomb gate, his hands in his pockets, his black head erect, his merry whistle floating back over his shoulder.

And he was going then to see Leah Foster.

It was a stunning thought. She had to get out of this dim stifling shack before it suffocated her, to get away from the sight of Hugo on the cot, and Johnny's impassive, wrinkled brown face watching her. She heard her undisturbed voice.

"Keep him here till he's fit to go home, Johnny."

With her smile very steady, she said good-bye and went on. In the clear golden light of the May evening, she walked along the road toward home.

18

IN THE NIGHT THE WIND SHIFTED, and there was heavy rain; Joanna awoke to see a thick white wall of fog close against her window. Downstairs in the kitchen the men ate a late breakfast by lamplight. They were deep in conversation when she came down, so no one noticed her, for which she was grateful. She sat at the table listening half-heartedly to their voices, watching Owen through her lashes. He was as light-hearted and cocksure as ever. Was it her imagination, she wondered, or had he been extraordinarily good-humored lately?

He feels pretty sure of himself, she thought scornfully. The world's all his, with a fence around it, because he's taken Hugo's woman. At the moment she disliked Owen intensely.

"Well, I suppose somebody'll be visiting our traps while it's thick," Philip said mildly. "Can't expect anything different."

"If we could just catch 'em once," Owen mourned. "Just once — to get the goods on those bastards. They've been out gunnin' for me ever since I took over Simon at the dance that night. He's been too damn friendly with that Brigport gang, and they'd just as soon haul hell out of us as not."

"It was a good thing you showed them you meant business," their father said.

"I'll say I meant business!" Owen was jubilant. "And if I ever catch one of 'em — Birds or Brigport — within ten yards of one of my pots, I'll do a little hauling on my own hook."

"You will not," said Stephen. "Owen, you're what Philip calls you — a rooster, always ready to rush into trouble head first and take everybody else with you. You're not happy till you've got us all by the ears." His voice was pleasant, but there was no doubting his look. "You'll haul your own traps and no others. When you have proof — and I've told you this a hundred times already — you can go to law. But meanwhile you'll behave yourself."

Owen's scowl slipped darkly across his face. Philip smiled quietly and stroked Winnie's ears. Stephen went on. "You cut off one trap and you'll start something that'll never end. It'll get more rotten every year, and drag the Island down to nothing but a muckhole."

He looked at them pleasantly, and went out to the shop. Philip said, "Well, that's that." He gathered up his oilskins. "I'm going out and pump out my boat. Coming, rooster?"

Owen picked up the latest adventure magazine, propped his feet on the oven hearth, and began to read. "All in good time, my boy."

When Philip had gone, Donna went to set the living room in order, and Joanna inquired acidly, "Doesn't the *Old Girl* need to be pumped out?"

Owen lifted an eyebrow at her. "Don't rush me. I work cheaper." He hunched up his shoulders and went on reading, tobacco smoke drifting around his absorbed black head. Joanna bit back the heated words on her tongue, and began to wash dishes. It took all her will power not to slat them furiously into the pan.

The teakettle sang, Winnie sighed under the stove, Owen read. Joanna finished the dishes and swept the floor, filled the lamps and polished the chimneys. Once Owen looked up, squinting at her through cigarette smoke, and said amiably, "What are you looking so ugly about?"

Joanna didn't answer. Stephen came in from the shop and paused by the stove to fill his pipe. "Working hard, son?"

Owen grinned up at him. "Cripes, you teamin' me around too? Joanna's been switching her tail around here for-god's-sakes."

"I don't like to team anybody around. But it seems to me your boat must have plenty of water in her, after the rain last night."

"I've just about decided the lobster business is going to hell. What's the use of fooling around with the damn boat?"

"What's wrong now?"

"I haven't had a decent haul in a week, and it's not because anybody's bothered my traps. There's just not lobsters enough to go around."

Joanna said scornfully, "He's plain lazy, Father. He doesn't want to take his feet out of the oven and look after his boat, so he's stalling."

"In the spring crawl," Stephen said pleasantly, 'you were spending money like a drunken sailor. Trouble with you, son, you're spoiled. You made a good dollar with your first string of traps, you've always had a roll in your pocket big enough to choke a cow — and the minute lobsters slack off a little, you think you're finished."

"Wait till lobsters drop down to something like twelve cents," said Joanna, "before you start howling."

"Twelve cents!" Owen laughed at her. "Where'd you ever hear of twelve-cent lobsters? Ain't no such animal. Well, I'll go down and pump out the blasted tub."

"I'm going with you," said Joanna. "I need a breath of fresh air."

He waited while she put on her boots and trench coat. "If you call this cotton-wool air, you can have all you want of it," he muttered, looking at the opaque whiteness that hid the harbor from them.

They walked along the road through the marsh that showed green now where it had been tawny with winter. The young birches at the foot of the meadow were unfurling their new leaves, their trunks were startlingly white in the dreary day. On the brow of Schoolhouse Cove there was more green; the wild rose bushes, the beach peas, the evening primrose, the tall coarse grass.

But the fog shut in behind Joanna and Owen, and hid the meadow and the beach, and then it parted before them to show the harbor, gray and tranquil at low tide. The ledges were black with rockweed and the gentle swell broke around them in a lazy curl of white. There was a smell of salt wetness, and the sound of gulls crying aimlessly and unseen overhead.

Joanna helped Owen to push a punt down over the wet stony beach. "You don't have to go out aboard," he said. "She'll be plenty wet."

"What's a little water?"

"I always knew you were first cousin to a duck." They pushed off and the oars cut soundlessly into the pale, glassy water. Joanna looked out at the *Old Girl*.

"Remember when you said you wouldn't have her?"

"Oh, she's not a bad old crate. After all, she's not the only boat I expect to have. Here we are, grab hold of her there!"

The punt made fast alongside, Owen began to pump, while Joanna sat on the damp engine box and smoked a hurried cigarette. Rain began to patter lightly on her sou'wester. She watched Owen somberly, wishing there were some way to approach him. But they had never confided in each other, even as small children playing together day after day.

He looked up and caught her thoughtful gaze. "Why so glum? You know one thing about the *Old Girl?* She's easy to handle. That thing of Philip's is stubborn. Bad as some women."

"What kind of women do you like?" asked Joanna casually. "The kind that's easy to handle, or hard?"

"Well, I couldn't say offhand." He looked at her mischievously, his grin putting a deep dimple in one brown cheek. "Some of 'em look difficult, but that's just on the surface. And some of 'em look as smooth as the ocean in a flat calm, but they're obstinate as hell. Either way you get a surprise. And that's what I like, kid.

Don't ever be just what people expect you to be."

Watching him as he talked, watching the way his right eyebrow quirked, the reckless, assured tilt of his head on his strong neck, she felt an odd little pang of knowledge; it was almost as if she understood how Leah Foster, married to an old man, must have first seen this rich and vigorous youth of Owen's. But the pang was quickly gone.

Across the harbor a man climbed down into a dory, over the side of a low-slung dark boat. He rowed among the moorings, the dory rising and falling in the long swell, and passed close to the *Old Girl.*

"Hello, folks!" he called, and Joanna called back. But Owen deliberately turned his head away.

"Why didn't you speak to Ned?" she asked quietly.

"That son of a bitch." The venom in his voice frightened her.

"What's the matter with him? I like him."

"You wouldn't speak to the bastard if you knew the truth about him. How a decent woman was fool enough to marry him — oh, I guess he put up a good front." Owen's mouth was thinned and pale. "He's the kind of guy who can put a woman through hell, and make everybody think he's the one who got the dirty deal."

"I've never heard of his making any talk. And Leah has everything she wants. She's got plenty of time to fool around with a kid like Hugo, I know that much."

"That's all you know about it! You damn women are all alike. Cats. Ready to pick another one to pieces just because you don't like her."

"That's not fair!" Joanna cried passionately. "How could I dislike her? All I know about her is what I've heard you boys say!"

For an incredible moment she thought Owen would strike her. His eyes widened and burned, red streaked across his face. "You never heard me say anything about her."

"Oh, all right," she said sulkily. "But you listened. The only reason you didn't say anything was because you didn't have anything to say. It was Hugo this time, for once!" Her voice gathered intensity as the pattern became suddenly clear to her. "It was Hugo who got there first! It was his turn to brag, and you had to listen. You didn't like it very well, did you?"

"Shut up your goddam mouth!"

They were abruptly silent, staring at each other from eyes curiously alike in their rage. Then suddenly all expression was gone from Owen's face. It was as blank as the unbroken wall of fog around them.

As they rowed back to the beach he looked through Joanna as if she didn't exist. She knew that look from past experience. It meant that at this moment he hated her. And she didn't care. She wished she could slap that locked dark face, beat the blind foolishness out of him, beat some sense into him.

The beach pebbles grated under the punt and she jumped ashore, ignoring the icy wash of sea water around her ankles.

19

THERE WAS NO ONE IN SIGHT, but smoke drifted down from the chimney of Karl Sorensen's fish house. If Philip were still at the harbor, he would be there, and she had to talk to him, right away.

But he wasn't there. Nils looked up from the workbench when she walked in, but she was too furious to be embarrassed. "Where's Philip?" she demanded. Sigurd, whittling a minute dory with exquisite precision in his big fingers, looked at her red cheeks and laughed.

"Philip's gone down to the Eastern End. Broke a connectin' rod this mornin' and went down to see if Charles had one."

Nils, watching her face, said, "Anything wrong, Joanna?"

"No, I—I just wanted to speak to him. Well, thanks, kids." She went out quickly and walked back along the road. Charles had come very infrequently to the harbor since his marriage. Maurice or one of the younger children, Rose-Marie and Pierre, came for the mail. Mateel had not come at all, and Joanna dreaded seeing her, when time had just begun to take the edge off that bitter day.

But she walked swiftly across the marsh, feeling the wet east wind against her face. Philip had gone to the Eastern End, and that was where she must go.

She moved through a deserted world, empty except for the surge and wash of water over the rocks below the path, the dripping trees, the foghorn at Matinicus Rock mooing like a disconsolate cow. Joanna usually loved the sense of mystery and adventure that surrounded her when she walked in fog; but today there was no joy in it.

The Eastern End houses looked forlorn. There was no sign of life as Joanna went through the gate and down the path. Even the old spaniel was missing. A faint wind eddied the fog and she glimpsed the boats in the cove, the filthy old *Cecile,* Maurice's weatherbeaten boat, Charles' *Sea-Gypsy.* Joanna's heart contracted. She was so pretty and pert down there between those other two.

The fog drifted again and hid the cove, and at the same time Joanna saw Philip come to the doorway of one of the old shops on the bank.

Then she needn't go in the house. She went over the wet grass, and the thought of telling Charles and Philip fanned her resentment against Owen. She was through with tact and silence. If Owen wanted to cut his own throat, that was his business. But he wasn't going to cut the family's throat as well.

She walked into the shop and slammed the door behind her.

Philip and Charles were alone, for which she was thankful. This was strictly a Bennett affair. God and the older boys willing, it would be over before one other person on the Island knew that Steve Bennett's boy had been making a fool of himself.

They stared briefly at her flushed cheeks and brilliant eyes. "Nothing like a little fog to make a beauty out of a woman," Philip observed.

"Did you know that Owen's chasing Leah Foster?" she said bluntly.

Incredibly, Charles laughed. "Owen, after that cold fish! I'd as soon make love to a corned hake."

Philip smiled, and she stared at their amusement with horror, as if they had suddenly become hostile strangers.

"It isn't funny," she said in a low voice. "Do you think it's funny?"

"Of course it's funny!" Charles looked merrier than she'd seen him look for a long time. "The rooster thinks he's going to show us a thing or two—no small fry for him!"

Philip's blue eyes had a look of his mother as he dropped his hand on Joanna's shoulder. "It's natural, Jo. It's part of growing up. Don't look so scared."

"But Leah — she's — " Joanna stopped, with anger a half wordless lump in her throat. Then she found speech again, in a hot torrent. "How do you think it'll be when the chew starts around the shore? How do you think it'll sound to Father when he hears it? Will he say it's natural, and grin like a fool? How will Mother like it, when Aunt Mary goes tearing up across the meadow with her mouth watering?"

She stood with her back against the door, her head high and her mouth furious. "Well, maybe *you* don't mind the grins and the looks and the talk about somebody with the same name as you! Maybe *you* don't care if your brother's ruining himself and disgracing the family!"

Philip shook her hard. "Hey, stop it, you young fool! Owen's not going to ruin himself. He's too damn selfish. And nobody'll know about it if you keep your mouth shut and don't go off half-cocked."

She felt resentment spread through her body like fatigue. They didn't care, they had laughed . . . Philip put his fingers under her chin and tilted it, smiling into her eyes.

"Listen, young Jo, we've been talking to him," he said gently. "But he thinks he's got hold of something good, and he's not letting go. So — " He shrugged. "How's for letting him stew in his own juice? He'll get over it all the sooner."

Charles, sitting on his heels by an old sea chest containing a jumble of small engine parts, muttered, "Here's a rod, Phil." He glanced up at Joanna with a quizzical look "Take it easy, Tiddley-winks. After all, the boy's only human. Wait till your turn comes."

"I'm not taking that kind of a turn, thanks!" she flared at him. "I hope I think enough of myself and the family, even if nobody else does!"

She went out, slamming the door behind her, and walked up toward the gate. The fog was cool and kind against her hot face. As she went back along the path, through the dripping woods, she thought about Leah Foster, who with her thin, slow smile and thick-lidded eyes had driven a man to kill himself; Leah Foster, who watched the boys as if their youth and vitality, their loud young voices, their big free gestures and supple bodies, were food and she starving. Joanna had seen that look, just as she had seen Hugo grow too thin, too jerky, too hollow under the cheekbones.

How long would it be before Owen began to look like that?

Joanna spoke aloud, and the wet wind pressed the words back on her mouth. "I'll have to do it myself," she said. "Alone."

The chance came sooner than she expected. For in the afternoon the wind changed again, and the fog scaled off, to show a blue and shining day, all the more radiant for having been thoroughly drenched.

The men went out to haul in midafternoon, and after supper there was a baseball game at the harbor, in the big grassy field where the village well was. When Joanna finished her dishes, she went down to watch the fun. As she came along by the fish houses the game had already begun, in the radiant ruddy light just before sunset. Shadows were long on the grass, voices rang in the clear, cool air.

Some of the girls sat on the granite outcroppings under Gunnar Sorensen's spruces. Kristi called to Joanna, and she waved back, but she didn't join them. For Ned Foster's boat was not at the mooring—he hadn't come back yet from hauling. And Leah must be alone, expecting him at any moment.

Joanna felt curiously calm, as calm and as cold as the shining harbor. The game was on the other side of the Binnacle, but as she waited for Leah Foster to answer her knock, she could hear Owen's shout. She pictured him leaping upward for the ball, his eyes alight and unclouded. They'd be stormy enough if they saw her now.

Leah Foster opened the door, smiling, her voice soft and crystal-clear. "Isn't this nice, Joanna! Come in!"

As always she gave the impression of having been just scrubbed, starched, and ironed. Her brown hair was as smooth as silk floss, her skin pale and clear, her tailored print dress smelled faintly of lavender.

She led the way into the sitting room, as incredibly neat as herself. Joanna didn't like it. It's because I don't like her, she thought uneasily. It's not the room's fault. It's not really bad, but it feels that way.

She didn't sit down at Leah's invitation. "What I've come for shouldn't take long," she said.

"I can't imagine what it is," said Leah. Her eyes were very bright. Joanna fought the weakening panic that threatened her.

"It's about Owen."

"Owen? Why, what do you mean, dear?" The smile deepened, the eyes—were they gray or green or palely blue?—took on a sheen like a cat's eyes, Joanna thought. Rage came instead of panic, warming her and sending a new glisten into her own eyes.

"You know what I mean," she said steadily. "Owen was here last night. And it wasn't the first time, was it?"

Leah's voice was light and precise. "I imagine that's Owen's business."

"He's my brother. That makes it my business, if he has anything to do with you."

"You'd better go," said Leah, smiling from beneath thick white lids. "You're acting like a rude little girl."

"Little girls can make a lot of trouble. They tell things." She felt a small surge of triumph as the lids lowered and the smile dimmed.

"What is there to tell, Joanna dear?"

"Enough. My father owns this house, Leah. If he ordered you out, there's not another place for you on the Island. And Ned would be mad because he likes it here. I heard him say he likes it better than any other place he's ever lived in. He'd probably ask my father why he had to go."

Leah forgot to smile. "You'd never dare to go to your father with a story about your brother!"

"Wouldn't I?" said Joanna softly. From her height she looked down at Leah with scornful black eyes. "I wouldn't stop at anything to get you out of here, Leah." She looked out at the harbor; in the clear pale light that follows sunset, Ned Foster was rowing ashore. She smiled a little. "I wouldn't stop at anything. Is it true, Leah, that Ned brought you here because it was the last place he could find where they'd let him come—with you?"

"Get out!" Leah whispered. "Get out before I kill you. If your brother comes here again—or any of your precious clan—I'll not even open the door to them. Now *get out.*"

Joanna paused in the doorway to look at the drawn face beneath the smooth bands of hair. "If you tell Owen," she said tranquilly, "that I came here, I'll go to my father—or Ned."

They both heard Ned's whistle. It seemed to Joanna that Leah was holding herself straight by a superhuman effort. Her eyes blazed darkly in the sockets. In spite of her triumph, Joanna felt a pang of pity. It was true then. Leah Foster was afraid of her husband.

Afraid of this little man coming up the path whistling. As Joanna passed him, he tipped his old felt hat and smiled vaguely at her. He looked as if he had been carved from some thin weathered bough of old wood. There was a grayness in his eyes, his hair, his voice.

Going around the house was like going into a different world. She took a long deep breath of cool air in this world where boys ran and yelled and swore happily at each other, two beloved mongrels yelping at their heels, and girls giggled on the knoll under the spruces. She had to pass Owen to reach them, and he threw out his foot to trip her.

"What deviltry have you been up to?" he demanded. For a moment black eyes laughed into black eyes, then he gave her a rough good-natured shove and spun around to shout encouragement at Maurice.

Not until she sat down by Kristi did she contemplate what she had done. If Owen ever found out—but he wouldn't find out. Not as long as Leah was afraid of Ned.

20

THERE WAS A WEEK WHEN JOANNA felt as though she were walking a tightrope. A week in which the men hauled their traps and planted their gardens, the woman washed and sewed and called on each other, the children filed in and out of the small white schoolhouse above the cove, and Joanna waited, fearfully and yet with defiance, for Owen's wrath to strike.

But it didn't strike. Leah had kept her word; she hadn't told him. Apparently she had given him no excuse or reason whatever for shutting him out, for sometimes Joanna, watching him covertly when he was silent at the table, seemed to see a furious bewilderment in his face. Once, walking to the store with him on boat day, she caught his bitter sidewise glance at the Binnacle. It was almost too quick to notice, but Joanna saw it.

Owen had his black moods that week, but Owen had always had his black moods. If sometimes they came thick and fast, the family left him severely alone. They rarely spoke to him about it. He'll be over it in no time, Joanna thought. Already it seemed to her that he glowered less.

And then, at noon on a breathless shimmering day, she knew it would take more than time to get him over it. It started so very innocently, with Philip tipping back in his chair, laughing, as Owen stopped halfway across the room to wrap his arm around his mother's waist.

"My favorite blonde," he said, and Joanna felt a little wave of pleasure, because for the moment he looked keen and kind and gay.

"Don't let him fool you, lady," Philip said, smiling. "He's butterin' up to you for a purpose."

"You can catch more flies with molasses than you can with vinegar," Stephen murmured absently to his pipe.

"Can't a man show a little honest affection without a lot of chew from you stump-jumpers?" Owen demanded, tightening his arm around Donna's slim waist.

"As long as it's honest," Philip drawled. "Nothing wrong with hugging up another man's wife . . . so long as it's your mother."

A whiteness sprang out sharply around Owen's mouth, and his eyes were narrow and shining slits. In one swift motion he let Donna go and reached for Philip, caught him by the shoulder, and pulled him up from his chair.

"For God's sake, Owen!" said Philip, laughing. It was Stephen who saw the virulent twist of Owen's mouth and caught his arm as it drew back and tensed to strike. It was Stephen's voice that rapped out sharply, "You young devil. Get to your room, or get out of doors!"

Owen stood motionless, his dark face darker with passion, his head lowered like a bull. Philip was slightly pale. "Wait a minute, Father. He was fooling."

"I was like hell," said Owen thickly. "I'd have killed you. I will, too, if I hear another goddam word."

Philip went even paler. He seemed suddenly taller than Owen, and his face was set in deep lines. "I'm always glad to oblige," he said quietly. "You won't hear anything else, Owen. *Anything.*"

He picked up his cap and left. Owen flung off his father's hand and went out of the kitchen, out of the house. They saw him go around the corner of the shop toward the point. Donna Bennett looked at her husband.

"Stephen—"

"I don't know, Donna," he said heavily. "I don't know." He took up the water pails and went out.

The house settled into early-afternoon silence, and Joanna, when her work was finished, slipped out through the back door. She wished achingly that she could tell someone. She had been so sure she had done right, and yet she felt so terribly young, so terribly lost. At fifteen she had thought she was a woman, and now at nineteen she felt like a bewildered child.

She was responsible for this, for Philip not speaking to Owen, and Owen going deeper and deeper into his own blackness. It would have been heaven to talk about it to someone. Nils, perhaps. But she had lost even that, and besides, this was Bennett business. She and Alec were friends, but even Alec mustn't know. She could only wait, and hope for the thing that would miraculously wipe the slate clean again.

David Sorensen was unloading driftwood from a dory in Goose Cove. Joanna walked down the slope toward him; the white beach stones were dazzling to the eyes in spite of the thick spruce woods that marched along above them, all cool green gloom and the voices of the birds who thronged the trees in May, little tuneful birds unafraid of gull and crow and hawk.

The May sun blazed in a brilliant unblemished sky, it drew a hot white glare from the beach. But the cove was a small, tranquil blue loop.

David worked swiftly, taking the crocus sacks from the dory; he must carry them across the meadow and through the alder swamp.

His yellow hair was bright in the sunshine, and his slender, yet strong body was stripped to the waist and shining with sweat.

And marked with something else . . . Joanna saw it in a brief instant, before he noticed her and reached quickly for his shirt—the long, pinkish strips laid unevenly about his shoulders, vivid on the boy's white skin. They must have been even more vivid when they were new. She wondered if David cried when his grandfather whipped him, and felt anger coming over her like a slow sickness. This was a worse ugliness than Owen swearing at Philip in the kitchen. David was so skinny and young, long-necked and big-footed like a pup. He seemed younger than Stevie, who was fourteen to David's fifteen.

"Hello, David," she said.

David grinned at her. "Hi, Jo. Hot, ain't it?"

"Uh-huh. What's the weather going to do?"

"Not so good." He squinted bright blue eyes at the sky and shook his head. "Today's a reg'lar weather-breeder." He pointed out at the place where sky and sea melted together in a shimmering mist. Above it the towers of the Rock light swam like a mirage. "That means storm."

"That's encouraging," said Joanna dryly. She walked down to the dory, and David hastily buttoned his faded blue shirt, leaving the tails outside his dungarees. Now all the scars were hidden.

"Jinx Pete, I was lucky today," he said eagerly. "Look." The bottom of the dory showed a rich harvest; three buoys picked up on one of the west-side beaches, a good oil can, two short but substantial pine planks. Joanna looked admiring and David went on with enthusiasm, "Nils will give me a quarter apiece for the buoys, and Sigurd wants an oil can. He'll pay me too. And my father'll buy the planks."

"Golly, you'll be in the money."

David's eyes were aglow. "Yep! I've got a lot saved up. I made me a bank—" He gave her a quick sidewise glance and went back to work.

Gunnar doesn't know about the bank, Joanna thought, and David's taking no chances. She sat on the gunwale of the dory while he worked. Above them the house stood against the sky. Three gulls sat on the ridgepole and brooded in silence, their plumage achingly white against the blue; a fourth, perched uncertainly near them, was gray-brown and awkward, an extremely adolescent gull.

The meadow drowsed; there was no sound anywhere. The young

boy and Joanna might have been alone in a hot bright world. At last David swung a sack over his sholder. "Well, I better start movin'," he said shyly.

"You've got to carry that stuff home, and then row the dory around the Eastern End?"

He nodded and started up the beach. "Look," said Joanna. "You've been working all day—I'll row the dory around. I haven't taken a good long trip for ages."

"Gosh, *no!*" His eyes widened. "I mean, it's too long for a girl."

You mean your grandfather would light into you if he thought you'd got out of any work, Joanna said silently. Aloud she said, "O.K., David. You're the boss."

When he had gone across the meadow she walked around the cove and into the cool gloom of the woods. She sat down on a fallen tree beside the path, hearing the small noises of birds around her and watching the glimmer of blue between the tree trunks. A hawk flew past her on soundless wings; he was intent and deadly in his silence, and though Joanna had seen hawks all her life, she felt herself shuddering.

The hawk was suddenly evil to her. He was like a symbol, sign of the evil that was here, on her Island. She had seen it herself, and the knowledge of it was a burden.

21

At supper time it was almost oppressively hot. The sun streamed across the Island and through the kitchen windows, beating in with unusual strength until Donna lowered the shades.

Beyond a few remarks on the unseasonal heat—even in midsummer the Island rarely had such weather—the family ate in silence.

They seemed to be caught in a spell, as if the scene at dinner still possessed them. At first Philip talked courteously with his parents. Owen looked steadily at his plate. Joanna, refilling plates, bringing more bread, pouring coffee, was grateful for the chance to move around. There was oppression indoors and out, tonight.

Suddenly, when the silence was becoming intolerable, Philip said in a quiet, unsurprised voice: "Look at the barometer."

Heads turned swiftly. All eyes lifted to the instrument hanging by the window that looked harborward; all eyes saw the needle gone crazy all at once, quivering madly back and forth.

"It's going to blow," Stephen said. "Westerly, I shouldn't be surprised. And soon."

Owen put down his fork. "That's fine, isn't it? Everything's hunky-dory. Boats and traps all stove to hell! When do we get that breakwater?"

"Never mind arguing. Just get through your supper. We've got work ahead of us."

It was then that the wind struck the house, with so violent a blow that Joanna's hands jerked and the coffee cup in her hand spilled hot liquid over her wrist. Donna said mildly, "Good heavens."

The windows rattled, the wind shrieked, the world was full of noise for one long instant, and then the roar subsided slightly. Joanna hurried to set the hot gingerbread on the table. Owen pushed back his chair noisily and went to the window that looked down across the meadow; the trees at the foot were tossing wildly, and the harbor, like polished glass a few minutes ago, lay open and defenseless to the wind. Now it was choppy and dark under a huge mass of scudding cloud that hid the sun; far to the west'ard there was a narrow brilliant line of silver on the horizon, but everywhere the sea was coldly gray.

The gulls soared high in hysterical arcs. Gust after gust crashed against the Bennett house, high and unprotected on its slope. The men finished supper in wordless haste, their faces unmoved. Donna, too, seemed undisturbed; she had been an Island wife too long to show alarm when a crazy westerly threatened the boats. It didn't help to be afraid. You needed more than fear to make the moorings hold.

While they were putting on their boots, Alec came in. His hair was wind-roughened, his eyes alight.

"I just lost my hat," he said cheerfully. "She went sailing out over the point."

"How's your mooring?" Stephen asked sharply.

"All right, I guess. Grant said the pennant was fairly new."

"Fairly new!" Owen snorted. "I guess you better keep your eye on it. You just got Jud Gray between you and the harbor mouth, and the way that old sea's pounding in —"

"Sure, I'll watch her," said Alec easily. His faint smile touched his eyes as he looked at Joanna, and she suppressed an impulse to ask him how he enjoyed his supper at Nate Bennett's last week. He leaned lazily against the doorframe, running a lean hand through his hair — the soft light brown hair that turned to bronze as the sun came out again and streamed through the kitchen.

"Well, let's be on our way, boys," Stephen said, and they went out, all four of them. Joanna and her mother watched them from the window as they went down through the meadow. The heavy clouds driving across the sky were storm-black, edged with silver; they hid the sun, then uncovered it again, and the long yellow light fell across the meadow and the four men, throwing their long black shadows behind them. Before them the harbor held a threatening darkness, lashing over the ledges, tossing the boats like chips.

Joanna's heart pounded with her excitement. "I'm going down! They'll need another pair of hands to help move the gear!"

"I need another pair of hands to clean up this gear," said Donna. Joanna flew at the sink like a whirlwind, and Donna laughed. "Too bad you couldn't have been a boy."

"That's what I always wanted," Joanna said, "but now . . . I don't know . . ." She was assailed by a sudden dreaminess, her hands were slow on the dishes.

"Oh, it's not too bad, being a girl." There was soft laughter in Donna's eyes as she looked at her daughter, and Joanna felt the color rise in her face, without knowing why.

The wind crashed against the house, and she hurried. Donna took pity on her when she had almost finished, and began to wipe the dishes. "Go on, go on!" she ordered when Joanna protested, without much conviction. "No sense trying to keep a gull inside four walls."

"You're — you're *swell!*" Joanna cried, and hugged her mother with all her hard young strength, before she grabbed her jacket from its hook and ran out, with Winnie barking behind her in furious excitement.

Down at the shore the men were working against time. Traps that had been apparently safe above the high-water line must be moved to the other side of the board walk; it took two men to carry a heavy trap with any degree of speed, so everywhere they worked together, brothers and cousins, fathers and sons, friends and enemies—Joanna saw Nils and Simon pulling up a dory together, with never a word between them.

The whole Island was there; women with coats hugged around their necks to keep out the chill wind as they watched their men, and talked in high, excited voices to each other, and lent a hand when they could. Children ran wild underfoot, shrieking; the steadily rising wind, the roar of water, touched them with the exhilarated madness of young animals. As Joanna stood in the shelter of Nathan Parr's camp, one of Marcus Yetton's little boys tripped, and sprawled at her feet with a startled squawk.

She set him on his feet. "Whose boots have you got on, Julian?"

"Pop's old ones!" With a whoop he was off again, darting among the men like a little harbor pollack among the moorings.

Peter Gray stood near her, smoking nervously; his new dory was safe, but he was worried about his traps, set out brand-new in April. Gunnar moved deliberately across the beach, his eyes blue pinpoints as he watched Karl and Eric work. Sigurd and Nils and young David didn't escape him, either. He saw Thea, too; she was taking an incredibly long time to pass the beach with the milk, and she was in Philip's way, or Alec's, or Tim Gray's, every time one of them came up the slope.

Gunnar approached her, smiling with deadly benevolence. "Ha, you come to help? Vall, I tell you. Get home, you young hussy! If you vass mine, I'd put the whip to you!"

Thea pulled back from the rosy, grinning face so close to hers, her eyes full of terrified tears, her lips trembling. Hugo grinned at her; she turned red, and hurried along the road.

Now the tide was racing in, a tumble and rumble of foaming waters up the beach where it usually crept so silently. Overhead the clouds scudded from the west, a violent, flaming west above a stormy sea whose waves were crested with fire. It was at once beautiful and terrible. The small boats leaped frantically at their moorings. Joanna felt pity for them; it seemed to her they were afraid. The *Donna* alone rolled gently, her masts brave against the sky.

Behind Joanna, as she watched, Nathan Parr and Johnny Fernandez carried on a stoical conversation.

"Last westerly we had," Nathan drawled, "I kinda thought I heard someone at the door. So I opened it, and pretty damn near the hull Atlantic came in."

"You boys better move out some of your stuff." That was Jud Gray, with no hint in his easy voice that his boat rode the outermost mooring. "Plenty of room in my shop."

"Me, I taka da chance!" Johnny exploded. "No storm scare old Johnny, after Grand Banks. Me I *speet* at it!" He did so, with emphasis.

Marcus Yetton came along the boardwalk in oilskins. "Three-quarters my traps set on the west side," he said, his face scared and old in the dusk. "And every one of 'em'll be stove to hell. I'm gonna bring some in."

Stephen stopped him. "Don't be so dumb, man!" he exclaimed. "Better the traps be stove up than you."

"Maybe you don't mind losin' gear," said Marcus bitterly. "You got money to build new with. Me, I got nothin'!"

"Susie'll have even less if you go out there." Stephen clapped the younger man on the back and smiled his quick, warming smile. "If it hits you bad, Marcus — well, don't worry."

Marcus will be another one of Father's lame ducks, Joanna thought with loving impatience. Another one to "borrow" money that would never be repaid. Not that Stephen ever expected it back . . . Marcus walked away, still sullen, but he didn't untie his skiff.

Joanna looked across the beach at the old wharf, staunch under the battering onslaughts of water. Spray flew over the spilings and touched the boys who stood with their backs against the boat shop. They had done what they could, and now they must watch the boats until the roaring dusk shut down. They would go home then, and not a man wouldn't start up in the middle of the night, wondering if his boat was safe.

Joanna took a long breath and plunged into the wind. But she was too late to join the crowd, for suddenly someone was shouting like a madman and the boys were running the length of the wharf, jumping down to the beach. Philip untied a dory and Alec and Owen came pell-mell behind him. Tim Gray and Hugo lent a hand, and almost instantly the dory was in the water.

No one, watching them go out, with Owen and Philip rowing and Alec in the stern, needed explanation. A boat was dragging her mooring. The Islanders thronged the old wharf and the whole wild harbor lay before them, ledges boiling with surf, boats dancing.

It was Alec's boat that had broken loose. The pennant was still fast to the paulpost, but one end of the ground line had given way and the boat had moved down the harbor until she had come up against Owen's boat. With each sea the two boats came together hard. The dory seemed small and impotent, fighting its way across the waves. Joanna watched it with parted lips, her heart big with pride. Those were her brothers out there, bringing such indomitable drive to the oars, sending the boat over the blown white crests and down into the gray-green valleys, and then up again, never failing . . . and spray flying all around them, and the wind catching viciously at the oars.

Alec crouched in the stern, his eyes never leaving his boat as it crashed again and again into the *Old Girl*. Let them bump long enough to start the caulking, and there'd be two boats lost in the harbor to-night. Joanna held her breath, thinking of it. The dory took an eternity to cover the last few yards, and it seemed as if the wind threw all its devilish strength into a final attempt to turn the small boat back.

Another dory fought its way toward the harbor mouth. Joanna heard someone say, "There's Jud and his boys goin' out!" She gave only a quick glance at Jud's boat, on the other end of the chafed ground line. Another boat to be brought in before the storm tore her loose altogether.

Stephen was beside her; she slipped her arm through his and held tight. Neither spoke, as they watched the boys approach the shabby gray boat that bucked like a wild horse. The dory slid alongside, the plunging bow reared high above them, paused for a second, and Alec was aboard in one scrambling leap, hanging on with a ferocity that must have broken more than one fingernail, while his long legs clambered over the gunwale and down into the cockpit. He had the painter in his hands, and pulled the dory alongside, holding it while the other two climbed aboard. Owen made the painter fast to the bit on the stern deck, and Alec started the engine. Philip went cautiously along the dripping washboards to the bow, and cast off the mooring.

The boat was no longer a wild thing, but something docile and trustworthy under Alec's hands. He swung her around until Owen could jump across into the *Old Girl.* Those on the wharf saw him as he dropped on his knees in the rolling craft, looking for a place where the caulking might have been started. After a few minutes he stood up again, shaking his head and laughing, and scrambled over into Alec's cockpit again. The gray boat shot forward across the water, making straight for the wharf.

Joanna felt her father's arm relax. "Now if Jud gets in all right—"

"He's making it," said Joanna. They stared out through the dusk, and the wind carried to them the sound of another engine, sure and strong. One by one the watchers left the wharf. Joanna was driven by a tremendous and jubilant excitement. She felt as if she were alive again, after the taut days of worry; it seemed as if she could never again be worried, or sad, or anxious. Nothing mattered now except that her brothers and Alec Douglass had conquered the sea, she had seen it happen before her very eyes. To the others it meant only that a boat had been brought in when she dragged her mooring; to Joanna it was living proof of the invincibility of her men.

Her men. She tasted the words on her lips, and knew shock; only two of them had been her men, her brothers. Her face began to burn, but she thought it was the wind.

They were hauling the dory up when she came along the beach. Alec's boat was made snugly fast, lines forward and astern, in the lee of the wharf.

"Did you leave some coffee on the stove?" said Philip, looming out of the dusk. "We want some."

"There's plenty. And fresh doughnuts, too."

"Come on, lads," said Philip, and Owen and Alec joined them. Owen was laughing and excited, and Joanna felt a deep wave of joy when she saw his hand close around Philip's arm, heard him say, laughing, "What's better than one Bennett in a tight spot?"

Alec said promptly, 'Two Bennetts and a Douglass. Where's that coffee?"

Like a triumphal procession tbey turned along the road for home. Lights streamed down across the meadow toward them.

In the entry the boys peeled off their spray-soaked jackets and wet rubber boots. Owen was through first and into the kitchen, shouting, "Ahoy the house! Where's my darlin'?" Philip said over his shoulder, "I'll dig up some slippers for you, Alec," and he too had gone. Presently their voices came out from the sitting room, where they were telling Donna about the boats.

Kitchen lamplight streamed into the entry, on Alec bending down to pull off his boots, across his damp soft hair, so different from black Bennett hair; and on Joanna, standing against the outer door, wondering why she didn't go into the house with the others.

The silence in the entry became an audible thing. Joanna's face burned, but her hands were cold, she thrust them hard into her pockets. In a moment she must say something, but what could she say? If only Alec would get his boots off, so she could go by him into the kitchen. Anybody would think he was being slow on purpose . . .

Her voice felt scrapy and unfamiliar. "Did you break any fingernails out there tonight?"

"Fingernails?" asked Alec. He straightened up and looked down at Joanna as if he had never seen her before. Then, with one swift motion, he shut the kitchen door, and in the sheltering blackness of the entry he took her into his arms.

His lips were warm and firmly gentle against hers. Gentle, but the touch of them sent a great tide of thanksgiving over Joanna. This is it, she thought, and her arms went around him. It seemed as if she could never get enough of the good clean smell of him, the wiry strength of his body, his arms tightening around her, and the way he put his face against hers.

She felt the deep thudding of his heart as they stood thus, and hoped passionately that he could feel hers. There was no word between them, nor any need of words; for a long time they stood together, with no speech or movement, until they heard Owen come whistling across the kitchen.

Without haste or alarm, they kissed and separated; Alec opened the door, and they went in.

22

At daylight, Joanna heard Owen stirring in his room, next to hers, and on a quick happy impulse she dressed and went downstairs. She opened the back door to let Winnie out, and stood for a moment looking across the point at Schoolhouse Cove, and the black loom of the Eastern End woods against the sky.

The world was tranquil and gray in the pale clear light; the scattered spruces on the point were etched black on a sky that would soon be flushed with the color of wild roses. Joanna stood on the stone doorstep and took a deep breath of the cool air, at once fragrant and salty. It was so still that the gulls' eternal chatter on the ledges came to her ears with sharp clarity, and the sparrows' sleepy twittering in the wild pear trees was loud and sweet.

The glow that had lain all night against Joanna's heart spread through her body until she seemed to feel its radiance go forth from her like actual light. Here in this entry, with the familiar oilclothes and rubber boots . . . She shut her eyes and lifted her face, remembering with an aching happiness his hard young cheek so warm against hers, the way their hearts had beat together.

She heard the stairs creaking under Owen's feet, and went back into the kitchen, discreetly shuttering her face. When he came in, she was building a fire.

"Hello," he said on a yawn. He noticed nothing, too intent on plunging his head into a basin of cold water. Joanna put the teakettle over the rising blaze and measured out the coffee, brought eggs and cream from the cold cellarway. Owen toweled his head vigorously, subdued his wet black hair, and presented a glowing countenance to his sister.

"How about some light here?" He lit the lamp on the table, and Joanna shrugged. "I was going to let the sunrise in."

"You and your sunrises!" Owen grinned at her. "I wonder how Alec's old tub got through the night."

Alec. She loved the very sound of it; it evoked him before her with his quiet smile, and the way his hair grew, and the feel of his arms tightening around her. She said, level-voiced, "Did the *Old Girl* have any holes knocked in her?"

"Couldn't see a damn thing. Oh, she's built to take it, that one." Vital, healthy, smiling, he sat down to his breakfast and Joanna forgot for a moment her own personal delight to half-wonder if this was the sullen, tormented Owen who would have struck down his brother yesterday. He looked as if there were nothing to cloud his universe — the universe that stretched over and around them now, the sky tinged with the delicate hue of sun-ripened apricots, tbe sea turning faintly, silkenly blue.

It was the boat that mattered most, not the women. They were brothers again when it was sea they must fight, instead of each other.

When they had finished breakfast, Owen put on his boots and Joanna walked with him down across the wet green meadow. A little breeze riffled Schoolhouse Cove and made a scalloped edge like white lace on the beach; the birds were active in the alder swamp at the foot of the meadow, and the first primroses were the color of sunlight on the brow of the beach.

The harbor lay before them, only slightly choppy now. The wind had risen rapidly until the tide turned, and now it was dying out as rapidly. Sigurd Sorensen's boat was passing the harbor ledges, and Joanna saw Nils dragging his punt down over the beach. Remembering Alec, she thought: This is how you wanted me to feel about you, Nils, but I couldn't.

They passed the anchor and had a full view of the harbor now. Alec's boat was high and dry, keeled over beside the old wharf. Owen looked out across the water and made a strange and furious sound.

"By God, she's gone!"

The *Old Girl*'s mooring was empty. Brother and sister stared, all speech forsaking them, until Joanna said slowly, "But where is she?"

"Sunk, damn her!" he said between his teeth. "She must be! She did take in water, after all." He strode down the beach, shouting at Nils. "Wait a minute, goddam ye!"

Nils grinned at him. "Got a big head this fine large morning?"

"Christ, my boat's sunk. Come on, let's get out there." They pushed off, Owen at the oars. Joanna would have liked to have gone, but some new shyness kept her from going where Nils was when her own happiness should glow so transparently in her eyes. It burned steadily and sweetly within her, and she thought how irrevocable it was; the flame had been lighted, and even if he never again kissed her or held her against his heart, the flame would always burn.

She sat on an overturned dory and waited for the boys to come back. Presently they beached the punt, their voices clear in the early morning silence, and Owen came up toward her. His mouth was grim, but there was a curious taut excitement about him.

"Sunk, all right. Gone down clip 'n clean on her nose. She must have filled up in the for'd compartment."

"Oh, Owen! What are you going to do?"

He laughed. "I'll do something, don't worry."

"You'll have to get her up, and dry her out."

"Yep, I'll get her up—and leave her in the marsh." He grinned at her blank look. "I've got my plans made already, young Jo. First I've got to round up Alec."

She stood up and took a deep breath. "Alec?" she said casually, and it seemed as if he must see the way her color grew. But he was lighting a cigarette.

"You know him. That long-legged gandygut you lugged home one night."

"Seems to me I met him, once." Joanna managed to look humorous without looking radiant, and they separated. Walking home, she wished it were she who was going to wake up Alec. She knew what it would be like to walk silently in the dew-wet grass, to go so quietly up the steps and slip through the door, to tiptoe through the cool bare rooms and come to the cot where Alec slept.

She considered this, her mouth curved with secret delight. Did he sleep on his back or his side or his face? Did he burrow down till you could see only a rough brown crest? Or were his arms flung above his head, his throat bare, so that he looked young and defenseless and remote?

And what would she, Joanna, do — now that she stood there? At the thought of his waking to her presence, she felt her whole body tighten in unbearable, exciting happiness. For she knew with her heart and soul what he would do. He would put out his arms to her and she would go into them.

Here was the house again, and Joanna, her face impassive, went into the kitchen to find Philip and her father washing up. She hurried with their breakfast, and waited until they were fortified with good coffee and bacon and eggs, before she said quietly, "The *Old Girl's* gone — sunk."

Philip said at once, "I knew the rooster should've brought her in last night. But he's so cussed stubborn."

"Where's Owen now?" Stephen broke in.

"Gone to find Alec," Joanna answered.

"We'll get to work on her this morning," Stephen said. "It's died down a lot — we'll have to get her up as soon as we can. At that, he'll lose plenty of good hauls."

"And Closed Season in three weeks." Philip was grim. "At the rate that boy's been hauling, this'll lose him a couple hundred dollars. He'll be broke all summer."

It was not a pleasant prospect. Owen could go handlining or trawling to keep some change in his pockets, but until now summer had always been more or less playtime for him. Beyond the necessary repairing of gear, he considered it his right to spend his money as he pleased; he didn't stint on his work the rest of the year. And there was always more money to be made in September. But if there weren't any money in his dungarees, and if there weren't any chance of a fling on the mainland — Joanna's mind didn't have to go into details. She knew, just as the others knew, what it would mean.

Philip and Stephen went to haul, Donna came downstairs, the routine of the morning went on, and Joanna couldn't worry much about the *Old Girl* when the thought of Alec was a little wordless song that went on and on.

Before noon the kitchen was suddenly full of men. Philip and Stephen, not too discouraged about their traps, since most of them had been set to the east'ard of the Island; Owen, coming in arrogantly with an unmistakable aura of triumph around him; Alec, not saying much, smiling a little; Nils.

Stephen said at once, "Well, what are you going to do about your boat, son? She won't be fit for a while—you can take my boat to haul this afternoon."

Owen didn't waste time with preliminaries. He said directly, "Thanks, Father, but I've got my plans made. I'm going out to Cash's. Alec's going with me."

Donna said in a low voice, *"Cash's,"* and that was all.

"How are you going?" Stephen asked quietly. "You haven't any boat. Alec's isn't big enough."

"What about Nils' boat?" said Owen, smiling. Stephen looked at Nils.

"So he's talked you into this, and I thought you had some sense in that yellow head of yours. Don't say anything—I know damn well it's all Owen's idea, from start to finish. Go out on Cash's with sixty-five pots, stay a week, haul three or four times a day, make stacks of money—maybe. If a storm drives you right back, you've lost gear, bait, and your expenses, besides maybe losing yourself. I'm not saying you wouldn't get back all right. But there's more men lost out by going to Cash's than those who've gained anything. That's a good boat of yours, Nils, I know that—"

Nils said quietly, "She's seaworthy."

"She's a big boat, too—she'd probably carry a hundred pots out there, easy. I'll grant you that. But you've never lobstered on Cash's. Owen and Alec don't know anything about it either, except what they've heard of all the money you can make . . . if you're lucky."

Philip said, "And maybe it's quick money, but it sure isn't easy money. You can take an awful beating in that shoal water."

"Bill Clark's boat caught on fire last time he was out there," Joanna volunteered. "He had to row home in a dory. Sixty miles. He lost his boat, engine, traps, everything."

"He's one of those Brigport numbskulls," Owen said impatiently. "They don't know anything. Nobody but a proper damned fool'd let his boat get afire. Listen, you can argue all you want to, but if everybody's said their five cents' worth, I'll say mine. We're going out to Cash's. We're going to get some of those lobsters that crawl around those ledges thick as flies in honey. And this summer I'm going a build me a boat."

His eyes were aglow and his color was high, and the poise of his head was the poise of a colt's head when he is about to take the bit in his teeth and run.

Stephen shrugged. "Well, Alec, I hoped you'd have more sense."

Alec shook his head, smiling. "I guess not, sir. Maybe it's a gamble, but everything is, to my way of thinking."

Joanna liked his adventurous spirit, for it was adventure to go out on Cash's Ledge, where it was always rough except in the finest weather, and men who had never been seasick in their lives came back gaunt and white, sore from the ceaseless pitching and tossing, swearing that three thousand pounds of lobsters in five days wasn't worth wishing every hour of those five days that you could quietly die.

Stephen played his final card—toward Nils, who owned the boat that would go. "What about a storm? It's sixty miles home, you know. You'd leave your pots out there, and a lot of your lobsters. And you'd be risking that handsome boat of yours."

"We've just had a good blow," Nils said. "There'll be a spell of fine weather for a while."

So they faced him, Owen defying anyone to cross him, Alec politely sure of himself, Nils not saying anything at all. But Joanna knew the obstinacy of his mouth. She glanced at Philip, who stood with one foot on the oven hearth, looking at Owen with indulgent amusement. She glanced at her mother, who didn't look up from her sewing. And at her father, who was saying:

"Well, I can't forbid you. You'll never learn till you find out for yourself. But you'd better get the *Old Girl* up first. She'll be dried out by the time you get back."

"I'll never haul from the *Old Girl* again," Owen said. "When I go out again in September, it'll be in a boat of my own, built the way I want her."

"Well, you're not going to start building her right now, are you?" asked Donna mildly. "Because it's dinner time."

For a moment Owen scowled, then suddenly he smiled at his mother. "Aye, aye, sir! Got room for a couple extras?"

"Not for me, thanks just the same," Nils said. "Kris'll be looking for me." He went out quickly.

"Now, what ails that boy these days?" Donna wondered aloud. "We hardly ever see him, and then he's gone again before you can say hello."

"He's a hardworking guy." Alec retrieved a spool of thread for Donna and sat down on the window sill near her. "I've never seen him loafing since I came here." Owen brought out a notebook and began to jot down figures for the trip. Philip and Stephen, having given up the argument, made amiable suggestions. Joanna put dinner on the table.

She felt an almost intolerable ache to be in Alec's arms again. She was so tinglingly aware of him that she didn't dare look at him. When would they have a moment alone? The thought ran wildly behind her quiet intent face.

She was beset by doubts and agonizing fears. She really didn't know Alec at all. Maybe he was in the habit of kissing a girl when he had a chance; any girl. Maybe she'd read a meaning into his gesture that he hadn't intended. The thought was a knife in her heart. She couldn't bear it, to know it was only a casual thing, as casual as the kisses Owen bestowed among the Island girls.

Quite suddenly she dreaded being alone with him.

Dinner over, the men went back to the shore and Donna lay down in her room. Joanna washed and wiped dishes in absent-minded fury. Not a word, not a look from Alec; he hadn't tried to be alone with her. He was like the others—he'd kissed her because she was a girl, and handy, and she'd fallen into his arms like a ripe plum. Oh you fool; you idiot! she thought, remembering the way ecstasy had lain all night on her lids, and how she had opened her eyes to it with the first glimmer of dawn.

The house was exceedingly still, except for the clock on the shelf and her own subdued rattle of dishes. Noon sunshine and fragrance drifted through the kitchen. It was June, and the Island was at its best. In a week or so the buttercups would strew the meadow in shining drifts, and already the first blue flag were out in the marshy spot between the fence and Goose Cove.

You could always depend on the blue flag, anyway, Joanna thought bitterly. She hung out the dish towels, took her mother's old shears, and went down toward the cove. The day glittered after the storm; the air held a blend of sweetness and sharpness, scented with sunwarmed spruce and early clover, and the racy pungence of the high tide that filled the cove with a shining and incredible blueness. High tide, and a golden noon.

And there, caught between the weather-silvered rail fence and the white beach rocks, bordering the path that curved into the deep sun-spattered shadow of the woods, the blue flag grew tall and stiffly elegant, the color of heaven.

Joanna loved them, but today she was preoccupied as she cut a good armful for the big earthen jar in the sitting room. Cold water seeped into her shoes, but she hardly noticed it; the persistent caroling of a song sparrow from the wooded hillside behind her went ignored, for Joanna, deep in confused and angry thought, was whistling absently under her breath. She realized suddenly that it was one of Alec's songs—"The Road to the Isles."

"Damn the *Scotch!*" she said aloud, and precisely at that moment she looked up and saw Alec Douglass coming around the corner of the house.

She had a moment of panic. He had seen her, he was coming down over the grassy slope—long-legged and quick—and her heart began to beat faster. At the same time she was quite aware of the fact that he probably wanted to know the whereabouts of the new manila hawser, and that was all.

He looked curiously sober as he came along the path. "Hi, Joanna."

"Hello.' Her dark eyes viewed him remotely across the brilliant blue of the flowers.

"I was going to help you with the dishes."

"They were done long ago."

They stood gazing at each other. Alec was pale under his tan, and not exactly at ease. He glanced around, and his eyes halted at the place where the path led into the woods.

"Does that go to the cemetery?"

Joanna nodded. "Haven't you been up there yet?"

"No." Almost, he fidgeted. She had never seen him so uneasy. "Look Jo—"

She lifted an eyebrow, and suddenly color came back into his lean cheeks, the twinkling smile into his eyes. "Don't look so dignified, Jo. Come up and tell me who's buried where."

In this new cool detachment of hers, born of a knowledge that men were all alike, she didn't wish to appear too willing. She considered, staring meditatively into space as if Alec Douglass were no more than a distant gull that floated, laughing raucously, overhead. But she was poignantly conscious of him, of the line of his jaw and neck, the way his mouth was cut at the corners, the way he stood watching her, his hands in his pockets and the wind stirring his hair, his eyes bright with imminent laughter.

"Well," she said slowly, "I was going up to get some apple blossoms, anyway."

They went silently along the path and left the shimmering cove and the flooding sunshine behind them for the cool green shade under spruces, with only the quick rush of small birds' wings, and their voices, for sound. The path turned and twisted upward, and came out by the great maple that Joanna loved. They paused, letting the silence flow around them. The little cemetery was washed with sunlight, but all around it the ancient spruces stood tall and very dark, their pointed tops seemed to hold up the June sky. The stones were small and gray, the older ones covered with lichen; the pansies and geraniums set out on Decoration Day were vivid against the grass.

Joanna and Alec sat down on the stile, built over a fence that had been made years ago, when part of the woods served as pasture for Grandpa Bennett's cows. Wherever they looked, except toward the cemetery and the blossoming orchard beyond it, there were green and shadows, and splashes of light like warm gold; and under the oldest spruces there was cool and mysterious darkness that had a silence of its own. There the hawks moved soundlessly, but where Joanna and Alec sat, there were continual soft twittering and elfin whistling from the small birds.

"Listen to them," Joanna said. "They sing all day, as if they never heard of a hawk."

"Maybe they're just whistling in the dark."

"Listen to that sparrow. If that isn't pure happiness—" She remembered her dignity. "Did you say you wanted to know who's buried where?"

"Yes. Who's buried there, where the apple tree is. There's no marker."

She glanced at the place where every breeze brought down a lazy drift of petals on the grass, a pink and white snowfall. "Five unknown sailors who were drowned in a wreck, right after my grandfather came."

"I wonder if there's room for one more," Alec said. He was watching the dreamy progress of the petals fluttering down to the grass. "Do you think they ever feel the flowers coming down on them like snow, and wake up and know it's spring?"

She thought with a curious delight, it's like poetry. She couldn't imagine Owen or Philip or Nils thinking of words like that. Aloud she said, "Maybe . . . and maybe when the wind blows the apples down they wake up and know it's autumn. . . . We used to think that tree had better apples than the orchard. Owen and I used to come up here after them — we called them the Sailors' Apples."

"I'd like an apple tree over my grave," he said mildly. She felt cold, as if the breeze had suddenly chilled.

"You don't have to think about it yet," she answered.

"Why not? According to Phil and your father, and Gunnar Sorensen and some of the others, we'll come back from Cash's all ready for the grave, if we don't end up in a watery one."

His eyes were twinkling, and with relief she shook off the odd mood that had seized her. "Alec, why in heaven's name do you want to go out there? It's foolish! There's only one chance in ten that you'll make more than your expenses."

"Don't you believe in taking chances?"

"Oh, I'm not a coward, if that's what you mean. But look, Alec, there's no need of it. You're doing all right with your trawling, doing better all the time. And there's enough boats in the family so Owen can haul until the closed time begins."

"Owen wants to build his boat. And I'm not making money fast enough to suit me." He said it calmly, as an irrevocable fact, but she challenged him.

"Not making money *fast* enough?"

Alec turned his head and looked down at her. "Well, if a man wants to buy furniture for a house, so it's fit to bring a woman into — if a man wants to settle down —" The color burned high on his cheekbones, and his eyes were very bright. There was a curious sensation around Joanna's heart, and she felt fire in her own cheeks, a smarting in her eyes . . . I don't know what he's talking about, she thought stubbornly.

She never knew which one of them moved first, whether without realizing it she swayed toward him, or he toward her; but she was in his arms, there on the stile by the cemetery, with the apple blossoms falling on the sailors' graves, and a song sparrow blithely singing his heart out over their heads.

It was just as she remembered it, the feel of his arms around her. Only this time they talked.

"I want to marry you as soon as I can," Alec said. "As soon as we've got something to start on."

"We don't need much to start on," she murmured, "only each other . . ." She fitted so perfectly against his shoulder, and she could hear his chuckle begin in his chest.

"I know, but you've got a family that's in the habit of being prosperous. I've got to show them I'm fit to take care of you."

"They won't think much of your fitness if you're going to keep risking your neck." She twisted her head to look up at him. "It's such a nice neck. I like it."

"I like yours." This was a curiously intent and somber Alec; somber, yet his eyes were shining, his voice faintly unsteady. The touch of his fingers on her throat sent fire along her skin. She turned up her face to him; a heaviness lowered her lids until the lashes were thickly black against the warm brown of her cheeks, and her mouth was soft and full, and waiting.

He said her name in something between a groan and a laugh of pure triumphant happiness, and buried his face in her neck. His arms grew so tight that she could hardly breathe, but this very breathlessness was a feeling of wonder and beauty. She was motionless in his arms, holding this perfect moment like water brimming in a cup. Then she felt his lips warmly on her throat, moving up toward her cheek, and when she could bear it no longer, when it seemed as if her whole body was one aching pulse, she turned her head and met his mouth.

This time it was not gentle.

23

MARK AND STEVIE CAME ON the *Aurora B.* for the summer vacation. Joanna was at the wharf when they arrived. They had grown just since Easter; tall and arrow-straight, they hurled their bags ashore and swarmed up after them.

Link Hall leaned out of the pilot house, a deeper red than usual, and said around his cigar, "Jo, see if you can't drown them two wild Injuns before next September."

"Drownin's too good for 'em," said Fred Bowers from the engine room hatch. "Though I recollect them Bennett boys always did raise hell when they come back from school."

"You, Ash Bird," Link yelled. "Look alive and grab that line! Look here, Jo, I don't mind common-ord'nary good spirits, but I can't say as I like findin' them boys up in the crosstrees every time I turn around."

"Can I help it if they're part monkey?" asked Joanna politely, and an appreciative chuckle rippled across the collection of Islanders on the wharf. Stevie grinned, thumbed his nose at Fred, and yelled at David Sorensen to wait for him. They went off toward the shore. Mark stopped long enough to give Joanna a mighty hug.

"Hello, fishface. My God, the girl's got handsome! Hey, where's everybody? Nils and Owen out hauling?"

"Gone to Cash's," said Joanna briskly. "Left at three this morning, in Nils' boat." And her heart had gone too, following across the starlit sea. . . .

"Cripes, why couldn't they wait for me?" Mark demanded.

"Save your fight for later. You march yourself along home and see Mother." Arm in arm they went up through the shed and found

Stevie sitting on his suitcase outside the store, explaining the intricacies of basketball to David, Pierre Trudeau, and an assortment of younger children. He had grown very tall, but his shy grin at Joanna was the same endearing one that he had possessed since childhood. No hugs on the wharf for him, but later he would seek her out and tell her in detail about his year at school.

When they had started along the road, attended by a retinue of youthful admirers, Joanna went into the store to wait for the mail. Quite suddenly these commonplace duties held a new zest; it was as if with the coming of Alec into her personal life everything had taken on new colors and freshness.

When she reached the house, Mark and Stevie, already in dungarees, were rolling around in the grass by the back door, an animated mixture of black heads, long legs, and Winnie. Joanna, watching them wrestle, knew exactly how they felt. It had been like that with her, too, when she came back from school. She wanted to run out and see the whole Island at once, take it into her arms; and if she couldn't do that, simply to fling herself to the ground was the next best thing. The breath and being of the Island came into you then, with the damp warmth of the earth, and the smell, and the sunshine.

Her mother, setting the table, said, "Joanna, I don't know whether to laugh or cry."

"Why?" Joanna put down her bundles and stared.

"Mark's got a girl."

"Oh, Mother!" Joanna began to laugh. "Are you surprised? He's sixteen, and you know the Bennetts! Stevie's got a new love, too."

Donna sat down. "That *baby?* Who is it?"

"Basketball."

They laughed together as they put dinner on the table for themselves and the boys. Philip and Stephen wouldn't be in from hauling till midafternoon. And Owen—

"They must be there by now," Joanna said absently, trying to see the boat in her mind, and the three boys eating dinner in the cuddy, laughing, joking, talking about the money they were going to make.

"Who? Oh, you mean this Cash's business." Donna shook her head. "I don't mind admitting I'll be glad to see that boat come into the harbor again, money or no money."

"Mother—" Joanna began, and hesitated. To her mother's inquiring blue glance she said briskly, "Do you want the cake or the
pudding for dinner?"

No, it was too early to tell her about Alec. He had only come
in April; they would think she didn't know him well enough, or that
she was too young. As if love didn't tell you everything! As if time
or age made any difference! But you couldn't explain to anyone how
it was when he kissed you there in the dark entry, how it was as if
you had always known what would happen. . . .

"Pudding, I think," her mother was saying. "Your Aunt Mary
brought up some heavy cream this morning."

The boys were gone all afternoon. They came in at supper, sun-
burned, sweaty, noisy; wrestling at the sink, filling the house with
their healthy and impudent chatter. It was their first day home, and
no one put a damper on them. Time enough to calm them down
tomorrow, when their regular tasks would begin. There was baiting-
up for them to do, painting, weeding in the vegetable garden, wood
to chop and water to fetch; they would go fishing with their father
during the Closed Season, and be paid for their share.

After supper Joanna walked around Schoolhouse Cove to get the
milk at Uncle Nate's, and the boys went with her, Winnie an ador-
ing shadow at their heels. As they went through the gate, Mark said
abruptly, "Listen, Jo, what's Charles done? Sure, I know Mateel got
caught on a stump—"

"Mark, if you say that again I'll slap your face."

"All right, then." He laughed. "I won't say it. But Charles married her. Does that make him an outcast?"

"He made himself an outcast if you want to call it that. He knew
how Father felt about the Trudeaus."

"Mateel's no worse than anybody else."

"She's not a bad girl. It's the family. Oh, when you've got boys
of your own, you'll understand better." She couldn't help being very
adult, and Mark flushed under his dark skin.

"I understand enough. I know Charles hasn't set foot near the
house since he got married." He flung up his head in the familiar
defiant gesture so like Owen's. "I'm going down there and see him
tonight."

He waited for Joanna to answer, his eyes very bright. Quite suddenly, she smiled. "Golly, he'll be glad to see you."

Stevie chuckled. "Fooled you that time, Marcus Aurelius. You were all set for a fight."

"Cripes, I'm going to have one, too," said Mark, and Joanna went suddenly sprawling over his foot. She reached up and caught him around his knees, and for a moment there was unbounded confusion in the midst of the evening primrose and beach peas, with Stevie helpless from wild laughter, and Winnie running in frantic circles around them all. All at once Joanna found herself sitting on Mark's chest.

"Can you breathe?" she asked him anxiously.

"Sure I can!"

"Then I'll sit here till you're cold and lifeless."

"Like hell you will!" With one mighty heave he rolled her off, and Stevie pulled her to her feet. Slightly out of breath, they continued across the pleasant meadow, their shadows long before them in the mellow sunset light.

Mark left them where the road turned off to the barn. He went on toward the Eastern End woods. Stevie looked wistfully at the vast bulk of the barn against the brilliant western sky and sea. "We could play basketball in there, if Uncle Nate—"

"Well, he won't," Joanna assured him. "And they've milked already, so we can just leave our jug on the doorstep and take our milk, and go home again."

"That's good. I don't want to talk to Aunt Mary tonight." Stevie was frowning. He picked up the warm full jug, and they went back to the road. "Nice gardens Uncle Nate's got laid out this year. Jo—"

"Mmm," she said absently. There was something on his mind, and she mustn't seem too eager.

"Know where I was this afternoon?" he said. "I went down and helped David clean up the barn. Gunnar was over at Brigport, or I couldn't have stayed."

"You had a good chance to talk, then."

Stevie nodded. His face was absorbed, he didn't know how closely Joanna was watching him. Mark had already taken on the taut, reckless look of Owen and Charles, but Stevie's long lashes, which he hated, and his shyness, gave him a very young air. It was an anxious air at the moment. Joanna waited.

"David's going to run away," he said at last.

"Tonight?"

"No," said Stevie, "but the next time Gunnar gives him a whipping." There was nothing childish about the dark rage across his face. "Gunnar beat him this morning, and it was awful. Right after the boat, it was—right after we were talking. That old bastard! He only did it because Nils was gone."

"What did he whip him for?"

"He told Dave to clean out the barn this morning, and when Dave heard the *Aurora B.* whistle, he beat it down to the wharf—just to say hello, that was all. So you could say it's really my fault," he added flatly.

"Maybe. But that wasn't bad enough to whip him for. So David's going to run away." She looked out across Schoolhouse Cove, dark blue in the lee; far out on the horizon there was a line of gold, and the Rock towers still caught the sunlight.

"He's desperate, Jo. Golly, every time he moved, it hurt him. Anna came out and brought us some lemonade, and she looked at him and began to cry, and Kristi was white as that schoolhouse there. They hate it when Gunnar lights into him, but they can't do anything about it." Stevie's mouth was tight. "Jo, I'm telling you this, because you'll take it right, and not make a fuss about it. When David runs away, I'm going with him."

Her heart gave a sickening lurch, but she said evenly, "Why?"

"He isn't fit to go alone. He'd get lost, and into all kinds of messes. He's so *little,* Jo."

She smiled at that. "He's older than you."

"But he doesn't know so much," said Stevie seriously. "He wasn't brought up like me, and he doesn't go to high school. Gunnar won't let him read anything but the Bible—remember when I lent him *Under Two Flags,* and Gunnar threw it in the fire? Gosh, Jo, David doesn't know half as much as I do."

They stopped by the gate to wait for Winnie; she was flushing ground sparrows in the marsh. Stevie said, "You see what I mean, don't you?"

"Yes, only promise me something, will you, Steve? Come and tell me before you go."

"I can't do that. I already promised David I wouldn't tell anybody, only I figured I'd better tell you a little about it. When we go, you can tell them up there." He nodded toward the house. "I wouldn't want 'em to think I wasn't happy, or something."

She wanted desperately to take him into her arms and hug him hard, but instead she snapped her fingers at Winnie and turned toward the house.

"You understand, don't you?" He was anxious. "I just have to go with him."

"Sure I understand, Stevie!" She looked back at him smiling. "Race you up the hill!"

The anxious look went out of his eyes and he began to run, overtaking his sister, with the dog nipping happily at their heels.

24

THREE DAYS WENT BY, three days of June at its loveliest. Overnight the daisies came out and whitened the fields; the barn swallows came back to Nate Bennett's barn and Gunnar's — sleek darting shadows, with eyes like tiny gems. The lobsters were crawling thickly, as if to give the men one magnificent series of hauls before the Closed Season began, when the lobsters could carry on their shedding and breeding without interference.

"The boys ought to do well out there," more than one man said, and Hugo talked urgently to Jeff and Philip about making the trip while the weather held good. Joanna hardly dared to think what it would mean if the boys came back with eight or ten hundred dollars' worth of lobsters. She only knew that the thought of marrying Alec in the summer filled her with a rapture that was almost too great to keep secret. And it seemed to her that the whole world unknowingly shared the happiness that burned in her like an unfaltering flame.

There were three days of beauty and richness and promise, and on the fourth day the wind rose. It came from the northeast, a cold, howling, wet wind without mercy or respite.

The Bennetts didn't talk about the storm, and to Joanna the silence was worse than talk. To see her father or Philip pause by the seaward windows and look out through the streaming glass, to see them turn away with only blankness on their faces, was enough to draw every nerve to unbearable tightness. The hours were endless, from the moment she awoke to the familiar assault of wind and rain against her window; not only for Joanna, but for them all.

Mark and Stevie came in at noontime, their cheeks fiery red from the cold rain, and hung up their streaming slickers and sou'westers in the entry, talking all the time. "Jeeley Criley, it's a humdinger!" Mark said with enthusiasm. "Pete Grant says he'll call the Coast Guard any time you say, Father."

"The boys can find their way home quicker than the Coast Guard can find them," Stephen said. Nothing else was said. The family sat down to dinner and talked casually about Island affairs. But Mark was obsessed with a desire to talk about the storm.

"They're all worried, down at the harbor. You know what that goddam—what Aunt Mary said when I was up there this morning? She says—" He minced into a crude but realistic caricature of his uncle's wife. "She says, 'I don't know why your father let Owen go. Then they'd none of 'em gone. Owen's the ringleader in all the deviltry, always was!' "

He broke off as he met his father's eye, shrugged, and began to eat busily. "I felt like kicking her someplace," he observed in muffled defiance to his plate.

Stevie grinned, but it was an anxious grin. He was too young and too sensitive to hide his worry behind an impassive face or a swagger. Joanna forced herself to eat. They were all thinking of Owen, and the Sorensen clan was thinking about Nils, but while she thought of her brother and her old friend, there was also Alec.

The younger boys were out again when dinner was over, and Philip went down to the shore.

"This weather will drive them in from Cash's," Donna said cheerfully. "I'm glad there's plenty of chowder left." She chuckled softly. "I'm thinking Cap'n Owen's going to know what it is to be seasick before this gale blows itself out."

"Take him down a peg or two," Stephen murmured. "He's a mite too cocky, that one. I wonder how Alec's taking it."

Joanna, wiping dishes, had an instant picture in her mind of Alec being washed overboard, lost at once between mountains of gray water, of the others circling vainly, calling against the howl of wind and the beating rain. No, he'll have to come back, she thought, setting her lips like steel. This can't happen to us, when we've just found out. But in the next breath she knew it could happen, and suddenly it seemed the most real thing in the world; almost she could see the boat limp into the harbor in the silence after the storm, she could see Owen and Nils, gaunt, unshaven, hollow-eyed; she could hear the way they would tell it.

I'd have to run away, she thought in panic. I couldn't listen to them. I couldn't tell them about us, knowing he'd never come back again.

She hung up the dish towels. "I'm going out for a while," she said.

"Put on your boots," her mother said. Joanna wondered if they would talk after she had gone, if they would speak of their anxiety.

Schoolhouse Cove was choked with breakers and foam, the air was filled with the heavy waves' thunder. The rain was needle-sharp on Joanna's face as she went down the road. By the Binnacle she met Kristi, on her way to Karl's fish house. Her face was pale under her grandmother's shawl, her blue eyes wider than ever.

"Jo, d'you think they're all right?"

"Of course they are," Joanna said scornfully. "Nils' boat is seaworthy, isn't she? It'll take more than a northeaster to hurt them."

"That's what I keep thinking." But Kristi's smile wavered. "Only Gramma's going around singing 'Precious Name,' and crying, and it gets on my nerves."

"Why don't you come up to the house?"

"I can't. David's waiting for me in the shop. I'm going to help him clean it up."

"Come up when you get a chance, then." Kristi nodded and went over the wet beach stones, splashed with black where tar had been spilled; the dripping wild caraway fronds and chicory made wet lines on her coat. She waved to Joanna from the doorway, and Joanna waved back from the path.

It was sheltered here at the harbor, but all around was grayness and a wet smell, from the drenched ground and green stuff and the little rocky beach between Karl's fish house and Pete Grant's big wharf. Somewhere in the misty vastness overhead a gull was crying; more gulls poised tranquilly on the shining tarred roof of the store. White water jetted high at the mouth of the harbor, and the roar of wind and surf seemed to fill the world.

The store was warm, and lit by lanterns that caused mysterious shapes to materialize where in brighter weather there were only prosaic coils of rope, and rubber boots. The glass toggles hanging from the ceiling gleamed crystal and amethyst and sapphire. Below the floor the water swished and chuckled.

Pete Grant was at the telephone, mammoth in wet oilskins. Nathan Parr sat on a nail keg beside the pot-bellied stove. He looked pleased to see Joanna. "Hello, young woman. How's that stubborn, stuffy old man of yours today?" Nathan had a particulariy disrespectful brand of humor.

"He's fine," said Joanna. "Good."

"Good, is he?" Nathan's laughter wheezed and rattled. "Are ye sure of that? Never knew there was any good Bennetts but dead ones. That's what my brother used to say after your gaffer run him off'n here."

Grant struggled with the telephone, alternately ringing and roaring "Hello!" with no apparent result. Joanna said above the uproar, "What did he do—your brother, I mean?"

"Somethin' about women, if I remember rightly. My brother had a fondness for 'em—failin' of the Parrs, only I didn't come by it. But Tommy—he'd chase a pretty petticoat from hell to breakfast." Nathan looked interestedly at the toggles. "Seems he went ashore with a load of mackerel one day, and after he sold it, and moistened his parched throat a mite, he went up 'n down Wharf Street invitin' folks to come for a sail. Mostly folks of the female persuasion."

"Hello," said Grant furiously. "Goddamit, why don't you *answer?*"

Joanna moved closer to Nathan. "What then?"

"Well, the whole kit 'n caboodle ended up out here, feelin' very mellow. And your grampa was on the wharf." Nathan rocked with reminiscent laughter. "He threw 'em out of here quicker'n white lightnin'—and every time I come up this wharf I think of it. Tommy down below with his ladies—Wharf Street variety—and the cap'n up there with that black Bennett face on 'im, and a way of usin' his tongue to blister the hide off ye without cussin' once. A proper gentleman, your gaffer was."

Grant slammed the receiver into place and stamped across the floor. "Now Pete here," said Nathan, "he ain't no gentleman, or he wouldn't of swore into that instrument."

"Goddam thing's always out of order," Grant rumbled.

"No wonder, with you always blattin' into it. If you stood on the shore and hollered across the bay, they'd hear you jest as good. Might have to do it yet—the gover'ment's liable to take out the cable if you keep on sullyin' the innocence of them young Coast Guard boys with your bad language."

"If I could raise one o' them young Coast Guard boys to answer once in a while, it'd be a help," said Pete. "Nary a peep out of them. What'll you have, Joanna?"

A moment ago she had been laughing with Nathan, but now she felt cold and humorless. "I was going to ask you to call up the Rock—maybe they can see the boys from there, if they're coming."

"Sorry, girl, I can't get a thing. Cable's out again."

Joanna turned toward the door, and Nathan said after her, "Don't worry, them boys is part gull. They'll be all right. And jest think of the fun you'll have when the Coast Guard comes to fix the cable."

Joanna smiled, but it was an effort. She shut the door behind her and stood for a moment looking across the harbor. The wharf cat came out of the shed and rubbed against her ankles, making inquiring noises. She leaned down and scratched his ears. A man came around the corner from the path, his yellow oil jacket and overalls bright and glistening in the gray day.

"Hello, Joanna," he said pleasantly. It was Simon Bird.

She straightened up and walked past him, saying, "Hello." It would have been superbly noncommittal except for one thing: the wharf cat had left the remains of his daily pollack in a usually secluded corner by the rain barrel. No one had ever before disturbed his fish when he left it there. Joanna, trying to walk between Simon and the barrel without brushing against Simon, stepped on the fish and slipped.

It was humiliating beyond speech to find herself thrown thus into Simon's arms. She thought distinctly, *damn* that cat! . . . and tried to twist herself free. Her face was as hot as fire, and Simon's arms were like steel around her. And he was laughing.

"Let go," she ordered him. If only she could get one hand free to slap his mocking grin from his face.

"Aren't you goin' to thank me?" he asked gently. "I saved you from crackin' your head open."

"Thank you." She was suddenly icy-calm, waiting for him to release her. For a moment that seemed like an hour he held her motionless, her arms pinned to her sides; the narrow, smoky-gray eyes looked down at her brilliant ones, and stopped at her mouth.

Simon Bird kissed her. She fought, but he only tightened his grip, and nothing could shake the hard urgency of his mouth on hers. She had never been kissed like that, with a savage hunger, with *hatred*. For it seemed to her, even as she pitted her slender wiry strength against his, that he hated her as much as she hated him.

At last he let her go. Shaken and breathless, feeling murderous, she stared at him. Her lips burned, there was a sharp stinging in the lower one. She flicked it with her tongue and tasted blood. Simon laughed, and there was unusual, excited color in his face.

"Yes, it's cut. It'll be a long time healing."

She turned quickly and walked along the path, her hands clenched into fists in her pockets. Some day I'll kill him, she thought with deadly clarity. Her lip hurt, and Simon's voice followed her.

"That's something to remember me by." She heard his soft laughter before a great gust of wind came across the harbor and drowned out all sound but itself.

Sometime in the night she awoke with a start from troubled dreams. There was something strange . . . She lay there in her little room under the slanting roof, and the close silence pressed against her face. *Silence.* That was it. It was perfectly still.

She slipped out of bed, and opened her window, left closed when she went to bed because of the beating rain. The breath of the Island blew gently upon her, cool and fragrant with the fresh sweetness that follows rain. There was still a subdued wash of surf on the Island's shores, but there were the stars, clear again. Orion had climbed high.

The rhythmic flash of the Rock light caught on Uncle Nate's white house. What time was it? Joanna wondered, kneeling by the window. According to the stars, it was long after midnight, and there was a ghostly streak of light over the eastern sea. And faintly—so faintly that if you strained to hear it you couldn't hear it at all—she heard a distant throbbing, as evasive as a failing pulse.

She dressed quickly and went downstairs, expecting to find the kitchen dark and cold. But the scent of coffee met her at the door, with lamplight and a crackling fire; her father stood by the stove, talking softly to Winnie.

He looked up at her and smiled, but she knew he hadn't slept much. "Father," she said swiftly, the words tumbling out in an eager rush. "Father, I'm not sure, but I think they're coming."

The streak over the eastern horizon had widened, and flushed delicately pink, and the darkness was fast melting away when the throbbing grew clearly audible to those on shore. Men who were going out early to haul, others who had awakened like Joanna to hear the distant engine, a few of the women and children—they stood about the beach talking and shivering a little in the cool air.

Kristi said jubilantly, "I knew they'd make it all right."

But *are* they all right? Joanna thought. Jud Gray said, "Comin' up Old Man's Cove now. Sounds weary, don't she?"

"Limping home." That was Karl Sorensen. "Just as I said."

Joanna stood rigidly still beside Kristi, who was shivering, and chattering about the big breakfast she'd fixed for Nils. The mention of food turned Joanna's stomach. And all the while the engine was growing louder, until someone on the old wharf yelled, "There she is!"

There she was indeed, coming in sight around the point; she was weary and slow in the gray light, a gaunt, tired shadow of the trim boat that had gone out so gaily a few days ago, with a fair wind to help her, and her jigger sail snapping. Limping home. Limping home with her dory gone, with a splintered stub of a mast, as if she was so tired she could hardly go the last few yards, as if she could barely slip toward her mooring; as if she would never again be a gay and leaping and vital thing.

She reached her mooring, and something like a sigh went up from the watchers. Joanna felt a blinding rush of tears. She could hardly see the figure kneeling on the bow to pull up the mooring chain.

"There's Nils," Kristi said. Now was the time for Joanna to steel herself, because Sigurd and his dory were alongside, and soon they'd be ashore. Three of them, back from Cash's. Or two . . . The sound of oarlocks was loud in the stillness as the dory slipped across the pale water, pink and mauve and silver in the growing sunrise. It came past the old wharf, it skirted Alec's boat, and a few more strokes brought it to the beach.

Besides Sigurd, there were three men in the dory. Joanna stood very still as the others went down to the water, as the hands went out to pull the dory up. She saw her father and Philip, down there, Kristi and David. Without moving, she watched and listened. Nils was laughing, and he looked natural. Tired, perhaps, but not too badly. Owen needed a shave—his beard was very black—and there was a rip in his damp jacket. He greeted his father sheepishly.

And then there was Alec. Owen took him by the shoulder and said, "Cripes almighty, has this boy been seasick!"

"I noticed you hanging over the side a couple of times, Cap'n Owen," Nils said dryly. "We're all pretty much of a mess. We thought we'd ride the storm out, but it pretty near rode us to pieces. Threw us all over the cuddy to hell and gone. We've been since noon yesterday coming home." He glanced out at his boat. "There aren't many can take it like her," he stated simply.

"Where's all them lobsters?" someone demanded maliciously.

"We had plenty, never fear," said Alec with a grin. "But they were so damn homesick we threw 'em all overboard again." A laugh went up, and even Owen smiled faintly. It had stung him, Joanna knew, to come home defeated, after all his planning and bragging.

He and Alec came up the beach with Stephen and Philip. "Jo's got a big hot breakfast ready for you boys," Stephen said, "and then you can get some sleep."

"That sounds good, sir," Alec answered.

Owen said, "It seemed out there as if there wasn't any such thing as sleep, or quiet, or being warm. The stove fell over—you couldn't keep a coffee pot on it anyway—and a port got smashed in so the place was awash before we could fill up the hole. It was pure hell!"

Joanna watched Alec move up the beach. She ached at the sight of his gaunt pallor and his weariness. Like the other boys, he wore clothes that had been soaked with sea water and were still damp. There was a bruise on one temple and a scratch on his cheekbone, with a trickle of dried blood. He stumbled once, and staggered. She wanted passionately to take him into her arms and cradle his head against her breast until he fell asleep.

He saw her then, and paused. "Hello, Alec," she said, her voice suddenly husky. "I see you got back."

"I got back," he repeated somberly. "But I haven't any money."

She was aware of her father and brothers watching them oddly. But it didn't matter. Nothing mattered except that her man had come back to her.

"Never mind the money. You're still alive and that's what counts. You're home again."

Alec smiled. It filled his tired, heavy eyes with light and sent a deep radiance across his thin face. "Home again," he said simply, and without hesitation she moved into the possessive circle of his arm.

25

IN OCTOBER THE ROSE HAWS BLOOMED red against the gray rocks where the wild roses had bloomed, fragile and pink. The gulls drifted high over Schoolhouse Cove, and Joanna watched them from her bedroom window, her hair loose on her bare shoulders. It was the afternoon of her wedding, but she could always find time for the gulls.

They were her friends, they had always meant freedom to her. They came and went, the whole wide universe was for them; space and sun and air, an eternity of sea and sky. They mated, and raised their awkward speckled young, but soon the young birds flew, and they were all free together.

As Alec and I will be free, Joanna thought. For she never once doubted that this day was a step into freedom.

She started as Kristi came in. "Joanna, aren't you dressed *yet?*" she asked in a shocked voice.

"I'm dressing, Kris," Joanna said guiltily. She had made the simple white dress herself, and she had small white chrysanthemums, from Donna's garden, for her hair. It was Alec who wanted the white flowers.

"I wouldn't be so slow getting ready if it was my wedding!" Kristi said. She left the room quickly, and Joanna was alone again. She finished her dressing without haste. She wasn't nervous, and that was queer, but there was really nothing to be nervous about. She was going to marry Alec, she had probably known it from the moment he set foot on the wharf at Bennett's Island, and that was nothing to have cold and shaking hands for.

The white dress slipped smoothly over her head, the fabric cool and silky against her warm brown skin. Joanna stood before the small mirror over the chest to put the white flowers in her hair, and remembered a night when she and Alec had walked to Sou-west Point in the moonlight, in a hushed and sleeping world. The woods were motionless and black along the Island's crest, and the rocks gleamed along the shore; the sea stretched toward the end of the world with a vast and infinite calm, but where it murmured around the rocks it was liquid light, forever changing and twinkling and whispering.

They came over the rise between two steep coves, caught in the dreamlike silence. Joanna, hearing their quiet feet on the short grass, feeling Alec's arm snug around her waist, and the soft touch of the night wind on her face, thought: This isn't the path I followed this morning, looking for strawberries. It's as if some magic thing happens after sundown, and then nothing is the same. . . .

"Smell the blackberry blossoms," she said dreamily, as the fragrance drifted in the air, intensified by night and dew.

"Look at them," Alec said. "White flowers in the moonlight." They stopped and looked down at the little gleaming stars that held a treasure of sweetness. On an impulse Joanna dropped to her knees in the grass and put her face close against the blossoms; they were cool and wet on her cheek, and the deep breath she drew was pure delight.

She sat back on her heels and smiled up at Alec. "I always wanted to do that. Did I look silly?"

"You look beautiful." Very tall he was against the moon-washed sky, before he bent and broke off a cluster and tucked it behind her ear. He cupped her chin in his hand and said gently, "My darling," before he kissed her.

The next day, when she saw him lounging across the beach, thin and lanky in his dungarees and rubber boots; when he came to the house and wrestled on the grass with Mark and Stevie — whenever she saw him as he moved among the Islanders, she felt her heart quicken. For this was the Alec they all knew and liked, but she knew a different one, and it was a secret thought, her knowledge of an Alec who tucked white flowers behind her ear and called her *darling*. It was with this Alec that she shared a dream, a world where no one else could ever come.

Just to think about it brought a lovely color to her face. She didn't need rouge or lipstick. Her mother and Kristi, who would be up here at any minute, were both pale today. It wasn't strange for Donna. And Kristi was pale from excitement and misery at once. She wanted to marry young Peter Gray, and Gunnar wouldn't even let Peter take her to dances. From the rainbow peaks of her own happiness, Joanna knew a deep pity for Kristi and Peter, but she couldn't think of it now. Not while the people of Bennett's Island were gathering downstairs to see her married, and the Island itself was so beautiful that it shook her heart.

For me, Joanna thought, standing before the mirror. Her red mouth shaped the words. *For me.* It was as if the Island knew, and had brushed its tawny fields with gold, and deepened the blue of its coves, and touched with flame the little vines and shrubs at the edge of the dark woods.

She heard voices at the foot of the stairs. They'd be coming soon. These few voices were almost the last she would know as Joanna Bennett. She touched her full lower lip with her finger. Yes, it had healed, though for a long time it had bled whenever Alec kissed her hard. He'd told her amiably, without asking what had happened to it, that it had better heal before October.

Simon Bird must know by now that she was out of his reach forever. He would be downstairs in the sitting room at this very moment; every one on the Island, old Johnny and Nathan, the Trudeaus, the Birds, had been invited to the wedding. So Stephen's father had always done; so Stephen would always do, and his sons after him.

Joanna herself had gone down to the Eastern End to ask Charles to come. He'd been knitting trapheads in the kitchen, and it had been a relief to see that he was as clean-shaven and neat as ever, his shirt just as white. Charles always wanted to wear white shirts for everything. The kitchen was very clean, and painted in warm light colors, and Charles had bought a new stove, and a vivid linoleum for the floor. There were starched curtains at the windows, and Mateel looked happy and no longer terrified. Color flashed into her face when Joanna told them about the wedding.

But Charles had shaken his head. Mateel said quickly, "But Charles —" and was silent. Later Charles walked up to the gate with Joanna.

"Charles, please come!" she pleaded. "We all want you — *all* of us. Don't be stuffy and narrow about it. It's my wedding, Charles, and I always planned on having all my brothers at my wedding."

Charles' dark face was impassive. "Sorry, Jo. But we're better off down here in our own neck of the woods, with the baby coming, and all. Thanks just the same, Jo."

"You damn stiff-necked Bennett!" she raged at him, but she could have cried as she walked home through the woods.

Her parents came in, Kristi behind them with Joanna's white chrysanthemums and her own bronze and rose armful. "Hello," Joanna said. "Where's Alec?"

"Gone out to haul a few to the south'ard," said Stephen dryly.

Joanna laughed. "I wouldn't be surprised if he did go out to haul at the last minute. He's been working so hard since he got his traps out that it's a wonder he'd take time off for his wedding."

"He's down there," said Donna, "looking as calm as if he'd been married twenty times before."

"Maybe he has, for all we know," said Joanna tranquilly. Kristi looked shocked, and turned pink as the others laughed. Donna kissed Joanna lightly and went downstairs. In a moment Miss Hollis, at the cottage organ brought up from the schoolhouse, would begin the wedding march. Joanna stood very still at the head of the stairs, her hand on Stephen's arm; Kristi, on the step below, looked up at her with wet blue eyes and a tremulous mouth.

"Weddings always make me cry," she said shakily.

"If you howl at mine," said Joanna, "I'll pinch you. Honest,

Kristi!" Kristi smiled waveringly, and then, with only the faintest preliminary wheeze, the organ began to play.

It seemed only an instant before they were in the big sitting room. It was crowded now. Young Julian Yetton's nose was running, Joanna noticed, and Rachel was spotty; she saw Nils standing back against a window, serious and scrubbed-looking in his dark blue suit. Nils, you wanted it to be you, she thought swiftly in that instant. But you'll marry some day, and she'll be a lucky girl, whoever she is.

Funny, the way some faces stood out so clearly before her eyes. She had one glimpse of Simon Bird. His color is very bad, she thought, and then she saw Alec.

He was standing by the fireplace, the mantel behind him garlanded in juniper and bittersweet. Mr. Guthrie, the minister from Brigport, was there too, the late sunlight shining on his glasses. Owen was beside Alec, darkly handsome, and nervous in spite of his stillness. But Alec wasn't nervous, Joanna thought with an inward chuckle, and neither was she. Of all these people, she and Alec were the most at ease.

He was waiting for her; he had that waiting look in his eyes and in the tilt of his head. Their glances met across the little space left between them, and they smiled. Her heart began to beat faster, her fingers tightened on Stephen's arm.

Why, I'm going to be *married!* she thought all at once, as if it were a new and tremendous thought. We're not just going out for a walk to Sou-west Point, we're going to live together for always.

She wanted to run the last few steps. But somehow she walked them, and the music was stopping, and at last, as if she had been journeying toward him for all her life, she reached his side.

26

IN THE COOL BLUE OCTOBER DUSK Joanna and Alec came alone to their house. It stood apart from the rest of the Island, as aloof in its way as the Bennett house was; backed by the steep dark hillside, cut off from the Bennett meadow by the woods and the orchard, with its field running down to a narrow rocky cove to the west, and stretching down to the village in front, it held a true feeling of solitude for Joanna as they went up the steps to the porch.

The door was unlocked. Alec opened it, and swung Joanna into his arms to carry her into the kitchen. He kissed her, and for a long moment their lips clung before he put her down.

"I can't believe it," she said.

"Believe what?"

"That we're alone . . . and when we take walks and go sailing we'll come home together. Not you up here, and me across the meadow."

He ran his lips across her cheek. "It's you and me, and the whole world before us. I'll light a lamp, huh?" He was gone for a moment, then she heard the sharp crack of a match, and light grew in the kitchen. They looked at each other by lamplight, and then at the room.

"It looks good," Joanna said with pride. She had made the curtains, Alec had done the painting and laid the linoleum; together they had done the papering. They had worked on the house all summer, when Alec wasn't fishing, or worklng on his traps. A great many people had helped them. Nils had rebuilt the very door through which Alec had carried his wife tonight.

They left the lighted lamp on the table and wandered through the other rooms in the dark. The front room was no longer Alec's sleeping quarters now, but a real sitting room, with bookshelves and pictures. Alec dropped into his new easy chair and pulled her down onto his knees.

"This is where we'll sit and listen to the radio," he said contentedly. "In Poppa's chair. I see where Momma's chair isn't going to get much use."

Joanna chuckled against his shoulder. Alec was all hers, and forever . . . all the world before us, he'd said. It was such a vast prospect that she couldn't take it in all at once. You will, Joanna, she assured herself. Little by little you'll know it's not really a dream, that you're married to the man. You'll wake up in the morning—

She pressed closer to Alec. Will I be as happy as this tomorrow morning? she wondered. But then she knew that she would be happy. The gods that Alec was always talking about had blessed them from the start; they would always be blessed.

She lifted her head and kissed Alec on the mouth, and felt his hand warm on her breast. The dusk crept around them, and the silence was immense. Even the sea was quiet.

"Isn't it *still!*" she whispered.

He answered against her lips, "But not for long. What about the serenade?"

She sat bolt upright and stared at him through the dimness. "Are they serenading us, Alec?"

"You didn't hope to get married without it, did you? Well, they kept it pretty quiet, but your two kid brothers gave it away."

"And I thought they weren't going to have a shivaree— usually somebody lets you know ahead of time. I haven't got anything to give them!"

"Did you think they'd let a Bennett get married without all the works? Come here and calm down, wench. Cigars, coffee, pop, stuff for sandwiches—the cupboard is full."

"Alec, you're wonderful!" She buried her face in his shoulder. The gentle pressure of his lips on her neck sent a sharp thrill across her skin. She lifted her face then, and they clung together in the warm, gathering darkness.

Wrapped in their deepening mood, intoxicated with their entrance into their new and personal world, they didn't hear the knock on the door until it turned into a persistent hammering.

"They'll go away in a minute," Alec muttered against Joanna's cheek. She lay against his shoulder, her eyes half-closed, her head heavy; she didn't want to move, ever. She only wanted to lie here with Alec in the warm dark, and hear his soft whispers, and know the joy of his touch.

But the hammering didn't stop, it grew louder, until at last the kitchen door opened and Mark shouted lustily through the house, "Anybody home?"

"That devil!" whispered Joanna, suddenly possessed with a fierce desire to murder her younger brother. "He only came up here for mischief. Don't go, Alec! Maybe Owen put him up to it."

They were very still, listening to Mark's feet in the kitchen. "Hey, this isn't a joke!" he hailed the silence. "D'you take me for a damn fool?"

"I'd better go," Alec said. He went out to the kitchen and Joanna followed him, smoothing her hair and wondering why she had ever been so generous as to have her wedding in Teachers' Convention Week, so that Mark and Stevie could come home from school.

Mark greeted them with extraordinary excitement. "Charles just came up to the house!"

"*Charles?* Really?" said Joanna happily.

"Yep. But it's nothing to crow about. He wants Mother to go down to the Eastern End with him—he thinks Mateel is going to die. It's the baby, I guess. She fell downstairs right about supper time." Mark's eyes were wide. "Charles looks like hell. He's some scared."

"I should think so." Joanna felt cold and wide-awake now. "Did Mother go?"

"Yep. She says it might not be as bad as Charles thinks, and then again it may be bad. Well—" For the first time Mark looked slightly embarrassed. "Well, I'll be going. Didn't mean to barge in on you fellas."

"That's all right," said Alec. "We were listening to the radio." Mark stared. "You haven't got one yet!"

"Well, if we had a radio we'd be listening to it," Joanna explained gently. Mark went out, and Joanna and Alec looked at each other.

"The next thing is the serenade," said Alec.

"Alec, what if Mateel's really dying?" Her fatally vivid imagination could see it all; a wedding, a birth, and a death in twenty-four hours. Charles left with a tiny baby, and the leaves from the big maple drifting down on a new grave. She shivered, and Alec put his arm around her.

"Mateel's as tough as they come."

"But a fall—and a baby. That's dangerous, Alec. And Mother's not strong enough to walk all that distance and then look after Mateel." Alec's arms couldn't warm her. Even her own joy wasn't enough to shut out the memory of Mateel's big frightened eyes and her twisting hands.

"Joanna." Alec said it very quietly. "Listen, dear, if it would make you feel any better to walk down there and see for yourself, we'll go."

"Alec, do you mind if we go?" she asked eagerly. "We only have to walk down and back. You married a worrier, Alec." She put her arms around him under his suit coat and hugged him hard. "I've got to fat you up, Alexander Charles-Edward Douglass. I put in a big order at Uncle Nate's for milk and cream." She tilted her head and looked up at him through her lashes. Her tongue was suddenly shy, trying to shape the words she had never said before, though she knew the truth of them.

"I love you, Alec."

"I love you, Joanna," he answered, and bent to kiss her throat.

The familiar sounds of an Island night in October had a new and intimate delight for Joanna, walking beside her husband. The distant screaming of the gulls, the surf on Goose Ledge, the smell of wet rockweed as they passed the beach, the scents of the marsh and the blessed darkness all around them, the darkness that would soon be starlight.

Joanna thought: Mateel will be all right, and in a little while we'll be home again.

Lights burned high in Nate Bennett's house, and the sound of guitar and accordion came through the closed windows, and the lusty singing of a melancholy tune.

> Down in a low green valley,
> Where roses bloom and fade,
> There lived a jealous lover
> In love with a beautiful maid . . .

"Sounds as if the gang moved up here," said Alec, "What kind of a song is that?"

"Don't you know it? He stabs her in the last verse—I mean in her snow-white bosom, but she forgives him, so it's all right."

"A fine way to celebrate our wedding, with a dirge like that."

When they came out of the woods and looked down across the rolling ground, with the Head bold and high against the stars, there were lights in both houses at the Eastern End. The old dog came to meet them, and escorted them to the nearer building—Charles' house. Charles himself opened the door to them.

"Mother's upstairs. Sit down. Take off your coats."

Alec put his hand on Charles' shoulder. "Sit down yourself. Hello, Maurice. How do the lobsters crawl for you, these days?"

Maurice was pale too; his mouth shook when he tried to smile. He was terrified, Joanna realized, and remembering the mischievous Maurice who had been Owen's equal in deviltry, she felt queerly hollow inside.

Men are always frightened about babies, she thought. But it wasn't very calming; she didn't like to see their fear.

She listened to the uneven talk that Alec tried to keep alive. Then her mother came down the narrow stairs from the open chamber overhead, and said, "What are you two doing down here?"

"Mark came over and told us. I thought you might need me."

"Mark ought to have his bottom spanked. Maurice, will you go to the harbor and call the doctor?"

Maurice took a step forward, his mouth moving before the words came. "She's—she's bad?"

"Yes," Donna said evenly.

Maurice took his cap and went out. Charles fumbled with his cigarettes and dropped them, and Alec handed him one. There was no sound in the house, no sound from upstairs.

"Mateel's the bravest girl I've ever seen," said Donna, and her quiet words broke the spell.

"Mother, *how* bad?" Charles said quickly.

"I don't know, Charles. But not too bad, I think. Mateel's sturdy."

"Does it hurt her much?" His words came harshly, with difficulty.

"Babies always hurt," said Donna in her most practical voice. "But Mateel's got grit. She won't make a sound."

Joanna sat very straight and trembled a little inside her coat. She didn't look at Alec, who was scratching the old spaniel's ears.

I was married tonight, and I've thought about having children, and upstairs a woman is having a baby. Upstairs a woman is in terrible pain.

She felt as if every nerve of her body was pulled taut. She couldn't stop thinking of Mateel. Sometime Alec might look as Charles did now, sometime she might be biting back her moans. But it didn't have to be like that, if she didn't want it that way. She and Alec didn't ever have to go through this ordeal.

And in the middle of her tumbled thoughts, she knew something else; that Charles had turned to his mother as he had always turned to her. And that there had been tenderness as well as admiration in her mother's voice when she said, "Mateel's got grit. She's the bravest girl I've ever seen."

The door opened violently and Aunt Mary came in with all the force of an easterly gale, Mark grinning over her shoulder and making wild gestures at the others. Her great voice and presence filled the tiny kitchen, making Donna seem twice as quiet, and twice as slender too.

"Well, I never!" Aunt Mary boomed at them. "A wedding and a baby in the same day!" She wagged a roguish finger at Alec. "Good thing you folks ain't responsible for the baby as well as the wedding — then there *would* be something to talk about on this God-forsaken place!"

Alec lifted an eyebrow at her. Donna said sincerely, "I'm glad you came down, Mary." Nate's wife was in her element with sickness and new babies, and most of the Islanders were willing to ignore her candid humor, at least until after the crisis.

"Well, when Mark come and told me, I knew you'd be needing me," she said without false modesty. "You can't tell about these things — all the Bennett babies I ever knew was in such a hurry to start raising a rumpus that they never waited for any doctor. Course none of 'em was ever way ahead of time . . ." Her eyes narrowed. "Just how much ahead of time *is* Mateel, Charles?"

Charles said, "Next month it should've been."

"Well, that's not too bad." Without invitation she went upstairs. Donna, smiling faintly, removed the singing teakettle from the flame and said to Joanna and Alec, "You two might as well run along. It was good of you to come down but I don't need you, now that Mary's here." The smile broadened. "The two of us should be able to manage a Bennett baby. We've had plenty of experience, God knows."

Charles ssid haggardly, "Yes, thanks, kids." Alec laid his cigarettes on the table. "Just in case you run out of 'em, son . . . Coming, Mark?"

"Mark, you go on back to the harbor and round up Stevie, and go home," Donna said.

"I been trying to dig him up all evening," said Mark sulkily. "I don't know where he is."

"He went down to take David some wedding cake and ice cream, don't you remember? That's where he is."

Joanna stopped, her hand on the knob. "Wasn't David at the wedding? No, he wasn't! I don't remember seeing him. Did Gunnar—"

"Yes, the old bastard," sald Mark simply. "He was mad as hell 'cause David went up in the woods with Stevie and me to get some greens for the house. Dave went off without asking . . . and him fifteen! The goddam old—"

"*Mark!*" said Donna.

"Well, he's worse than I could ever think up words for," said Mark candidly. "I bet he was good and mad when Stevie went down with the eats, too—it's a wonder he'd let Dave have 'em."

Donna sighed. "I know. But we can't interfere. And Karl was such a nice young man, too, when we were all young married people together. I don't know what's come over him. Go along, Mark, and see if you can't find Stevie."

"Am I my brother's keeper?" said Mark in a pained voice, but he unfolded his Bennett length and went out with Joanna and Alec.

They walked briskly back through the woods. The wind was rising, and though it came from the north, so that the path was sheltered, it hit them with a chill breath when they went down through the field. There was still music at Uncle Nate's, but Mark and his air of martyrdom accompanied Joanna and Alec to the harbor.

"I suppose I've got to find that kid," he muttered.

"Cheer up," said Alec. "We'll walk around the shore with you." Facing the sharp wind, they went down the road through the marsh. As they reached the shore, they heard the dories and punts rolling and bumping at the water's edge, and the rattle of beach stones as the water pulled back, gathering itself to leap forward again.

"Making a little surf, isn't it?" Joanna said. She felt cold, yet her hands were sweating. She was nervous with the long excitement of the day behind her, the worry about Mateel, and the sharp anger that had come over her like flame when she found Gunnar had kept David from the wedding.

And then there was the serenade; she'd have to make sandwiches as soon as they got back to the house. Mark would find Stevie and pretend to go home, but they'd come through the woods with their firecrackers, and the others would come up from the village. And then the women would sneak upstairs—you weren't supposed to notice them sneaking—and do crazy things with the bed.

Joanna sighed. Just that to go through, and then she and Alec would be really alone.

Out of the darkness, as they passed the bait house, there was the sound of feet on the stony path, and a voice hailing them. It was Nils.

"Mark, is that you?"

"Yep!" Mark sang out. "Hey, have you seen the kid brother?"

"Have you seen *mine?*" Nils reached them now, and recognized the others in the starlight. "Hi, Jo . . . Alec. Mark, where'd those kids go?"

"How should I know?" Mark was injured. "Aren't they at your house?"

"I was just up there. They've all gone to bed, but David's gone. He sleeps with me, so I ought to know." Worry made him curt. And suddenly Joanna knew where the young boys had gone. She heard herself saying, "What if they've run away? Are all the boats in?"

Mark was off with a whoop. "Hey, wait a minute, I'll get Nathan's flashlight—he's got a new one with a long beam." They heard his feet running away from them on the stones. The other three waited in the chill autumn darkness, listening to the rising wind.

"But those kids, in a boat—" Alec began.

Nils said, "It's crazy. Only I was always going to run away too, but I never did. Do you think David—Oh, Christ, they're probably rammin' around the Island somewhere."

Joanna had never heard his voice so jerky and uneven. Then Mark came back with the light, and they went out on the old wharf. Boat by boat the harbor fleet was picked out at their moorings by the long finger of light; Nils' boat, Sigurd's, Karl's, Owen's,

Stephen's—but Philip's was not there. The *Gull* was gone.

"They took Phil's boat because they knew he'd be easy on 'em," said Mark. "Young sons o' bitches. Why didn't they take me along?"

Alec took him by the shoulder. "You go home and round up your father and Philip. Then go up to your uncle's and get Owen and the other boys. And no side trips down to the Eastern End to tell you mother what's going on."

"What do you think I am, a damn fool?" said Mark indignantly, and left them. As the others went back to the road, they almost collided with Maurice.

"What goes on?" he inquired with interest. "Me, I got to 'ang around till the Coast Guard brings the doctor. I don't know 'ow Mateel is, or anyt'ing."

"She's doing all right," Joanna said. Nils went to find his father and Sigurd, and Alec sent Maurice back to the store, to have Pete Grant call the Coast Guard again and give a description of the *Gull* and present crew.

For a moment Alec and Joanna were alone in the lee of the boatshop. He put his arms around her and tried to stop her trembling. "We'll all have to go out, Joanna, and comb the bay for those kids. You'll remember your wedding night for a long time, honey."

"Alec—"

"It's not like you to take on like this, Jo. Remember what I said. We've got the whole world before us, and the rest of our lives." At the gentle reproach in his voice, she stepped back from him and put her hands on his chest.

"Don't talk as if I was a weak fool!" she said scornfully. "It's just that— Alec, Stevie told me a long time ago they were going to run away. Don't you see? I *knew!*"

"Well, somebody couldn't always be watching the kids," he said sensibly. "Even if you'd told 'em. So don't fret. Here come the others." He kissed her hard, a long hungry kiss as if it must do him a lifetime, and then they were going out to meet a swinging flashlight— Philip, the first of the searchers.

He said easily, "Looks like they've stolen a march on us, all right. Father went down to the Eastern End before Mark came, he's going to keep Charles company. No sense bothering him about it. I'll take his boat."

Stephen had gone to the Eastern End—he'd put out his hand to his eldest son at last. But where was the youngest son now—the baby, with his puppyish awkwardness and the long eyelashes he hated, and his love of basketball?

27

THE NORTHERN LIGHTS, STREAMING HIGH over Brigport, sent a weird light over the harbor as the boats left, one after another. There was no possibility of keeping the story quiet when most of the men had joined the search. Only the Eastern End remained oblivious. Maurice knew, and wanted to go too.

He stood beside Joanna on the wharf, watching the lights flash in the harbor, and said wistfully, "I could get my fadder to come up and wait for the doctor."

"I don't want anybody down there to know!" Joanna's voice was sharp. "My father and mother and Charles have enough to worry about. So you needn't go down there and tell anybody."

"All right, all right, Jo! Don't fly at me!"

She had to laugh at him, in spite of her anxiety. They went back to the store, which Pete had kept open because of the emergencies. He was doing a rising business in cigarettes, pop, and candy. There was a festive air about the place, a sharp excitement in the voices of the women who spoke to Joanna.

"My lands, I hope Jud don't catch his death of cold runnin' around the bay tonight!" Marion Gray said. "Those two boys need their bottoms warmed, that's certain."

Susie Yetton was loyal. "They ain't no worse than any other kids. What about the time your Peter set the Western End on fire?"

Thea and Maurice had wandered outside, looking casual. If Joanna hadn't been so upset, she would have been amused. Maurice had stopped worrying about Mateel; he had called the doctor, and that was the end of it, as if the mere act had accomplished some magic down at the Eastern End and removed the danger. That was the way with men.

The women's acid voices were maddening, and she went outside again in the cold windy darkness. She had not forgotten Mateel, nor the silence from upstairs, that had struck on her ears with the impact of a scream. She had not forgotten Charles' gray face.

Perhaps Mateel was dying now. Perhaps the two boys were already drowned. No, don't think of that, she told herself harshly. It's wrong to think that. They know how to run a boat. It's just the ledges, and the wind rising. It's getting colder, too . . . There it was again, the terror that wanted to spread like smoke through her brain.

Mark had gone off around the shore somewhere, furious because the older boys had refused to take him. Joanna walked down to the wharf and stood in the lee of a stack of Pete's lobster crates. It seemed to her that she was always waiting somewhere, alone.

She touched the wedding ring on her finger, and knew she was not really alone now. She was a married woman, and yesterday she'd been Steve Bennett's girl, nineteen years old. Now she was Mrs. Alec Douglass.

The water chuckled and banged under the wharf, and the lobster car thumped against the spilings. Over the long black ridge of Brigport the northern lights shot up long fingers of light, pale green and rose. Joanna watched them, wondering why David had chosen tonight to run away.

There were firm, heavy steps in the shed, and she knew, before he came toward her and flashed his light on her, that it was Gunnar Sorensen. His son Karl walked behind him—he hadn't gone out with the others.

"Ha, Yo, your man gone on the vedding night, huh?" said Gunnar.

"Hello, Mr. Sorensen. Hello, Karl."

"Oh, hello, Joanna," Karl said vaguely. He leaned against a hogshead and lit a cigarette. In the glow she saw his features, strong like

Nils', yet not strong; as if there had once lived in him a loyal, reso-
lute spirit that had marked his face, but had since died, leaving only
the imprint.

"You better do to dat Stevie what I do to David." Gunnar said,
chuckling. "I von't say Stevie made David a bad boy—David vass
plenty bad to begin with."

"I always liked David," said Joanna stiffly. In a minute now she
would walk away—she couldn't stand the sight of that old man with
his Santa Claus face, gloating so cheerfully over what he would do
to David.

"They've got courage, haven't they, Karl?" she said to him. "You
can't say they're cowards. I'm proud of them."

Karl said nothing. His profile was unreal against the starlit sky
behind his head. Gunnar cleared his throat, sniffed, chuckled. There
was a lantern coming down through the shed now, and above the
sound of wind and water, a high plaintive voice arose.

"Kristi, can't you valk faster?"

"*Anna!*" said Gunnar sharply. "Karl, take your modder home."

"He vill not take me home," said old Anna. Leaning on Kristi's
arm, she confronted her husband and her son. "Do you hear anyt'ing
of the children?"

"No, no," said Gunnar. "You go home, Anna. Get to bed. No place
for a voman. Kristi, you take her—"

Anna Sorensen was little and rosy. In the lantern light Joanna
saw the shawl wrapped around her head and shoulders, and the short
wrinkled hand she laid on her husband's arm. "Gunnar," she said
in her soft anxious voice, "you are cross with David, you are more
than cross. Please, remember your Bible, Gunnar, and forgive the
boy."

He shook off her hand. "Anna, go home as I tell you. If the
boy is bad, you have made him so, always spoiling him, so soft. Beg-
ging me to not punish him. I vass beaten, Anna. My modder begged
for me, too, but my fadder knew how to raise a boy." His voice was
thick with rage. "Anna, vill you do like I tell you?"

"Yust the same, Gunnar, you should have let him have the cake
Stevie brought him, and the ice cream. You t'rew it in the pigpen,
and you know it vass not *right*, Gunnar."

"Mother," Karl said evenly. "I'll walk home with you."

"Karl, if only I vass big enough to shake you like I did when you vass little!" She began to cry. "David iss your little boy!" She went away between her son and her granddaughter. After a moment Gunnar went up to the store, muttering to himself. And Joanna, alone on the wharf again, realized she was taut with rage. So that was where the ice cream and cake went—into the pigpen.

Tears swam in her eyes. If those two boys are lost, he'll have killed them, she thought. There alone on the wharf, she cried with a passion of anger, and of sudden loneliness for Alec.

The sound of a heavy engine vibrated through the night air. Joanna went to the end of the wharf, hastily drying her eyes, and saw the lighted Coast Guard boat coming past the western end of Brigport. Well, that takes care of Mateel, she thought. The boat was making good time; already it was coming past the harbor ledges, pitching in the tide run. Some of the watchers were coming down through the shed.

Joanna went around by the other side of the crates, and when the shed was quite empty, she walked up to the store. She was not in a mood for any more quips about being left alone on her wedding night. She remembered suddenly that there was the serenade to go through when the men came back, and already she was so tired she wondered how she could bear it.

Pete had gone down to the wharf, so the store was empty. She sat down on a nail keg beside the stove and warmed her hands. It seemed like a year ago, those few heavenly moments with Alec in their own house, before Mark came in. Mark, with his loud and cheerful voice—

"Hi, Jo!"

Her heart seemed to come into her throat. Stevie shut the door behind him and leaned against it. "I didn't mean to scare you," he said meekly.

"Stevie, where did you come from!" Yes, he was real, she put her hands on his shoulders and shook him. "How did you get here?"

"Coast Guard." He grinned nervously at her. "Something went wrong with the engine. Philip'll be mad, but honest, Jo—"

"Stevie, you picked out an awful night to run away in. I don't know whether to slap you or kiss you. Everybody's out looking for you."

Stevie looked suddenly very young and weary. "I know it. Gosh, don't *you* start in on me, Jo! Everybody else got a dig in when I came up the wharf."

"You'd better go home and go straight to bed. And don't get up when Mother and Father come in, because they don't even know you've been gone." They went outside, and heard the others coming up from the wharf. She gave him a little shove toward the path, then caught his sleeve as Gunnar and Karl came around the corner.

"Where's David?" she asked swiftly.

"He's coming with the crowd, I guess. Thea grabbed him and was hugging him. Gosh, she's sappy." He blinked as Gunnar's light picked him out.

"Ha! The vanderer returns. Velcome, my boy!" Joanna felt Stevie's arm tighten under her fingers. He jerked free and walked swiftly toward the path, and was lost in the darkness.

"And here iss my fine grandson!" crowed Gunnar, and the light fell full on David as he came out of the shed; a blinking, white-faced David shivering in his jacket, his yellow hair tumbled. He stood still and looked at the light, while Gunnar's voice came out of the darkness and curled around him like the tongue of his whip. Those who stopped behind David didn't move; Karl, behind his father, was a motionless shadow.

"So you come back to your grandfadder, did you? You couldn't stay away from him because you love him so much. And your grandfadder love you too, my boy." The words were honey-sweet, but when Gunnar was honey-sweet the Island walked warily. "Come, my boy," said Gunnar, and David, his eyes widening, took a jerky step forward.

Somebody moved. Somebody said quietly, "Come here, David." It was Karl. In quick bewilderment, the boy turned his head as a dog does. Karl stepped into the light.

"Come on, David," he said. He was smiling, and it was odd, what a smile could do to a voice. Karl's voice was suddenly warm and pleasant; it was a voice to trust. He sounded a good deal like his son Nils.

Gunnar said coldly, "Leave the boy to me, Karl."

"You'd better go home, Father. It's cold down here." Karl's tone was level. "David's going to help me in the shop for a while. Then we'll come home."

Joanna wondered if anybody else felt like cheering, if anybody else felt this devilish delight in Gunnar's silent rage. It had to be silent, for almost the whole Island was looking at him, the whole Island could see how his flashlight trembled in his hand. He made a harsh, grating sound in his throat and walked away. For a moment there was complete stillness, then the tension broke, and everybody was talking at once about the Coast Guard, the doctor, Mateel. Nobody mentioned Gunnar.

The women who had been waiting for their husbands went home to wait; now that the boys were safe, there was nothing to worry about. Pete Grant locked up the store. Down at the end of the wharf the Coast Guard boat waited for the doctor to come back. The men had tied up Philip's boat, and in the cutter's snug cabin they were drinking coffee and playing cards.

The Island seemed asleep. Joanna walked around the shore; she too could go home, but she dreaded entering the empty house. The thought was like a chill going over her, as if it would be bad luck to go up there alone. No, she would wait until Alec came back. It wouldn't be so long, now. She turned up her coat collar as the wind struck at her through a space between the fish houses.

The boat shop on the old wharf was open, the door was always unlocked. Jud Gray was building a new boat there, and when Joanna slipped inside, the air was warm and aromatic with new wood. Shavings were soft around her feet. Above her, the hull loomed whitely in the gloom.

She heard an engine in the harbor; the *Donna* was coming back, with Philip. It meant the others must be on the way. They would see the Coast Guard boat at the wharf, and go alongside, and then find the *Gull.*

She stayed in the boat shop, sitting on a box in the wood-scented darkness, listening to the water gurgle under the wharf and to voices on the beach outside, the sound of a dory scraping over the stones. She wondered how Mateel was coming along. She put the thought of Mateel's death from her mind. She couldn't die as quickly as that.

Perhaps she dozed a little, there in the warm dark. But it seemed to her all at once that she'd been there a long time, and there was another engine coming into the harbor. She sprang up wildly. What if Alec had come back, and didn't know where she was? She ran outside, and the cold wind was bitter around her body, the stars seemed very far away, with the distant frosty twinkle that meant a cold snap; her teeth were chattering as she went out on the end of the old wharf and strained to see through the darkness. Alec's mooring was so far from the wharf, and the northern lights had died out to a pale, curved glow. She heard the familiar clink of the mooring chain, the clatter of oar blades striking the thwarts—and she knew a joyous surge of relief.

Alec was a quiet, slow-moving figure in the starlight as he pulled the punt up and made it fast. He was the last man to come in. There were no lights around the harbor now; it was a desolate prospect of black trees against the stars, of blackness everywhere, that greeted him as he came slowly up the beach. Joanna remembered the return from Cash's, and how she had wanted to cradle his tired head in her arms.

Tonight she could do that; tonight she would hold his head against her breast. For he was hers, and the world belonged to them. The Island itself was theirs tonight—an island floating in a dark sea spangled with stars, an island where there was no one but themselves.

"Alec," she said quietly, and walked toward him. He put his arms around her and held her close to him in a long and silent embrace; she felt his tired breathing, and the deep steady rhythm of his heart.

"So the boys are all right," he said at last. "I met the Coast Guard going back, just off Brigport. I hailed them—the doctor said Mateel's got a fine boy."

"I'm glad," said Joanna peacefully.

"Me too . . . Well, let's go home."

They walked slowly through the sleeping village, his arm around her shoulders. They hardly spoke until they had come to their own steps. Joanna stumbled a little, and he caught her to him. "Tired?"

"A little. I know you are."

They opened the door and went in; warmth and lamplight spread about them. Joanna stood without taking off her coat, and watched Alec kick off his boots. He looked so utterly tired and worn out, and she felt like that too. A little depressed. What a way to feel on your wedding night.

Alec looked at her suddenly, a merry grin slipped across his face. "No serenade!"

It broke the spell. Joanna was laughing all at once. She ran across the room and put her arms around his neck, her face turned up to him with tears of laughter and love glittering on her lashes. She loved him so, and there was no gesture, no word big enough to show the bigness of her love for him. It filled her heart and her head and her throat.

Then she saw the light come into his wind-reddened eyes, and knew that he felt the same.

"Mrs. Douglass," he said in a faintly unsteady voice. "Did I ever tell you I love you?"

28

THE LAST DAHLIAS FLAMED on their tall stalks as Joanna walked down from her house to the gate, where the wild pear tree was fragile and bare except for a few tattered leaves and a brave-hearted sparrow. But anyone could be brave-hearted on a day like this, brilliant and blowing, with the dry tawny grass rippling in the wind like a golden sea, the clouds whiter than a gull's breast as they drove across the sky.

It was noontime, and the month was almost November. Joanna and Alec had been married a year. A year, and still his name was a little song that ran on and on inside of her, and still he came home to her as a lover would come. A year, and still Joanna walked down to meet him when she saw his boat go past the cove, and he looked for her on the beach when he rowed in from the mooring.

Walking down to the harbor now, she thought without smugness: We've been blessed from the start. Some people are cursed, and nothing ever goes right for them, but it'll always be right for us.

Everything in the past year had been as she had known it would be; indeed there had never been a doubt in her mind, never an instant of fear. It had been meant that Alec should come to her across the bay, it had been meant that she should never want to love anyone till he came. It had been planned from the beginning, so there was no reason for doubt and fear.

Now, at the beginning of their second year, they were even more deeply in love than they had been when they married.

Joanna Douglass, walking down the lane by the clubhouse, thought only distantly of a young girl's terrified flight along this lane, of the thick shadows under the trees, of the cold sickness that had lived with the girl for so long afterwards. It was almost as if she hadn't known that girl. Even when she turned at the end of Gunnar Sorensen's spruce windbreak and met Simon Bird coming from the well, she could smile as she spoke to him.

"Hello, Simon!"

"Hi, Jo." His lips flickered in a smile that didn't touch his eyes, which glanced almost imperceptibly at her mouth as he passed with his brimming pails. But it meant nothing to her now, when she could see Alec's boat at the car. She walked faster.

As she passed the Binnacle, she met Ned Foster, who spoke to her in his gray voice. He always spoke to Joanna, but Leah never spoke. She never spoke to Owen, either, and it was Maurice who now carried a bucket of water for her sometimes when Neddie was away.

On the beach Nathan Parr and Johnny Fernandez and Theresa sat on Johnny's doorstep in the sun, the two men smoking while Theresa took an absent-minded bath.

"Here comes that girl lookin' for her man again," said Nathan. "Too bad Steve Bennett never had but the one girl."

"Why?" asked Johnny obligingly.

"Cause there's plenty other young ganders'd like to marry into that family. They got the golden touch, that's it. The golden touch."

"Well, her Alec's caught it, from the looks of things."

Joanna laughed and shrugged, and went down the beach, but her pride was a warm and satisfactory thing. Yes, Alec had done well; her family said as much and the Island admitted it too. Alec belonged, at last. She remembered that first night, when he had told her over the dishes that he wanted to belong. Well, he had succeeded now. Not just because he married me, she told herself, but at the same time that counted. He had wanted to prove his worth to the Bennetts, because they were her family.

I would have married him anyway, she thought now as she waited for him to come from the mooring. With or without a cent.

But she was too honest not to admit she respected his capacity for work. She had been brought up in a family of men who neither shirked nor stinted. Consequently it was no poor living that the sea had yielded up to them; the sea, and the Island, which would never fail them. It won't fail us, either, she thought confidently, and here was Alec's punt coming past the old wharf.

They walked home sedately through the village, not arm-in-arm as they walked at night. "Hello, sweetness," Alec murmured.

"Darling," she whispered. Then aloud, "What kind of haul did you get today?"

"Fair. The fall spurt can't last forever. And they've gone down two cents."

"They'll go up again."

"They always do." They went up the steps, and in the kitchen they went into each other's arms, their bodies seeming to merge into one, their lips like one mouth. Their embrace was long and silent, and it ended in Joanna's little broken laugh as they separated.

"Back to work," said Alec. "Where's my dinner, woman?" He laid a handful of bills and change on the table. "I'll bet I was low man today. Only forty-seven pounds." He took a five-dollar bill from the handful and laid it beside Joanna's plate, but she pushed it back.

"Let it go this time, Alec. You'd better put it all in the money box."

"But what about that order you want to send? That dress you've had your eye on—"

"It can wait. I'm not buying dresses while the lobsters aren't crawling, Alec."

He shrugged, grinned at her, and put the money back in his pocket. "You're the boss, honey."

When dinner was over and the kitchen set in order, she went into the sitting room where Alec lay on the couch reading. He shut his book when he saw her, and moved over; she lay down beside him, her head on his arm. For a few moments they lay without speaking, caught up in a warm, half-drowsy contentment.

"Alec, I'm not going to get any new dresses for a while," she said at last. "I've got more than enough now. We spent a lot on clothes this year. Now let's spend on something else."

"On what?" he said lazily. "New radio? There's a peach of a set in the new catalog."

"Not a radio. What's the matter with the one we've got?" She turned over and burrowed against him, and his arm tightened around her. "Not a radio. Not a new rug, or a set of dishes. Nothing like that."

"Your hair smells nice. You want a dog? One of those collie pups over at Brigport?"

She rose up on one elbow and looked down into his thin dreamy face, his eyes narrowed and half-asleep, but bright between the lids. She was conscious that her heart was beating very fast because of what she was going to say.

"No, a baby, Alec."

He wasn't half-asleep now. "A *baby?*"

"You know what a baby is, don't you?" she laughed down at him nervously. "Little gadget with arms and legs. They holler. Alec, I'd like one before we're two years married."

He pulled her down and hugged her tight against him. He kissed her soundly and then, looking down into her entranced, flushed face, he said seriously, "Well, listen, Jo, I want a baby too. But look— we're just starting out. You're not even twenty-one yet, and we haven't got any bank account. And I made up my mind a long time ago, when I was a kid and there wasn't enough clothes to go round, and sometimes not enough to eat, that when I had a family, there'd be something to raise it on, first."

"But Alec, we're not poor!" she protested. "We could sort of start the baby, and save while we're waiting for it."

"That's no way to do. Lobsters went down two cents today. What if they keep going on? What if there's a spell of bad storms this winter and we keep losing gear? Honey, you know what condition my boat's in. Any day I expect to start a couple planks in her. We've got to have a good boat to make a living for children."

She had never known him to be so pessimistic. *The gods will provide,* he was always saying gaily. Now she said, "If everybody went on like that, nobody on the Island would have any children. Of course lobstering's a gamble, but I thought you liked taking chances. What about the time you went out on Cash's?"

"That was different from having a baby. Your life wasn't mixed up in it. Joanna, do you think I want you going through what Mateel went through?"

"I won't, unless I fall downstairs."

"I don't mean that. I mean that my wife is going to have our baby in the hospital, and she's going ashore in plenty of time, and she's going to have somebody to help out with the work afterwards. Joanna, can't you see what I mean?" He tightened his arms around her. "If you'd seen my mother dragging around doing washings, with a baby only ten days old . . . and they thought they'd have plenty to feed and dress those babies right. But when the time came — well, it was a different story."

"Yes, but we're not going to be poor. Nobody's ever really poor out here on the Island. Mother raised all six of us with plenty to eat and wear."

"You ask your father — I'll bet he had money in the bank long before Charles was born."

She looked at him silently, too disappointed to speak, and he kissed her mouth. "Jo, you think I'm just talking, don't you? Beating around the bush. I do want a family, only let's wait a while, honey."

When he was like this, his voice, his eyes, his touch all loving her, she couldn't be stiff and resentful against him. Besides, she understood his viewpoint. He was just as positive as she was, only he was positive of the need for *waiting*. After all, she reminded herself, his childhood hadn't been like hers, happy, sheltered, and abundant. She could understand and be patient with him. She put her hands behind his head.

"I guess we've got plenty of time to have babies, darling. But we can start the bank account right away, can't we?"

"Sure. Next time we go ashore we'll go to the bank." He gave her a breathtaking hug and stood up. "My God, I hate to go back to the shore and leave you. You don't know how you look, lying there."

He stood looking down at the warm clear color of her skin and the blackness of her hair sprayed over the pale cloth of the cushion under her head, the dark curl of her lashes, the way her mouth curved as she smiled up at him.

There was a crash and a clatter in the kitchen, and Owen's voice burst through the silence. "All hands on deck! Hey, Alec! You to bed?"

He laughed at his unsubtle humor, and waited. "Leave it to a Bennett," said Alec briefly, and went out to the kitchen. In a few minutes the two men had gone down to the shore, but Joanna still lay dreamily on the couch.

She was disappointed about the baby, but since it was his baby too, she must consider his views. Only she wished now that she had taken the five dollars at dinner time; it would have made a good beginning for that bank account.

Before she went over to see her mother, she went upstairs to take a final look at the spare room. Margaret, the elder sister with whom Alec had lived in Jonesport, had written that she was coming for a visit as soon as she could manage it. It all depended on whether another sister would come and keep house for Jim and the children. It was rather an exciting prospect for Joanna, to entertain one of her husband's family, though she wouldn't have admitted it to anyone. And it was a good excuse for a frenzy of painting and papering, which Joanna loved. The spare room, as she now beheld it, was pure delight.

She smiled as she caught herself rearranging the starched curtains and straightening an imaginary wrinkle in the bright bedspread. She had hated housework ever since she could remember, but it was always there to be done, and it was silly to slop through it. If you had to spend precious time sweeping floors and doing up curtains, you might as well get some satisfaction out of it. And in your own home, that belonged to you and your husband, *and* the bank-account babies, it was surprising how satisfactory housework could be, if you didn't let it tyrannize you.

So even if the unknown Margaret was one of those fanatical housekeepers who bowed down in worship of spotless paint, and "floors you could eat off"—the Island standard of cleanliness—she couldn't possibly find any fault with her brother's home. Most of the time there was a pleasant clutter of books and magazines left wherever Alec and Joanna happened to drop them, but not today, or tomorrow, or any day when Margaret was likely to arrive on the mailboat. Joanna was taking no chances on being caught at a disadvantage.

Alec told her at supper that he was going out in the evening.

"Poker game down at the Eastern End. Why don't you come along and keep Mateel company?"

"I'm too tired, Alec. Me for bed and a book. You go ahead and have your poker game. It's only once a week, and it's all the social life we've got around here, except for the clubhouse in the summer." She added seriously, "Only don't let the stakes get too high, Alec."

"We never do."

"I know, but with all the money everybody's making, I should think it would be a temptation to be reckless. Really gamble, I mean."

"Don't worry, honey." He shaved and put on a clean shirt while she washed the dishes. When he was ready to go, he came to where she stood on tiptoe before the cupboards, and caught her around the waist. "What'll I give you if I win a lot tonight?"

She leaned back against his shoulder. "Would it be sinful and scandalous to start a bank account for a baby with the money you won in a poker game?"

She watched him from the corner of her eye, her mouth ready for laughter, but he said seriously, "You really want a baby, don't you?"

"Don't *you?*" She turned in his arms to face him. "Alec, I don't want a baby just because it's a baby — I'm not one of those born mothers who marry just to have children. I want your baby."

He caught her to him, kissing her forehead and the widow's peak so sharply black against her smooth warm skin. "Don't be too tired when I come home," he said, his lips on her cheek, and was quickly gone.

29

MORNING DRIFTED OVER THE ISLAND as lightly as fog; or else it came like a trumpet call. On these days, before the winter set in, that burned in one triumphant burst of flame, it was the trumpet that awoke the Islanders; a trumpet whose notes were rose and gold and scarlet, streaming across sea and sky, exciting the gulls on their barren sanctuaries until they launched on strong white wings into the brilliant air, and began the day.

It was the gulls, screaming and fighting overhead, that awakened Joanna to sunlight on her eyes and Alec in deep sleep beside her. There was not much of him to be seen but a sandy chest, bronze as the sun slanted across it; but one arm was under Joanna's neck and the other flung over her body. She lay contentedly for a few minutes, listening to his breathing, the wind roaring through the tall trees behind the house, the gulls. The mailboat would have it choppy today.

"Alec," she said.

Almost instantly he awoke. "What's the matter?"

"It's late, and it's boat day today." She rose up on one elbow and looked down at him. "Aren't you a mess," she said fondly. She kissed him, and then snuggled against his chest. "We've got to get up. Alec, how much did you win last night?"

"Momma, Poppa didn't win. He lost."

She felt a twinge of disappointment. It was silly, because at the most he would have won or lost only a few dollars. But it would have been an omen—a sign from Alec's gods—if he had won. She slid out from under the quilts into the cool bright air, and began to dress.

Alec lay cornerwise across the bed so he could look up into her face with twinkling hazel eyes. "Momma love Poppa?" he asked pathetically.

"Sometimes. Right now Momma needs some money to pay a bill Poppa forgot."

"Which one was that?"

"Montgomery Ward—the last order you sent, the heavy shirts and socks." She pinched his chin. "You're a peach of a manager. If you're taking care of the bills, you're not supposed to forget them, so they'll write stern letters."

"I suppose a Bennett never forgets, like an elephant." Alec's eyes laughed up at her. "Joanna my love, haven't you any money left?"

"You haven't given me my housekeeping money yet this week, and I couldn't save anything over from last week, with fixing up the spare room and all. And I don't want to touch the money box."

"Well, darlin' mine," he said lightly, "Montgomery's will have to wait a day or two. I'm a little broke."

"Did you play with *all* the money you got from your lobsters yesterday?" He'd never done that before. She didn't know why she felt so empty, all at once.

"It was only about fifteen dollars, Jo. If I'd won—"

"But you didn't win, and something's got to be paid on that bill, and besides—" She couldn't keep the bitterness out of her voice. "I was going to put a dollar or two aside for the baby."

"There's plenty of time for that, honey." He pulled her down close to him. "I'm going out to haul this morning, and you can send off the money next boat day. How's that?"

"Next boat day is three days away," she reminded him. "There'll probably be another stern letter by then, only worse."

"We'll smooth 'em down. Mad with me, Jo?"

She couldn't be mad with him, ever. But she couldn't help this baffled feeling. She pulled away from him, gently. "I'm going down and start breakfast. You'd better hurry if you're going out to haul."

He came down quickly, as amiable and carefree as if he had a pocket full of money. "I ought to get plenty today. Only hauled about forty pots yesterday. I'll go all around the Island today. And I'll bring something for you, something for the box, and something to win back my fifteen dollars with."

"Do you think you ever really win anything back?"

"Sure! Win it back twice, three times!" On his way to the table he stopped to kiss the back of her neck. A great wave of tenderness swept over her, strong and warm, driving away some of the baffled feeling. Alec was Alec, and he was all hers.

When he had gone out, whistling, she did her small quota of housework, and sat down at the desk in the sitting room to make out her grocery list. When Alec gave her the housekeeping money, after he came in from hauling, she would go down to the store and stock up for the next week. Then she wouldn't have to buy anything else, unless Pete Grant got some fresh meat in, or something else that was out of the ordinary. She had learned from her mother to plan out a week in advance, and with her cellar shelves full of the things she had canned, she managed very successfully. She was honestly proud of her ability to serve good meals on little more than a shoestring; she herself had limited the amount of money Alec gave her.

"It'll be more for the money box," she told him. "More for the new boat."

As she sat at the desk now, her mind seemed oddly vacant of ideas about food. She looked out at the bright windy day outside, the dark blue water whipped into whitecaps beyond the little cove, and remembered the odd, empty feeling she'd had when she and Alec were talking before they got up. It had been a silly way to feel, she thought now, smiling a little at her foolishness. It didn't hurt if Alec was reckless once in a poker game, or if he didn't have anything in his pockets when he went out to haul. Probably it would never happen just that way again.

Only she wasn't going to wait till next boat day to pay that bill. The letter had startled her more than she would admit, even to herself, especially when she'd believed Alec had paid up. She had left the bills to him from the start of their marriage, and it had only been by accident that she'd opened the letter.

There'd be no harm in taking the money from the box. She would put it back this afternoon, after Alec came in. She didn't want to touch the money box, for she never had; it was Alec's personal concern, set aside for their savings toward the new boat he needed so badly. But once wouldn't count, and the bill would be paid today, and off her mind. She took the small metal box from its drawer. It was never locked.

There were papers lying just under the cover, some with envelopes, some without. Receipted bills, she thought carelessly, laying them aside. But as she put them down, she glanced at the top one, picked it up and read it with rueful amusement. Another one Alec had forgotten, she thought he'd sent off the money for the kitchen cabinet months ago.

"Please Remit," said the black letters across the paper. She riffled through the others, feeling strangely cold. The new engine for his boat, the studio couch, the pictures, radio repairs, the flannels he'd bought in the summer, three barrels of bream from a man in Port George . . . there were bills a year old. Bills dated from just before and after their marriage. They sifted through her fingers and she stared over the desk top at the brilliant day outside, seeing nothing but the words and figures that leaped at her from the papers.

"Please Remit" — "No further extension of credit" — "will be forced to put this bill in the hands of a collector" —

Alec had blithely put the bills out of sight and forgotten them. True, he had kept his Island bills paid up, but any man, getting a foothold, would do the same. She shook her head impatiently. That wasn't Alec, deliberately building up good will and ignoring the obligations that weren't near at hand. Alec wasn't sly. But he'd been working hard, and they were so desperately in love. How easy to let things slide for a little while, put the bills aside.

She remembered her father saying, "Bills are the easiest things of all to forget." For that reason he always paid them at once . . . the empty feeling had come back to Joanna, a coldness came with it.

She added up the figures swiftly. When she had finished, the total was seven hundred and sixty-nine dollars. Almost eight hundred. Almost a thousand. She felt slightly sick. She turned back to the money box and began to count the boat savings. Fifty-five dollars.

There should be a lot more than that, an astonished voice said in her brain.

She looked back again at the past year. There was a depression on the mainland, but not in the lobster business. The hauls had been phenomenal sometimes, and the prices were good. Once a buyer had offered eighty cents a pound! Those men who had carred their lobsters, and had a thousand or more pounds to sell at a crack, had come home with rolls of bills.

She remembered with fantastic clarity Alec's brilliant eyes, the excitement in every motion of his lean body, his gay voice. "Fifty dollars for the money box, and what do you want for a present, Jo?"

Of course, eighty was an extraordinary price, but even in the slack times, when the tides were wrong and lobsters weren't crawling, thirty cents was the average, and the hauls were always good enough to keep a man's family clothed and fed. All this Joanna knew, as well as she knew that there was no reason for eight hundred dollars' worth of bills and only fifty-five dollars in the money box. You couldn't blame it on losing traps; there'd been only one storm bad enough, in the past year, to smash any of Alec's gear, and then only a few ten- and fifteen-fathom traps.

She felt alone and lost. Alec had become a stranger. She tried to picture him, out in the rough sun-flecked waters off the Souwest Point, with the boat rolling in the white wash from the ledges as he hauled a heavy trap dripping to the gunwale, brushed off the sea-urchins, measured his lobsters with the gauge, and tossed them into a keg. As if she were perched on the engine box, she saw the way he tilted his head back and watched the seagulls soar up from the rocks in a shrieking rush. His eyes would be narrowed against the sun glare, his mouth shaped for his constant whistling. He would whistle all the time he was out there, even when he couldn't hear himself through the heavy drone of the hauling gear and the noisy chuckle and run of water against the sides. After he'd worked around the Island and about the ledges where the seals tumbled in the surf, he'd come whistling home, shaking out the bait bags and looking back at the gulls who came down like a winged snowfall in the wake.

He'd whistle when he came up the path; he wouldn't stop until he came through the door and took her into his arms. Joanna, sitting at the desk, knew how he would come in. She knew almost everything about him. But she hadn't known about the bills and the money box. And because of that, it wouldn't be her Alec who came whistling home tonight.

She would have to talk to him, she thought, walking nervously through the rooms. Tonight she must ask him about the bills and the money he'd made in the past year, and it was going to be the hardest thing she'd ever done.

She would have given anything to forget it, but she knew that for the sake of their future together, she couldn't forget it. It was something to be brought out into the open. If she concealed it, it would poison their life together, and wipe out the unclouded happiness of the year gone by.

It was suddenly torture to stay indoors. She put on her jacket and went out into the crisp afternoon, to walk in the autumn sunshine and wind along the west side of the Island. Here the spray flew up from the red rocks, flashing in the sunlight, and the air was cold and rough and strong against her face, and the gulls rode high overhead.

When she came back to the house the lamps were lit, their yellow light streaming out into the salt-scented dusk. Alec was boiling lobsters in the kitchen. He waved one at her.

"How's for some chowder tonight? You don't have to do anything—just sit down and let the old expert take over."

He dropped a swift kiss on her nose and went back to the stove. Joanna knew by his manner that he had made a good haul. She didn't object to his getting supper; working around the kitchen, whistling, talking, he didn't notice her restraint. She knew that sense of strangeness would lie upon her until she had talked to him, but she couldn't do it now, while he was happy and proud to be waiting on her. After supper, she promised herself.

After supper Owen drifted in with Maurice Trudeau. Later Mark and David Sorensen, David with his accordion under his arm. He worked for his father now, and had bought the accordion with his earnings. Last of all Sigurd arrived, with his guitar. Alec brought out his fiddle and they made music around the kitchen stove.

Ordinarily Joanna loved evenings like this, there was something so richly satisfactory about having the crowd come to Alec's home and hers. But tonight she was on edge. Always, in the back of her mind, she was saying what she must say to Alec when they were alone. Always she was seeing the laughter go out of his eyes and from his mouth when he heard her words. The music, the singing, the stamping feet, and the laughter were simply noises clashing against her eardrums.

It was only when she looked at Alec, his cheek against his fiddle, his fingers flying over the strings, that she felt almost eager to tell him. She loved him so much that this thing must be straightened out between them; it couldn't stay to cloud the shining, flawless surface of their love.

She made coffee for the crowd, and brought out gingerbread. They departed at last. When Alec went out to bring in some wood, she heard them singing, the sound sweet and clear in the cold stillness. She stood on the back steps, looking up at the thick, twinkling brightness overhead, the Milky Way spattered across the sky, and waited for Alec to come in from the woodpile. In a little while now, they'd talk, and she'd find out there was no reason for distrust and suspicion. Already her heart lightened miraculously.

Perhaps he'd lent the boat savings to someone who'd been in a tight spot — Forest Merrill, perhaps, or even one of her brothers — and he'd been afraid to tell her. That was so typical of Alec, helping somebody out, and how could she be angry with him for that?

When she stood back to let him pass with his armful of wood, and then followed him into the kitchen, the restraint was lifting, as fog burns off before the sun. She was glad when he put his arms around her.

"Time for bed, honey."

"I've got to wash up those cups, first—"

"Oh, leave 'em!" Alec's lips brushed hers. "Come on, you're tired tonight."

She laughed up at him. "I hate to have dirty dishes staring me in the face when I get up in the morning. You go along up, and I'll be there in about five minutes."

"Is that a promise?"

"Promise." They looked gravely at each other, and then Alec laughed suddenly, and kissed her hard. He went upstairs, whistling.

Joanna washed and put away the dishes, rinsed out the percolator, and set the table for breakfast. She hummed a little under her breath. Queer, how much better she felt, all at once. Of course it was some foolish, generous thing Alec had done. Letting the bills go was foolish, too. But not criminal. They'd talk it over, and straighten it out.

The lamp still burned on the bedside stand when she came into their room, and Alec was asleep. Deeply and soundly asleep, his face buried in the pillow, just his sandy cowlick showing. Joanna leaned on the foot of the bed, her new-found peace of mind ebbing away. She couldn't wake him now and talk to him, and she was still nagged by that maddening uncertainty.

She undressed and slipped into bed beside Alec. Something— she didn't know what—kept her from snuggling up to his back. For a long time she lay awake in the darkness, not moving, not touching Alec. Wondering.

30

IN THE MORNING ALEC HAD GONE before she woke up. He didn't come in from hauling till midafternoon—he shifted one of his strings out toward the Rock—and when he did come in, Donna had come down to spend the afternoon with Joanna. Alec ate his dinner and went back to the shore again. He brought Mark home to have supper with them, because Joanna had baked beans, which Mark would eat, cheerfully, seven days a week. Mark stayed late, and again Alec fell asleep as soon as his head touched the pillow.

Tomorrow, Joanna thought. Tomorrow we can talk. But the next day brought a northeast wind and a battering rainstorm, and Owen and Hugo spent almost the whole day in Joanna's kitchen, yarning and spinning cuffers as they'd always done. At length they went, but Alec went with them, down to the shore to see to his boat, thence into Karl Sorensen's fish house to yarn some more around the pot-bellied stove. In the evening he wanted to go up to the big house, and Joanna couldn't refuse.

I've got to talk to him, she thought desperately, when the right time comes, the exact moment. But what if it never comes?

Until now she had always awakened in the morning with an eagerness to live this new day. Now she awoke with a shadow across her mind, and she knew it would be there until she sent it away. On the third day—boat day again—when she was brushing her hair in front of the mirror, she could see faint shadows under her eyes. She hadn't slept well the night before, she woke up every hour, it seemed, and her sleep had been full of vague, troubling dreams. Not enough to frighten her, but enough to leave her heavy-footed and tired in the morning.

It was calm and clear again, as warm and mild as a spring day; the sea outside the little cove was the soft, pale blue of forget-me-nots, and it made hardly a sound as it washed against the rocks. Alec left early to see how his traps had fared in the storm, but not before Joanna had made him promise to take a walk with her toward Souwest Point in the afternoon. It would be easier to talk out of doors, she thought.

Before he went out he had given her money for the bill, and she took it without a word of reference to all those others. She went down to the post office early and sent a money order; then, relieved by the certainty that they could talk over their finances, she went home and decided to do a washing. Activity was better than just waiting.

She was sorting the wash in piles around the kitchen floor, and the boiler was steaming on the stove—Alec had promised her a washing machine for next year—when she heard Mark's voice outside the house. Joanna remained where she was, sitting cross-legged on the floor as she separated Alec's dark socks from his white woolen ones. She wished Mark didn't have a genius for dropping in when she didn't want to talk to anyone. It had been enough strain to make Alec think there were nothing on her mind. Yesterday, with the boys under foot, had been a dreadful day. Now Mark was coming in, to sit around and talk.

She sighed, and bit her lower lip, just as Mark came through the front door and sang out, "Company, Jo!"

A terrible knowledge assailed her, even as she kicked the soiled socks under the table and got quickly to her feet. Alec's sister had come. Margaret was here.

* * *

Mrs. Jim Coombs, born Margaret Douglass, was a tall spare woman with eyes and hair the color of Alec's, but without his rather shy and good-natured charm. She looked as if life had not been easy for her, as if she had learned early to tighten her lips at it and not allow it an inch of leeway.

Though the sea was quite calm, she had been seasick. And here was her sister-in-law looking at her with startled, almost unfriendly eyes, apparently not expecting her. It was a white and taut-lipped woman who stood in Joanna Douglass' sitting room, where Mark had put down her suitcase and left her.

It was true, Joanna was startled. But only briefly. Then she went forward smiling, her hand out. "You're Margaret, and I'm Joanna. I'm awfully glad you've come. Come out in the kitchen where it's warm, and I'll make you some good hot tea!"

She had the older woman's coat and hat almost before Alec's sister realized it, and the rich, warm charm of the Bennetts, that seemed to glow out with extra power under just such circumstances, flowed around Margaret in Joanna's voice, her manner, her gestures. When a guest arrived looking as wretched and unfriendly as Margaret did, a true Bennett always rose magnificently to the occasion. It was necessary to make the guest forget that she'd been cold and seasick, that neither her brother nor her brother's wife had met her at the wharf, that she wished she'd never left home.

At length, when she was established in the rocker beside the stove, with the added warmth of sunshine streaming across her, a cup of tea in her hands, her pale mouth unclamped and she said unexpectedly, "This is a very pleasant room."

"Yes, we think so." Joanna gathered up the soiled clothes again, smiled at Margaret. "I was going to wash, but now I shan't. I'd rather wait a few days, anyway. Alec ought to be in from hauling pretty soon."

"He works hard, does he?" Margaret's voice was pale and dry, like herself. Joanna thought her eyes were like chips of green-brown stone. No wonder Alec hadn't been happy with her.

"Oh, he works like a Trojan," she said. "He's never been lazy."

"You don't say." Margaret stared into her teacup, and the conversation waned. What'll we have for dinner, Joanna thought frantically. She'd planned on leftover fish hash, but not for company. She could put on potatoes, anyway. She took them out of the bin and began to scrub them.

"Do you have to lug your water?" Margaret asked.

"From the well in the village. But Alec's promised to build a cistern."

"Promises," said Mrs. Coombs grimly, "butter no parsnips."

Joanna conquered an impulse to say she didn't like parsnips, especially with butter, and wished Alec would come soon. "How are Mr. Coombs and the children?" she asked pleasantly.

"They're all good." For a moment the dry, harsh voice hesitated. "Yes—good." She went on rocking. Joanna put the potatoes on the stove and began to set the table. Before her stretched a long weekend of Margaret. It was a weary thought. And she wouldn't be able to talk to Alec this afternoon.

Alec himself was coming up through the gate. "Here comes Alec now!" she exclaimed thankfully.

"Is that so?" said Margaret dryly. No joyous start, no flash of light across her face, no eagerness in her voice. For a moment Joanna seemed to feel a cold wind blowing. Then Alec was standing in the doorway, saying happily:

"Hello, Meggie! So you got here at last—after a year!" He bent over the rocker and kissed her, but even then there was no softening of her austere face.

"Alec, maybe you'll carry my bag up to my room for me," she said abruptly.

"You bet. Wait'll I kiss my wife." He cupped Joanna's face in his hands, winked at her, and kissed her mouth. Then, talking eagerly, he escorted his sister upstairs. After a few moments he came running down again.

This time his kiss was more thorough. "Love me, honey?" he asked. "Did you miss me today?"

"Yes, dear, only what are we going to have for dinner? Look, run down and see if Pete got any meat today."

Alec twinkled. "And get it for my sweet smile? I didn't haul this morning, Jo. And I cleaned out my pockets before I left the house."

"All that went to Montgomery's." She stepped back from him. "If you didn't haul, where have you been all morning?"

"Don't look at me as if you suspected me of murder," said Alec merrily. "I got down to the shore and Marcus Yetton was having a hell of a time with his engine — hadn't been to haul for a couple days — "

"So you spent the morning working on it."

"Yep. She purrs like a pussycat now. He's going to haul this afternoon."

"Well, if you fixed it up for him, then you got paid," said Joanna confidently. "You've got enough for some meat for you sister's dinner, anyway." She turned back to the table, but Alec didn't move.

"How could the man pay me when he didn't have any money?" he asked simply. "Besides, I told him to forget it. He's got a big family there."

"And you've got a wife and a sister who are hungry." Joanna tilted her chin. "It's dinner time. There's nothing but potatoes and last summer's greens. What are you going to do about it, Alec?"

She realized all at once that she was furious. All the accumulated strain and worry of the last few days were rising to a climax now, as she stood looking at him. She felt her lips stiffen, and heat climb into her cheeks. Alec seemed totally unaware. He lit a cigarette, flipped the match neatly toward the stove, and said, "We'll have harbor pollack for dinner. They're good, and Meggie likes fish."

"Well, don't tell her it's the same kind you use for bait sometimes." Joanna clattered the frying pan.

"Nothing I like better than a good mess of pollack," Alec said, and departed, whistling "The Road to the Isles."

The little harbor pollack were crisp and brown, the potatoes mealy, the greens tasted fresh and good. The apple pie and coffee were just about perfection, Alec assured Joanna. Margaret ate with a good appetite, and Alec was always hungry. Joanna was glad the food tasted good to them; it was so much sawdust to her. But she ate and talked and laughed, and wondered if Alec's sister disliked her as much as she seemed to.

Margaret offered to help with the dishes, but Alec wouldn't let her. "You go up and have a nice nap, Meggie," he urged her. "I'll help Jo."

"I don't need any help," said Joanna, but Alec ignored her. He walked to the foot of the stairs with Margaret, and came back to the kitchen to take Joanna into his arms.

"What are you thinking?" he whispered to her dark, locked face. "Thinking *damn?* Thinking *goddam?* Meggie's not so tough as she looks, honey. Wait till she thaws out."

"It's not Margaret." She leaned back in his arms and looked steadily into his eyes. "Alec, I don't like it, not having any money in the house when we've got company, and your family at that."

"Didn't you like my little fish?"

"We can't eat pollack every day."

"I'm going out to haul this afternoon, and we'll get a chicken from Uncle Nate tomorrow."

"You'll stop on the beach and overhaul somebody's engine."

Alec's eyes danced. "Walk down with me then, and row me out to the mooring. Then you'll be sure."

She twisted in his arms, trying to hold her anger, but her laughter spilled through, and for a blessed moment as they clung together, there was no cloud of doubt between them.

Margaret napped for the greater part of the afternoon. Joanna went outdoors and walked down to the little cove to see if she'd missed any cranberries. When she came back to the house she gathered the last of the dahlias and took them into the house. As she clipped the stems at the sink, she heard Margaret coming downstairs. When her sister-in-law came into the room there was no trace in Joanna's manner of anything but a happy young wife who was at peace with the world.

"Did you have a good nap?" she asked.

"Yes, a very good one." Margaret looked better; there was color in her face and in her voice. She sat down by the sunny window that looked out at the harbor. "You have a lovely view."

"One of the best in the world," Joanna said. "I wouldn't swap it for anything. Would you like to go for a walk before the sun goes down?"

"After a while." Margaret seemed uneasy. Joanna felt the older woman's glance touch her and then move away, then come back.

"Joanna," the older woman said unexpectedly. "I might's well admit it. I came here in an awful frame of mind. A downright ugly frame of mind."

Amazement made Joanna forget for an instant her own frame of mind. She looked at Margaret with widening eyes, and Margaret nodded her sandy head vehemently.

"I didn't know what Alec had gone and married, I didn't know what condition I'd find him in, or what kind of place this was. I guess I just about expected the worst, and I told my husband so."

Joanna laughed. "Well, every sister feels that way when her brothers get married. They always think that the girl isn't good enough—I've got brothers, you know."

"It wasn't that," said Margaret. "It was—well, after I'd got rested up in that pretty spare room of yours—I began thinking I owed you an apology for coming in here looking like the Great Stone Face. That's what Alec used to call me when I was on the warpath." Her fleeting smile softened the angular frame of her face. "You see, it wasn't that I thought you weren't good enough. But Alec was always an awful problem to me. I guess you know he lived with me from the time he was sixteen."

"Yes, he told us that."

"Well, even with all my family to think about, I'd lay awake nights thinking about Alec, until my husband used to say we'd get rid of him, if he was going to make trouble—"

"What kind of trouble, Margaret?"

"Now don't look so white, child." Joanna didn't know she was white; she made herself relax, leaning back in her chair. "It wasn't girls, though I wished sometimes it *was* girls instead of cards. In love with 'em, he was. There was always a pack of cards in his pockets, and sometimes more money than a boy sixteen or seventeen had a right to have, when he was just handlining for a living."

"He gambled?" said Joanna.

"I should say so!" Margaret rocked, and her voice gathered enthusiasm. "He got more fun out of a poker game than from taking out the prettiest girl in town. Why, one night Jim and I came home and found him teaching the young ones how to play penny ante—he was giving 'em money and pleased as punch because young Jimmy kept winning. Well, we put a stop to *that!* But there were plenty of people in town to keep a young boy gambling, even if *we* wouldn't allow it."

Joanna said quietly, "I haven't seen any signs of it in him." One poker game a week through the fall and winter—you couldn't call that gambling. Only what about the boat savings? Where had they gone? She felt that vast emptiness again. Margaret said, "Of course you haven't seen any signs! Because he's cured, that's why. He's learnt his lesson. When we sent him down here—"

"*You* sent him?"

"Sure. Us. The family. We didn't know what else to do with him, and since Jim and my sisters' husbands paid up the debts and saved his boat for him, he had to do as we said." This isn't true, thought Joanna sickly, but Margaret's voice went on and on. "He was good and scared when he almost lost the boat, so he promised to turn over a new leaf. But like I said this morning, promises butter no parsnips, and many's the night when it's been cold and rainy I've waked up wondering if he'd kept away from the cards, or if the fever still had him so he'd gambled away his boat, and the house here—"

She leaned forward and put her hand on Joanna's knee. "Let me tell you, girl, I feel as if somebody had just given me a million dollars. I always knew there was good stuff somewhere in that boy, though sometimes I got downhearted about him. And now I know he's all right, and I give most of the credit to you, young woman. Alec's married a good girl from a good family. Oh, I used to hear my mother and my grandfather talk about the Bennetts, and Stephen Bennett! I couldn't wish anything better for my brother than to marry Stephen Bennett's girl. You're the one who's saved him from the cards and the gambling."

Her eyes were suddenly wet as she glanced around the room. "He couldn't buy all this for you, if he was wasting his youth and money away in gambling. Just wait till I tell Jim Coombs! He was always saying there was a weak, rotten streak in Alec—just you wait till I tell that man a thing or two!"

Joanna sat stiffly in the big chair, trying to smile. Yes, he's given me all this, she thought, but it's not paid for. Then with a sudden revulsion of thought: How does that Jim Coombs dare say Alec's weak and rotten?

Never mind the bills and money box; there were men who paid their bills and kept up their savings, and weren't half as kind and sweet-tempered as Alec. Her Alec. She lifted her chin defiantly, and smiled at Margaret. Color was a flag flying in her cheeks.

"Yes, there's good stuff in Alec. You've seen for yourself. Let's go for a walk now, while there's still some sunshine."

31

WHEN AT LAST JOANNA AND ALEC lay in bed, side by side, the curtains blew inward in the sweet frosty air, and the stars twinkled coldly against the panes. From the other side of Brigport came the occasional moan of the whistling buoy; that meant the weather was right for a fine day tomorrow.

"Meg's a good scout," Alec murmured, reaching out to draw Joanna close to him. "Like her better now, Jo?"

"Yes, I like her a lot . . . Are you hauling again tomorrow?"

"Yep, I set the alarm for five o'clock. Philip got a hundred pounds today on a one-night set. What do you bet I can beat him?"

"I never bet," she said. "Alec, did you get anything for the money box this afternoon?"

"I sure did, honey. And enough for you to feed Meggie like royalty all the time she's here."

This was the time. Right now. If she didn't speak now, she never would. Her mouth dried suddenly and she had to moisten her lips; it was not for herself that she was nervous, but for him. "Alec, I opened the money box a few days ago. I needed some money."

"Well?" he asked levelly.

"I didn't take any. There wasn't much, Alec. Not half what there should be in it." Alec, don't try to kiss me and laugh it off, she begged him silently. Be straightforward, for once. "There were more bills than anything else. I thought they'd been paid. And I thought there was more saved toward the boat. Alec, you've made a lot of money this year. Where is it?"

"Honey, it takes a lot of money to run a house!"

"But I know what I've spent for food, Alec. We get our milk

here, and our vegetables from our own garden, and enough to put up for the winter. We don't have meat much—mostly fish, or a chicken from Uncle Nate's. Our wood doesn't cost us anything."

He hugged her close to him. "Snuggle down, sugar, and keep me warm." His voice argued tenderly. "What about fixing up my gear, and our clothes, and things like that? You just don't realize . . . being married costs money, Jo."

"I know it does." She turned suddenly and put her arms around him. "I want to know something. Please tell me the truth, Alec."

Be honest with me, she begged him from her heart. Because if you lie, I'll know you're lying, and I'll never be happy again. She said aloud, "Never mind about the bills. We've got to start paying them up, and going without a few things, but I'll take charge of them so you won't have to bother. But there's the box. Alec, did you take money out of the box to play poker with?"

The silence in the room was loud against her ears. She could hear her own heart beating. Alec lay still in her arms, and she put her lips against his cheek, and felt the tightened muscles there. Please don't make any excuses, just tell me if it's so, she pleaded silently, and waited.

"Yes, I took it," he said evenly, after a long time. "Not to play with. I had to pay up."

"I thought the stakes weren't high."

"Sometimes they were. When the boys were flush." How rigid he was. She tightened her arms around him and said bitterly, "Owen, I suppose, Hugo and Sigurd. They're the worst ones for throwing their money away."

"You don't have to blame anybody else. And you didn't have to open the box."

"I suppose you thought if I never opened it, I'd never know about the bills and the money." She let go of him and moved away in the darkness.

"You didn't have to know," Alec said shortly. "You left the business to me from the first."

"But I thought—" She stopped. It was useless to tell him she'd trusted him to look after their debts as her father had always done at home. There was nothing more to say, and anger and doubt lay heavily between them, pushing them apart. Miles apart. A world apart. Her throat was clogged with bitterness. She turned over on her side, and looked up at the frosty twinkle outside the windows.

"I was going to pay for everything," Alec said. "Those people expect to wait for their money."

"They sounded kind of tired of waiting. 'No further extension of credit—' "

"Talk," said Alec. His sulkiness was unfamiliar. "It's just so much talk. And I've been putting back the boat money, too. My God, Joanna, you act as if I was a thief!"

"It's not that!" Her voice was passionate against the cold anger in his. "Alec, don't you see? I thought we were all free and clear—we didn't owe anything, and pretty soon there'd be enough for your new boat. And then, all at once, I find out it's not like that at all. We haven't got *anything,* Alec."

She turned back to him, trying to break down the wall between them. "I don't blame you for anything, darling. I just wish you'd told me."

"In other words, you don't trust me to handle the money."

She was furious again. Let him deliberately misunderstand her, put wrong meanings to her words. Let him try to make her feel miserable and ashamed of hurting him: it didn't change the truth.

"I didn't say I couldn't trust you," she told him coldly, and was shocked to realize that was exactly what she had meant. She couldn't trust him.

Alec said nothing. His breathing was deep and regular. He had fallen asleep in the middle of the argument, or he was only pretending. Either way, she felt like slapping him. It was a much more invigorating feeling than sorrow. And why had she been sorry for him, anyway? She lay in the dark and contemplated the situation. It certainly wasn't too much to expect her husband to take care of his money. *Poker!* she thought scornfully, and fell asleep.

She slept heavily, without dreaming. She awoke to find gray daylight in the room, and Alec drawing her gently into his arms. Sodden with sleep, she murmured his name and burrowed against him; her mind was not enough awake to remember the quarrel, only her body knew his touch and responded to it without thought or hesitation. Drifting back into sleep again, she felt the light warmth of his lips on hers. It called her back, and her mouth looked for his and found it.

Somewhere a sparrow was singing.

When she woke up again, Alec had gone to haul, and sunlight had again turned the tawny grass to a golden sea. As she began to dress, she was conscious of a deep-welling serenity, of a firmer grip on life than she had ever known—her life and Alec's. It was not complex this morning. It was the simplest thing in the world. She wondered why she hadn't seen it so clearly before.

I'll take care of the bills from now on, she thought. He'll give me more money. I'll make him put back the boat savings, he'll take no more from the box for his poker games.

That was all there was to it. Lots of men were like Alec; married to a strong woman, they turned out all right. Her Bennett blood pulsed strongly through her body, she glowed with health and confidence. She was supremely sure of herself.

She was happy as she went down to get breakfast for herself and Margaret. It was a wonderful world that flashed and glowed outside her kitchen windows. A wonderful world, and it was all hers.

32

THERE WAS A GIRL ON BRIGPORT who was telling around that Owen Bennett would have to marry her. The story reached Joanna by way of Mark who, though he considered himself a man grown at eighteen, still clung to his old way of being a bird of ill omen. If there was a tale to tell, Mark was the one to tell it first. Joanna never saw him lounge through her kitchen door, with a preoccupied glint in his dark eyes, without feeling a slight depression.

This time there was reason to be depressed. When Alec came home from the shore, she asked him if he'd heard anything. He laughed.

"Lord, yes. She's been talking that way for a month. Nobody ever pays any attention to her. She's always after some poor fish."

"Is there any truth in it?" she persisted.

Alec twinkled at her. "Ask Owen."

"It could be true, Alec." She tried not to sound worried, but she couldn't help it. "Owen's just foolish enough to get mixed up with something like Trudy Loomis. Especially if he's been drinking—oh, you know how crazy he can be! And Trudy'd give her eyeteeth to get her claws into him."

"I'm betting Owen's not that foolish. Buck up, honey." He hugged her and rubbed his cold cheek against hers. "You're so warm and smooth. When I was out hauling today I thought I'd never be warm again. Vapor flying till my face felt frozen, and now it's blowing a livin' gale of wind."

They listened to the sweep of the March wind coming in from the cove and roaring through the trees behind the house. "Never mind, darling, you're home now," she said against his cheek. "And we've got a special supper tonight. Mother and Kris baked beans and brown bread today, and sent some down to us. I've fixed pickled herring and onions, too."

"Kris was in the store when I went in," Alec said, looking appreciatively at the table. "She looks swell. Your mother's done a good job on her."

Joanna nodded. Donna had needed someone, and Kristi had seized with both hands the chance of freedom. She had defied Gunnar at last, and now she was a new Kristi, whose wide blue eyes weren't so easily frightened, and who laughed a great deal more.

"Peter's courting her like everything," Joanna said. "When he's hauling outside Goose Cove, he rows ashore and drops into the kitchen, and sits there watching her while she works. The boys ride him, but he doesn't care."

"That's because he's in love," said Alec, and gathered his wife into a mighty hug.

Owen came in after supper, looking extraordinarily handsome. His red plaid mackinaw set off his bright dark eyes, and his brown cheekbones were whipped scarlet by the wind. In his extravagant vitality he seemed to tower over Alec. Joanna couldn't blame Trudy Loomis for wanting him.

As she cleared away and washed the dishes, she listened to the men's easy talk of lobstering and weather, Washington and politics. Traditionally the Bennetts were Republicans; Owen was convinced, he told Alec profanely, that Bennett's Island wouldn't get a breakwater in a Democratic administration.

She was always contented to listen to her menfolks as she worked, but tonight she was frankly worried. It was just possible Trudy wasn't lying; Owen was crazy and reckless enough. Look what had happened to Charles. . . .

She hung up the dish towels and walked over to where Owen sprawled in a rocking chair, one long leg over the arm. He looked up at her, smiling. "Hi, Tiddleywinks. What's on your mind?"

"Is there anything to this story about Trudy Loomis?"

Owen laughed. "What kind of a damn fool do you take me for?"

"A proper damn fool," said Alec. "She's been worried sick."

"Only because I didn't want Mother to hear the story," Joanna defended herself sharply. "If it's all a lot of hot air, why do you let her talk like that?"

"Oh, it makes her happy," said Owen benevolently. "She's a forlorn little bitch. And if the rest of 'em want to talk about me, they'll give somebody else a rest."

"If you wouldn't hang around Brigport so much, there wouldn't be any chance for chew."

Owen was in rare good temper tonight. He laughed at her. "I've found out all I want to know about those Brigport tramps. I'm in love with a new *she.*"

His smile tried to be casual, but it was suddenly eager and excited. He reached into the pocket of his plaid shirt and took out a folded paper. With a curious gentleness in his big brown hands he unfolded it and laid it on the table. Alec and Joanna moved close to look, not knowing what they would see.

It was a drawing of a boat, neatly and painstakingly done. Such a sleek, handsome boat as Owen had always dreamed of. He had been forever drawing her, from the time he was twelve years old. She changed occasionally in the flare of the bow, the sheer of the bilge, the type of cabin, the placing of the wheel; but Joanna knew that in her brother's heart it had always been the same boat, the one boat. And she was on paper again, and lettered tidily on her bow was her name: *White Lady*.

It was a strangely self-conscious Owen who said, "I figured I'd been running the *Old Girl* long enough. She's a tough little critter. Tomboy, sort of. I'm going to have a lady for a change."

"Tough little tomboys can take a lot of punishment," said Joanna loyally. But she leaned over to admire the drawing; Alec and Owen were engrossed in it, their eyes following the long, harmonious lines of the hull.

"I'm going to start her in April," Owen said with quiet assurance. "Oh, I've said that a hell of a lot of times. But this time I mean it. Jud Gray's renting me his place. I know just how much lumber to get, I can build a model from scale, and I'm ready to go."

Alec put his hand on Owen's shoulder, his face alight with enthusiasm, and Joanna had a sudden sharp image in her brain of the money box. Since Margaret's visit Alec had made a sincere attempt to clear things up, giving her extra money when the hauls were good, playing poker only seldom, and then not going above the five-dollar limit, as far as she knew. She hadn't begrudged him his card games; he showed no signs of the gambling fever Margaret had told her about. But since she'd taken the money from the box to pay the most urgent bills, there hadn't been much to put back. And how could Alec face another winter in that old boat, which he called *The Basket* because she was forever springing a new leak?

There was always some part of her engine to be brought home and thawed out in the oven, there were precious hauling hours lost when, on a good day, he couldn't start her up, and must work on her while the other boats left the harbor. And if it wasn't Alec's own engine, it was somebody's else's, she thought with grim humor.

Owen and Alec were deep in technical talk now. Joanna listened; Alec was telling Owen what sort of engine he should have, and the exact details as to how it should be placed. She marveled at his happy, unselfish interest in Owen's plans. Didn't it bother him, didn't he feel the slightest envy because Owen had three hundred dollars saved to start the *White Lady*, while he had nothing at all except what was in his pockets and Joanna's purse?

Owen was smiling at his plans with the expansive pride of a new father, and Alec gave all indications of being a fond uncle. They looked as if they saw her in the drifting tobacco smoke. The wind was howling outside, and the day behind them had been long and cruel, but they had gone ahead into April now, into the long, soft blue days when the Island's breath would be warm and sweet once more. It was taken for granted that Alec would work on the boat, along with Nils.

"And we'll turn a hand when you get yours underway," Owen said. "Seems to me it won't be long now, will it?" Alec said easily, "Oh, not so long. But you'd better get the *Lady* launched before you start building mine."

"And we'll launch her by midsummer." Owen stretched with the slow and powerful grace of a big man. Beside him Alec was slight and almost pale; but Joanna, looking at them both, loved the gentleness of her husband's look, the quick humor in his eyes. Humor that was always kind. Owen had plagued her so many times into furious tears.

But tonight he radiated good nature. "I'm going down to the Eastern End," he said as he put on his mackinaw. "Coming, Alec?"

"In this gale?" Joanna asked, and Owen gave her a rough squeeze.

"Not half so bad as it sounds. Don't be one of those Aunt Mary wives, Jo. She won't let Uncle Nate stir."

"Alec can go from here to Portland for all I care," said Joanna with dignity.

"I'm only going as far as the Eastern End, my dear." Alec rumpled her head. "We'll see how Charles thinks the *White Lady* stacks up with the *Sea-Gypsy*."

"The *Gypsy*'s a sweetheart," Joanna warned them. "Take that bunch of magazines down to Mateel, Alec."

"You ought to get down and see her, Jo," Owen said. "The kid started walking last week and she wants to show him off to you."

"When the weather clears," she promised vaguely, and Owen gave her a sidewise glance.

"Never knew the weather to hold you up when you really hankered to do something."

She felt the blood in her cheeks, but she only smiled, and held up her mouth for Alec's unabashed kiss. He was so completely unabashed that Owen had long since given up his sardonic observations. When they had gone out she sat for a long time staring at the pages of her book without really seeing them. Owen was right, she didn't really want to go down to see Mateel, and watch young Charles stagger across the floor to clutch his mother's knees with a chuckle of mad delight. She didn't want to see Mateel, shining-eyed, bury her face in her son's neck and kiss it on what she called "the 'oney-spot."

She told herself now that it was foolish and selfish to feel that odd nagging pain in her breast, to shrink from picking up her nephew's warm little body and holding it close to her. It wasn't as if she wasn't going to have children of her own; it was just that she wanted them *now,* and the boat must be built first, and sometimes it seemed as if the money box would never be full again. And sometimes she felt a queer coldness, almost like terror; terror that Alec's child would never be born to her.

And then, when she was in despair, the natural buoyancy of the Bennetts bore her to the surface again. It always happened like this; for no matter how she might worry, no matter how many moments of panic she knew, she knew something else too—that she loved Alec with her whole heart and soul and body, that he was her man just as she was his woman. And they lived on the Island; it was enough to make her grateful for living. What if there was a little wind and weather in these first few years? A chop wouldn't necessarily drown you; you kept your bow pointed into it, and laughed at the wind, and before you knew it there was smooth water under you.

Joanna went to bed, feeling a quiet but radiant peace. In moments like this it seemed as if the smooth water was just a boat-length away. Any time now, they'd reach it. . . .

She woke up with the sensation that she'd been asleep for a long time. The wind still battered at the front of the house and the surf made a constant hollow booming in the little cove. Alec hadn't come in yet. She smiled in the darkness, imagining them sitting around Charles' kitchen talking boats, not knowing how bone-weary they were from the long day of off-shore hauling. These days they went out ten or fifteen miles to the east and southeast of the Island, out beyond Matinicus Rock, in the lanes where the big fishing trawlers passed. There the fifty-fathom traps were set. It was an hour's run in the bitter cold, with the freezing vapor flying against their faces. Then there was the long day under lowering skies or wintry sunshine webbing the rolling sea with a gunmetal gleam, the soaked mittens, the water freezing on the washboards, the boat pitching and wallowing under cold feet all day; and then the return in the late afternoon, with a purple dusk creeping over the sea, and perhaps a rising wind and a cold spit of snow.

They came into the harbor, past the white fury of the harbor ledges, wondering if they'd ever been so cold before, but by the time they reached the car, and had swung the heavy crates and kegs of lobsters onto the scales and received the slip with Pete Grant's scrawl on it — thirty-five or fifty or seventy-five dollars to be collected when they went into the store — they knew it was a good life. They cursed it sometimes, and swore they'd never put in another winter like it, but somehow they could whistle as they rowed in from the mooring.

And you forgot about the burning cold of the vapor, and the everlasting wind, in the evenings when you had the plan of a boat laid out on the table before you, to talk about now, and to build come April.

Joanna lay in bed and thought about the men. They didn't know what time it was when they were talking boats. She turned over and burrowed down into the warm bedclothes like a kitten and fell asleep again.

When she woke up, the first gray light, faintly flushed with rose, was filtering through frost-brocaded windows. She knew before she opened her eyes or moved that Alec wasn't beside her, but from the kitchen she heard the sounds that go with building a fire. She must have been too sound asleep to wake up when he came in last night, or when he got up this morning; and he was going to surprise her with coffee and hot muffins that were amazingly light.

But when she opened her eyes, she saw that he hadn't slept in the bed at all. She lay there for a moment, not liking the way she felt. Little by little the cold sensation faded away. Of course they'd talked till all hours and suddenly realized how tired they were, and bunked on the couch in Charles' kitchen until daylight. She'd have some fun with Alec about this.

Moving swiftly in the chill air, she slid into her bathrobe and slippers and ran downstairs. The coffee was bubbling and aromatic, and Alec was taking cups out of the cupboard. In the pale light he looked gray with weariness, his eyes red-rimmed and dull.

"Hello, darling," she said, going confidently toward him for his kiss.

"Hello, Jo." He smiled at her, but it was an effort, and she knew it.

"Have you boys been talking boats until you're out on your feet?" she asked. "After you worked all day, I'd almost think you'd be ready for bed at night."

"Well, we didn't notice the time. Maurice and Jake came in, and . . . oh, you know how it is." He gave her a shamefaced grin. "A little cold water will fix me up."

He turned icy water into the basin and splashed his face. Joanna brought him a fresh towel. "Mateel must think she's running an all-night dive."

"Oh, she went to bed early. She doesn't care, and even if she did, Charles wouldn't give a damn." Before the mirror, he parted his wet sandy hair and brushed it back, his eyes narrow with concentration. "Charles is the head man down there."

Joanna leaned against the wall and smiled up at him. "Well, aren't you the skipper aboard this vessel?" she asked demurely.

Alec laughed. "Sometimes I wonder."

"You wonder! And here I stand, mine not to make reply, mine but to do or die—"

He leaned over and kissed her. "Yours but to pour some coffee. And then I'm going to climb the wooden hill."

"You're a disgrace to the clans of Douglass and Bennett," she told him, shaking her head. "Rolling home at dawn, after a boat-building spree. Here's your coffee." She looked at his fatigue with tender eyes, wanting, as always, to cradle his heavy head in her arms till he fell asleep.

When he put down his empty cup he kicked off his boots and started toward the stairs. Joanna, laying her clothes over the oven door to warm them before she dressed, grinned at him. "Wait a bit, Cap'n Alec. If you're going to sleep till noon, I need some money to get your dinner with, unless you want boiled salt herring again."

"What's the matter with herring?"

She went to the foot of the stairs and looked up at him, her black hair tumbling over the shoulders of her dark red robe. "Alec, you growled when you said that. What *isn't* the matter with herring when we've been eating it for almost a week? And Pete's getting some meat today. Think of it, Alec, nice juicy steak!"

It sounded wonderful to her. Alec looked over her head and sighed. Apparently it didn't sound wonderful to him.

"I know you're tired, Alec," she said quickly, "but just toss me down one of those bills you had last night. We've lived off the pantry and cellar shelves for a week, and we deserve something special today."

Alec said heavily, "Joanna, we can't afford steak."

"Why?" she asked blankly. Before this it was always Alec who brought home the expensive luxuries from Pete's store, and looked blank when she said they couldn't afford it. "Why, Alec?"

"Because I haven't any money. No more than two bits. We'll eat herring and like it till I haul again."

She leaned against the wall and said in a flat voice, "Why haven't we any money, Alec? You had plenty left from your haul yesterday."

"If you have to know, we had a little poker game last night and they cleaned me out."

She said, still tonelessly, "I see." He ran lightly down the stairs to her. His hands gripped her shoulders warmly, and he put his cheek against hers.

"Don't look like that, Jo. Sure, I know I should've held on to some of it, but I was winning like crazy, and I kept thinking of what you'd say when I woke you up and showed you the roll."

"Why didn't you stop then?"

"Aw, honey, I couldn't! You can't stop when you're winning."

"Are you supposed to play till you've lost everything? Alec, if they'd known that money was all you had, you could have stopped."

She knew better, but she had to keep talking without looking at him, pretending his hands weren't trying to turn her toward him. She wished he would go to bed and leave her alone. She didn't know whether she was angry or hurt, or upset because this wasn't a way of living that she liked.

"The wind's still blowing," she said dryly. "The weather report last night said storm warnings were out along the coast. It'll likely be three or four days before you get out to haul again. You'll be sick of herring by then, Alec."

He took his hands away from her shoulders and she felt him

grow stiff and distant. She was vaguely sorry for him, through her anger. He'd been without sleep for twenty-four hours, and yesterday had been a windy and hellish day; she could have waited until he napped a few hours before she talked like this.

"Do you have to act as if I'd killed somebody, or been out all night with a woman?" Alec said coldly, and she stopped being sorry for him. She felt her chin tighten and go up, as she turned toward him. Whose fault was it that he hadn't slept? Not hers, certainly. No one forced him to go down to the Eastern End, no one pointed a gun at his head and told him to play poker.

"Why don't you go to bed?" she suggested.

Without another word he went up the stairs. Halfway to the top he spoke to her with remote politeness, as if they were strangers. "Call me at noon. I'm going down and work on Jake Trudeau's engine after dinner."

She nodded, and the upstairs door shut behind him, with a sound of finality. She dressed before the oven door, but though her skin was warmed by the glow of heat, she felt cold. . . . You went along serenely, thinking you knew a man, and then you found out you didn't. You loved him, and you felt you were a part of him, and he was a part of you, and then all at once you were alone again, and it was a bleak, desolate feeling.

But why couldn't he have *thought?* she asked herself. He knew that money was all they had for the next few days. He knew he could very easily lose it all, if he were careless. But she could answer her own questions. Alec was too sweet-tempered, too social, too hopeful. The very qualities that had endeared him to her were the factors that made trouble for him.

But he'll have to learn, she thought, her teeth tight against her lower lip. Her mind was made up about that.

33

JOANNA BROUGHT UP HERRING from the cellar and put it to soak, and opened a jar of beet greens. At the rate they were using the canned stuff, it wouldn't last very long. She thought of the days during the summer and early fall when she had stayed in to can fruit and vegetables and fish, and had gone up to the big house to help her mother and Kristi, and the Island had been so lovely that she ached; she had wanted to stay out in that radiant world for every waking moment, she had wanted to go fishing and hauling with Alec, she had wanted to lie in the warm tawny grass on the west side watching the gulls and listening to the loons.

But she had spent those waking moments—all of them, it seemed—standing over a stove, sterilizing jars, ladling hot jam, salting fish, while the last blaze of summer drifted into the nostalgic, dreamy peace of autumn.

Donna was the only one who guessed Joanna wasn't as whole-hearted in this phase of housekeeping as she appeared. The others, coming in, looked at her apron and flushed cheeks, and neat ranks of jars, and said, "Old married woman now, ain't ye?" But Donna, who saw everything, said to her once, "It won't hurt if you run away once in a while."

"What do you mean?"

"Go down to the shore and take a skiff, and go rowing around the harbor. It's high tide."

"I've got to start dinner—" Her protest was feeble.

"Dinner!" Donna looked as scornful as her inherent quiet sweetness would allow. "Dinner can wait. Jo, I know you're in love with Alec and you'd like to wait on him by inches, but I'm telling you because I know — you'll have to run away sometimes, even if it's just down to the gate and back. Women aren't born housekeepers and wives. You're not helping anybody by cooping yourself in a house and letting it run you."

She smiled at Joanna. "If some of the women on this Island heard me talking like this, they'd be horrified, but underneath they'd agree with me. Start Alec's dinner, and can beans this afternoon the way you planned. But take yourself rowing first. It's noon, and high tide, and that's the time you like best."

They were not a demonstrative pair, but Joanna, in passing, stopped to kiss Donna. "I've known you twenty-one years, and you still surprise me," she said, and went out as if her feet had wings, straight down to the gate and from there to the beach where the skiffs were tied.

But she hadn't run away often, and she hadn't shirked on her canning, and she was glad now. They had lived for days from these jars, but by April the shelves would be almost bare.

At noon she set the table, looking at it with distaste. Herring were good when you wanted to eat them, but not when you had to. Tomorrow it would be creamed codfish and pork scraps — also good when you ate it from choice. She had two eggs to put into it, and there wouldn't be any more eggs until Alec hauled again. She could get them any time from Uncle Nate, but to charge them would be an admission to the whole Bennett family that she and Alec were short. More than short. *Broke.*

There was always the money box, but she put the thought out of her head. The money box was not to be touched until the time came to pay for the lumber for the boat. She remembered what Alec had said about Jake's engine, and the tight wire of anger, that had kept her tense, loosened. Why, Alec had taken on a job to tide them over, and she'd been calling him careless and improvident.

She ran upstairs and called him, feeling a sweet rush of penitence. She'd behaved like what Owen called one of those Aunt Mary wives.

He looked faintly surprised as she leaned over and kissed him, and then he reached up to pull her down against his chest, his eyes alight with their curious radiance.

"Love me?"

"I love you," she said meekly. "Do you love me?"

"Sometimes. Right now is one of them. Jo . . . still mad at me?"

She traced his nose with her forefinger. "I wasn't mad."

"You were damn mad, and I don't blame you. But I won't do it again, Jo honey." His voice pleaded to be believed. "Honest, I promise —"

She didn't know what whim, what impulse, made her put her hand over his mouth. "No, Alec. Don't ever make promises."

The storm broke that night, and was a week blowing itself out. At the end of the week, there were no herring left, and very little dried fish. Also, it seemed that Jake Trudeau couldn't pay Alec right away for the six hours' work on his engine.

Alec was lighthearted about it. "He'll pay me when he can," he told Joanna. "But if he'd given me anything, it meant the youngsters would go hungry till he got out to haul again."

"Did he offer to pay?"

"Oh, yes. Sure, Jake's all right. He looks like a hi-jacker, but he's straight." Alec wandered to the stove and looked with interest in the kettle of fish chowder. "I told him not to worry about it."

"I suppose you didn't tell him we'd go hungry too."

"What, with a cellar full of grub?" He twinkled at her, but she turned away from him.

"It's not very full, I can tell you that." She felt tired and dispirited, as she stood by the window, looking down across the sodden brown field toward the gate. Beyond the dark barrier of Gunnar Sorensen's spruces, the harbor was slate-gray in the growing dusk. There was no one to be seen, no sign of anything human except the lighted window of Gunnar's kitchen, down there beyond his garden.

Alec was whistling softly, and she heard him sit down at the table. Still watching the coming dusk outside the windows, she said, "Alec, do I sound as if all I cared about was money? Because that's not so, and you know it."

"Sure I know it, honey. You feel low because you think it's not decent to live without plenty put away in the teapot in the cupboard." His voice was soft and warm around her heart. He did understand, then, and it was good to know. "Give me time. We're in the doldrums right now, but what I said goes — I'll be good. Believe me?"

She smiled out at the barren field. "Uh-huh . . ."

"And we'll have a big steak dinner tomorrow, and you'll forget all about herring. I'm damn sick of 'em myself."

She couldn't resist it. "What'll we buy it with? Charm and a sweet smile?"

"Money, my dear!" he said gaily. "Because I'm going down to the Eastern End tonight and lick the pants off Charles and Owen, and get back all I lost."

She spun around and saw him sitting at the table, his hair bright in the lamplight. He was playing solitaire. Almost, in that instant, Joanna heard Margaret's voice. "I wished it was girls instead of cards. In love with 'em, he was. There was always a pack in his pocket."

Joanna found her voice. "You're going to play again, after you told me you wouldn't?"

"Well, I meant to get my money back first." He leaned back in his chair. "I've got a quarter and Owen'll give me something to make a start with, and the Douglasses will be in the money again. Don't look like that, Jo, honey." He stood up and came toward her. "Don't you believe me when I say I know when to stop?"

His eyes, his voice, his mouth appealed to her, and she wanted with all her heart to tell him she believed him, to send him out tonight with a flip "Good luck!" and to stop this nagging anxiety in her brain. Now he was hugging her with a rough, little boy's hug, rubbing his cheek against hers.

"Believe me, honey?" he whispered. "Tell me you do."

And then she knew she couldn't tell him that she was afraid. It was selfish and suspicious, not to have faith in him. She wanted to have faith in him. With a small, unheard sigh she said, "I believe you, Alec," and felt the pure exuberance of his kiss.

While she set the supper table, he sat at the end of the stove playing his fiddle for her, one old song after another; sad ones, melancholy old ballads whose bitter words he sang as he played, his Scotch jigs and reels, Swedish tunes learned from Sigurd, and pure Yankee ones. Whenever she looked at him, soft brown hair tumbled over his forehead, green-brown eyes narrow and bright, she felt with new force her love for him. But it was mingled with something new and confusing. Something like sadness.

She went up to see her parents while he was out, and when he called for her, and came into the warm sitting room, he wore the air of taut and jubilant excitement that told her he'd been winning. Owen wasn't so good-natured. Apparently he'd lost.

They had no sooner got away from the house than Alec told her. "Enough for steak?" she said dryly.

"Steak, and that suit I've seen you looking at in the catalog, and all the stuff to go with it. And a new sweater for me, maybe."

She halted in the path, regardless of the sweep of wind from Goose Cove, and looked at him in the clear starlight. "Alec, how much did you get?"

"Thirty dollars. More than I lost last night."

"Thirty dollars is a lot," she said without enthusiasm.

"Owen was flush. Charles dropped out—it was Owen and Maurice and me." He laughed aloud, it was an exultant sound on the wind. "Lord, it was some game! Here, Jo, you take it. Come on, open up your hand."

Her fingers seemed cramped and unwilling as he forced the money into them. "Tomorrow you make out the order and get that suit, with shoes and everything to go with it. We're going ashore on a spree when the weather comes good, and I want you to look special. You've worn that old sweater and skirt long enough."

"Oh, Alec," she said softly, and felt the sting of tears in her eyes. He thought it was pleasure in her voice, and he put his arm around her shoulders and hugged her. They walked like that all the way home, through the woods and past the bare apple trees, out to their own house again.

He slept in her arms that night, his face warm against her throat. She knew that he was completely happy when he fell asleep, and thought she was happy too. But she lay awake for a long time, her arms tight around him even when she could have let him go. It seemed to her as if she must hold him fast, as if her arms could protect him. Against what, she didn't know.

34

ALL AT ONCE, AFTER A WINTER that seemed to last forever, it was April. It was still cold, but on a gray and streaming day the bluebirds came to Joanna's field, winged jewels of heartshaking blue against the drab, sodden grass; they perched on swaying reeds, and for all they cared, the sun might have been shining and the sea as blue as they were.

They were only the beginning. As April slipped into May, there were mornings when the woods behind the house were alive with bird calls and flashing wings. It was migration time, and the sparrows, nuthatches, kinglets, and crossbills, the finches and the warblers, and many an unfamiliar stranger who was only stopping for a night in his northward flight, came to eat from the feeders Alec had made. When the back door was open, they flew into the entry, and more than once Joanna and Alec captured in their hands some small creature whose wings had been beating frantically against the window. The ruby-crowned kinglet was tiny and warm in Joanna's cupped hands, as she carried it to the open door and let it go. The white-crowned sparrows walked around the yard, and their voices were like elfin flutes through the woods.

By May, Owen's boat was well under way. The *White Lady* was shaping up to be a beauty; the whole Island was agreed on that, and almost every family felt a proprietary interest in her, since the Sorensen boys, the Grays, the Birds, the Trudeaus, and Alec spent most of their leisure time in the boat shop. The older men stopped by to look on and smoke and offer casual advice. But it was the young men who built the *White Lady*.

Owen's feeling for her made the family bear with his black moods, which seemed to them blacker than usual. If something went wrong, if some new tool or material didn't come when he expected it, if one of the older men implied that he was a raw amateur at boat-building, and that the *Lady* would probably show him up, he was almost insane with fury. He would walk away without speaking and tramp for hours through the woods or over the steepest, ugliest rocks on Sou-west Point, until he had walked some portion of his rage out of his system and could endure people again.

He took to wandering around the Island long after everyone was asleep. What he thought as he wandered, no one knew. But his walks always ended in the boat shop, and there in the darkness the *White Lady* loomed above him, a pale and towering shape. The air was warm, and aromatic with new wood, and shavings were soft under his rubber boots. He would walk around his boat, needing no light to show him the gallant, lovely line of her stem, the smooth, perfectly proportioned flare of her bow.

If ever dreams were built with timber and nails, it was during those months when the *White Lady* was coming into being.

There was a long fog mull toward the end of May. For a week the Island was shrouded in mist that blew back and forth as the wind shifted. Sometimes in the morning the sun burned through, and showed a patch of luminous blue. Sometimes at night one saw the stars. But always the fog stayed, and after a while the Islanders hardly heard the foghorn out at the Rock, they were so accustomed to it. The grass was wet and the woods dripped. In the harbor, the water was a motionless silvery gray; in the patches of slick, the trees on the point were perfectly mirrored, as if in the most tranquil lake.

At night, Owen walked in the muffled silence. Leaving Joanna's house one evening, he took the long way home, through the village, so that he could stop in the boat shop. There was a faint chuckle and swish of the incoming tide around the old wharf's spilings that hid the slight sound of his feet on the path. The shop door was usually ajar, and he stepped inside without moving it — stepped into the warm, wood-fragrant darkness to see a slowly moving light playing over the *White Lady's* rounded side, far aft.

He stood motionless, watching the flickering light, the play of shadows around it, until it glinted on something red. It was just for an instant, but he recognized in that instant Simon Bird's red hair.

He moved forward through the muffling shavings until he could see the hands working swiftly and deftly in the circle of light. Simon's hands; he could tell by the ring on the hand that held the knife. Then it would be Ash who was holding the light. He could see its faint glow on the front of the red and black plaid shirt Ash wore. That was why the light jumped so. Ash was always nervous, afraid of his own shadow. But Simon worked steadily, his knife driving the oakum deep into the seams, the long ends of oakum that Nils and Hugo left trailing when they finished their day's stint of caulking, so they could tell where they'd left off. A boat whose caulking had been persistently tampered with would cause trouble from the moment she was launched.

There was no rage in Owen, only a cold elation that he had caught them. He walked forward through the shavings, noiseless as an Indian, and with one powerful surge he drove his fist into Simon's intent face.

Simon reeled backward, swearing from a bleeding mouth. Almost simultaneously Ash dropped the flashlight, and it went out. But Owen had a grip on the front of Simon's shirt that no one could shake, and in the pitch blackness he hit again and again, without speaking. He heard, through Simon's hard breathing and the scuffling of their feet, young Ash running for the door. He chuckled, and his hard hand made one more contact with the side of Simon's head before Simon wrenched himself free. Owen let him go.

"The bastards," he said softly, stepping over to the *White Lady* and stroking her with his hand. "The sons o' bitches." It was almost as if he were trying to comfort her.

In June, the *White Lady* was launched. They had a pretty day for the event; a blue and shining day, when the tide was high in midafternoon, the wind northwest, the sky flawless. The whole Island came down to the beach to see Nate Bennett's tractor haul the *White Lady* out of the shop and into the light of day.

Joanna stood by the anchor, near her mother and Mateel, watching the men as they worked around the boat. She felt a constriction in her throat, her eyes smarted. How lovely she was, how big, how shining and white and untouched. She saw Alec straighten up from adjusting a roller; his thin face was gay and proud and excited. There was pride and admiration in her father's face too, and in the other brothers'. But Owen looked stern and dark, and hardly spoke. It was no time for talk.

Every man on the Island, with the exception of Ash and Simon Bird, was gathered around the boat. Even George Bird was there, lending a hand. Not working very hard at it, but still, he was there. Old Gunnar stood on the wharf, hands on his hips, and said nothing; it was an Island proverb that when Gunnar couldn't find anything bad to say, he didn't say anything.

The *Lady* was on the sloping beach now, she wouldn't have far to go to reach the water. Stern first, that was it; her bow towered above Joanna and the others who watched from the road. Launched bow first, she'd bring bad luck to everyone who ever owned her. Out by the end of the old wharf, Philip's boat idled; there was a line from the *Gull* to the stern of the *White Lady*.

The men lined up on either side of the new boat to hold her upright, rubber boots digging into the beach stones. Owen and Alec put the heavy pole under her bow and leaned all their combined weight on the other end of the pole, lifting the boat enough to give her a start. There was a creaking and a rumbling, and the *Lady* moved on the rollers. Lifted hands on either white-painted side held her steady when she would have heeled. Slowly, yet irrevocably, she moved down the faint incline of the beach, until the clear green ripples lapped against the coppered bottom. As she slipped easily into the water, Owen scrambled over the side and into the cockpit.

The *White Lady* was afloat. Like a gull resting, she lay on the water, her white sides reflecting below her. For a moment she was uncertain, dancing slightly, moving timidly with the current. Then Owen shifted the line from her stern to her bow, and Philip headed the *Gull* out into the wide harbor. She followed, gliding docilely across the bright water.

Something like a sigh went up from those on the beach. Joanna tried to force the mist away from her eyes. Behind her, Nathan Parr blew his nose.

"With all I seen la'nched in my day," he muttered to Johnny Fernandez, "it always gits me just the same. They seem so young-like — scairt, and yet they knew they was goin' where they belonged."

He blew his nose again. Out in the *White Lady* Owen stood by the wheel. His face was set and grim, locked lest his fierce exaltation should show through and be seen. But Joanna knew that it was beating like drums through his body.

35

IN JUNE, STEVIE GRADUATED from high school. The Bennetts were all together on the Island, and true to form, Stevie began to build his pots for the fall. He recaulked and painted Owen's old peapod, and seemed perfectly happy and contented. Joanna and Donna, picking the wild strawberries on the point, talked about it.

"We're all alike," Joanna said. "We want to be on the Island."

"Still, I wish one of the boys had wanted to go to college," Donna mused. "I had an idea Stevie — oh, well, if he didn't want to be a fisherman, people would think he was a queer sort of Bennett."

"It's not so much being a fisherman as it's staying where you belong — in your own kind of air, along beside your own special piece of ocean." Today that ocean was a tranquil Mediterranean blue beyond Goose Cove, dark green in the shallows where the rocks loomed above the still, cold water, and the spruces came down to the very edge. The sky was the lovely tender color Joanna had dreamed about all winter long, and it seemed as if wild strawberries had always a warmer, more melting tenderness than she'd remembered. She sat cross-legged in the grass, eating berries from a cluster, and said, "Stevie knows he'll never be any happier than when he's rowing his own peapod across that water, and hauling traps he's built himself. Maybe it isn't ambitious, but it's darned satisfactory."

"And it's one more to worry about when the Closed Season's over," said Donna briskly. "There are times when I just don't feel romantic about the lobster industry."

They laughed, and at the sound of their laughter, Winnie got up from where she lay panting under a wild pear bush, and came over to them, amber eyes and waving tail asking to be let in on the joke.

With the Closed Season, the men were busier than ever. Their traps had to be brought in, dried out, repaired, and stacked in trim rows around the shore. They brought their boats up on the beach to be painted and overhauled. They helped in the gardens, reshingled their roofs and painted their houses, built new chicken yards, and managed to keep busy until the Season was over.

But most of the men, either through necessity or choice, went fishing. Alec went trawling for hake outside the Rock, so far from the Island that *The Basket* seemed like a brave little cockleshell alone on the sea. Joanna went with him sometimes; she liked the feeling of being suspended in a great and shining blue world. She lay on the bow, feeling the gentle and persistent motion of the boat as it drifted on the smooth water, and shut her eyes against the sun as she listened to Alec's contented whistling.

The summer was like a long breath after the winter. The biggest debts were paid, and the fishing was good, so that they could order something new from the catalog once in a while. Alec worked hard and long, came home to go to bed early and get up at daylight. Joanna and the rest of the women picked water pails of wild strawberries that would bring a breath of summer sweetness into the next winter. They weeded their gardens, they guarded — unsuccessfully — their cucumbers from the young crows who had considered cucumbers legitimate booty since time immemorial. They cooked their husbands' meals, washed the blue shirts and scaly dungarees and thick socks worn under rubber boots. They sewed, and talked, and dressed in fresh prints to go to the dances in the clubhouse on Saturday night. Owen planned to go deep-sea fishing, now that the *White Lady's* massive marine engine had been installed, and he wanted Alec to go with him on shares, out to the Blue Ground and Jeffrey's Bank, far beyond the Rock. No idling for Owen this summer; he had to pay for that engine, which was one of the most expensive the Island had ever seen. Stephen Bennett shook his head over it, but the *White Lady* now had enough power in her to outrun every boat in the harbor, and to Owen, that justified any expense.

Joanna didn't begrudge the two or three days at a time when

Alec was out on the banks with Owen. Sometimes he came home unexpectedly to wake her out of a sound sleep and tumble money into her hands, his eyes tired and excited, his beard two days old. Having him come home, money or not, was always such a joyful experience that it was almost worth missing him for a few days.

And so the summer went on, in the way all Island summers went, punctuated with occasional fog or a bad blow. But always in between those times there was the sun-drenched brilliance, the glitter of dew, the sweet scent, the procession of dawns and sunsets that shook the heart and soul and could never be forgotten, so that years later you might say to someone who had been with you, "Remember the night the sky was—"

You could go on and tell as best you could of that unearthly blaze of red-gold and violet and of the evening star shining serenely in an apple-green lake above flames. You would find it had been remembered, not just this once, but many times. And the blackberry blossoms had been remembered too, and the song of the white-throat, and the way the gulls called over the harbor in the early morning.

There had been many summers that Joanna had thought were her happiest, but it was this one that she *knew* was the loveliest. When she looked back on it, it seemed to her that all the small and exquisite delights of an Island summer had been intensified for her and Alec; there was a deepening, a sharpening, a more luminous quality to all that they said and saw and did. Even their lovemaking shared it. And it seemed to Joanna that the Island must spread out from its very heart some mystic force that caused all these things.

The Island . . . As long as she never left it, there was nothing that could harm her, or hers.

The lobstering was always good after the end of Closed Season. After the dreamlike pace of summer, there was a quickening of tempo all across the Island, as the traps went overboard again and freshly painted buoys dotted the water in vivid bobbing shapes red and yellow, blue and white, orange and green—every conceivable combination of color.

The earliest morning silence was broken by the sound of engines in the harbor as the boats went out, one after the other. Between midmorning and noon, when the nip was driven from the air by a kindly warmth, the boats came back again, and Pete Grant went up and down the ladder to the car, cursing good-naturedly.

Fog hung around the Island persistently, melting away at noon each day, dissolving in luminous trailing tendrils. In the morning sometimes it was thick and opaque against the windows. Joanna awoke to stifle the alarm clock and prod Alec.

"It's thick o' fog. Going out today?"

He would yawn and stretch. "Hell, yes. What's a little fog?"

And by the time he was at the shore, lugging his bait box across the beach to his punt, the sun would be striking through the white wall. Alec had no hesitation about going out in the fog. He had learned well the ledges that made the Island waters treacherous to strangers, and the other men said he was half fish, half gull.

Toward noon Joanna walked down to the beach sometimes to wait for him. She would sit on the chopping block outside Nathan Parr's camp and watch him and Johnny mending her father's biggest seine with nimble, gnarled old fingers. Or if they had gone out to haul in their peapods—Johnny with his cat Theresa sitting proudly on the stern thwart—she sat cross-legged on the beach and scaled flat pebbles into the water, or watched the young gulls squabble and shriek over a dead fish.

One noon there were medricks skimming over the harbor, white and soft gray, with little orange feet, and forked tails like the swallows which lined the telephone wire these days, talking about their autumn migration across to Africa. The cries of the terns were shrill and tiny, and the gulls looked huge among them. Sometimes a single swallow shot out among the sea birds; he would be a minute and darkly shining speck, magnificently unafraid as he circled and banked and skimmed impudently under the very beaks of the big gulls, then soared high above them toward the sun.

Like a growing pulse then, there was an engine somewhere. Jud Gray. And the raucous hammering right behind it would be Marcus Yetton. And from the west side, the *Donna* was beating her way home, unfaltering and graceful across the jade water in the Island's shadow.

One by one the boats came in, stopped at the car, returned to their moorings; one by one the men rowed ashore to the beach. Marcus Yetton stopped to speak to Joanna, his bony face sulky and pale as usual.

"The little kids is sick, Jo. Susie's about crazy."

"What's the matter with them?" she asked in quick concern.

Marcus shrugged. "Hot, 'n runny nose. Won't eat nothin', not even fried bread 'n coffee, and that'd always put 'em on the mendin' hand before now."

Fried bread and coffee, thought Joanna, and the oldest child wasn't fourteen yet, and all the others under twelve. Coffee meant fisherman's coffee, strong and black enough to float the spoon.

"My mother will come down and look at the children," she told him. "She can tell Susie what the matter is."

"Thanks, Jo." He went up the beach with his discouraged walk.

She saw *The Basket* coming in, her shabbiness accentuated painfully by the clean brilliance of the September sea and sky. Joanna felt a twinge of sadness. No chance now of building a boat before cold weather, and there wasn't nearly enough in the money box for all the material, if he wanted to build his boat in the manner which had created the *White Lady*. The best thing was to take the money and try to pick up a good second-hand boat somewhere.

The *White Lady* followed *The Basket* around the point, the water flashing back from her bow in two glittering crystal wings. She was so lovely and so triumphant, her voice was so silken-strong that Joanna's heart sang at the sight of her. But at the same time she was thinking: Why should Owen have everything just a little better than anyone else?

That eight-hundred-dollar marine engine with an appetite for gasoline that would discourage anyone else—Owen had to have that, because nobody else on the Island could come up to it. Oh, he could pay for it easily enough. But why did those things come to him when he had only to lift a finger, while she and Alec seemed to have been rowing against the wind ever since they were married?

But she could answer that for herself, as she watched her husband and brother race their punts toward the beach. Owen had a convenient little gift for looking out for Owen. It would always get him what he wanted, whether it was a new boat or a girl. All the Bennetts had it in some degree; that was what made them as they were, had given them the Island and the life they lived on that Island.

But Alec didn't have it. Some day he would have a boat like the *White Lady,* and money in the bank, but he'd never do it alone.

God and the Island willing, Joanna would have enough iron for them both.

They came up the beach toward her, Alec smiling at her and Owen scowling. He hauled her roughly to her feet.

"Come up to the house and have a mug-up."

"But I've got dinner ready—"

"Forget it. Come on!" He linked arms with her, and Alec took the other side. For some unknown reason, Owen was in a difficult temper, so she didn't argue. They went up the road through the marsh that was turning red-brown at the edges now. The Bennett house stood high and white against the luminous aquamarine sky. Like the old Captain, who had built it, there was no nonsense in its straight New England lines, erected for service but somehow achieving an austere beauty. Now the dahlias blazed in a pagan fire of wine and scarlet and gold against the clapboards; and the sun-warmed perfume of the last white roses on the tall bush by the front door was anything but austere.

Alec broke off one to tuck behind Joanna's ear. Owen went on into the house, banging the screen door and kicking a chair out of the way. When Joanna and Alec came in, the whole family was assembled in the kitchen, having coffee and fresh doughnuts. And Owen stood back to the stove, legs set wide apart, chin out-thrust in the familiar attitude of black defiance.

"I waited a week before I said anything. I wanted to be sure," he said. "I've gone out every day, thick or no thick. I've gone out as soon as it was light enough to see my way past the harbor ledges." He looked around at the family, his face tightening. "If it just happened once or twice— well, Christ, that's bad luck! But when it happens *every goddam day*—"

"That's not luck, it's the Birds!" said Mark.

"You're damn right." Owen looked across at his father. "You know what folks have always said about us—that we could set traps in the dooryard and find lobsters in 'em. Even Stevie here, with his measly thirty traps, has made a good dollar this fall. But *me*—" His eyes burned in his furious dark face. "*Me!* They're hauling hell out of me. And the company's dunning me every mail for more money on that engine. If those bastards hadn't been sneaking around in the fog, trying to get even for the time I caught them in the shop, I'd have had that engine paid for now!"

"How do you know it's the Birds? How do you know it isn't somebody from Brigport?" Stephen asked quietly.

"What other son of a bitch would put the buoy inside the pot and sink it for good after they'd hauled it?"

Stephen set down his coffee cup, his face tightening and darkening as Owen's had done. Mark was on his feet.

"Let's go down there right now and clean up the lot of them, once and for all!"

"Sit down and stop waving your arms around." Philip spoke for the first time. "It wouldn't do any good to take them over. They'd have us up for assault and battery and everything else. But we've got to do something." He looked at his father.

"Yes, we've got to do something," Stephen said. "But it'll be something lawful. I'd like to tell you — God knows I've felt like it plenty of times — to go out and sink every last one of their pots. But I *won't.* It's just one family raising hell now. But if we make one move the wrong way, the whole Island'll be up to its neck in the worst mess of robbing and bedeviling and cutting off that's ever happened in Penobscot Bay." His voice was irrevocable; his eyes met Owen's steadily. "There'll be no way of stopping it. It'll go on for twenty years or more and every family on the Island, instead of just the Birds, will be ruined."

"And George Bird's got plenty salted away to keep traps in the water," Philip said. "Looks like we've got to keep on looking for proof. We're damn sick of that word, but we've got to take notice of it."

"I don't have to take notice of it!" Owen's nostrils were rimmed with white. "I'll be goddamned if I'll sneak around trying to catch them in the act! They're too smart for that, anyway, or they'd have been caught five years ago."

Stevie said mildly, "It's about time for the warden to be out here again. Can't we talk to him?"

Owen turned on him savagely. "What about my engine? Let 'em come and take it back again?" He gave them all one long black look, his mouth twisting. Then, without a word or a backward glance, he walked out of the house.

Stephen shook his head and went to stand by the seaward windows. Donna collected the coffee cups. Joanna joined her at the sink to wash and wipe the china, while the boys talked and argued behind them, Mark angrily demanding action.

"Owen's gone off to the woods, probably," Donna murmured. "He'll be back when he's walked it off. But I don't like it, Joanna."

"Those rotten —"

"I don't mean the Birds. It's Owen, and the way he's been about this boat. If anything ever happened to her, I don't know what he'd do." Donna shook her head. "He's got some notion that it'll be unlucky for the *White Lady* if he doesn't pay for every bit of her himself, without even borrowing, and if they ever tried to take that engine away . . ."

Her voice trailed off. The two women looked at each other for a long, apprehensive moment.

Joanna and Alec walked home across the meadow without speaking. Alec was lost in thought, and Joanna's mind seemed heavy with an unknown oppression. Steadily before the eye of her brain she saw Simon's thin-chinned face watching her, mocking her from narrowed smoky eyes that told her that there would never be an end to this. She knew it was a crazy fancy, but she couldn't escape it. When they spoke of the Birds, she thought of Simon alone.

Everything he did was aimed at her. Of that she was sure, and as she walked home through spattered shadow and sunlight, past the orchard where the apples hung like golden fruit from twisted boughs, she felt strange and alone. She wanted to shake this oppression, but there was no one to help her shake it.

No one but Nils, who was the only other person who knew what she knew about Simon. For an instant, as she glimpsed the gray Sorensen house among the trees, she wondered if she could find him and talk to him. But in a moment she knew it wasn't possible. And Alec was close beside her, his arm snug around her waist, he was saying close to her ear:

"What are you thinking about?"

Joanna tilted her head to look up at Alec. "Thinking about my husband. What else would I be thinking about?" she answered lightly, crinkling her nose in a grin.

36

THE APPLESAUCE HAD BEEN PUT UP, and the blackberry jam, and it was almost time to pick cranberries. The slopes of Sou-west point were wine and bronze with them. With everyone on the Island picking water pails full, there were still enough for Stephen to send two or three barrels across on the *Aurora B.* to a store in Port George. But up at the big house they were still making pickles, and Joanna awoke one day with an infinitely pleasant sense of leisure. For a few days, until Kristi was free to go cranberrying with her, she didn't have anything to do. And she was going to spend every available moment aboard the boat with Alec.

She'd go with him to haul in the bright blue mornings, and they'd go fishing in the quiet afternoons, when sea and sky melted together in a dim violet haze on the horizon, and the big cod swam lazily upward through the sun-shot water to nip at the black lobster on the hook. She and Alec would soak in gallons of sunlight, and talk sometimes or be peacefully silent, with only the gentle chuckle of the water against *The Basket*'s hull, and the infrequent voice of a gull floating overhead. They might see some ducks and old-squaws paddling contentedly along, too. . . .

It was a good prospect for Joanna to think about when she woke up in the morning. In this golden fall it seemed as if there'd never been anything but perfect harmony between her and Alec. Those days and nights at the trailing, stormy end of the last winter were something unreal. The Douglasses had crossed the choppy stretch and come into the slick, and except for the Birds and Owen life was almost completely satisfactory. And in another year there'd be the child. The circle would be complete.

For a few days after Owen's outburst, they saw little of him. Mark and Stevie were in and out, Philip dropped in, once Charles and Mateel came up from the Eastern End with young Charles, who was almost two now; square, determined, with his father's eloquent dark eyes and his mother's shy sweet smile and bronzy curls. Joanna was undemonstrative with him, but he loved her, he demanded to be held, and talked to her in remarkably clear language, except for the Trudeau way of dropping h's and adding them where they shouldn't be.

"Damned little Frenchman!" Charles said affectionately, piling his son onto his shoulder, to take him through the woods up to the big house to see his grandmother.

But Owen stayed away and Alec said he was working very hard, trying to send off a big payment on his engine. Philip reported that the rooster was so mild in the house that Donna thought he might be ailing, but Stephen said not to worry, but to be grateful for small mercies.

All in all, it seemed very peaceful. It was young Stevie, usually without much to say, who told Joanna it was almost too peaceful. "Like the way it is just before the wind starts up in a squall," he told her. "Know what I mean, Joanna?"

She laughed at him. "You're all Bennett. If there isn't any excitement, you try to make it. Owen's just decided to use common sense for a change, that's all. We'll get rid of the Birds sometime, but we can't just go and blast them off the face of the earth."

Stevie shook his head. "You feel it yourself, but you won't say so."

"Well, I'm not crossing any bridges till I come to them, Stevie lad. How are you getting along with your pots?"

"Bought some new ones this week from Nathan Parr." He scowled at her. "Only lobsters've gone down to twenty-five and that's something else I don't like much. Nathan Parr says it means trouble."

"You're a regular bird of ill omen, aren't you?"

Stevie said gloomily, "Just you wait."

One morning, when a small chop made a dancing edge of lace against the rocks, Joanna, out hauling with Alec, saw the *White Lady* idling in a tiny cove between jagged walls of rock. Gulls roosted on the cliffs and rose into the bright air in a cloud if a boat came too near; they were wheeling and shrieking above the *White Lady* when Alec and Joanna saw her.

Joanna looked past Alec's shoulder and said, "Has he any pots set in there?"

"Not that I know of, unless he's shifted some. Maybe he's fouled up in somebody's warp. That's a hell of a note." He turned *The Basket*'s wheel and she obeyed him, heading for the *Lady*. "That's no place to be stuck."

"What's he doing with that trap on the washboards? He *must* be fouled up."

Alec yelled to Owen above the roar of the water. "Need a hand?"

They saw Owen grin. "No, thanks!" He waved them away, but *The Basket* was closing in already and Joanna noticed, hardly realizing, that it was a blue-and-white buoy he'd caught with his gaff—George Bird's colors. "You don't want to come too close," he called to them cheerfully.

"Fouled up?" said Alec.

"Fouled, hell," said Owen merrily. "I'm having the time of my young life." He coiled the warp neatly, dropped the buoy into the trap, and fastened the button.

Alec said, "My God! What are you doing, you crazy fool?" He sunk his gaff into the *White Lady*'s washboard and held the two boats together. "Are you going to sink that pot?"

"I am!" He stripped off the thick white canvas gloves, wrung them out, and took out his cigarettes. "In a minute I'm going to sink it. No hurry. I've been sinking them all morning. Sunk some yesterday, and cut some off day before that."

Joanna wondered if the motion of the boat made her stomach feel so queer, and her hands so clammy. She said, "Owen, are you drunk?"

He laughed at that. "I'm not drunk, but I'm having a hell of a good time. I've wanted to do this for years, and it's a damn sight more fun than a quart or a woman."

Joanna sat down weakly on the engine box. Alec said, stiff-lipped, "How many you done away with?"

"I lost count, but I treated 'em all alike—Ash, Simon, and dear old Dad. I guess they've started missing 'em, too. I noticed they were going around the shore with a sort of bewildered look."

"Well, you'd better stop right now," said Joanna. "I don't blame you, Owen, but you know it's wrong—what'll Father say?"

Two spots of red burned suddenly on Owen's brown cheekbones as he leaned toward her. "I don't give a good goddam what he or anybody else says. That goes for you fellas, too. I've listened to this so-called common sense all my life and it never got me anywhere, so I'm using my own brand of sense."

"And you'll get us all into trouble!" Joanna was furious. "We were brought up to have some decency—not to be thieves and cheats and liars. And maybe *you* don't care how much mud gets thrown at your name, but the rest of us care!"

"Aren't you a cute little devil?" said Owen benevolently, and blew a mouthful of smoke into her face. Alec pushed her aside and sat down on the washboard.

"Look, Owen," he said confidentially, "you've had your fun, and got even, and scared them off for good, most likely. Now it's time to stop fooling around, before you go too far."

Owen grinned at the trap on the *Lady,* ready to be pushed overboard. "Did you ever sink anybody's traps, Alec? More damn fun!"

There was a clatter of an engine to the eastward of them, and all three turned to see Hugo's boat, black against the sun glare, heading straight for them. They were quiet, watching him come. Joanna glanced at Owen, feeling the same strangeness and distaste she knew when she saw him drunk, and then at Alec. His thin face was grim.

Hugo grinned at them merrily as he edged alongside *The Basket.* "Hell, what is this? Family conference?"

"Yeah," said Alec grimly. "Owen'll tell you all about it."

Hugo's eyebrows lifted. "Well, what is it? Christ, Jo, you look ugly as a basket of rattlesnakes."

"They're all ugly, Hugo my boy." Owen threw away his cigarette butt with a flourish. "They're ugly because I'm besmirching the honor of the family—or something."

"It all adds up to this," said Joanna crisply. "Owen's been cutting and sinking the Birds' traps. Talk about a Roman holiday!"

There was pure dismay in Hugo's answer. "Jesus, Ash and Simon were just going gunning when I left. They're down here on the point somewhere! And Ash had his father's field glasses. My God, Owen, if they saw anything this morning you'll be in court and there'll be hell to pay!"

"Listen, Owen, take the buoy and warp out of that trap, and set it again," said Alec. "It's time to stop being a damn fool."

Owen was white around the nostrils. "So they're sneaking around the point, are they? With glasses! Trying to see who's bothered their traps — well, I hope they see a hell of a lot!"

Hugo stared into the *Lady*'s cockpit. "Where'd you get all those lobsters? From their traps?"

"You bastard, I'm not a thief!" He swung around, caught the heavy trap in an instant, and slung it overboard. He threw back his head and looked up at the towering rocks and the screaming gulls. "If you're up there, you sons o' bitches, I hope you saw that! Sure I sunk your traps, and I'll sink every one I get my hands on, till you get the hell off this Island."

For once Hugo was speechless. Without a backward look he took his boat through the reef, and Alec followed him. Joanna lay flat on her stomach on the bow, and felt furious and sick and dismayed.

And Alec didn't whistle.

By nightfall the whole Island knew that George Bird had met Owen Bennett at the wharf, and told him that unless he paid for the damage to the Bird traps, the sheriff would be called; and when Owen looked at him with blank insolence, George told him, there in front of the store with half-a-dozen men and children listening in gape-mouthed amazement, that Ash and Simon had watched him through the glasses, and that when the time came Joanna, Alec, and Hugo would be subpoenaed as witnesses. They had been with him when he was seen to toss overboard and sink a Bird pot.

Owen looked down at him, brushed him aside as if he were a fly, and walked away. The story came to Stephen, who found Owen in the bait house, and asked for the truth. Donna, taking a chicken and some oranges down to Marcus Yetton's children, heard the story from a gasping and pop-eyed Annie. Only it was slightly distorted; Annie quoted Owen as saying he was going home to get his gun and shoot it out with the Birds.

That night Alec and Joanna walked up to the big house, feeling as if there had been a death in the family. "Worse than that," Joanna said tautly. "Murder."

"Everybody's with him," Alec said.

"Yes, but that doesn't make it any better. Owen'll never pay one cent and they'll drag him into court—" Her indignation choked her. "All these years they've been stealing, and then when somebody has the courage to hit back—the Birds set up a holler and you'd think they'd never done anything but good works."

Alec hugged her close to him. "You were mad with Owen this morning."

"Because he was so foolish, and I knew there'd be a stink, and hurt Mother—hurt all of us. But I don't blame him."

Alec stopped under the ghostly glow of the northern lights streaming over Brigport, and turned her face up to his. He kissed her hard, on her cheeks, her chin, her nose, her lips.

"Listen, honey," he said gently. "You've been wound up like a top all day. Relax, will you? If you go into that house with your nerves all tied up in knots, you won't be any help at all."

"It's those Birds," she whispered against his throat. "I hate them. You don't know how I hate them."

"Yes, I do, honey." He stroked her head. "I don't like 'em myself."

You don't know, she thought, with a long quivering sigh that made him tighten his arms. You don't know how I hate Simon. It was a hate that sickened her, like poison running in her veins instead of blood; hate and fear mixed together in deadly proportions. She didn't think of it often, only when something like this happened, and then it seemed to her that she could never feel free and happy and unafraid again.

Even in Alec's arms she didn't feel safe and comforted. She clung to him, there in the meadow with the surf roaring in Goose Cove, and the lights of the house looking down at them; she clung to him because he was hers, and she loved him. But he didn't know, he didn't understand how it was with her and Simon.

When they came into the kitchen, Nils was there. She hadn't seen him to talk with for a long time, and there he stood by the end of the stove, one foot on the hearth. He had come to try to persuade Owen to pay for the traps.

He smiled at Joanna and Alec, and she was suddenly conscious of a loosening of the iron band around her chest. "Hello, Nils," she said casually.

"Hi, Jo." That was all, that and his calm friendly blue gaze. But Nils was someone out of that long-ago time. Even if she never spoke to him about it, never again exchanged more than the time of day with him, she could always have the comforting knowledge that if she were to go to him and say, "Nils, I'm afraid. There's something evil in this and Simon's behind it all —" why, if she said that to Nils, he would nod, and understand.

37

IN THE MORNING SHE WAS ASLEEP when Alec got up, and he didn't call her. She didn't wake up until the October sun was a bright golden bar across her face, and downstairs someone was kicking the kitchen apart.

"Who's that?" she called sharply.

"It's me. Cripes, you gonna sleep all day?"

Me was Mark. Joanna said with some spirit, "Well, stop shacking the furniture and make some coffee. I'll be down in a minute."

When she came down, she found Stevie there too, long legs folded over the arm of a rocker, nose buried in *Popular Mechanics*. "Hi, Jo," he said vaguely, and went on reading.

"Isn't this a hell of a mess?" Mark said.

"Don't mention it till I've had some coffee. I can't face it right now. Go get a pail of water."

"Kind of high and mighty, aren't you?" But he went, and Joanna washed her face. Odd how you could feel so desolate and worn-out and look like a blooming rose, she thought, stopping in front of the mirror. Behind her, Stevie put down his magazine.

"Jo, we have to do something. I don't know what, but the three of us together ought to be able to figure out something."

Her mouth felt too tired to smile, but somehow it did. Stevie was so earnest and so eager. At seventeen he still kept his open-eyed interest and amazement at the world, and the shyness that the others had all left behind them at a very early age.

She said gravely, "Don't you think Owen should take his medicine?"

"Well, if it was just Owen, I'd say yes. But it's more than Owen; it's all of us. Father and Philip and Charles say there isn't anything to do, but I still figure we have to stick together."

Mark kicked open the screen and came in, splashing water from the door to the dresser. Stevie said nothing more, as they drank coffee together and toasted bread on a fork over the stove. The boys did away with half a jar of plum jam. They discussed everything but Owen until the dishes were washed and put away.

"Can I talk now?" Mark asked.

"Let's go out, it's easier to think that way." They went out to sit on the doorstep, the October sunshine mellow on their black Bennett heads, the nuthatches noisily at work in the woods. Mark passed around his cigarettes. There were no other preliminaries.

"Look," he said directly. "It's ten to one that there's some pots stacked up in the Bird's fish house with somebody else's name on 'em. They keep it locked tighter'n a drum all the time."

"Well?" Joanna said. "What good does that do us?"

"Well, if we was to see those pots with our own eyes, and could talk about it plenty if we had a mind to, George might find out that if he opens his mouth too big he's likely to put his foot in it."

His black eyes were shining, his mouth quirked with suppressed excitement. The battle-cry had been sounded and the Bennett flags were flying. And all the time that she was saying in her most skeptical, adult manner, "You've got a lot of *ifs* there, Markie boy," she was conscious of that excitement creeping into her own blood. She was going to be sensible for as long as possible, but already she knew she was on the brink.

"Never mind the *ifs*," Mark said bluntly. "Lookit, Jo. We're gonna get into that fish house and see for ourselves. And then we'll talk to George."

"And what are you going to say when he asks how come you got into his shop? It'll be breaking and entering."

Mark was triumphant. "That's all figured out. We'll find out if any of our pots are there—or anybody's that shouldn't be there—and then we'll get somebody to go in while the place is open some time."

"Who?" she gave him a sidewise look. "What do you think about it, Stevie? Don't you think Mark's kind of foolish in the head?"

Stevie flickered his lashes at her and grinned. "For God's sake," Mark said. "Stevie thought up the whole idea!"

"*Stevie?*" She caught her breath. "You thought up this breaking and entering business? Stephen Bennett, you're every bit as bad as Owen, out there sinking those traps yesterday."

"Mad at me, Jo?"

"I should be. I shouldn't sit here and listen to you. But you'd better tell me the rest of the mess."

"Mark talks better than me. Take over, Mark."

"We figured we could get Peter Gray, on account of him being a cousin to the Birds, even though he's not what you'd call proud of it. See, when George or the boys are working around the shore, they leave the shop open—you know how. Well, Peter comes along and says to George can he borrow a wrench or some other damn thing, and George, not thinking anything of it, says sure." Mark paused dramatically. In the brief silence two crows began to shriek at each other from the treetops.

"Well" said Mark, "I'm around somewhere too. Peter comes up from the beach and gives me the high sign, and we go in. George doesn't see us—or if he does, he's too far away to stop us without coming up from the shore. So we go in, Peter gets a good look at the pots, on account of I know just where they are, and we go out." He shrugged, and his grin held sheer delight. "Like it?"

"It's wonderful," she said dryly. "And it would probably shut George up for quite a while. But you have to break into the shop in the first place—"

"And find out where the pots are! Cripes, they aren't going to leave 'em right out in the face and eyes of anybody that might come in." Mark was disgusted with her stupidity. "If we know where the stuff is, we can show Peter."

"I see," said Joanna meekly. "But what if Peter won't do it? Maybe he won't be ready to get up and swear he saw those traps—after all, blood is thicker than water."

"He'll do it," Mark stated in dark tones. "Because he wouldn't want Kristi to know about him and Thea."

Stevie's sweet smile told her to mind her own business. "And don't ask what that is, because it happened about a hundred years ago, and Peter was drunk as a coot, and nobody else knows about it but Mark and me."

"I didn't want to know anyway," said Joanna. "When are you going to do all this? If you get caught, there'll be three Bennetts in court instead of just one."

"They won't know," said Mark, "and we won't get caught, because there'll be two of us inside to lift the stuff around if we have to, and somebody outside to watch."

Joanna felt a definite apprehension. "And who's going to watch?"

"You are. Well, me for the shore. Come on, Stevie." They stood up and she looked at them, tall and black-haired against the blue October sky, and thought how calmly they had brought her into their plot, and how calmly she was accepting it, when she should be telling them they were crazy, that she forbade it, that she'd have no part of it.

"Me," she said. "Nice you've got it all settled. So long, kids. Hope you bring in a lot of lobsters. . . . When does this little picnic come off?"

"Oh, tonight," said Mark, grinning down at her. "We'll be around and pick you up."

They went down the path to the gate, trying to throw each other in the tall timothy, their laughter coming back to her on the light wind. She had a moment of sharp astonishment as she thought: What am I letting myself in for? What will Alec say? And then she knew Alec wouldn't say anything, because he wouldn't know. It was rather shocking to realize she was going to deceive her husband, but there was nothing else to do. If the boys were right, and there were stolen pots in the Birds' fish house, the mess would end tomorrow, and the Birds would know at last that it was time to stop hauling other people's traps—the Bennetts' and the rest of the Island's.

She had no choice. She couldn't back out now.

After supper the seiners went out. Charles brought the *Sea-Gypsy* up to the harbor to pick them up; Alec, Philip, Tim and Peter Gray. Maurice was on the seining crew too this year, he came along from the Eastern End with Charles. At sundown they were all aboard, with food and coffee for a midnight lunch, full water jugs, and oilskins. The *Gypsy* headed out of the harbor across an apple-green and amethyst sea, and she wouldn't be back till long after midnight. If the ocean were willing, the dory and the seine dory and the big boat's cockpit would be brimming with silver — the silver of herring. On the beach the next day it would be divided among the crew, and the rest would be sold to the other men.

So far it had been a good autumn for herring, and it looked as if the men of Bennett's Island would have a good supply of bait salted away for the winter.

Joanna watched the *Gypsy* leave the harbor, and settled down to read. She avoided carefully any twinges of guilt about not telling Alec; and she refused to worry about the consequences of being discovered by the Birds. They wouldn't be caught. They couldn't be.

The boys came in shortly. "We're going to keep you company till ten o'clock," Mark announced. "Then we have to go home. But we thought you'd be kind of lonesome, with Alec out every night."

"You were nice to remember me," said Joanna innocently. "Want to play pinochle?"

It was not till the end of the second game that Mark said, "We came round by the shore to get the lay of things. The Birds were fixin' to go torching, around Goose Cove Ledge, I heard Ash tell Karl. They ought to be around there by now."

"Then let's go," said Stevie. His cheeks were flushed with excitement. So were Mark's, and Joanna's heart was pounding. But they were laconic as they put on their jackets and turned down the lamp.

"New batteries in my light," Mark muttered. "I've got a chisel too, but maybe we won't need it. There's a window you can open, and it's away from the road."

As they opened the door, Joanna stopped them and they all three looked at each other in the weird, dim light of the turned-down lamp. "What if we get caught, kids?" she asked them.

"You scared?" said Mark suspiciously.

Joanna laughed. "I'm having the time of my life!" She meant it. The boys' white grins flashed, and Stevie caught her arm in a hard and loving grip.

The night was very dark and the stars were tiny frosty pin-points;

and for once there were no northern lights. When they came out of the lane the wind from the harbor struck them, a bone-chilling, salty wind. The water was noisy on the ledges.

Though it was early yet, it might have been midnight. There were no lights to be seen, and for Joanna, the complete blackness made it a hundred times more dangerous; it looked as if everyone but the seiners and torchers were in bed, but you couldn't tell who might be wandering around in the darkness, you couldn't even hear a warning footfall on the path, when the sea was so loud on the shore.

Mark didn't dare use his light, and when they reached the black bulk of the Bird fish house, they stumbled through a knee-high growth of wild rose bushes and wild caraway, avoided by some miraculous sixth sense the old dory hauled up outside the door, and walked as stealthily as Indians around the other end of the shop, out to a small wharf and the edge of the harbor. The water slapped and chuckled at the spilings, and there was no shelter from the cutting wind. But the sound of wind and sea covered the slight noise of Mark's chisel, and he had the window loosened quickly enough.

Joanna held it up whlle the boys climbed in. There was one heart-stopping moment when Mark stepped in a paint bucket, but it was empty, and again the restless water had veiled the clatter. Joanna let the window down behind them and began her watch. The chances of discovery were small but they still existed. Hugging the tarpapered walls, she went around to the front, and crouched behind the old dory to listen. She was shivering, her teeth wanted to chatter, but it was neither fear nor cold.

Her mind raced at an unnatural speed, it seemed to her. What were the boys doing now? Had they found anything? Supposing they dropped a trap? Supposing the Birds couldn't find any herring and came back early? The thought sent her creeping around the fish house again, to scan the blackness that was the harbor; not complete blackness, for the sea had fire tonight, a greenish-white fire like luminous lace around the shore.

She looked cautiously through the window and saw the moving light. The boys' shadows were looming dark shapes on the walls as they examined the traps stacked against the front wall — in which, fortunately, there was no window. They were looking for burnt-in numbers and names that didn't belong to the Birds.

Time to go out front again. And it seemed to Joanna that she dropped down behind the dory just in time, that no darkness was thick enough to hide her, for someone was coming along the road from the shore.

Lying there uncomfortably in the chicory and beach peas, she recognized the step as it passed on the other side of the dory. Halting, almost limping — that was Nathan Parr, going home from his nightly game of cribbage with Pete Grant. He went on, unsuspecting of the eyes that strained to pick him out of the darkness, and Joanna breathed again.

Back to the little wharf . . . Above the roar on the ledges, she heard an engine. She knew, with a sick drop of her heart, that it was the seiners, coming back in the *Sea-Gypsy*. They hadn't found any herring. She tapped on the window and Stevie came quickly. The window stuck when they tried to raise it, and it meant some pounding, while the engine's pulse grew steadily louder.

Mark joined Stevie at the window. "For Christ's sake, what in hell are you two doing?" he demanded in a furious whisper.

"The seiners are coming back," Joanna hissed at him. "Get out of there, quick! They can see that light of yours when they get to the wharf."

"I guess we've got enought to go on. Climb out, Stevie." As each one of the boys dropped softly to the beach stones, all three were motionless for a moment, listening. For an anguished interval the window wouldn't come down again, and when it did, after frenzied tugging and much cursing on Mark's part, it came with a crash that convinced them each pane had been broken. It was too risky to use the light, and they passed their hands quickly over the window, expecting at any moment to sever an artery on a jagged edge of glass.

The *Sea-Gypsy* was coming into the harbor, her masthead light swaying as she rolled in the tide rip, when they slipped between the Birds' fish house and the Grays', and came out into the road — to collide with Jud Gray.

"Hi, Jud," Stevie said in a smooth young voice. "We've been watching for the seiners — here they come now."

"Yep! Thought I'd go down to the shore and see how much they got. Can't be a hell of a lot, when they're back so early." He peered at them. "Oh, it's Jo you've got with you — thought it was another boy!" They laughed obligingly with him about his mistake, and went on. Not until they reached the well did they dare to speak.

"Two minutes earlier and he'd have heard that window drop," said Joanna. "Well, what did you find?"

"Wait till we get to the house," Mark warned her, but the triumph in his voice was hardly hidden. She knew then that they must have found enough to stop the Birds. In all these years there had never been one atom of proof; men had guessed that the locked fish house might hold a few traps lifted from another man's string, but no one had ever found out anything. They were smooth and skillful, their stories were always plausible, there was never a chance for conclusive evidence.

"Not a goddam one of those traps under the tarp belonged to a Bird," Mark told her when they reached the house. He stood with one foot on the stove hearth, watching her make coffee; Stevie lounged in the rocker with his legs over the arm, reading *Popular Mechanics* as if he hadn't been out of the chair all evening.

"Not a goddam one," Mark repeated, almost admiringly. "Three of them were Owen's. And there was a good one, almost new, belonged to Jud Gray. Wait till Peter sees *that!* And a couple Karl Sorensen thought he lost in the last gale o' wind we had." He blew out a long mouthful of smoke. "Two of Marcus Yetton's — can you beat that? Marcus with all those kids, and almost too dumb to make a living anyway."

Joanna glanced down at Stevie's absorbed face. "You must feel pretty proud of yourself and your idea, Stevie."

"Huh?" He winked. "Oh, Mark was the skipper. He did all the work. Did you see this old auto engine a fella made into a battery charger?"

When Alec came in, there was coffee and pie on the table, two boys reading magazines, a wife knitting tranquilly on a new sweater for him. He looked with pleasure on the scene as he warmed his cold hands over the stove and kicked off his boots.

"I guess you didn't miss me tonight, sugar," he said cheerfully. Joanna tilted back her head to smile at him from luminous dark eyes above the deep, lovely color in her cheeks.

"No, darling. To be truthful, I didn't miss you at all."

38

IT WAS QUEER, THE ISLAND AGREED, how George Bird stopped growling about Owen Bennett. Just stopped talking about those traps Owen'd cut off, and never said another word about it to anybody.

The Island waited in breathless anticipation for the sheriff to arrive, but he didn't arrive. In fact, nothing at all happened, and by the time November blew down across the bay, the Island stopped wondering. The incident was closed, and no one ever knew why.

But Donna had begun to show the worry and strain of those days. She couldn't sleep, and her headaches became more frequent and more painful. Early in November, Charles, Philip, and Stephen won out by sheer force of numbers, and sent her ashore to see a doctor.

At the very last minute, Joanna went with her. Alec had two good days' hauling before she went, and made her take most of the money. He wanted her to go, he said; she deserved a little spree. As the *Aurora B.* went around the point, out of the harbor, Donna turned to Joanna with her gray-blue eyes shining, and said, "Your father and I think of Alec as one of our own boys. I couldn't have asked anyone better for you, Joanna."

Joanna, standing up against the mast in her trench coat and red beret, smiled and didn't answer. She knew she couldn't ever tell her mother the little fear that nagged her constantly, even when she was happiest with Alec. Those nights when he went to play poker frightened her, though they were few and far between. And when she had been going through his corduroys before she washed them, she'd found a pack of cards, and remembered with a little chill around her heart what Margaret had said. "In love with cards, he was . . ."

Most of the time she could shrug off these little pricks. Margaret had talked of gambling fever as if it were a disease, but you couldn't call Alec a gambler. He played solitaire a lot, at home, and sometimes he and Owen and Sigurd matched pennies, just for fun; and she knew Hugo carried dice in his pockets. But Alec was all right. She repeated it stubbornly to herself now. *Alec is all right.*

She looked up at the gulls circling above the tawny cliffs of Tenpound, against a sky of purest turquoise, and the crystal cold of early November flowed against her face. One thought followed the first; there was something else she would rather die than admit to any one of the Bennetts. She and Alec had been married for two years, the times were prosperous, and yet there was nothing put by. But whose business was it but hers and Alec's? She tilted her chin at the world. There was plenty of time to build new boats and have babies.

She and her mother didn't go back to the Island the next boat day, after all. A storm blew up — one of the worst in the year — and it was two weeks before there was a fair chance over on the *Aurora B.* Stephen called up the rooming house where most of the Islanders stayed when they were ashore, and told Donna not to try to come back; she had plenty of money, she wasn't to be afraid to spend it. Alec told Joanna the same. He sounded very cheerful, despite the fact that the gale was probably tearing his traps to pieces.

When they finally went home, the weather was soft and gray, like a day in early spring. The sky had the lustrous color of pearls, the water was silvery, breaking lightly against the bow in little curls of white. Joanna, watching the dim blue shape of Brigport rise on the horizon, felt her heart beat faster. She was going back to Alec, and the thought of being alone with him again, of feeling his arms around her, was unutterably lovely and exciting.

Charles was at Brigport to sell his lobsters when the mailboat put in there, and they went home with him in the *Sea-Gypsy,* leaving the *Aurora B.* to follow along in her staid fashion. Charles stowed their bags and packages in the cabin, spread his oilclothes over a box for his mother to sit on, and told Joanna to take the wheel. She felt like singing at the top of her voice as she headed the *Gypsy* out of the harbor. This was heaven, flying toward home and Alec in a big white boat that might have been winged, so lightly did she skim over the silvery water. The gulls were gray and silvery and white, too.

Charles stayed in the lee of the cabin, talking with his mother, until Tenpound loomed before them. He came to the wheel. "Tide's going, Jo. Take her around the other side of Tenpound."

"So you can wave at the Cove!" she said laughing. "Well, Cap'n Charles, what have you boys been doing in all this stormy weather?"

Charles grinned down at her. "Playing poker," he said candidly. "Longest poker game in the history of the Island — we played every goddam night for almost two weeks."

Alec, too? The words came to her lips, but she didn't say them. Instead she said lightly, "What does Mateel say about it?"

"Nothing. She knows better. Besides, I get out when it goes too high. Wife and kids to support."

"Kids?" She stared at him, and his black eyes danced. "You mean — when is it?"

"March." They were passing the Cove now, and he waved at the houses above the bank, on the chance that Mateel or young Charles might be looking out. "Maybe it'll be a girl this time, huh?"

Joanna looked straight ahead at the *Gypsy's* forepeak against the line of gray sea and sky. She didn't know why she felt so cold and empty inside. So Charles could afford to have babies and play poker too — because he got out when the stakes went too high. And she knew, with a sudden wave of bitterness, that she needn't ask him about Alec. Alec would stay in till the last card was played.

Charles said mischievously, "I'd almost think you and Alec would be about ready to start a family. Been married two years now, haven't ye?"

She looked squarely into his dark merry eyes. "Tell me something. Alec's been playing, hasn't he? How much has he lost?"

"The son of a gun just about won the pants off the rest of 'em! *Lost!* Maybe a little at first, but then he got a winning streak, I never saw anything like it, Jo!"

"You sound as if you admired him."

"Well, we've always played a little poker on the Island, but I've never seen a guy yet who could charm those cards like Alec did. Of course it was luck — pure luck — but it was something to see, just the same. He cleaned out Owen and Hugo and Sig. Maurice was like me — he got out while he could."

"Charles," she said levelly. "Do you think Alec is a gambler?"

Charles said slowly, "He's got it in him to be one, Joanna. But

I'll tell you — it'll be a good while before we have a spell of poker like this one again. It was just the goddam weather, nothing to do, nowhere to go, and Alec missed you like hell, too."

She wondered what Charles would say if she told him Alec's family had sent him to the Island to get rid of him. She wondered what she would say to Alec when she reached the house. And she wished with an aching intensity that she hadn't left the Island at all.

Almost everybody at Bennett's Island was out to haul, on the first good day after two weeks of wind, but Stephen was in, and so was Alec. Joanna reached the top of the ladder and was in his arms, her face was against his neck, but she felt none of the happiness she had expected to feel. Rather it was a sadness, a weariness.

When they reached the house and came into the kitchen, his arms went suddenly and tightly around her again, holding her close against him. His face was taut and stern, his voice harsh. "My God, I've missed you, Jo. Don't ever go away like that again."

She felt tenderness flow over her in an infinitely sweet wave. Oh God, he needed her so. She shouldn't have left him, without her he was a ship without a rudder. "No, I'll never go away from you again," she promised with passionate honesty. "Never. As long as I live."

Alec didn't want to go out to haul that afternoon, but Joanna hardened her heart and told him he must. "When was the last time you went out?" she demanded.

"You think I've been out in this williewaw we've been having?"

"That just proves you can't afford to miss today," she said triumphantly, and he tried to pull her down to his knee. But she wouldn't be pulled.

"Time for you to be going to the shore," she said.

"You're a bossy little devil," he muttered, as she set his boots down by his chair. "But I'm crazy about you. And I'll be back."

"And I'll be waiting," she promised, standing just out of his reach. Her eyes glinted and shone, her mouth teased him.

"I'm not going out there this afternoon," he said between his teeth.

"Yes, you are, my little man!"

For an instant he stared hard at her, his eyes narrowing. Then he burst into laughter. "So you're getting tough with me! Gunnar's going to do a little prodding, is he? Well, maybe I need it." He chuckled as he pulled on his boots, and Joanna felt slightly annoyed. It was going to be hard to handle things if he only laughed at her.

When he had gone whistling down the path, she tidied the kitchen and went down cellar for a soul-satisfying look at her shelves of canned stuff. It meant plenty to eat this winter, anyway. But they needed heavy clothing and shoes, right away. Frowning, she went upstairs again and into the sitting room. No use to take the money from Alec's hauls; and she didn't want to charge the things, when they'd just got the other big bill paid up. There was nothing for it but to make up an order and pay for it in one fell swoop from the money box. There wouldn't be any new boat this winter, anyway.

She felt tired and dispirited as she took the box from the desk. This was no way to live, forever worrying about money, knowing that if you spent it on winter clothes, there'd probably be an emergency — some new part for the engine, new trap stuff after a storm, a sudden sickness.

Well, she had made up her mind. She would talk to Alec about his card-playing when he came home, she thought, as she opened the money box. She looked with some pride at the receipted bills, and lifted them out.

There was nothing else in the box. There was not even a handful of change.

When Alec came home, she faced him. She forgot to be gentle or tactful. Her voice was chill.

"Alec, where's the money that should be in the box? Where's the money you won playing poker while I was gone?"

His cheekbones glowed scarlet, and his lips were stiff. "I squared up some bills, and I got some new trap stuff. I lost almost a dozen traps in the storm."

"And how much money did you lose, before you started winning? Plenty, wasn't it? You gave me all you had in your pockets before I went away, so you took the boat money to play poker with, and lost every cent of it, didn't you?" She walked up and down the kitchen. She had never been so furious with Alec before. She felt as though she hated him, as if he had caught himself in a trap and pulled her into it too, and then smashed her every effort to get them out of it.

He stood by the stove watching her, rigid and straight, his eyes like green-brown stone. Yes, he was furious too, because she'd saved up those things to say to him. And maybe if she'd said them before, they'd be a little better off. She stopped in front of him.

"Alec, it's coming winter and we haven't a cent. All you got to-day was enough to pay for your gas—you couldn't even get around the Island to haul because your engine broke down off Sou-west Point and you had to be towed in. And she's going to break down all winter, isn't she?"

"All I need is a new connecting rod—"

"You're always needing new connecting rods, because you need a new engine. And how long does it take to put in a new connecting rod? It means you lose a day, doesn't it?" She began to pace again, too enraged to stand still. "And how are you going to send off for a new connecting rod when we haven't got any money? I suppose you can go out and win another poker game!"

"My God, Jo, what makes you take on like this?" He followed her, trying to turn her toward him. "I've never seen you like this before!"

"But I've felt like this, lots of times!" She faced him, shoulders rigid under his hands, head flung back. "Alec, you're not slow-witted—you're supposed to be smart! Don't you see that we can't live forever from hand to mouth? I've struggled and saved, and got those bills paid off, and the minute I turn my back you throw away enough money to dress us for the winter and buy new connecting rods and anything else we need in a hurry—Alec, can't I *trust* you?"

Her eyes searched his face, the face she had loved from the very beginning; her lips had traced every line and bone in it, her hands had lain against his cheeks, had pushed his hair from his forehead; but yet, as he looked at her, it was the face of a stranger. And she knew, with the terrible clarity her anger had given her, that she had read into that face something which wasn't there and would never be there: *strength*.

"Joanna," he said quickly, and she knew he was holding his mouth steady only by an effort. He was unhappy, but it was no good. He couldn't be anything else but what he was. And suddenly she was terribly tired.

She turned away from him and his hands fell from her shoulders. "We're broke, Alec. We've got food in the cellar, and the clothes we stand in, but you need new rubber boots, don't you? And woolen socks, and heavy work pants, and flannel shirts, and all the rest of it." Her voice went back to him wearily, where he stood behind her. "You need a lot of new stuff for winter hauling, but even if you had it, it wouldn't do you any good, because after a couple of weeks of rough water *The Basket*'ll start her caulking and leak like a sieve, and you'll have her on the beach for a week, fixing her up again. Then there'll be a storm, and you can't haul anyway. Then you'll go out, and break a connecting rod. And lobsters are going down, Alec. Did you know that? How much were they today?"

He answered reluctantly, "Twenty-three cents. Jo, listen. I can't stand having you like this! What do you want me to do, honey? What can I do? You know this lobstering business — there's times when everything goes to hell. But we've always got along, Jo."

That made her mad again. "Got along! Yes, we've always got along, Alec, and that's about all! If you broke a leg tomorrow, we'd have to go up to our necks in debt. If *The Basket* sank in the harbor next week, we'd go to hell fast enough!"

"What do you want me to do?" He asked her steadily, and once more they faced each other, white-lipped and stony-eyed.

"You can't afford to play poker," she told him. "Not ever. Not every night for two weeks, not one night in two months. You can't afford to even touch a pack of cards, Alec Douglass, and you'd better burn the pack you've in your pocket right now!"

"It happens that I cleaned out Owen and the rest last week. They're looking for their chance to win back."

"Let them keep on looking."

"I've got to do it, Joanna. Good God, your own brothers — I've got to keep straight with them."

"They can afford to throw their money away, but you can't." Her chin went up. "They can afford to do a lot of things we can't do. Charles can have children. Owen can build himself a decent boat —"

"I've had about enough of this!" said Alec furiously. He strode away from her and took his mackinaw from its hook. Joanna folded her arms and watched him.

"That's right," she remarked approvingly, "go down to the shore and match pennies in Sigurd's fish house, and you won't have to listen to me. You'll never have to listen to the truth as long as you can run away from it. But you can't run away from this, Alec. Give the boys a chance to win their money back," her voice was quiet now, almost gentle, "and then they'll give you a chance to win back, and it'll keep up like that forever — maybe. Until the time comes when you have to choose between poker and me."

He was halfway to the door; instantly he turned, and came back toward her, his eyes wide with furious unbelief. "What's that you said? *Joanna* — " He put out his hand, almost gropingly, and her heart quailed within her. He looked stricken. She could have taken him in her arms, but she kept them folded tightly across her breast, and sweetly, sharply, through her loving pity ran a bright ray of triumph. This, then, was it. She had known there was something that would reach him.

"You heard me," she said. "I won't live like this forever."

He reached for her then and pulled her into his arms, buried his face against her hair. "You darling," he muttered. "Joanna — my God, Joanna — " His voice was quick and unsteady; pressed against his chest, she felt his hard breathing, and thought in sudden panic that he was crying.

She forced her head upward, her own eyes flooding, and caught his face between her hands as he said, still in that queer voice, "You sweet little brat, you know damn well you couldn't live without me!"

Alec went out laughing.

Joanna went upstairs and flung herself face down across the bed. The coverlet was cool against her burning cheeks, but there was nothing to cool the burning ache she felt inside. It was an ache compounded of grief and anger; which was the strongest, she didn't know. She did know that to argue with Alec was to argue with the east wind; to pin him down to anything, to make him listen and understand, was to try to catch one of the humming birds that flickered on lightning wings around Donna's honeysuckle.

Margaret had been right after all when she said gambling was a disease. It was a fever that came back again and again, and nothing was strong enough to stop it, not even love like the love she and Alec carried for each other. *Nothing.* She rolled over and looked up at the ceiling with widening eyes. Wasn't there anything in the world to knock sense into him again, and make of him the man he should be?

Alec was kind-hearted and gentle, he loved little, young things that were small enough to be protected. Foolish downy infant gulls, children. She had seen him pick up young Charles after a tumble, and wipe the button of a nose as carefully as any woman. Alec loved children; he should have some of his own. A baby that must be clothed and fed; a helpless baby whose very life depended on him — surely even a gambling fever must give way to that.

But we can't afford to have a baby, thought Joanna, looking at the ceiling. And then she said aloud, very clearly and very positively, "We can't afford *not* to have a baby."

39

BUT THERE WAS NO BABY. Alec was too stubborn, too canny.

In the lilac dusk of a soft April day, Joanna sat on a rock in the little cove, her knees drawn up to her chin, the mild night wind stirring her hair, the green smells of the Island spring lifting to her nostrils, and decided to leave Alec.

It was not a shocking decision. She realized that she had probably been thinking about it for a long time, all through the winter that lay behind her now, that winter of fret and strain and worry, of quarrels that left her exhausted but still raging. They didn't leave Alec like that, because he didn't quarrel. He only caught her in his arms. And she hadn't known, till that ghastly winter, that she'd ever strike his hand away.

But it wasn't kisses I wanted, she mused now, hugging her knees and listening to the soft sighing breath of the sea below her. But I never could make Alec see it. He thinks if we stay lovers, that's enough.

But how could you stay lovers when there was never a moment's peace, never an instant when you weren't worrying — when fear followed you deep into sleep and then you dreamed? She thought of those dreams now; there was one that came often, especially after *The*

Basket had to be towed in so many times. She would awaken crying, night after night, because she had seen too vividly the small, gray boat drifting helplessly toward the black ledges of Sou-west Point, battered brutally by winter surf that broke it into matchwood; and Alec's body lying on the shore with the gulls wailing overhead.

Sometimes there was no body or boat, only an upturned punt floating aimlessly on the water.

She couldn't tell Alec about her dreams, when he woke up and tried to draw her into his arms. It wouldn't have helped anything. She couldn't tell him about the dreams of bitter cold, or hunger. He would have laughed at her and said, "We're getting along, aren't we?"

Yes, getting along because of the cellarful of canned stuff (it was empty now), and the short lobsters, and the ducks shot around the shore. And warm because she sacked home driftwood from the lonely coves on the west side, so they wouldn't have to burn too much of their precious cordwood. He had the heavy workclothes he needed, bought one article at a time, when he had a lucky streak and won a lot. He certainly wasn't making enough, lobstering, to buy much. And she had clothes enough to do; it wasn't as if she went without. But her things were on the shabby side.

It had been a lonely winter too. Gradually she had stopped going up to the big house. The frequent storms made a good excuse. It wasn't so easy to go up there and be her confident self when she knew what they were thinking, though they never gave any sign. The whole Island knew that Alec Douglass loved playing cards more than anything else in the world; that he was either playing because his luck was good and he couldn't stop, or playing because his luck was bad and he expected it to turn at any time.

Owen had come to her once in February, while Alec was out in the harbor pounding ice off his boat. Owen hadn't come to the house for a long time, neither had any of the other boys, except Philip occasionally, or Stevie. She'd been fixing salt fish for dinner when Owen walked into the kitchen, big and handsome and prosperous in a new mackinaw and moleskin breeches.

"Why haven't you come before?" she demanded.

"Sorry, Jo. I'd like to come in oftener, but—"

"But what?" She faced him, hands on her hips. "What's eating you, Owen Bennett?"

"Well, I came this morning because I saw Alec down at the shore."
He looked oddly uncomfortable. "I might's well tell you first as last.
Alec don't think much of me these days. Don't think much of any
of us guys."

"Why?"

"Well, Jo, it's hard to say this to a kid sister, specially when I
thought she'd married a fella who could give her more to eat than
salt fish and potatoes all the year round, and keep her in shoes at least."

She blushed furiously, conscious of the battered saddle shoes she
had worn for two years now. They were getting thin in the soles, and
the cold struck through them when she went out. But she'd thought
Alec needed new rubber boots more than she needed shoes.

She tilted her chin at Owen. "Yes, go on," she said dangerously.

"Now don't get mad with me, darlin' mine!" He grinned at her
affectionately. "You see, we been playing poker with Alec off and on
for a couple of years, and never thought much about it. But it seems
like this winter Alec's gone kind of crazy on the subject."

She nodded, and he went on. "Well, all of a sudden we came
to and found out how things were going. That boat of his is no better
than paper—she can't stand anything at all. And he hasn't been tend-
ing his gear, making up for pots he's lost, so what used to be a pretty
sizable string that brought him in a good dollar has dwindled down
quite a bit."

So they were talking like this about Alec now; it was there for
the whole Island to see, the way he was going to pieces.

"So we figured he couldn't afford to play, and we been edging
him out. Lots of times when he felt like it, we haven't played, so as
to discourage him." He stared meditatively at the cigarette smoke.
"But it's a funny thing about gambling. It takes hold of a man. Looks
as if Alec fought it pretty good when he first got here, and then it
snuck up on him."

She said from a dry throat, "I shouldn't have gone ashore that
time with Mother."

"Maybe you're right. I don't know, Jo. But after a while Alec
began to guess what we were doing, and he didn't like it. He's got
to play, like a man has to have his liquor. Me, for instance. Only,"
his smile flashed, "I can afford it. I haven't got a boat that needs a
lot of fixing, or a broken-down string of traps—or a wife."

"What's a wife supposed to do?" she asked lightly.

"Just hang on, I guess, Jo. We're doing our part, and maybe the craving'll wear off, if there's nobody to encourage it." He rumpled her head with a big, kindly hand, and the rough affection of the gesture made her eyes sting. "We're looking out for you the best way we can, Jo. Well, I'll move along. Alec ought to be back pretty soon, and he won't take kindly to meeting me here."

She went to the door with him, hating to see him go, yet wanting to be alone with her shame and her bitterness. "But Alec's *good*," she protested. "You know that, Owen. He's always been fond of you! But it's just as if he wasn't himself."

"Sure, Jo, you don't have to explain. He'll come along all right." Owen went away. Alone, she paced the floor, facing her despair at last. In this moment there was no way out. But she had reached the bottom of it, she thought, and now she must go up again. Owen had said the craving would wear off, if it weren't encouraged. . . .

Well, it hadn't worn off. In the bad spell that came in March, when the wind blew constantly for almost a month, day and night, and Joanna never left the house except to wander along the west side looking for wood, Alec was out almost every night. What he was playing with, she didn't know, because he wasn't going out to haul and bringing in any money. And she didn't know with whom he was playing, either. Sometimes he said he was going to the clubhouse to play pool, and from the sitting room windows she could see the light among the trees. He usually didn't come home until long after she had gone to bed.

She had new shoes at last, though; sturdy, stout shoes such as she had always worn in the Island winters. It was Nils who was responsible for that; Old Faithful, she thought with a rueful twist of her mouth as she sat in the cove in the soft April dusk, this night when she had decided finally to leave Alec.

She had seen little of Nils during the winter, until one night when she sat alone in the kitchen reading. He came in, as fresh and ruddy and yellow-haired as ever, except that his face was set in leaner, more mature lines. He brought two balls of marlin with him. He wanted her to knot some trapheads for him, he said. Kristi always did it for him, but she was so busy working up at the big house these days, she didn't have time. Nils was so simple and unembarrassed about it that it was easy for Joanna to accept the job. After that, there were always trapheads to knit. It took her two or three days, after her hands toughened up, to knit up a ball, and there was two dollars' worth of heads in it.

It was Nils, too, who told her where Alec found his card partners these days. It was the night he first brought the marlin.

"I noticed Alec in the clubhouse when I came up the lane," he said mildly, "playing pool with Ash and Simon."

The words caught her like a blow to the stomach. Her eyes never shifted from Nils, but he must have caught a movement of her lips, a narrowing of her lids, a change of color. He said instantly, "I wouldn't think anything of it, Jo. They just dropped in, most likely."

"Most likely," she repeated. But there was no one else on the Island who would play with Alec . . . none of her brothers or her friends . . .

She had wondered afterward if Nils were trying to warn her, somehow, thinking she could do something. But what was there to do? Could you catch the east wind and tie it in a sack? Could you keep Alec from going his own way? No more than the east wind.

And now it was April, and she was going to leave Alec. She had felt for a long time as if she were caught in a trap, and the steel jaws had tightened on her when she found out about the Birds. All the revulsion she had ever known for Simon was intensified now. If she met him in the road she felt a sick inarticulate rage. He came into her dreams at night; she awoke in the morning wanting to fight and knowing with utter despair that there was nothing she could openly fight against.

And now she was worn out, and there was nothing else to do but go away. She couldn't live like this, with a man to whom she was nothing but the woman he slept with. It sounded ugly, but it was true. He wanted to kiss her, to caress her and make love to her, but he didn't want to listen to her when she tried to make him understand what was happening to them.

She would tell him all that when he came home tonight, and she would be cool and dispassionate and final, and tomorrow she would go away on the boat.

Where she would go, she wasn't sure. The Island would buzz

louder than it had ever buzzed, but she wouldn't be there to hear. The thought of escaping filled her with a strange relief. She had struggled and fought for so long now. It was good to give up.

She put her forehead down on her knees and let the Island breathe softly around her. The sea crept quietly up the little pebbly beach, edged with white fire in the dark, and chuckled around the rocks. There was a scent of growing things in the little cranberry bog behind her, and of damp earth. The darkness was a hushed but real thing, soft as a breath.

How long she sat there she didn't know, but her legs cramped when she slid down off the rock and went up to the house. She lit a lamp in the kitchen, and sat down to read until Alec came. Sometimes he stayed out all night, and came in with his face set against her, already on the defensive. After tomorrow he wouldn't have to feel like that, because there'd be no one to set his face against.

It was curious how alone she felt as she sat there with her book in her lap. But it was not the aching loneliness she had lived with for so long. Everybody, even the family, seemed far away in little worlds of their own. And as she waited here, in her own little world, she must have slept, for suddenly she was waking up with a start, her heart pounding. and Alec was coming through the door.

The lamplight was a sickly thing, with the spring dawn flushing the sky outside the windows. She sat up, rubbing her cramped neck, and her book dropped to the floor. The fire was out. Without a word Alec went to the stove and began to put kindling into it. His face was a queer gray color, his eyes strange. She watched him calmly. He had been staring at cards too long, she thought.

He got the fire going and put the teakettle on to heat. Still there was silence in the kitchen; he seemed not to realize she was there. Joanna wondered how to begin to tell him about her decision. Perhaps she had better wait until he had coffee. He looked as if his head ached terribly. She stood up and went over to the sink to wash the sleep out of her eyes.

"Joanna," he said, and the strangeness of his voice turned her around. He came toward her, so the light from the east window fell full upon his face, and she caught her breath.

"Are you sick, Alec?" she asked him swiftly.

"No." His eyes were bloodshot, and there were deep lines carved from his nostrils to the corners of his mouth. "No, I'm not sick, Joanna. Just not crazy any more."

She didn't know what to say to him, so she waited. His words came from his throat with a harsh weariness. "I'm not playing poker any more. Not any game of cards. Remember when you told me to burn the pack I carried?"

He went back to the stove, took the cards from his pocket, and dropped them in. She saw the flames leap up, then he put the cover on again and came back to her. "I'm through, Joanna," he said.

She put her hands on his arms and looked at him, trying to read what lay behind the gaunt weariness of him. He looked ten years older than the Alec she'd married, and this was still a new Alec; neither the lover, nor the man in the delirium, but someone else.

"What's happened, Alec?" she asked him quietly, and he shook his head.

"I've told you." A gleam of the old smile struggled through. "Turned over a new leaf, if you want to call it that. Let's have some breakfast. Then I'm going to bed for a few hours before I go out to haul."

"The boat's on the beach—"

"Where she always is, poor critter. I'll go out in the peapod, if I have to. *But I'm going to haul.*"

They ate breakfast together in the early morning, with the sun coming up over the trees and setting the dew afire with diamonds in the grass. It was an odd and silent meal. He ate like a man starved, but his strangeness held, and Joanna couldn't speak. Somehow there was nothing to say, not even the most casual remark, and all the things she had planned to say were far out of her throat's reach. She couldn't say them now. Not right away.

Breakfast over, Alec went upstairs. "Call me about half-past nine," he told her. "Looks like a good day to haul." The door shut behind him. Joanna, clearing the table, knew that whatever had happened, she couldn't go away today. She would have to wait a while, until she had things straight in her head again.

40

THE SPRING CRAWL CAME, and the Island was plunged into a fever of activity. New traps of yellow wood slid overboard from the washboards, set close around the Island now, among the rocks where the kelp grew the thickest. After the long winter, when the lobsters went out to sea and lay in the mud at bottom to keep warm, some unknown instinct sent them toward the mainland to spawn, and the men on the outer islands made good on this mass migration.

The Island was up and working at dawn these days. There was a joyful stir everywhere; the women felt it, and turned their houses almost inside out to let the sunshine reach every corner. The children felt it, and Miss Hollis found them more than usually fiendish to handle in school.

The hauls were good and the weather fine. The price was not as high as it had been a year ago. Some of the older men worried. It wasn't natural for prices to stay down so consistently, they said. Jud Gray, always a worrier, said that if they didn't come up again in the fall, he'd have to move off to the mainland. It was expensive, keeping his girls in high school.

Alec had never offered to tell Joanna what had happened that strange night, and she didn't ask him any questions. He worked hard, much harder than he had ever worked before; a twenty-four hour day seemed too short for him. He kept *The Basket* on the beach, giving her the most thorough overhauling of her career, while he hauled his traps from a peapod. It was cruelly hard work, and long. He came home to his dinner, handed over his entire receipts to Joanna, and went down to the shore to work all afternoon on *The Basket* and bait up for the next day. At night he slept like a dead man, but he was up again at dawn. Once Joanna tried letting him sleep — he was driving himself too hard and he needed the rest. But he was furious when he woke up.

"I can't waste time sleeping!" he told her impatiently. Then he smiled at her frown and kissed her hard, and strode off to the shore without any breakfast other than coffee.

She wondered about him sometimes, but it didn't do to question the gods, she would think ruefully. It should be enough for her that he was working with the drive and energy of five men to regain all the lost ground. It was painfully slow progress; they needed so much that every bit of profit was swallowed up immediately. And *The Basket* wouldn't stand much more patching, no matter how thorough he was. But already there were a few dollars in the money box, and this time she dared to hope.

To be proud of him; to know the Island and the family were watching him and seeing how hard he worked — and to know in her own heart that there was truly iron in him somewhere — it made the scrimping and saving as easy as a song.

Little by little the boys started to come back to the house. She never forgot the intense gladness that flooded her when she looked down toward the gate one day and saw Alec, Owen, and Philip coming up the lane. Her eyes stung, and she knew then how much it had really hurt her when there was trouble between her brothers and her husband. Seeing them together like this, seeing Owen walking with his hand on Alec's shoulder, watching them laugh together in the clear April sunshine, she felt a tremendous lift of her heart.

She had coffee ready for them when they came in, and fresh cookies. The cookies were a symbol of the new order of things. It had been a long time since she'd dared to use eggs and shortening and sugar for something that was purely a luxury.

They sat around the kitchen talking as they had always talked. Owen groused good-naturedly; this time it was the price of lobsters.

"What are you growling about?" Philip asked lazily. "You brought in your hundred seventy-five pounds, didn't you?"

"Yes, but listen — last year at this time they were thirty-five, and now it's twenty-five. They haven't been up to thirty for a hell of a while, and they never used to go below it!"

"They'll go up again," Philip promised, and Alec said, with a rueful tilt of an eyebrow, "I wish they'd be quick about it, then. Pete's charging a god-awful price for pot warp, and if I don't get a new suit of oilskins pretty soon, I might's well go to haul in my undershirt."

"Pete's making a damn good living out here, running the only store," said Owen.

Philip tipped back in his chair. "Good coffee, Jo. I don't know about Pete. There's a lot of bills owed him. He's carried Marcus Yetton along for years."

"So has Father," Joanna put in.

"Well, that's none of our business," said Philip, smiling at her. "Listen, Alec, there's some oilclothes kicking around up at the house, nobody wearing them."

Alec shook his head. "Thanks, but I'd rather buy and pay for 'em. Pay as you go, that's what I'm sailing under." He looked pleasant but firm, and Joanna was proud of him. This was the Alec she had looked for a long time ago.

"Stiff-necked son of a bitch, ain't he?" demanded Owen. "I been talking to him all day, trying to convince him there's no sense hanging on to that old engine of his."

"What's he supposed to do, send off for a brand-new Kermath or something?" Joanna asked him hotly. "She'll do all right with a little care and attention."

"Like you, huh?" He grinned at her. "I notice you're kind of blooming these days, since your old man took to staying in of nights." He laughed at her sudden angry flush, and turned back to Alec. "Now that engine I took out of the *Old Girl*—she'll run like a bird with half the fussin' you've done over that wreck of yours. Just try her out, that's all! Rent it if you don't want to borrow it—but just try it."

Alec stared at the table, ran a lean hard hand through his hair. There were drawbacks to this new Alec; Joanna didn't know what he was thinking, she didn't know what changes had taken place behind the curiously bright hazel eyes and the easy smile. And this man who drove himself from dawn until long after dark was not a man to talk about himself.

"Listen, Alec, you can haul twice as much," Owen said. "Sure, a peapod's all right for a kid with fifty traps, but how many new traps did you put overboard this spring? You must have well over a hundred, and building more all the time—" He leaned across the table.

"I'm not trying to give you anything, if that's what you're scared of. But rent it, like I said, and see what happens."

Alec looked at him, then at Joanna, whose lips quivered a little in excitement and eagerness. He said, smiling, "It's a deal, Cap'n Owen."

They had fresh coffee all around to drink to the bargain. Then there was a new problem to discuss. Alec was running short of bait. Back in the fall, while he was on the seining crew, he had laid in a good supply of herring. But he'd let Jake Trudeau have some when he was short, and Marcus Yetton, and Forest Merrill—in fact, all the usual bad providers, who were perpetually short of something. The boys had warned him against it, but it seemed to be an utter impossibility for Alec to say *no* to anyone.

"I suppose it won't do any good to tell you to help yourself to mine, said Philip. "But if you want to get your own bait—well, what about the flounders down at Pirate Island? Nobody ever goes after 'em, and it's coming time—in May they come to sun themselves in Spanish Cove. It's shallow there, and the bottom's flat, and you can go along in a peapod and spear the things."

Alec stood up. "How long will it take us to set that engine of yours on the beds, Owen?"

"Couple of days. Why? You in a hurry?"

"Let's get started, then. Those flounders won't wait forever." The others went through the door, but Alec held back until he and Joanna were alone for an instant. He took her into his arms.

"Love me, Jo?"

"What do you think?" She hugged him with all the hard, passionate strength of her young body. "I love you more all the time." Words trembled on her lips, words that must be said. She whispered, "Alec, I'm so *proud* of you, too."

She saw for an instant the way his face changed, before he tightened his arms and crushed her head down against his shoulder. He kissed her neck, her cheek, her hair, with a sudden desperate hardness, and then as suddenly let her go. He went out without another word. But she could still feel the pressure of his arms and his mouth, she still saw that strange look, and wondered at it. It hadn't been a happy thing.

She went out to walk in the May afternoon. The wild pear tree at the gate was in bud, and soon the strawberry blossoms would cover the ground in little white stars, promise of fragrant red sweetness to come in June. The harbor shimmered and rippled in alternate sunshine and shadow as the clouds moved in dazzling masses across the sky.

She stopped by the gate to look around and sniff the ineffable scent of May on the Island. Her own house gleamed whitely against the dark spruces on the hillside, there was a sheen of blue through a break in the trees above the little cove; the Sorensen house and barn looked somnolent in the afternoon sunshine, a gull chanted lazily overhead, the sparrows twittered and chirped in the wild pear tree, and Gunnar's cow lifted up her voice in a paean of thanks as David came across the field with a pail of fresh water for her.

Joanna watched the yellow-haired boy and the cow in their silent comradeship, felt the sunshine warm on her face, and the clear green-scented breath of May, and she knew in that instant something which hadn't come to her for a long time; it was as if the presence of the Island slipped into her again. She stood in a little hush at the very center of this glowing world, not wanting to move or speak.

David saw her, whistled and waved; she waved back, and the instant had gone. She walked down the lane toward the harbor. Things are right for us now, she thought. Really right. The Island will look out for its own.

As she came past the Birds', Simon was coming down to the lane, Ash a little behind him. Joanna met him face to face. For a second they looked at each other without speaking.

Quite suddenly she smiled. "Hello, Simon . . . Ash." She nodded, and walked by them. She was inwardly rejoicing; she knew just how Owen and Mark felt when they walked down the road as if the world were their exclusive property—and fenced in, too. At this moment the world belonged to her, Joanna Douglass, and Simon Bird didn't exist in it any longer. He had been shut out of it forever in a dawn she would remember till she died; the dawn when Alec had come home and dropped a pack of cards in the fire.

41

Pirate Island gleamed in the May sunshine; it rose, a long barren ridge of yellow rock, out of the sapphire-blue bay five miles to the north of Bennett's Island. Joanna and Alec went there in *The Basket* one brilliant morning with a good lunch stowed forward, the peapod riding astern, and Bennett's Island like a blue-violet cloud on the horizon behind them.

They anchored outside the Spanish Cove. Facing open sea, with no land between it and the coast of Spain, the cove had been scooped out of the side of a hill; steep grassy banks like the curve of a bowl went down to a small pebble beach. Everywhere along the water's edge, the same giant hand that had scooped out the cove had flung down great boulders in untidy confusion. In an easterly, when the seas broke into the shallow cove like a thousand wild stallions, the surf roared and hissed and jetted high over these boulders. But when Alec and Joanna rowed in through the mouth in the peapod, the water curled itself glitteringly around the rocks, as ingratiatingly as a cat weaves around friendly human legs.

The cove itself lay placid and bright in its solitude. The tide was low, and there on the flat rocks on bottom, basking in the sun-warmed water, they saw the flounders. It was something to see. Alec stood in the bow, and speared with his homemade harpoon the flat and sleepy fish. It was quick and easy. Poling the double-ender along was like canoeing on a millpond, and it seemed as if the bottom of the boat was deep in flounders in no time.

The bare, deserted island towering over them, the peaceful little cove, the windless sunshine, all held a queer charm for Joanna and Alec. They hardly spoke. It was as if they could relax at last, after the long hard battle of the winter. Besides, words would have spoiled this half-enchanted serenity that had caught them up.

They rowed ashore, finding an opening in the rocks big enough to let them pull the peapod up on the beach, and took out the lunch.

"Want to stay here on the beach?" Alec asked.

Joanna looked up at the curving grassy walls and shook her head. "Let's climb up there!" she suggested, a quick tide of excitement running through her. "Let's see what it's like. I'll bet you can see the whole bay."

Alec shrugged. "You fixed up the grub, I guess you can say where we'll eat. Lead on!"

Feeling wildly happy, she attacked the slope. She had on a pair of Alec's dungarees, with the bottoms rolled up, and one of his shirts. With her strongly slender brown arms and hands, her long legs and narrow hips, she looked like an agile young boy as she went up the bank. It was steep, but there was juniper to cling to in the worst places.

She looked back over her shoulder to see Alec coming with the lunch. "Ahoy, Creepin' Moses!" she shouted down at him, and scrambled upwards. A little ground sparrow rose chirping from a clump of bushes, and she said, "Hi, there! How's the wife?" A gull went overhead, laughing, and she mimicked him. She felt half-drunk with the bright winelike air, the sunshine, the challenge of the climb . . . and being with Alec, like this, away from everything and everybody, as if they were the only people in the world. Of course Alec was quieter than he used to be. But he was still her own dear love.

Quite suddenly she reached the top, or rather a little grassy plateau with the highest ridge of the island rising above it, shutting off the wind. And in this sheltered spot, high above the blue tranquillity that was the cove, the strawberry blossoms dappled the grass like a thousand tiny fallen stars. Joanna stood still, breathless with the climb and with delight. It was like finding a grassy carpet spread for her and Alec, a carpet spangled with flowers.

She dropped down on it and shut her eyes. How nice it smelled. How warm the sunshine was on her face. When Alec came, she opened her eyes and put out her hand to him.

"Lie down and rest a while," she murmured.

He stretched out beside her, and propped himself up on one elbow to look around. "Did you know this place was here?"

"Second sight. I'm fey."

"You're fey, all right. Your shirt tail's out."

Joanna promptly pulled it out all the way and rolled it up. "I want the sun to shine on my stomach. It feels good," she explained to Alec's amused green-brown glance.

"Why don't you take it off altogether?" he asked. He pulled his own shirt off; his body was lean and muscular, and fine gold hairs glinted in the light.

"I always wanted to go sunbathing," said Joanna, and shed her blouse. She lay back again, feeling the grass cool and prickly against her bare shoulders, the sun like a caress on her skin. Alec looked down at her, his eyes narrowed against the bright daylight, his mouth softening. She stretched luxuriously and smiled back at him drowsily between her lashes.

"It's kind of nice to loaf for a while, isn't it?" she said."

"Seems to me I haven't loafed for a long time."

"You haven't. You're either working your head off, or sleeping like the dead. I was beginning to wonder when you'd stop to take a breath and say hello to your wife."

Alec smiled, and picked a strawberry blossom. He tucked it over her ear. "Now you look like one of those girls in the South Seas."

This was the old, gay and romantic Alec. It was fun to have him back for a day, this run-away day that felt like an adventure even if they were only five miles from home, catching flounders. She said lazily, "And who are you?"

"I'm a beachcomber."

"Kind of hard work, beachcombing in rubber boots—"

He pulled them off, and his socks too. "That air feels good. Those girls down there don't wear shoes and socks, either." He took off Joanna's sneakers and she wriggled her toes ecstatically.

"Alec, do we look like a couple of old married people?"

"If Bennett's could see us now, they'd chew about it for the next six months."

Joanna giggled. "Isn't it fun?"

"Mmm," said Alec, and bent his head. She felt his lips on hers, gentle and firm, and her heart quickened. He kissed her twice, and lifted his head, and she took his face in her hands, and looked deeply into his eyes.

"We haven't had a lot of those lately," she said in a low voice.

"There wasn't even time for that, Joanna," he answered her.

"There's time today." Her hands tightened, as she pulled him gently toward her. He slipped one arm under her head and laid the other across her body to hold her firm and close to him. This time, as his mouth came down on hers, the heart that had already quickened leaped with a sudden wild happiness. And lying as she was, against his breast, her skin warm and brown against the warm fairness of his, she felt the fierce thudding of his heart too.

"I love you, Alec," she said against his mouth. She took his hand, the one that held her so close, and held it against her breast.

He lifted his head a little at that, and through her lashes she saw his face for an instant before he buried it against her throat. "I love you," he answered. "Don't ever forget it, Joanna."

It was somehow a holy instant. Joanna's fingers were quiet in his hair as she felt his mouth against her throat, his hand curving over her breast. "I love you," he had said. "Don't ever forget it."

She didn't know why her eyes were stinging, all at once.

For a long time they lay like this. The gulls aloft in trackless sunlit space must have seen them there, lying so close together on the tiny carpet of grass starred with white blossoms; the bare rocky ridge of the island rising above them, the cove sloping away from them below. They lay there with no thought of time. For all they cared, it could go on like this forever, brilliant and fragrant and shadowless and unpeopled, except for them.

Presently Alec stirred, lifted his head, and looked down into Joanna's face. They smiled at each other, a long slow smile without haste or urgency in it. With a small, sighing sound of content, Joanna put her arms around his neck. And his warm fingers tightened over her breast.

After sunset the west was jade and gold, the eastern sky was a pale glow of rose and lavender, melting into an amethyst sea. When the boat slipped quietly across the serene water, it left a wake of deeper amethyst and jade. The peapod astern ruffled the wake into gold.

Joanna, standing beside Alec at the wheel, said, "I've never seen it like this before. Have you?"

Alec shook his head. They stood close together against the after-sunset chill. They were quiet; their silence held more than words could ever hold. We don't need to talk, Joanna thought. We don't want to talk. But it's as if we're saying things to each other, just the same.

It was a strange but wonderful feeling. Dusk slipped down from the east, the line of sea and sky became indistinct. The amethyst was turning to gray by the time the boat slid under the shadow of the Head, passed Eastern End Cove, where the lights were already lit, and the boats lay peacefully at their moorings. The woods were black against the sky, and as the afterglow faded, one star after another came twinkling over the trees.

"Home again," said Alec, as *The Basket* reached the mouth of the harbor. *Home again.* Lovely words, thought Joanna. A day of loveliness, and then coming into the Island's harbor at dusk. Coming home . . .

With Alec.

42

THE FOG IN JUNE was a thick and windless hush, an opaque silence. You could hardly hear the foghorn at the Rock, and the sea was very calm. The men went out to haul around the Island, grumbling a little because the lobsters were falling off — it was almost time for the Closed Season and shedding — and the prices were falling off, too. Joanna and her mother listened to their menfolk and took the grumbling lightly. Island women were used to this.

They were used to the fact, also, that some of the men were always in debt by the beginning of summer and the Closed Season. Joanna, going into the big house one day during the fog mull, heard Stephen on the other side of the front door, talking to someone; she stopped on the doorstep to smell the budding white roses and in a few minutes Forest Merrill came out. He looked sheepish and relieved. She knew that look.

She spoke to him and went into the house. Her father had gone back to the sitting room; he stood by the mantel filling his pipe and looking down at it thoughtfully.

"What's the matter with Forest?" she asked him bluntly.

"Oh, Harpers' is pressing him a mite too close for the trap stuff he bought in there last winter." Stephen shook his head. "Pete's after him too, but Harpers' is the hardest nut to crack. Pete'll still let him have food, for the kids' sake."

"And you'll keep on letting him have money for the kids' sake," said Joanna. "Father, if he and Marcus didn't know they could get money from you every time they got up a tree, they'd do things themselves—for the kids' sake."

Stephen's fine black eyes crinkled in affectionate humor. "Looking out for your old man, are you? Well, Joanna, Marcus and Forest are the way they are, and a man with a little extra in his pocket doesn't like to stand around and see people in want—especially children and women that can't get out and dig for themselves."

"Susie Yetton does a lot of digging in Johnny Fernandez' pockets!"

Her father laughed. "Susie's a case, poor fool, and Marcus is shiftless. All the more reason the rest of the Island's got to look out for the young ones."

"Father, what if you're out on a limb sometime? You know darn well they don't intend to pay you back."

"You're a hard-boiled little cuss, aren't you? Well, Jo, when I let 'em have it, I don't look very hard for it to come back. I've got it, and I'm not using it—"

"But you might want to use it sometime!" she said passionately. The meals of herring and potatoes were not so far behind her that she didn't remember them with humiliating clarity. "Father, I'm not stingy or tight, and I believe in helping people out, but you never refuse them *anything!* And I say they think you're an easy mark, and it's just throwing good money after bad."

Stephen laughed at her, the deep and infectious Bennett laughter, and after a moment she had to laugh too. "Well, just the same, Cap'n Bennett—"

"They'll be calling *you* Cap'n next, the way you team folks around.

The way you drive that man of yours down to the shore is a sight to behold." He watched her quizzically. "Y'know, Jo, I always had a little hunch Alec had a lot of Scotch obstinacy—wouldn't do anything he didn't have a mind to."

"He's working hard now because he's got a mind to."

"I'm glad to hear it," her father said quietly, and then Donna came in from the kitchen with Kristi and they began to talk about the strawberries on the Western End, and the possibility of the fog spoiling them.

Later in the day Joanna walked down to the Eastern End. Mateel hadn't been up to the harbor since she came back from the hospital in March, with the new baby. She'd had a hard time, and now in June she still tired easily. She worked too hard, Charles said, and it was true that their little house, at some distance from Jake's weather-beaten place, showed the affectionate care she gave to it.

Charles had shingled it and re-roofed it the summer after they were married, and they'd kept the inside painted and papered like new. If the Bennetts had been afraid Charles would go slack down among the Trudeaus, here was evidence of the truth. Young Rose-Marie, out of grammar school now and keeping house for Jake and her brothers, was so enamored of her big sister's house that she had badgered Jake into letting her and Pierre do some fixing-up in their own house. And there was a rather splendid vegetable garden in the field below the Head.

The place was quiet and sleepy in the fog when Joanna went through the gate and down to Charles' house. Young Charles played around the doorstep; the old half-blind spaniel, guarding him, flew at Joanna and then subsided into fat wigglings when he recognized her voice. Young Charles greeted her with a crow of happiness, and Mateel came to the door with the baby on her shoulder.

Her pleasure lit up her face. "Come in, come in! Oh, I'm *glad* you come down!"

Joanna followed her into the small kitchen, bright in spite of the fog. She felt rather ashamed that she didn't come oftener. Though she hardly admitted it to herself it had been the children who kept her away; or rather Mateel's radiant, open pride in Charles' son and this new little girl, Donna.

Mateel was in the midst of a huge ironing. As she put Donna

back into her basket, Joanna said, to her own surprise, "Let me take her, Mateel." And there was the baby in her arms, gossamer fluff of black hair on a bobbing head, an unsurprised blue gaze, and a wide mouth that curved in an enchanting, drunken, toothless grin.

Joanna looked back at her, her own mouth twitching in an uncertain smile, and her eyes feeling queer. *Oh, darling, darling,* she thought with sudden incoherent delight, and the light warm burden in her arms, the fragrance of clean healthy baby, was intolerably sweet. But it had no evasive ache for her now, no sense of hidden hunger. Rather a new excitement pounding through her body. It was so new and strange that she was almost afraid to think about it; but it was still there, and try as she might, she couldn't look stern and uncaring and insolent when she met Mateel's eyes over the baby's head.

"You look good, wit' the baby," said Mateel shyly. "Why don' you 'ave one, Joanna?"

Joanna laughed. "There's plenty of time."

Young Charles and the dog came in; he clamored at his mother in a garble of French and English baby talk, and she said *no,* he was to stay by the house. Charles went out with a miniature Bennett scowl on his young brow, and a cookie clutched in his fist.

"What did he want?" Joanna asked curiously.

"To go down in the shop wit' the boys," Mateel explained. "Mark, Stevie, David, Pierre. They talk an' fool—you know 'ow they do. The baby come 'ome and say *goddam* all over the place."

They laughed, and talked inconsequentially while Mateel finished her ironing and made tea. Sitting in this pleasant kitchen, with the baby in her lap and Mateel the picture of contentment, Joanna remembered that other day when she had come to see Mateel; how sunk in misery they'd both been, how they had hidden it—or tried to—each from the other! And it was all for nothing, because this was how it had come out. Donna and Stephen had a warm tenderness for their oldest boy's wife.

We Bennetts have a way of falling on our feet, she thought. The teakettle sang, Mateel hummed under her breath, the baby dozed against Joanna's arm; its hands were little pink starfish, but their texture was that of flowers.

Into this peace the boys came noisily, Mark and Stevie, David Sorensen, and Mateel's younger brother Pierre. The house was sud-

denly crammed to bursting with boys' arms and legs, boys' exuberance. Mateel, flushed and laughing, set out more cups, and Joanna
protested.

"When they're hungry they drop into the nearest house for a mug-
up. Why don't you make them bring their own grub?"

"Why didn't you bring yours, then?" Mark demanded. "Seems
to me there was a time when you ate like a damn gannet!" He held
the baby high over his head. She began to cry, and Stevie took her.
He went over to the couch in the corner and sat down with the baby
cradled in the curve of his arm, talking to her quietly. Joanna, watching his bent dark head, had a sudden vision of Stevie with a child
of hers.

Pierre sprawled beside Stevie, with the inevitable harmonica making a sweet sharp thread of sound through the babel; David was as
silent as ever. Mark said, "Know what we been talking about?"

"Women," said Joanna.

"Women, *hell!* We been making plans. Big ones."

"You're going to make a summer colony out of the Island."

"Nope. Can't do it. No plumbing, no electricity. Nope, Jo, this
is it. Steve and me, we're going ashore and buy a truck. Dave and
Pierre will handle the business from this end—car their lobsters and
we'll get some other guys to do it too, and send 'em ashore to us,
and we'll peddle 'em." He looked at her expectantly, waiting for her
praise and admiration.

"Where's the profit?" she asked shrewdly. "The truck costs something. You won't get the gas free. And you have to pay for the lobsters."

"Profit! My Jesus, woman, where's the profit in lobstering out
here, with prices dropped down to sixteen cents?"

"They'll go up in the fall."

"Sure. For about twenty minutes." He paced the crowded kitchen,
black brows heavy. He was Owen all over again. "Look, we can get
a hundred per cent profit peddling lobsters ashore. The truck and
the gas—that's easy handled. Once we get the business under way,
it's all as simple as billy-be-damned."

"What about Stevie?" she glanced across at him. "Do you want
to leave the Island!"

Mark said impatiently, "Of course he doesn't! He's been arguing like a bastard for a week. But he's got to go where I go."

This wasn't anything to shrug off, Joanna knew. Mark was serious; he'd go in a minute, leave the Island and drag Stevie with him. She could see his point—it was going to be hard if the lobsters kept dropping—but if these young Bennetts left the Island, what would happen to its future? She forced herself to say lightly, "When do you plan to start up this business?"

"That's the hell of it. I won't be twenty-one till next year."

She felt an instant relief. By the time he was of age, prices would be up at their winter heights, and when he was getting seventy-five dollars at a haul, he wouldn't want to go ashore.

"Mug-up's ready!" Mateel sang out, and young Charles echoed her, scrambling up into his high chair. They drew together around the table, to drink tea and coffee and eat cold biscuits with homemade strawberry jam, and there was no more talk of plans.

43

WHEN THE FOG MULL WAS OVER, Brigport celebrated with a supper and dance. There was a good-sized summer colony on the larger island, made up of teachers and artists, and by the end of June enough of them had arrived to make a considerable difference in the population. Most of the Bennett's Islanders went across to these affairs, if the weather was fine.

Joanna and Alec decided to stay home this time, though at least three boatloads were going

"Let's go for a long walk and make believe we're alone in the world," Joanna said at noontime.

He smiled at her, the gentle, gay smile she loved, his eyes full

of tiny lights. "You're the skipper, honey. Y'know, Owen's right —
you are sort of blooming."

"Owen ought to mind his own business."

"Not that boy. He couldn't do it to save his life. He's going across
tonight, with bells on. Seems there's a pretty little schoolmarm on
Brigport for the summer, and she came over on the *Aurora B.* this
morning, just for the ride. She was flitting around on the wharf, cute
as a hummingbird, and Owen struck up an acquaintance. She'll be
looking for him tonight."

"Well, it's about time for him to break out with a new woman,"
said Joanna philosophically. Alec took the empty water pails down
to the well; she watched him go toward the gate, lean and erect and
springy-stepped, his hair ruddy in the noon sunshine. She dreamed
a little, watching him. They were out of the woods now, they were
seeing a little profit. Saving a dollar here, a dollar there, and they
didn't need new clothes this summer. Oh, they were getting ahead
now. No doubt of it.

There was something else she knew, too. That was why she
wanted Alec to stay home tonight. They would take a long walk in
the clear June starlight, the way they used to walk when they were
first married, and stop to rest above one of those little coves on the
west side, where the sea would be so still they could see the stars
shimmering in the dark water, and the woods would be black and
listening behind them, and then she could tell him that she was positive about the baby.

She dreamed about this baby too, as she saw Alec coming up
through the lane again. Sunlight filtering through the trees glinted
across his head; light and shadow dappled him alternately as he walked
along swinging the pails. She saw him now as the father of their child,
sharer with her of something they had themselves made. It was queer
to be watching him and thinking of him like this, when he didn't know
about it yet. But tomorrow he would know, and he would see her
in her new part, as she was seeing him now.

She could hardly wait to tell him, but tonight would be the time.
She remembered with a smile how he had objected when she first
talked to him about a baby. But he'd been like a child himself then,
unwilling and afraid to be responsible for another life. In the past

few months he had grown so much older that he was almost not the same Alec at all.

She watched him coming up toward her, and heard his sweet, sharp whistling. It was one of those old Scotch songs of his, about Bonnie Prince Charlie. "Will Ye No' Come Back Again." Her lips phrased the words, fitting them to the music.

> Better lo'ed ye'll never be,
> Will ye no' come back again?

This baby would be happy and blessed, growing up a child of theirs on the Island. It had been blessed already, from that day on Pirate Island. It seemed to Joanna as if her child must be born with a memory of flooding sunshine and the shy fragrance of wild strawberry blossoms. And an amethyst sea at nightfall.

Her heart seemed full to bursting. This was what it meant, in the Twenty-third Psalm . . . "My cup runneth over . . ."

Alec's feet were on the steps, and the whistle was clear and loud.

> Better lo'ed ye'll never be,
> Will ye no' come back again?

Joanna, looking every inch the practical wife of a fisherman, began to take up the potatoes.

In the late afternoon, Joanna walked down to the shore to see why Alec hadn't come home yet to supper, and found him on the wharf, lounging against a hogshead and watching the exodus of Islanders. Joanna was in time to wave off Stephen and Donna. One by one the boats were leaving the harbor for Brigport, lying long and serene across the glassy smooth Gut. Almost everyone was going to the supper and the dance. As the *Donna* slipped away from the wharf, Leah and Ned Foster were coming through the shed.

"Summer's here," said Alec cheerfully as they came out into the late sunshine. "You can tell what time of year it is when they start gadding around."

Leah Foster's smiling glance touched Joanna and moved toward Alec. "Are you two people too old and settled to gad around?"

"Yep!" Alec smiled back at her. "What's on Brigport that we haven't seen already?" He put his hand lightly on Joanna's shoulder, and with that warm pressure, she looked back steadily at Leah Foster, with pity behind that look. But it was never Joanna's way to pretend friendliness where it didn't exist.

Ned was more like a piece of old gray wood than ever. He touched his hat and nodded to them with his faint smile. Leah, pausing there a moment to speak to them, looked exactly the same as she had always looked, hair like smooth silk floss with not one thread of gray in it, head carried in the same way on the plump white neck — Leah never tanned up like the other Island women — eyes smiling as they had always smiled from under the thick white lids. There was not one new line in her face.

When they had gone down the ladder, and Ned's gray boat had skimmed across the mouth of the harbor, quiet came down on the Island again like a veil of warm gold light. The western sea was a sea of blazing bronze; the harbor itself lay cool and still and blue, but the few boats left at the moorings caught the late sun until it seemed to wash their white sides with gilt.

"You don't like Leah much, do you?" said Alec with a chuckle. "I've noticed it more than once."

"Maybe I'm jealous of her charm. There's always some numbskull waiting to get her a pail of water and chop her kindling."

"It's Ash Bird, now." Alec's fingers turned her face toward him. "What would you say if I started being helpful to Leah, huh?"

Joanna wrinkled up her nose at him. "I'd say any man that left me for the likes of her could leave me for keeps, and I'd say good riddance!" She grinned at him. "But out of the kindness of my heart I'd warn you 'Look out for Neddie!' "

"That old man?" Alec looked skeptical. "Why? Look, she's been raising hell right under his nose and he doesn't do a goddam thing about it."

"Maybe so," Joanna murmured. She'd never told him about the Port George story Hugo had told her on that May afternoon so long ago. She'd never told him about Owen and Leah, either. She was half-minded to tell him now, but she had never told yet, so she shut her lips on the words.

Owen's *White Lady* was still on her mooring.

"I thought Owen was going," she said.

"Sure he is. The schoolmarm's waiting. Only he's got a quart from somewhere this morning and I guess he and Hugo are killing it. With Mark's kindly assistance."

"*Mark!* I don't like that. Mark's Owen all over again, only he hasn't got me to keep him out of Father's way when he's drunk. If they go over there and start acting up, it'll be a mess."

"I'll go stir 'em up. They'll miss the supper if they don't shake a leg."

Joanna tilted her head impatiently. "It's a fine thing when I have to ask my husband to keep tabs on my brothers. No, leave them alone, Alec. Let them miss the supper. And if Father catches Mark drunk — well, maybe that's what Mark needs."

"Tough little nut." Alec's hands gave her shoulders a loving shake. "You used to have such a time about it when they raised hell, and now you don't give a damn. But I don't want to see them get into a chew, for your mother's sake anyway. So you go along and get supper on the table, and I'll round 'em up and get 'em under way. I bet Stevie's worn down to a nub trying to drag that gorm of a Mark home to clean up."

He leaned forward and kissed her swiftly, and there was no one to see them but a gull on a spiling, watching them with a beady and wicked eye. They went up through the dark shed, arm in arm, and parted by the store.

"Be along pretty soon!" he called over his shoulder and swung along the path that led by the fish houses to the beach. She waited a moment to watch him, wondering how she had ever thought he was weak. Well, he *had* been weak once, but that was a long time ago. Now his very walk showed the difference. He was like a slender steel blade, as straight and as strong, walking as if at last he was sure of himself and his place in the world.

A ground sparrow rose up fluttering from the Queen Anne's lace as he passed it. He watched its flight as he walked, his narrow alert head turned to burnished bronze in the slanting light. Some impulse made him stop and turn around, by the Birds' fish house; he saw her standing there at the corner of the store, and waved. It was like a salute.

As she turned toward home, she was aware of her passionate eagerness to tell him about the baby; it seemed as if she could hardly wait for him to come. The walk they were planning, the first one they had taken for a long time, became vastly and thrillingly important. The Island would be all theirs tonight.

She hoped it wouldn't take long to get the boys started. They didn't deserve to have someone caring about whether they missed the supper or not. She was sorry Stevie had waited to go with Mark. As for Mark, he needed a good thrashing, even if he was twenty.

The long yellow light slanted into her kitchen and filled it with a warm and tranquil glow. When she looked out, the harbor and the village lay under that light too, the houses buried among their climbing roses and lilacs, the spruces that looked black, the mass of the Eastern End woods over there, Gunnar's cow grazing in the field beside the lane, her hide red in the warm light. There was hardly a sound in this hushed and peaceful hour; the cow's bell sounded clear and sweet when she moved her head, but it only sharpened the stillness. Even the eternal duet of gulls and sea was silent.

She sang to herself while she waited. One little tune stayed in her mind, she couldn't get rid of it. She'd ask Alec to teach her all the words, so she wouldn't have to go around singing over and over again:

> Better lo'ed ye'll never be,
> Will ye no' come back again?

She'd get Alec to teach her how to play the fiddle, too. It would be something to do when she couldn't get out and ram around the Island like a tomboy. She'd always wondered why women wanted to get heavy and out of shape with carrying a child, and then to have the agonizing business to go through at the end of the time. But now she knew.

"Darling, will you hurry up?" she pleaded soundlessly, and then chuckled aloud from sheer happiness. He was coming through the gate. She felt like running down to meet him, as she'd done when they were first married, and she was halfway down the steps, and the perfume of her pet white lilac bush was strong in her nostrils, when she saw it wasn't Alec coming up the path. It was Stevie.

She sat down on the steps and thought, What is it now? On this night of nights, was Alec going to fool around half the evening?

She grinned impishly at Stevie as he came toward her, tall, and still carrying his teen-age gawkiness in his long arms and legs. He had on his best blue suit and white shirt, but it looked funny. Decidedly funny. Queer. Stevie looked queer too, hesitating there in the middle of path, running a hand through his damp black hair, almost as if he were afraid of her.

"Well, young Lochinvar," she said, "would you mind telling me if you know why my lord and master hasn't come home to his supper yet?"

Stevie didn't answer her. He came to the steps, his eyes set very deeply between brow and cheekbones that were bloodless under the tan. And then she knew what was wrong with his suit. It was wet. Drippingly wet.

"Have you been overboard?" she demanded, and even as she said it there was a constriction in the pit of her stomach, a sudden, sickening tightness. Stevie opened his mouth and shut it again. His eyes clung to hers with a desperate, wordless pleading, and she said, carefully, "Where's Alec?"

She knew when he answered that he hadn't meant to say it the way he did, that the words came straight and without mercy from his shock and horror.

"He's dead."

"Oh, *no!*" she cried, her voice shaking, the words mingling with the echo of Stevie's voice in her ear, He's *dead* . . . it kept echoing; her head was ringing with it. *He's dead, he's dead.* But of course he wasn't dead, and this wasn't true. She was dozing, there on the steps.

Stevie's voice went on, uncertain, ready to break. "He was going to row us out to the *White Lady* in his peapod—Owen and Hugo and Mark and me. We were almost out there, we were fooling, and you know how tittleish that peapod is—well, she capsized. I guess Alec—" His voice rose ludicrously, "He cracked his head on the side, and he—and he—" She saw as from a great distance that he was fighting to keep from crying. "He went right down, Jo! Mark and I, we got him up, as soon as we could—"

"Where were Owen and Hugo?" She cut across his rising panic.

"Hugo started to drown and Owen was trying to hold on to him—and Christ, Jo, there wasn't a soul—not a living soul around the harbor! They were all gone!"

He sat down on the steps, his head in his hands. Joanna put

her hand on his shoulder, hardly knowing what she did. A coldness
had followed the tightness in her stomach. A coldness that crept
through her until she seemed to feel nothing. Her head wasn't ringing now. It was very clear. Alec was dead. A half-hour ago he had
turned and waved to her, and now he was dead.

"I'm going to the beach, Stevie," she said. "Are you coming too?"

"Back there?" His eyes widened. Then he stood up. "Yes, I'm
coming. Pete Grant's called the Coast Guard, they'll bring out a pul-
motor and stuff. And Mark's doing that artificial respiration we learned
in school."

"Then you're not sure!" Her heart pounded violently. "There's
a chance—"

His strong young hands tightened on her arms. He had control
of himself now, he would control her. "Don't hope, Joanna," he said
gently. "Don't look for a chance."

They walked down through the lane without speaking. Everything was the same: the harbor still shimmered out there, the gulls
still drifted in the same unclouded sky. But now she saw a hundred
things she had never noticed before; they intruded themselves on her
mind. A mole on Stevie's brown cheek; the dark down on his upper
lip. A patch of ripe strawberries in the grass beside the lane glowed
up at her, incredibly red. And she heard a cuckoo from the woods
behind the clubhouse. You didn't hear them very often.

As they reached Gunnar's spruces, she said suddenly, "Stevie?"

He looked at her, his young face stern and pale, his dark eyes
soft with his helpless sympathy. They looked strangely alike at the
moment, except that her eyes were dry and blazing; but the pallor
and the sternness were the same.

"Stevie, were they drunk? Owen and Hugo and Mark, I mean?"

Instantly she saw him withdraw from her. It was as if a shutter
dropped over his open look. "They had a little, but they weren't drunk,"
he said, and nothing more. She knew he would never say anything
else. It was Bennett lying for Bennett, even to her, another Bennett.
Besides, what good would the truth do?

They had taken Alec into Jud Gray's boat shop. At the end over
the water, where a window on the west side let in the red light of
sunset, they all stood—all but Alec and Mark. Alec lay face down
on an old sprayhood spread on the floor in the midst of curled yellow

shavings, and Mark was astride his back. His eyes were like black coals and his face was ghastly in the ruddy light. He looked at Joanna as if he didn't see her and went on counting in a toneless voice, swinging forward, pressing down, swinging back. She saw them all, before she moved where she could see Alec's face, turned from her.

Someone was very sick in a dim corner. Hugo. Between spasms he moaned. Johnny Fernandez was holding him up, crooning to him in a low, unending murmur. Owen leaned against Jud's bench, staring at Mark, smoking in long, famished drags on a cigarette. His suit was wet, too, the coat tossed into a corner, his black hair drying into a wiry crest. Nathan Parr stood beside him, watching Mark, with his thin, sunken old face set, his eyes queerly bright. He saw Joanna and spoke to Owen, who came toward her, skirting Alec's feet, and put his hands on her shoulders. How terrible he looks, she thought in some remote corner of her brain. Like Death.

And Death was here in this shop, with the half-finished hull of a boat towering above them and a red light flooding in on them. With Alec lying there, so flat and thin, his head turned away from her and the back of his neck so young.

"You shouldn't be here, Jo," Owen said to her. "Stevie, take her away."

She moved Stevie's hand gently from her arm and lifted her head a little higher. "Why shouldn't I be here?" she asked him clearly. "With Alec?"

He shrugged and turned away from her. She walked around Alec's feet — they'd taken away his rubber boots, and his socks were gone, and the sight of his narrow bare soles brought back a sharp, lightning image of the day on Pirate's Island. But only for an instant. She knelt on the sprayhood and looked down at his face.

Why, he's asleep! she thought with something like shock. How many times had she waked up to see him like this, lying on his stomach with his head on his hand, his face absorbed and remote from her, his mouth crooked in the faintest ghost of a smile, his hair tumbling across his forehead. Only then his skin had been bronze against the white pillow, and now it was white against the dingy gray canvas.

It was that, and the pallor of his lips, merry and mild even now, that told her he was gone. She looked at Mark. "You're tired, you'd better stop," she said.

He shook his head. "Not till I drop," he said between stiff lips. "Mark, it's no good. Don't do it any more."

"*I — won't — stop.*"

It was then that the doors at the far end opened, and they heard Pete Grant's voice, subdued now, but still resonant. "Down here, boys. Down at the end. I hope to God you can do somethin'."

The Coast Guard had come. The group in the fading light from the window looked toward the men who came past the raised hull; white caps showed in the gloom, and an officer stepped out of the shadow of the boat and looked down at Alec. Joanna, on her knees, looked back at him. Then she leaned forward and kissed Alec's mouth.

"That's one to sleep on, darling," she said to him without sound, and then Stevie whispered behind her, "Come on, Jo . . . *Please.*"

She went away from Alec then.

44

IN THE LONG SITTING ROOM in the Bennett house, the windows were open; three to look out on a blue sea and cream-and-amber ledges, on gulls drifting in a light-drenched sky. Three to look down on the meadow, ripe with summer, and to let in the scent of ripe field strawberries and Donna's white rose bush. At the foot of the meadow the Islanders had come through the gate in little groups of two or three, the men in their good dark suits, the women in their good dark dresses.

Joanna Bennett Douglass, wearing a new black dress, sat in the little ell chamber among her parents and brothers, and her sister-in-law Mateel, who was crying softly into her handkerchief. Joanna heard the minister's voice going on and on. The minister hadn't known Alec at all, so how could he talk about him like that? And besides, she had a strange certainty that this was not Alec at all. She had kissed

Alec good-bye there in the boat shop, and pushed his hair back from his forehead, and the Coast Guard had taken him away. But this man they had brought back, who lay there with his eyes shut, not caring about the minister and the women who sobbed—Joanna had looked at him remotely. She couldn't make this out to be her Alec, who'd waved to her from the road.

While the minister was talking, a song sparrow flew into the rose bush and trilled out his song. If that were really Alec, Joanna thought, he'd wake up when the sparrow began to sing. There'd been one they used to hear at dawn.

It was when they reached the cemetery that feeling came back to her. It was as if she had been chilled to numbness, and then with an aching rush the blood came back. One moment she was standing passively between her father and Charles, grateful for the soft little wind that blew a scent of sun-warmed spruce to her nostrils. In the next moment, she knew. Alec was gone, he was dead, in a few minutes now the earth would cover him.

She stood without moving a muscle, her face like stone, but inside she was crying out that she couldn't bear it, she must run, run—

It was the apple tree that did it. The petals drifted down on the wind, like snowflakes on the turned brown earth. She looked across the ugly hole at her feet and the tree stood white and radiant and lovely in her sight. Each blossom, each petal, was edged with light; and as they floated down and touched the earth, she felt each one on her heart.

"Do you think they can feel the flowers coming down?" Alec had asked once. "I'd like an apple tree over my grave." His voice was in her head now, with its undertones of laughter. But she couldn't hold on to it, and she would never hear it again. There had been two people sitting on the stile once, looking at the apple tree, and now, standing by the grave, she remembered his lips against her throat. And she would never know them again. *Never, never, never.* The word clashed through her head till she thought she must cry out, and run away from it.

But she stood erectly between her father and her oldest brother, and there was not a quiver of her lips to betray her, nor the faintest moisture in her eyes. Her head was as high as it had been when she had walked toward Alec Douglass to become his wife. No one should pity her. She hated pity.

The family wanted her to come back to the big house and sleep again in her own small room. She would be the daughter of the house again; caught up in the whirlpool of activity, of argument and laughter, she wouldn't brood, they thought.

But she wouldn't come, and Philip took her side. He said she'd be better off to go back to her own house if she wanted to. Didn't they realize she was as much Bennett as the rest of them? he asked. If you were a Bennett, you'd sooner undress in public than show the way you felt. You wanted to be decently alone with your troubles, until you knew how to live with them. So Joanna spent the summer alone in her own house, and if the family worried about her, they knew better than to let her know about it.

If they'd known about the baby, they would have worried more. But she wasn't ready to tell them yet; she wished she need never tell anyone. If Alec couldn't know, why should anyone else? Knowing she must go through the long wearisome pregnancy alone, and face the ultimate agony without Alec, knowing he would never see his child, she wished more than once that she could die too. But there was no chance of it with a strong, healthy girl like herself. So she ate for the child's sake, and made herself sleep, and gave way only a few times to the wild, passionate storms of grief that tried to sweep her away. Though she had no joy of the baby now, she couldn't forget her responsibility toward it.

The summer was too long, too intolerably beautiful. She thought it would never end. She longed for the winter when she could shut herself in, and the harbor would be hidden by snow and flying vapor, and she wouldn't have to see the boats coming home to their moorings.

She woke in the early dawn to lie there and think about Alec, going over and over their time together, every quarrel, every embrace, every joke . . . and the day on Pirate Island. She would lie there quietly as the day crept into the room, with tears welling and falling as if they would never stop. But they were silent tears.

She would wipe them away at last, and get up to begin her day. Nobody else knew about those tears. The Islanders shook their heads

at her still-lipped poise. "You'd think all that trouble, losin' her husband and everything, would pull that chin of hers down a mite,
wouldn't you?" they said.

The boys came by daily to see how she was, bringing some special
dish down from the house, filling her water pails, splitting kindling.
She was quieter than she had ever been, but she could still joke with
them, and they were relieved. She was always carefully natural in
her manner, wherever she was, so that no one would show pity for her.

So she tended her garden and canned her vegetables and berries, and the fall came at last, sweeping down on the Island in the
worst equinoctial gale the coast had seen for years. The crashing wind
on the hill behind the house, the foam flying in the little cove, gave
Joanna a strange comfort. She drew the curtains early that day and
lighted a lamp, and sat down to sew. She had the radio in the kitchen,
but she didn't touch it very often. The inner silence of the house didn't
bother her. Rather, she cherished it. Sometimes, even after almost
three months, she thought she heard Alec's whistle outside, and then
she would remember that it couldn't be Alec; but she had a feeling
that something of him stayed in this house, that some essence of him
was in the air, in the very walls. So she wasn't afraid of solitude,
nor of silence.

Besides, she had the baby. Now it was a living presence. She
would have to tell the family about it soon, but not yet. There was
an odd security in sitting here by the lamp, with the curtains drawn
against the late, stormy afternoon outside, hemming diapers that nobody knew about. She smiled faintly, remembering Stella Grant's frank
curiosity about the money order she sent to Montgomery Ward. She'd
talk enough about Jo Douglass sending off for stuff when she'd just
been left without a cent to bless herself with — well, almost without
a cent, just the boat and the house. The way that Alec rammed around
playin' poker, he couldn't have left her much else.

Oh, Joanna knew, without bitterness, only with a tiredness, just
how they talked. But Stella and the rest would talk more if they knew
what came in her packages. They'd know soon enough because she
couldn't hide it forever, but she didn't care. When she was a young
girl, she'd carried a chip on her shoulder; their talk made her furious, fighting mad. But now it was no more to her than wind blow-

ing. The gale crashed and moaned in the trees on the hill, but it was only a noise that couldn't hurt anyone. It certainly couldn't hurt her, shut into the magic circle of lamplight in the house that still held Alec for her.

Mark had been down to see how the woodpile was, and fill her water buckets. Charles had come up to the mailboat this morning, and dropped in on her with an armful of the last glads from Mateel's garden. Philip had come in to smoke and talk for a while in his pleasant, quiet voice about the Island, the lobstering this fall, the recent departures—Jud Gray had kept his word and moved his whole family to the mainland when the prices hadn't come up as expected in the fall spurt. His going left quite a hole: Jud had lived on the Island for years, raised all his family there. And he'd had tears in his eyes when he left, Philip said.

"If he felt so bad, why is he so hell-bent on moving off?" Joanna asked, and Philip shrugged.

"Scared, I guess. Lobsters never dropped down like this in the fall spurt. They been down a long time, Jo. And he's got those girls to put through high school."

"I thought the Grays had more loyalty," she said bitterly. "He couldn't stick it through with the Island, could he? Had to run!"

"Well, if lobsters come up again the laugh'll be on him," said Philip mildly, and changed the subject. "Still not ready to move up with us?" he asked her, his blue-gray eyes steadily on hers, and she shook her head.

Now, alone at last, she thought of it and shook her head again. No, she wasn't ready yet. She supposed she'd have to go, sooner or later. She couldn't keep up the house on nothing. Her father and the boys had bought Alec's pots from her, but the money wouldn't last forever. "But I won't go till I'm ready," she said to the diaper she was hemming. Almost at the same instant, through the unending roar of the wind and the crash of rain against the windows, she heard someone knocking at the door.

Involuntarily she put her sewing out of sight before she went to answer, wondering who would knock—none of the family would. Maybe it was Kristi, on her way home from the big house. Her lips framed a smile, and she opened the door.

It was Simon Bird who stood in the entry in his dripping oil-skins. She stared at him in surprise and he said in the soft, familiar voice, "I didn't aim to scare you, Jo."

"What do you want?"

"Nothin'. Just a little friendly call, Jo. I knew you was alone, and with this livin' gale o' wind, I thought you might kind of appreciate a caller." His slate-colored eyes smiled at her as he took off his sou'wester and hung it on a nail in the entry. "Well, can I come in, Jo? You ain't goin' to keep me standin' here while we talk, are ye?"

Speechless at his sheer effrontery she stepped back, and he came forward to lean against the dresser. His dark red hair gleamed like mahogany under the light; the bones in his narrow face were sharper than they used to be, his mouth thinner. His oilskins were new and shining, brilliantly yellow. She remembered Alec had never been able to afford the new oilskins he'd wanted.

"It's kind of you, Simon, but you're wasting your time. The storm doesn't bother me. So thanks just the same." She waited in chill courtesy for him to go, but he didn't move. He smiled as he opened the neck of his oil jacket.

"You wouldn't turn me out into the rain again, would ye? When I walked up here on purpose? Besides, it's time you saw folks again. A young woman like you hadn't ought to bury herself."

"There's no call for you to come up here, Simon."

"I don't see why, seein' you ain't a married woman any more." He lounged against the dresser, lighting a cigarette. " 'Bout time you started havin' company. Funny Nils ain't been up—I been watchin'." He gave her a sidewise glance, his mouth quirking, and she felt a tremor of rage run through her body.

"Will you please get out?"

"I ain't in any pucker to move," he said pleasantly. "Don't look so stuck-up, Jo. I don't smell like a bait butt. You know damn well you're lonesome up here. You got used to havin' a man around, you know what it's like, and you'll be lookin' around for another one pretty soon. No harm in me keepin' you company of an evenin', is it?"

The soft, persuasive voice wound itself round and round her brain until she would have done anything to stop it. She could hardly believe it was true, that he had the incredible nerve to come like this.

She stood watching him, her hands at her sides, her eyes dark and unreadable and steady on his narrow bright ones.

"Are you going to get out of here?"

"When I'm ready." He smiled at her amiably as her chin tilted. "Look, Jo, you got no call to be uppity to me, or anybody. When you goin' to find out that it don't count much to be a Bennett nowadays? Or a Douglass?" His smile deepened as he watched her. "You oughtn't to go around the Island with your nose in the air like that. Folks don't like it. They ain't nobody but what don't know what Alec put you through last winter, and then left you without a cent."

"Simon, I'm warning you. *Get out of my house.*"

"I'm gettin' out," drawled Simon, "when I'm damned good and ready."

"I'm not strong enough to throw you out. But if you don't go, you'll be sorry for the rest of your life." Her voice was very quiet. "My brothers don't like you, Simon. And there's five of them all bigger than you."

Simon laughed. "Aimin' to scare me, Jo? Look, darlin' mine. You can't tell me to get out of your house . . . because it ain't *quite* yours." He fumbled in his pocket and took out a billfold, opened it with maddening care. Joanna watched his calloused fingers with eyes strained wide by unbelief. His words still rang in her head, they hung in the hushed room . . . *because it ain't quite yours.*

The words on the slip of paper he handed her danced before her eyes, then steadied. PAY ON DEMAND . . . Simon Bird . . . five hundred sixty-five dollars . . . and Alec's familiar gay scrawl at the bottom, striking at her as sharply as if she'd heard his voice.

"Poker," said Simon with laughter behind his words. Laughter at her, Joanna Bennett Douglass. "I kept lendin' your fine husband money fast as he lost it. He was always waitin' for his luck to turn. It never did."

He took the paper from her fingers and put it back in the billfold. "Got to keep this safe. You oughtn't to take this too hard, Jo. Tain't as if you didn't know what he was up to, what kind of gamblin' fool he was." He blew a long cloud of smoke into the room, smiled at her through it. "Everybody else knew it too, seein' the way he let his pots go to hell, and you rammin' around in shoes with the soles goin' through. Course you never knew he'd get in so deep he'd put up the house as security."

"*The house?*" The words scraped her throat.

"Yep. Then he was scared. Left off the poker and went to work like a son of a bitch. Thought he'd pay up everything, and then he could start all over again. You been lookin' down your nose at me for a long time, Jo, but I'll be damned if I'd ever treat a wife of mine like he treated you."

"You're not fit to talk about him," said Joanna. There was a rod of steel where her backbone used to be. Whatever incredible thing he had told her, one thing was still clear. She would kill him if he didn't stop talking about Alec. "Where do you get the idea this house is yours? The note doesn't give it to you!"

"But you can't pay," he said easily. "I know that much."

"My father will pay you. I'll see him tomorrow."

"Do you think your old man can lay hands on five or six hundred dollars cash, right off?" Simon laughed. "Why, girl, he's been throwin' away his money so long on dead wood like Marcus Yetton and some of these other fools around here, and lobsterin' fallin' off anyway, that he's right on a level with the rest of us now. I know damn well he can't do a thing. And the boys can't either. Maybe they make money—seems to me that's somethin' the Bennetts like to rub in on the rest of us—but they throw it away as soon as they make it, drinkin' and whorin' around. They ain't no help to ye, Jo."

She stared at him, feeling the blood leave her face.

"You like this, don't you. You're having yourself quite a time. Why did you wait till now to tell me? Why didn't you come up right after the funeral? It would have been lots more fun."

"Oh, I had my reasons. One of 'em was, I kind of liked thinkin' about you so near, movin' around in my house. I'd see you up here in the garden an' all, made me feel good." He gave her a gleaming sidewise look. "Got used to thinkin' about it as my house, y'know—always liked it, 'specially after Alec got it fixed up—and I knew you couldn't ever pay. Course, it warn't as if I needed the money. Times ain't never been so bad but what I couldn't tide me over. Look after myself, and a woman, too—if I had one."

He put down his cigarette on the dresser and straightened up.

"I always knew Alec Douglass was a fool. Married to you and spendin' his nights playin' cards."

"Keep on talking," she said in a voice as soft and level as his own. "Have your fun. You'll get run out after a while. No matter what kind of filth you drag out, you can't touch Alec and me. Go on and talk, Simon."

He walked toward her, his smile never failing. Would nothing ever get rid of it? Wouldn't his voice ever stop? . . . "Jesus, but you're handsome when you're mad, Jo."

He won't dare touch me, she thought, and stood her ground. He won't dare go that far . . . "Look, Jo, don't worry about the house, I'm willin' to tear that note up. Tonight. Maybe I want you to keep on livin' here. It's handy, too. I can come up when I've a mind to, and never bother anybody."

Joanna looked at him as if he were a new and loathsome sort of insect. He *was* an insect, she thought: a creepy thing with gleaming slits of eyes and red hair and a narrow mouth twisting in mockery. A thing that came close to her now. It turned her stomach. She looked at him with ineffable disgust. If she reached behind her now, there was a flatiron on the stove. It was good for mashing creepy things.

"And you ain't goin' to be stuck-up about it, Jo. You can't afford to be stuck-up any more. You've got nothin' to put your chin up about! You ain't even had a man you could be proud of talkin' about," said Simon. "You're lucky he died young. You still got a chance to have a real man for yourself."

Joanna took a step backward, toward the stove. Nothing moved in her face. Simon kept coming. "You don't like me here, tellin' you the truth. But you can't do a goddam thing about it. You got to stand there and take it, for once, because you can't do nothin' different."

The lamplight slanted across his face, the lean sharp bones, the hollowed cheeks and eyes, the pallor of excitement. She put one hand behind her. Simon moved like a cat, and had her in his arms, his mouth choking off the cry from hers. He was hard put to hold her, but all at once she felt as though she had no strength; the child moved within her, and made her feel faint. With a final despairing effort she got one hand free and went for his eyes. She felt her fingernails rip the skin of his cheek, as they had done once long before. Simon lifted his mouth from hers and swore, but his eyes were shining.

"All right, all right, now just calm down. One kiss'll do me for tonight. Next time things'll be different." He held her shoulder with one hand and touched his scraped cheek with the other. "I like lots of life in my women, and you've got plenty, darlin' mine."

He let her go, and as she reached for the iron he jerked her away and pushed her into a chair. "Don't be so foolish! What'll that kind of actions get ye? Well, I'll be goin' along. Need any wood or water?" He cocked his red head at her as he fastened his oil jacket. "No answer? Well, sulk then. You'll get over it quick enough."

Let him laugh, Joanna thought. *Some day I'll laugh.* Swinging his sou'wester from his fingers, Simon came back across the room. There was triumph in every line of him, the way he stood, the poise of his head, even the way his fingers dangled the sou'wester. "You don't want to fight me, Jo. Won't get you nothin'. Might as well make up your mind to like me." He patted her cheek and she didn't flinch away at his touch. "I can do a lot for a woman if I've got a mind to, and the woman happens to be you. I'll be up tomorrow night for a while. Like some candy?"

Joanna said nothing, and she realized he took her silence for defeat. He went to the door in his brilliant, rustling oilskins and then looked back.

"Night, Jo. I'll bring some candy anyway. Be sure and have the coffee pot on."

The door shut softly behind him.

45

FOR A MOMENT SHE COULD HARDLY BELIEVE she was really alone. It seemed as if the kitchen was full of Simon's voice and laughter. The things he had said battered at her brain and reverberated in her ears. Without moving, she looked around at the bright, lamplit kitchen. *It wasn't hers.* It hadn't been hers for a long time. Alec hadn't told her because he was working so desperately to redeem it before she should ever know.

Strength came back to her on the great wave of returning rage. She wanted to kill Simon. If she strangled him, he would stop smiling. She began to walk back and forth the length of the kitchen. I must do something, she thought. I can't go on like this. It seemed to her that such fury as she felt must be like a poison flowing through her veins. It would be bad for the baby.

She wanted to go out and walk in the rain till it soaked her to the skin, she wanted the wind to blow its wild coldness across her, she wanted to walk all night; then, perhaps, she'd feel clean again. She didn't feel clean now. The very air in the room was tainted. She stopped by the sink and scrubbed her mouth violently until she tasted blood.

Yes, get out, that was it. Get out before the four walls converged on her and suffocated her. Already it seemed as if she couldn't breathe. She'd get out and walk in the storm for a while, and then she'd be tired enough to sleep, if she could ever sleep again in this house, after tonight.

She was putting on her boots when the realization came to her that she needn't ever again sleep in this house, not even tonight. She couldn't and she needn't. She had kept something of Alec here, and she had been happy, in a way. But whatever memories it held for her were gone now. Simon had done that, without knowing it. It was the cruelest thing he could have done, but in the same way he had defeated his own purpose. For the house meant nothing to her now. Nothing at all.

What she had left of Alec now were the things in her head, and the child who grew beneath her heart. The house was . . . just a house.

She went upstairs and began to put clothes into her small suitcase. A few things would do for tonight and tomorrow. The boys would help her move out her other things — there wasn't much. Downstairs she put on a jacket and her trench coat, her boots, and sou'wester, took a flashlight, and blew out the lamp.

Outside there was a roaring and immense darkness. Rain blew its silver lines through the ray from her light; it was icy, pelting her face. The wind in the tall old spruces on the hill seemed to grow louder and louder as she listened, it mingled with the thunder on the ledges, and she felt her heart quicken and pound with the old familiar excitement. She walked along the sheltered path through the woods, the tall grass soaking the bottom of her coat, and came out in the Bennett meadow.

Here the storm reached out for her, a shrieking force in the blackness, driving in from Goose Cove with a howl and a whoop. Joanna felt very small and alone as she fought her way across the meadow and up toward the house, her suitcase banging against her legs, her trench coat soaked through, her face stinging, the rain beating on her sou'wester. As she reached the slope below the house she was bitterly cold and out of breath. But she was triumphant. This was something you could fight against; you could pit your slender strength against the wind's strength and plunge forward with all your might. This wasn't someone who came to mock you with soft laughter, and words that made you feel sick and impotent and soiled.

There was a light in the kitchen, and she went around to the back door. It was never locked. As she came through the inner door into the warmth and glow, Winnie crawled out from under the stove, wriggling and whining, and came to nuzzle her hand with a moist nose. Philip, fixing the fire for the night, turned around with a stick of wood in his hand. His smile broke across his grave astonishment.

"Hello, Jo! What's up?" Then he saw her suitcase. "Come to stay with us a while?"

She nodded, stripping off her wet things. Philip pulled off her boots for her; then, still kneeling, he looked up, and his eyes were thoughtful on her face. She was glad she looked breathless and storm-beaten. She didn't want him to guess tonight that something had driven her out of that other house. She didn't want to talk about it. She only wanted peace and quiet.

"Storm too much for you down there?" he asked. "Still, you don't get much of it."

"The wind made me nervous. Philip, look . . . I guess I'll move back again. Up here, I mean. It's lonely down there."

He nodded. "Sure, I know. It'll be swell to have you back. Kristi won't mind, either. Peter Gray wants her to come ashore and get married."

"And leave the Island?"

"Well, you ought to know she's been cracked about Peter ever since they were kids. How about some coffee to warm your bones?"

He went to the dresser and began to measure coffee into the pot. Joanna put her stockinged toes on the oven hearth and clasped her fingers in her lap; she gazed at her distorted reflection in the shiny teakettle. "The Grays gone, and now Kristi," she said slowly. "Why do they want to go?"

"There'll be others, too," her brother answered. "This Island life is old-fashioned, Jo. They want movies and stores. They think they're not living when they're out here."

"What do *you* think?"

"Me?" Philip's eyes smiled down at her. "What do you think I think? I'm a Bennett. I've got to stick, come hell or high water. And there's a lot of people think it'll be hell, in the lobster business. We've been riding high too long."

"Philip, it can't hurt the Island, can it?"

"How could it hurt the Island? Nope, the old place'll hold out, way it always has. Say, Jo, you ought to turn in. Your eyes look like two burnt holes in a blanket. Finish up your coffee."

He was the big brother again, who used to whisper to her at the table to eat up her greens, because he happened to know there was chocolate pudding for dessert. She smiled at him in sudden, weary affection and stood up.

In the familiar darkness of her room, she felt her way to the narrow bed and sat down, shivering a little. She pulled her knees up under her chin and hugged them hard. The little red sailboats on the wall seemed to glow at her through the blackness. The rain blew in pattering gusts against the window, and the wind tried to shake the walls. The sound of the sea was very loud. She had lain awake listening to it so many nights before she married Alec, smiling into the dark, dreaming with open eyes.

And here she was back again. Without Alec . . . She fell over in a little heap on the bed and thrust her face hard into her pillow. *Alec, Alec* she wept in soundless desolation.

The next morning at breakfast she told them she had come to stay. Her story was neat and brief, her manner composed. She'd found out, she said, that Simon held a note on the house. He needed the money, and she couldn't pay it. The only thing to do was to turn the house over to him. The boys could help her get her things out. She didn't mention Simon's visit last night; she wasn't quite ready to tell anyone about that, and she was sure that Simon wouldn't advertise it around the shore. After all, it didn't put him in a very good light.

Oh, if she told the family about it, she'd have revenge — of a sort. But a man got over a thrashing too quickly, and he'd haul them more than ever, afterward. No, she'd save her story, for now.

Her father was quiet about the note. They all were. There was no breath of criticism of Alec, though it had been torture to tell about it because she knew what they were thinking. When she had finished, Stephen said mildly that it was unfortunate it was Simon who held the note. But they'd pay him off, and that would take care of it.

"I don't want you to pay it off," Joanna told him bluntly. "I don't want the house."

"Don't be so dumb, Jo," Owen protested. "Even if you stay here, it won't do any harm to hold on to that property. Cripes, we don't want the Birds to have any more foothold than they've got now!"

Joanna shook her head. "They can't do any more damage than they've done already. Look, if you boys and Father get together and pay off that money, you put yourselves in a hole, and it's coming winter."

"Jo's right," said Philip. "We'd better see how the winter comes out. May be a good one, with plenty of hauling days, but it's just as likely to be tough. When you get just about two hauling days a month, you have to live on what's in the sugar bowl."

Stephen said thoughtfully, "Well, Joanna, if you feel like that about the house, we'll wait a while. No hurry."

"Sure, we can get it back any time. Simon loves a nickel like his right eye, the bastard," said Owen. "I'm going down and pump out my boat. You coming, Phil?"

The four boys went out, and Joanna was left alone with her parents. Donna was quiet, as she always was, but her joy at having Joanna back showed in the way a certain taut anxiety had left her face. They washed the dishes and tidied the kitchen together, while Stephen stood by the window smoking, looking out at the ledges that were buried under tons of white water.

"I feel sort of funny," Joanna said hesitantly, "coming back like this in the middle of a storm, walking in and turning things upside down, instead of coming when you wanted me."

"*When* we wanted you!" exclaimed Donna. "Don't you think we've always wanted you back up here where we could keep an eye on you?"

Joanna felt a queer constriction in her throat. Golly, was she going to cry? She hoped not, because she had to tell them now, these two beloved people of hers; Donna humming to herself as she polished lamp chimneys, her eyes as clear and youthfully blue as ever, though her tidy brown head was feathered with gray at the temples. And Stephen, giving her a swift, twinkling grin . . .

She took a long breath and said, "Well, it's not just me you've got to keep an eye on."

The silence was immense. She felt her face burn scarlet. Why didn't they say something? Were they too busy thinking about the mess their only daughter had made out of life? Oh, this was a shabby homecoming for a Bennett woman. She wished she could drop through the floor.

And then she met Donna's eyes, and Donna's broadening smile. "You've taken long enough to get around to tell us," she said. "I was wondering when you'd get ready."

"You knew!" Joanna accused her. "You knew all the time!"

"Well, only for a little while," said Donna modestly. Stephen, on his way out to the shop, put his hand on his girl's shoulder and gripped it hard. Donna said with radiant mischief, "You know what I've been doing? I've got out all Stevie's baby clothes, and now that you've told us yourself—well, I can bring them into the open and put them out to air."

Joanna did cry, then.

46

OTHERS BESIDE THE GRAYS LEFT the Island that fall. The Areys, who had always boarded the teacher, decided suddenly to spend the winter ashore; Mr. Arey had enough laid by to put his traps on the bank, and Mrs. Arey was ailing. The teacher—new this year, since Miss Hollis had reached the retirement age—was sent to Pete and Stella Grant. Pete was the school agent, and it was up to him to keep the teacher anyway, the Island contended stoutly.

Miss Adams was a slight, timid-eyed girl just out of Normal School and rather terrified at the prospect of living all winter on an island twenty-five miles from the coast. She was also startled, Joanna guessed, at the array of frankly admiring young men lined up on the wharf when she arrived. A young slip of a schoolmarm coming out to Bennett's was something that hadn't happened before in their lifetime. It looked as if there'd be compensations for winter weather and the steadily dropping price of lobsters.

As soon as her chum, Mrs. Arey, left on the important business of being under a doctor's care, Nate Bennett's wife developed an astonishing array of complaints for one who had always been so offensively healthy. One day after she had just left Stephen's house, while the room seemed to echo her saga of headaches and hot flashes, Donna said quietly, "Mary wants to get off the Island. That's what all this is leading up to."

"Uncle Nate won't go!" Joanna flashed back. "He's never gone off in the winter! She can't make him go."

"Can't she?" Donna smiled. "You know what an afternoon of Mary and her headaches does to us. Suppose you had to listen to it day in, day out, like Nate. Maybe you'd do anything to stop it."

"I'd put a pillow over her face in the middle of the night and stop it for good," said Joanna. "Mother, Uncle Nate wouldn't know what to do with himself ashore! He won't go."

But he did go, at last, his dark Bennett face deeply lined and impassive as he boarded the *Aurora B.* Mary was blooming. They were going to live with Rachel and her husband during the winter. Jeff and Hugo would keep bachelors' hall at the farm, and tend the milk. It turned out that they ate most of their meals up at the big house, and spent most of their evenings there, those evenings when fall was deepening into winter.

It was a bad fall for herring, and the bait problem would arise before the winter was out. Those who'd laid down plenty felt duty-bound to sell to those who went short, and then they shortened themselves. And sometimes you couldn't get more for love nor money.

Joanna heard all about this, and other ins and outs of lobstering, in these long evenings. She'd sit with her feet on the oven hearth, her sewing in her lap, and listen, while they sat around smoking and talking and drinking coffee after Stephen and Donna had gone to bed. Her brothers would be there, Jeff and Hugo, the Sorensen boys. Maurice and Pierre came up from the Eastern End with Charles.

They talked about everything: boats and women and engines, radio, the movies someone had seen the last time he went ashore, the Island and the Islanders, the world, the things they'd like to do in it. Their talk ranged far and wide, but it always came back to the immediate and urgent problems of living. It always came back to lobstering.

"Jeeley, the damn bugs been readin' up on birth control," Owen grumbled. "We hold off all summer so's they can shed and breed, and what do we get for it? Just about enough to take us out and to haul the next time!"

"I'd give plenty to know what makes good years and bad ones," Nils said slowly. "Must be they follow different routes when they come in from deep sea. Now they're having a swell year up around Isle au Haut. But the last year or so they've been tapering off around here, all the time."

"It's the kelp," said Mark. "You get the best lobsters in the pots you set where there's plenty of kelp. Well, the kelp's almost gone from around here."

"Oh, you and your kelp can go to hell," said Owen rudely. "You don't know a thing about lobstering. Not the way it used to be, a few years ago."

"Strikes me none of us know," said Nils dryly. "My grandfather says that when he first came here you could go down to the beach at low tide and pick lobsters out of the rockweed, the way the kids get crabs now. This place was crawling with 'em. And look at it now. What makes it? That's what I want to know."

"I've heard about that too," said Philip. "Well, either we've caught 'em all, or it's like you said, Nils—they're coming in by a different route. Maybe sometime they'll hit the Island again—"

"I'd hate to be hangin' by the neck till they do," muttered Hugo. It was very late, and he was half-asleep in his corner. Jeff had gone home an hour ago. They had all gone except Nils and Hugo, who now murmured plaintively, "It ain't bad enough to have no lobsters, no bait, and no money when you do get 'em, but my God, no women!"

"I thought you were making time with the schoolmarm," said Philip. "Been up at Grants' every night for a week, haven't you?"

"So's that grinnin' critter over there!" Hugo jerked his head at Owen. "And he can outsit me every time, damn his hide! He don't have to get up at five every morning to milk a couple bitchly cows. I wonder if there'll be a woman he'll let me keep to myself."

"You want to polish up that technique of yours, son," Owen admonished him paternally. "It's a mite rusty, ain't it?"

Hugo swore at him, long and brilliantly as he pulled on his boots and put on his mackinaw, climaxed his recital with a cheerful smile at them all, patted Joanna on the head, and went home. When he had gone, Philip said around his pipe, "Good kid, Hugo . . . Nils, anybody been bothering you lately?"

Nils gave him a sharp blue glance and leaned forward, his elbows on his knees, his fair head yellow under the lamp. "What makes you say that?"

"It's most likely my evil mind," Philip drawled, "but when I came under the Head yesterday Simon Bird was right spang in the middle of your string. When I came up alongside he was hanging head down over the stern with a gaff—said he'd got his wheel fouled in one of your warps."

"Well?"

"Well, when I first laid eyes on him he didn't look to be fouled, unless he'd got his fingers tangled up with one of your buoys. But he certainly got shed of it quick—I saw it fly overboard."

"I figured that was it," said Nils. "Or else the lobsters have got educated, and know how to get back out of a trap." His blue glance was unclouded and cold. "Well, Simon's hauled everybody else on the Island—I knew it'd be my turn sooner or later. Can't figure out why, though. I haven't been doing any better than anybody else this fall."

Joanna looked across at him, and her hatred of Simon, something that was always ready to surge up in her like the comber that rears without warning over a hidden shoal, rose now. She knew why Simon was hauling Nils. A week or so ago when she'd been coming back from the shore, she'd met Nils on his way to the house. They had walked along together, past the beach where Simon and Ash were painting Ash's boat, and Simon had seen them. He probably knew, too, that Nils came up to the house almost every evening.

It came to Joanna with something of a shock that Simon really believed what he'd said that night . . . "You got used to havin' a man around, you know what it's like, and you'll be lookin' around for another one pretty soon . . ." Her disgust burned her face and thickened her throat, as she sat there quietly sewing, with the young men's voices around her. He'd think that about her, a woman with a baby coming in January; a woman who'd loved her husband in a way she would never know again, or want to know again.

Simon had trapped Alec and hounded him, played on his weakness till Alec with one vast final effort had freed himself—only he had never completed that freedom. He had died too soon.

Hate was wrong, hate was evil, hate was a poison. But she had reason and right to hate—

"What are you going to do about it?" Owen demanded, and she started violently. But of course he wasn't speaking to her. He was watching Nils eagerly. "You better do what I did—cut him off. Cut off the whole bunch."

Nils smiled. "I haven't got the Bennett luck. I'd be hauled again—right into court. Nope, I'm shifting that string next week, anyway, out toward the Rock, and I'll watch him if I have to keep right on his tail."

"They're all acting up," Mark said. "Nathan Parr says he knows somebody's after him, and all he can think of is Ash. Ash was hanging around the camp shooting off his mouth one day, and Nathan told him to shut up and git, so Little Blisterbelly's got to get even."

"Every little bit helps." Philip looked a great deal like his father. "Not enough to have storms and tides and no money, no bait, no lobsters, to contend with, but we have to have the Birds. Like fleas on a dog."

"Well, there's such a thing as washing a dog with flea soap," said Joanna violently, "and drowning the fleas!"

The boys looked at her with startled amusement. "Darlin' mine, we can't take that crew out and drown them. That's plain murder," said Philip.

"But you could get rid of them, couldn't you? Clean them off the Island?"

"How do you want to do it, Jo?" Owen put one foot on the stove hearth and looked down at her with brilliant black eyes. "What's your idea?"

"Run them off. It's been done on Brigport."

"That's Brigport for you. We've never copied them yet, and we never will," said Philip quietly. "We can't run a man and his family off when they own their place and their shore privilege. We're supposed to be civilized over here."

Joanna put down her sewing and looked around at them. "Listen," she said. "Maybe there's such a thing as being too civilized. Maybe there's such a thing as being *soft,* when all you can think of is cutting off a few traps, or just shaking your head about it. Traps don't matter to the Birds, they can always get plenty more. Lift 'em right out of another man's string if they feel like it. And you scare them for a little while and then they start up again. The Island's bad enough off this winter without having them on it."

She looked up at Owen, sure at least of his agreement. But to her angry disappointment, he shook his head. "Nope. Can't do it, Jo. Phil's right about that — there's a law."

"I don't think you were always so careful of the law," she said scathingly, and two stains of color spread on Owen's brown cheekbones. He looked angry as he lit a cigarette.

"I suppose you're afraid to do anything, too," Joanna said to Nils.

He smiled at her. "Do I have to tell you right off? Can't think about it a mite?"

"That means you won't do it." She shrugged. "All they can do on this Island is chew, and never lift a hand to help themselves — except the Birds."

"I'm with you, Jo!" said Mark, and in a burst of impulsive comradeship he gave her a mighty hug. "And Stevie'll be with us, too. Cripes, what did he have to go to bed so early for? Us three, we've always stuck together. Remember?"

She looked up into his gay, handsome young face, and memory was a quick strong current between them, memory of a dark fish house and a roving flashlight, a pried window. She knew then that the Little Boys would back her in anything and everything. But at the same time, she knew that the burden lay almost wholly upon her. For an instant she felt a heavy weariness, but it went quickly. Her hatred of Simon Bird mingled with the thought of Alec and her all-enduring love for the Island; together they made a brilliant and steady-burning flame.

47

SHE WAS FEELING HEAVY AND cumbersome now, but there was nothing heavy and cumbersome about the way she talked to the boys. She always thought of them as the boys, though they were men grown.

She talked to them a great deal on those winter nights, after her father and mother had gone to bed. Sometimes, knowing what she wanted the boys to do, she had a twinge of guilt, as if she were betraying her father, but she deliberately ignored it. There was a time to talk about law, and a time to forget there was law.

There were many nights when she went to bed feeling baffled and furious. Either they shook their heads or they laughed at her, like Sigurd Sorensen, who would watch her with his bright blue eyes dancing and his grin broadening, as if she were one of the youngsters playing around on the beach, and he'd toss her a nickel in a moment because her prattle delighted him so. Or, like Jeff Bennett, they weren't interested in her opinions simply because she was a woman, and in Jeff's world women didn't tell men what to do. She didn't know which attitude made her the more furious. And in her own brothers' glances she sensed that nothing, not even the child who would come in six weeks' time, could make them see her as anything else but the kid sister who always had a chip on her shoulder.

But night after night she sewed and listened, and then she talked.

"It would be one thing if you hadn't been chewing about them all these years," she said scornfully. "Sit around and tell what you'd like to do, and call them all the dirty names you can think of, while they go their own merry way. Why, they're the only ones who've got the *guts* to do as they please! And the rest of you sit around and take it."

"Jo, listen," Philip said. "Don't you think we'd like to run 'em off? But we can't walk up to a man that owns his house and shore privilege and tell him to git."

Hugo said from his tilted chair in a warm corner by the stove, "Cripes, Jo, those Birds are pure brass. You couldn't keep them off the Island, short of murder."

And Owen, who'd been so hot-blooded and vehement about the Birds once, talked of proof until Joanna flared at him, "Oh, you make me sick! If they were bothering you right now you'd be hot enough! Only you're so damned busy chasing those Brigport girls and coming home drunk that the Island can go to hell for all you care!"

Charles said he had family to take care of, another baby coming. Lobstering was bad enough this winter—he couldn't take any chances on getting into trouble. As far as the Island's going to hell, it looked as if it was on its way without any help from the Birds.

After all, they didn't have anything to do with the way the dealers had brought the lobsters down to twelve cents, or the way the lobsters themselves weren't crawling, no matter how far out you set your pots. He admonished Joanna, as one of experience, not to get so worked up. She should take things easy, he said. Like a cow.

Sometimes she thought she couldn't stand it. She'd always been so proud of her brothers, and now she half-despised them, even Philip. And all Owen's big talk didn't mean a thing; the way he held his head was just an empty gesture.

Once, going over to the Grants' place to spend an evening with Miss Adams, she met Simon Bird in the chill December dusk. He spoke to her, but she didn't answer. When he'd gone by, she leaned against the wall of Karl Sorensen's fish house and fought to get her breath. Just meeting him like that had choked her with a feeling she couldn't endure. She knew then that she couldn't live on the Island while he was still there; and it was her Island, therefore she must drive him off.

Afterward she laughed at her fancies, but the obsession stayed. The boys would have to do it for her. They *shall* do it, she thought. They *shall.* I'll make them.

One night, when the younger boys were down at Gunnar's with David, Charles came up to the house, along with Jeff and Hugo and Nils. Owen was in fine fettle. He was making time with Miss Adams, and there was a girl on Brigport who was silly about him. He was candid in his boastings. Miss Adams was a good girl, sure enough, but he could stand that. The one over on Brigport, now—she wasn't in a class with the schoolmarm, but she had her points.

Joanna listened. She watched him, watched the gleam of black eyes and white teeth, the rich healthy color of his skin, heard the vigor and energy in his voice. But the things he was saying, and the comments the others threw in, sickened her suddenly; she felt nauseated. This was what they would rather talk about—Owen and Jeff and Hugo—than something that meant stirring themselves a little, doing something for their own good and the Island. Philip and Nils weren't saying much, and being a family man had tamed Charles down; but they weren't any more eager than the others to listen to her, to take a drastic step forward.

She said suddenly, in a quiet, dreamy voice, "Simon was right after all, when he said the Bennetts didn't have anything to hold their heads up for. We haven't."

"When did he say that?" Charles asked sharply,

"Oh, a long time ago." She didn't look up from the baby shoe she was crocheting. "The night he told me he held the note on the house. He said all you boys cared about was drinking and whoring around."

"What else did he say?" Owen's voice was slow and quiet in the suddenly hushed kitchen.

She smiled up at him. "Oh, that was all he said about you boys. It made me mad, of course. But I guess he was right. I've been feeling bad because folks are moving off, and more people are talking of going, but I guess it doesn't matter much — even if they stayed, the Island would still go to hell. Charles was right about that."

"It's not the Island, it's the whole lobstering business —" Philip began.

"The Island's seen trouble before, hasn't it? I've heard Father and Pete Grant, and Gunnar talk about it. But it always held together, because of the Bennetts. Well, now there aren't any Bennetts to hold it together. A fine crew Father and Uncle Nate've raised for themselves! Simon spoke the truth for once in his life!"

Words rose to her lips in a tumbling tide. "You sit up here and call the Birds bastards and bitches and everything else you can think of, but they sit down there and *despise* you, a hundred times more than you despise them!" Her eyes swept around the room, burned on Owen and Philip and Charles, and didn't spare her cousins or Nils. "You know why? Because they know no matter how much you talk you'll never lift a hand to stop them! They can do just as they please on this Island. Bennett's Island — it ought to be Birds' Island," she said with rich scorn. "And it will be, some day, when the Bennetts fall apart altogether. The Birds'll have it, and everything Grandpa Bennett and Father and Uncle Nate built up will go to pieces, and it'll be like some island the gulls have taken over. They'll destroy it, the way they're destroying it now, while you sit around on your backsides and swear."

She took a fierce triumph in their startled faces. They didn't like what she was saying, and she was glad, glad.

"You keep talking about Father," Philip said quietly, "but he's held us back more than once, Joanna."

"You fool, I thought you had more sense than the others!" she lashed back at him. "He held you back because you were kids, you wanted to go off half-cocked. But don't you think he's been wondering when you'd show some signs of life? Don't you think he's been wondering how long you'd let somebody rob you, and take the bread out of old Nathan Parr's mouth, and from Marcus Yetton's kids?" She put her work in the basket and stood up. There was a strange dark dignity in her figure, straight and strong even with its heaviness.

"And you, Nils — maybe Gunnar wasn't so wrong after all, in the things he used to say about you. I used to think that if you ever got mad, you could pick up a mountain and throw it. But it seems as if you don't know when to get mad. And I thought you had some feeling about the Island, even if these brothers and cousins of mine haven't."

His cool blue gaze didn't falter away from hers; his face was impassive. She went across the kitchen in a heavy silence, but her soul was singing. At the door, she stopped. "Don't worry," she told them. "I'm not going to fuss you with any more talk. I can't do anything alone, and I shan't bother you with it." She sounded very remote from them. "If the Island doesn't mean anything to you now that the lobsters don't crawl so good, I can't make you think about it. So I might as well stop thinking about it too."

She paused, then added with a little quirk to her mouth, "The only thing that gowels me is that I have to admit that Simon Bird was right about you."

Up in her room, she lay in bed in the darkness, hearing the murmur of voices in the kitchen below. The winter wind battered against her window pane, and the stars had the distant twinkling brilliance of frost; she could hear the sea, the Island's voice, a subdued thunder on the ledges.

Excitement that approached exultation beat through her body. Whether she had done it or not, she didn't know. But she had said all the things that had been fermenting in her mind for so long; she had told them what she thought of them. And now they could think about it for a while. It wouldn't be very comfortable. . . . She smiled in the darkness and snuggled down. Her bed hadn't felt so good for weeks. She'd probably sleep very well tonight.

She knew the instant she walked into the kitchen the next morning that the boys had decided what to do, and that Stephen Bennett knew. They were still standing around the big room, lamplit against the gray morning outside, when she came down. Mark and Owen, who were going out to haul together in the *White Lady,* were putting on their extra wool socks, while Donna mixed hot coffee for their thermos bottle. Stevie, the family's slowest eater, tried to make his doughnuts last while he finished an article in *Popular Mechanics.* Stephen and Philip stood by the stove, smoking.

She didn't know how she guessed, unless it was the way Mark looked at her, with a swift sly grin. But when she went to the stove to pour out her coffee, Stephen looked at her gravely and said, "Well, I suppose you know what's in the wind. You always did."

"What's the matter?" she asked innocently.

"Don't lay it on too thick, my dear," he advised her. "I guess you know what it's all about. You ought to know, the way you've been sitting up every night till the last gun's fired. But I'll help you remember. They're planning to talk to George Bird, more or less, and I can like it or lump it, I guess." His mouth twitched in a wry smile. "They're all over twenty-one, except Stevie, and they've got a right to say how things should go on the Island."

"What do *you* say?"

Her mother and the boys were silent, listening for his answer. She guessed that he'd said nothing at all when he was told. He looked out now at the sea, took his pipe from his mouth, and said, "This is more than a family touse, Jo. The rest of the Island's in this. I've been wondering if the Birds would have the common decency to mind their own business now when lobstering isn't good, but it seems as if they don't know what decency means. So I'm leaving it to the boys here to sound out the rest of the Island. The majority rules."

"What about proof?" Joanna asked warily. Stephen shrugged.

"Circumstantial evidence is more like it. Nobody on the Island has a big string of traps out this winter — the price of gear being what it is — and everybody knows just how few pots the Birds have got between 'em. But they do pretty good out of that handful. Pretty *damn* good."

"The bastards," said Mark with enthusiasm. "Walkin' around here too big for their boots, grinning like fools because they don't think anybody's got the guts to say anything—wait till they see us come in—"

"With the tar and feathers," finished Owen.

"Hold your horses, now! None of that talk even in fun," his father said. "First thing you know some numbhead like Forest Merrill will show up with a pot of hot tar. Remember what you told me this morning. Make it plain what the idea is—to tell George and his crew they've either got to walk the straight and narrow, or else."

"Can't we even take a piece of manila rope along, just to make it look good?" Owen put on his long-visored plaid cap, picked up the dinner box, and jerked his chin at Mark. "Come on, Bub. Let's get started. Sooner we're back, sooner we can start in on some of these has-beens that only know enough to sit around on their backsides and chew, instead of doing something about it."

Joanna's mouth quirked. Owen certainly sounded bold and reckless this morning, using practically her own words. Carefully avoiding anybody's eyes, she carried her coffee and fish hash to the table. Stevie emerged from his magazine as from a dream, gave her a vague smile, and moved in the direction of his rubber boots. He was going out with his father in the *Donna;* in the winter, they doubled up to haul. Mark and Owen went out noisily, the two Stephens put on their outdoor clothes, Donna poured more coffee into a second thermos bottle. Philip went out to the shop to work on some damaged traps. He and Charles had hauled their complete string the day before.

By the time Joanna had finished her breakfast, there was no one left in the kitchen but herself and her mother.

"You never know what those boys will think of next," Donna murmured. "And it's about time they thought of this." She met Joanna's eyes, flushed deliciously, and added, "Not that I approve of violence! But sometimes, with people like the Birds, a little fear works wonders."

In the middle of the morning Joanna carried a mug of hot coffee out to Philip, in the shop. He grinned as he took it from her hands.

"Well, you certainly took us over, last night. Got results, didn't you?"

Joanna put a stick of driftwood in the stove, and stood watching the blue and green flames. "Looks that way. What did you tell Father?"

"We left you out of it, darlin' mine. Doesn't sound exactly womanly, and besides, it doesn't make us exactly heroes, either — admitting we didn't think of it ourselves." His thin face sobered abruptly. "Oh, hell, Jo, you know we've talked about it enough, but how in the devil did we know what tack the old man would take? How did you know?"

"I didn't. I just guessed." She looked at him with a little smile. "I guessed right, didn't I?"

"Uh-huh." Philip finished his coffee and lit up his pipe. Over the puffing flame he watched her closely. "Jo, what set you going against them, anyway? Simon holding the note on the house and turning you out?"

"I told you he didn't turn me out," she said patiently. "I moved out because I wanted to. It wasn't the note, Philip." For an instant the words quivered at her lips; if she let them go, it would all be spilled out, all the things that no one knew but herself. But she couldn't tell them and make anyone — even Philip — see what they really meant. She could perhaps tell him the things Simon had said at the house that night, and that he'd laid hands upon her; but there was no need of it now. She was getting her way, and that was all that counted.

"Well?" Philip said.

She grinned at him. "Remember what I said about washing fleas off a dog? That's all it is. Or like father spraying the orchard every year, to keep the trees healthy. The Island needs to be healthy now, more than ever."

"I guess you're right there. Did you know Jeff's talking about shoving off? And Mark's got that lobster-peddling business on the brain." Philip shook his head. "They've got the idea, along with a lot of other crape-hangers, that this place is just about wound up."

"Fools! What if they are only getting twelve cents now? Wait till April and May — they'll be flocking back like ants after honey!"

"I don't know," said Philip. "I don't know, Joanna."

When she left the shop she went around the corner and looked out across the point at the sea. The scrub spruces were black against a pearly sky, the water quiet and leaden beyond the brown, wind-flattened grass. The rose bushes that were skeletons now would be flowering in six months, the hollows would be marshy, and blue with wild flag. And in July the strawberries would come. Her body strained against its burden, and for a moment it felt slender and free again, leaping ahead into summer. What right did Philip have to shake his head and say, "I don't know . . ." As long as summer still came to the Island, it must hold together. As long as the world still turned.

Alec, wherever you are, you must hear me, she thought. You must know what I'm doing. Can you imagine the Island without the Birds? And they'll go, they'll have to go, because they'll never be able to straighten out. They won't want to go, they love it here in their own way—Simon loves it with that twisted brain of his—but he's got to pay for everything he's tried to do to me, and for what he did to you.

They've got to get off this Island, Alec, Joanna thought, before your baby comes to it.

48

CHRISTMAS CAME AND WENT. It was Christmas on a smaller scale than usual, and the vivid illustrations in Montgomery's and Sears' gift catalogs were only an irritation to most of the Island. There was a run of bad weather so that the *Aurora B.* missed a couple of trips, and there were some bad moments when it looked as if the turkeys wouldn't arrive in time for dinner. But the *Aurora* chugged into the harbor after dark, Christmas Eve, all lit up like a steam yacht.

There'd been the party the teacher always gave the pupils before she went home for the holidays, and the party the whole Island went to, in the clubhouse, with Pete Grant for a Santa Claus who didn't fool anybody. They had carols and refreshments, and Owen and Hugo had gone halves on a goodly quantity of apple brandy, which had a mellowing influence on the men who sampled it. All in all, Christmas was successful.

It was successful in more ways than one. The Birds broke out in a rash of new and luxuriously thick work pants, leather jackets,

bright wool plaid shirts. This was adding insult to injury, and it per-
suaded the last reluctant souls that it was to their common interest
to join with the rest of the Islanders. If they demanded more evidence, this was it. Credit wasn't given easily to lobstermen nowadays, and if the Birds paid cash for everything—which was George's
boast—how in hell did they get enough out of that handful of pots
to spend money like drunken sailors?

Never had the Bennett boys been more persuasive with their
gift of gab. "Look at how many years these Birds have been getting
up so goddam early," they said, "and going to haul before anyone else
was stirring! Look at the hauls we're bringing in, and look
what they get! How come lobsters crawl for them and not for the
rest of us? And it's funny—*damned* funny—how much engine trouble
their boats have lately, that keeps 'em out so much longer than
anybody else!"

So it went, around the shore and in the fish houses, in the camps
where the men yarned and played cards through the stormy afternoons, until right after New Year's, when a night was set for the "visit."
Forest Merrill, who had a permanent feud with his wife's cousin
Sigurd, didn't join, because it smelled too much of the Sorensens for
him, he said. Ned Foster stayed out, too. He said no one ever bothered
him, and he didn't aim to bother anybody. Apparently he didn't know
that Leah was supplied with her chocolates by Ash Bird, who kept
Pete Grant's candy stock pretty well cleared out.

But two men didn't make much difference. Everybody else, in-
cluding Gunnar Sorensen, was enthusiastic. Gunnar cautioned his
sons and grandsons, however. "Dem Birds is clever. You t'reaten,
dey can go to law. You lay one finger on dem, dey can go to law.
You be careful, but give dem *hell!*"

"They've picked out Karl to do the talkin', Father," Eric said.

"You do what I say, Karl. Be careful, but scare dem good. Of
course—" The russet-apple cheeks split into a grin—"of course, you
take a gun along and clean em up, nobody left to go to law!"

They all met in Stephen Bennett's kitchen after supper on the
chosen night. The wind was from the northeast, spitting snow. The
men stood around the warm room in their mackinaws and boots.
Joanna, in the sitting room, listened to their voices out in the kitchen.
Old Johnny's dry, laughing, broken English, Nathan's wheezy chuckle,

Jeff Bennett's deep brusque tones, Philip's quiet ones, and all the others.

The Trudeaus were there, the Sorensens, Marcus Yetton, as well as all the Bennetts but Uncle Nate. He'd have liked this, Joanna thought, feeling sorry that he was missing it. She didn't feel half so demure as she looked, with her head bent over her work and her hands busy with the needle. Excitement flooded her cheeks with color and her eyes with brightness. Her body resented its load. If only she could go with them! But she had to sit at home and possess her soul in patience, and she would know only from what they told her how Simon had looked.

"We'll have a mug-up ready when you come back," Donna was telling them out there, and then they were going out. The younger boys were exuberant with a sense of high adventure. When the door closed behind the last one, Donna came into the sitting room with Winnie at her heels, and sat down. Her eyes were very bright in her clear pallor.

"This is a night we'll remember, Joanna," she said.

The men weren't laughing as they went down the road. It was as if suddenly the meaning of their errand settled heavily upon them. They walked almost in silence, even the younger ones were quiet now. They were going to do something that never before had been done on the Island, and it stifled any desire for careless talk.

There was moonlight — winter moonlight picking out the boats in the harbor, and the long combers that broke on the harbor ledges gleamed and frothed like silver. The north wind whetted its edge against their faces. Chins dug into collars, caps and hats pulled low, they walked through the village. Sometimes from lamplit windows women and children looked out, and saw the silent procession, and understood it; were not their husbands and fathers there?

They walked across the moonlit clearing, past the well, and toward the Bird house, set back against the woods. They would go to the front door tonight; no back-door entrance for such a visit as this. Karl Sorensen and Stephen Bennett walked ahead, not speaking. The frozen boards creaked under their feet. Stephen knocked on the fancy glass panes in the door, and George Bird opened it.

"Evenin', Steve!" he said heartily. "Come in! Hello, Karl — who's that with ye — Eric?" The heartiness ebbed away a little as he saw them all on his porch. "Say, this is quite a crew. But nothin' I like better than lots of company! Come in, boys, all of ye!"

He stood back and they filed in past him, through the dark sitting room into the kitchen, where Mrs. Bird and Ash were, and Simon, who was reading. George brought up the rear, rubbing his hands together and smiling. But it was as if he were only pretending he thought this was a social call. Surely he must have known, when almost every man on the Island stood now in his kitchen and met his smile with a grim silence. If there had been anything likable about George, any slight redeeming feature, they might have felt a stirring of pity for him. But they didn't.

After a moment of awkward silence, he moistened his lips. "You fellas come for something special?" he asked huskily.

Karl stood facing him; Stephen was slightly behind Karl. The other men and boys filled in the room behind them. There was no lounging against walls or dresser, no foot propped on the stove hearth, no lighting of cigarettes. Quiet and straight in their heavy clothing, they waited. The lamp on the table threw their crowded shadows on the cupboards and the ceiling.

Mrs. Bird tried to keep on with her mending, but her hands trembled. Ash sat down again. But Simon, in a rocking chair at the end of the stove, hardly looked up from his magazine. George said again, "Come for something special, boys?"

"Yes," said Karl. "Pretty special, George. I'll be short about it." His eyes were cold and steel-blue, holding George in one place. "There was a time when we didn't miss — much — what we lost out of our pots. But things are different now. We need every lobster that's coming to us. Nobody's got a lot of pots overboard, and nobody can afford to lose anything that crawled into 'em and didn't crawl out again of its own free will."

George was suddenly the color of a codfish belly. "What do you mean?" he got out at last.

Karl said quietly, "I mean you and your boys either start out to haul when the rest of us do, instead of a couple hours earlier, *and tend your own pots,* or you'll stay to hell ashore. Is that clear?"

"You can't talk to me like this in my own house." The sweat was easy to see on George's forehead. He looked around wildly at Ash, who stared down at the floor, biting his lips, and then at Simon, who didn't glance up from his magazine. "You can't walk into a man's house and accuse him and his boys of stealin'—"

"Nobody's accusing you of anything," Karl said. "We're just telling you, George. Just telling you what we'd tell any other man who'd been going to haul hours ahead of the rest of us for years, and bringing in lobsters when the rest of us find our pots as empty as if they'd just been hauled." Karl's eyes were like blue ice. "Nobody's saying you or Ash or Simon hauled those pots, George. But they look mighty empty sometimes when a man's paid out money for gas, and goes out five, ten miles in a stiff wind, with vapor freezing his face, and then gets nothing."

"By God, it's goin' some when a man gets abused like this just because he's not one of these lazy bastards who lays abed half the mornin' instead of doin' his work!"

"Save your breath, George," Karl advised him. "And just remember what I told you. If nobody else starts hauling before noon, you and the boys will wait till noon, too. Understand? Then nobody can say you bothered his string." Karl looked over at Ash, who was trying to smoke an unlighted cigarette. "Got it straight, Ash?"

Ash drew his light brows together in a scowl, thought better of it, swallowed his Adam's apple. "Yes," he muttered sullenly. Karl looked at Simon.

"You too, Simon?" he asked pleasantly. Simon looked up and blew a perfect smoke ring at the ceiling. Then he returned to his magazine.

"I guess Simon's got it straight," said Stephen Bennett. "He's no fool."

There was nothing more to say. The men filed out again. Most of them nodded and murmured, "Evenin'," to Mrs. Bird. There was something piteous about the way she stared up at them from her bloodless face. She looked terrified, Stephen Bennett told Donna and Joanna later.

They went back to the Bennett house in the winter moonlight, the frozen ground ringing under their feet. Some of the men dropped out and went home. The others began to talk, gradually. The way

George and Ash had behaved was no more than they had expected; it was Simon who puzzled them. Surely he wouldn't have the brass to go ahead as if nothing had happened.

"We'll see," said Owen Bennett, and more than one echoed him. By the time they reached the Bennett house, looming white in the moonlight, their somberness had gone. Their action tonight had lifted a load from their shoulders that had been there too long.

"Why didn't we ever do this before?" somebody sang out. They had just come to the house, and Joanna, setting out coffee cups, heard the exultant question and smiled to herself. She felt relaxed and peaceful now, as if she had reached the goal she'd set for herself. It would only be a little while, perhaps a matter of days, before Simon overstepped himself.

Then he would be gone. He would go far away, and never come back.

49

IT SOMETIMES HAPPENS that in midwinter the wind lulls, the sun shines brilliantly for a week and goes down each night in a mad glory of fire; all day long the water is the color of sapphire and ultramarine, dark jade in the shallows, purple close to the rockweed-covered ledges. The gulls wheel in great circles over the spruce-crested islands that dream in the bay. In storm the islands are fringed with flying white spray, but in these periods of calm, they seem to float on the surface of the sea.

It's easy to find the buoys then, and from Grand Manan to Casco Bay the lobster boats are out, dories and peapods, scrubby little power-boats and big graceful ones like the *White Lady*.

One of these rare weeks began the day after the visit to the Birds.

For two days of this heaven-sent weather, George Bird and his sons didn't leave the harbor until most of the other boats had gone. On the third day, just as the Island was beginning to say, "By God, they knew we meant business —" on the third day Simon Bird went out before daylight and didn't come back until midafternoon.

The Island seethed. George and Ash were too scared to do anything but obey, but Simon was a different breed o' cats, for all he was a Bird. Somebody would have to tail him, the Island decided. On the beach, in the fish houses, in the store, over the pool table, the men talked it over. There were volunteers — Owen was one of them, but Nils was chosen. The Sorensens lived the nearest to the Birds, and Nils' room looked across the field and the lane so that he could see lights in the Bird kitchen when they were up early in the winter darkness.

When Nils came up to Stephen Bennett's house to tell them about his new job, he was quietly pleased. "Kind of like the idea of pestering Simon," he admitted. His eyes said nothing at all as they met Joanna's, but she felt the strong link of comradeship between them that had existed all through their growing-up. Nils hadn't forgotten, any more than she had; he would gain revenge for them both.

Now Nils was up every morning long before daylight, fixing his own breakfast and eating it by lamplight while the rest of the house slept above him; then he dressed in his heavy outdoor clothing and went out into the sharp cold hush before dawn, when the air stung his throat, and the stars burned with a white brilliance over the Island. Brigport was a long, crouched shape across the sound, like a sleeping animal. There was hardly a sound anywhere, except his own feet on the ground that creaked with frost. The wind died down sometimes in this last hour before daybreak, and the water on the rocks was like breathing. He walked down to the shore in this silence, keeping close to the fish houses and not walking on the beach stones.

When Jud Gray left the Island, he had sold his boat shop back to Stephen Bennett, who'd owned it first, and Marcus Yetton now had his shop at the farther end, which rose flush with the outermost end of the old wharf. This was where Nils went, threading his way among the hogsheads and traps like a shadow among shadows, his rubber boots uncannily noiseless; he never stumbled, or rolled a stone under his foot, or bumped against a hogshead. He waited, in the dark doorway of Marcus' place. The cold struck through his clothes; the water gurgled and bumped under the wharf, and the sky was pale over the Eastern End woods.

He never had to wait long before there was a faint rattle of beach stones, a bump against wood, a punt being slipped lightly down to the sea's edge; then the clink of oars in the oarlocks, and the whisper of water about the blades. The punt would glide past the end of the wharf, and Nils would wait a little longer until he heard, clear in the silence, the shipping of oars, the heavy clink of the mooring chain. Then the throttled murmur of Simon's engine, thrown back by the rocks as it passed them.

Nils could tell by the sound whether the boat turned to the east'ard or west'ard when it left the harbor. Then, moving fast, he clambered down over the spilings to the beach and untied his own punt.

By now the winter dawn threw a paling light across the Island; the spruces were very black against the eastern sky, the world was drained of all color. On the water the wind was sharp. There was a stiff chop in the rip tide at the harbor mouth. Nils' boat rode it steadily, responsive to his hand on the wheel. And when daylight was a reality, and not just a promise, he saw Simon ahead of him, bow pointed out to sea. If Simon looked back, he could see Nils.

Nils stayed behind him all day. Sunrise touched the sea with gold as far as he could look, and sometimes he had to narrow his eyes against the glare in order to see the tiny, dancing black speck that was Simon's boat. Simon roared to the east'ard, spray flying in a rainbow glitter from his bow, and Nils roared behind him. When Simon at last reached his string and began to haul, Nils cut off his engine and sat on the engine box, smoking, sheltered from the wind by the sprayhood, drinking hot coffee from his thermos jug. As the sun climbed toward the zenith, and struck up sparks of silver fire from the whole tossing, blue-green expanse, it was easier to watch Simon work along his string. The boat was at some distance, and Simon was only a minute dark figure moving back and forth in the cockpit, gaffing buoys with a venomous thrust, slamming the lobsters into the box, and throwing the traps overboard again as if it were Nils himself he had there, bound hand and foot and weighted down with a weir stone.

Perhaps there would be no sunshine, but snow on the wind, and foreboding black clouds driving across the sky, and a steadily roughening sea to wash over the decks, so that the boats would be iced before they reached home. But it was never too rough for Simon to go out, or for Nils to follow him. It became a strange, silent duel, with no signs of exhaustion on either side.

Simon didn't have reason to stay out all day when Nils trailed him so closely. Sometimes, to Nils' amusement, he invented side trips—apparently hoping to make Nils run out of gas. But Nils had prepared for this. He kept his tank filled, and two extra cans of gas in the cuddy. He was ready and willing to stay out all day—round and round the Rock, the boats wallowing in the wash from the steep shores of the ledge. The keepers and their families came out with glasses, to see what sort of hare-and-hound chase was taking place around their barren stronghold. Nils took off his cap and waved it at them, yelling greetings through the bitter-cold, sparkling air.

Nils' happy attitude, as if he were on a pleasure sail in the middle of summer, was usually too much for Simon. He would start for the Island. His boat was narrower in the beam than Nils', and when he reached Sou-west Point, where the red rock cliffs gleamed in the winter sunshine, half hidden in boiling surf, he skirted close to the ledges or between them, his engine wide open. He was tacitly daring Nils to follow him, but Nils was no fool. Eventually he must start for the harbor along the west side, and then Nils was with him again.

Simon wouldn't go to the car with his lobsters these days, not with Nils coming up alongside to shout cheerfully, "How they crawlin', Cap'n Simon?" No, Simon went straight to his mooring and gaffed up the buoy with a vicious thrust, and had reached the shore and disappeared before Nils rowed to the beach. Later, Simon would sell his lobsters.

The Island was laughing. They hadn't enjoyed anything so much for years.

"Simon knows they're laughing," Stephen told Nils one night. "Watch out for him. He won't take this forever."

"That's what my father and grandfather tell me. Well, I don't want any chew with him. If I can handle him without exchanging any remarks, that's the best way."

Joanna walked to the door with him that night when he left, and stood for a moment on the step, watching the sparkle and blaze of stars in the cold night.

"What'll happen between you and Simon?"

"I don't know, Jo. Wait till he makes a move."

"You've been waiting a long time," she said simply.

Nils looked down at her. "You've been waiting, yourself. I know about that poker rig, Jo. The debts, and all . . . and then the house."

"You know a lot, don't you?" She tilted her chin at him, defying him to be sorry for her.

"I know you've got guts," said Nils with simple eloquence, and stepped down into the path. "Night, Jo. I've got to turn in early and turn out early on this job. I expect our friend to start out at midnight, first thing I know."

"He can't keep this up forever. Having to be honest in spite of himself will strike in on him and poison him," Joanna called after him. She was laughing as she came back into the kitchen, and Mark said with frank interest, "Hey, Jo, are all women supposed to look as good as you do, when they're going to have a baby?"

"*Mark,*" Donna reproved him, and Joanna grinned.

"Golly, Mother, he's going to be its uncle—I'm glad he's interested in it."

"Me too," Stevie chimed in. "Will somebody tell me why I'm getting a lot more kick out of being an uncle to this one than Charles' kids? Say, Jo, are you going to keep on calling it *it?*"

"Itsie," said Joanna. She went up to bed, smiling. In spite of her aching back, an odd and somehow satisfying peace lay upon her these days. She thought of Uncle Nate's cows in the time just before they calved; nothing bothered them, they stood knee-deep in meadow grass and looked at you with buttercups sticking out of their mouths, and switched their tails languidly. Perhaps this quietness was nature's way of making you rested and ready for the business to come. But whatever it was, she was thankful for it.

The baby was going to be born on the Island. She had settled that when she first came home to live. Donna wanted her to go to the hospital, and Stephen agreed that it was safer to be ashore, in case anything went wrong.

"But," he added, "Nate and I were born out here, and Charles, and Joanna herself."

"You see?" Joanna faced them triumphantly. "It's right that my baby should be born here, if I was. What can happen to me? I'm strong and husky. Look at Mateel, she got along all right, didn't she? Oh, women make too much fuss about having a baby nowadays! Me for the good old days when you dropped them between the rows when you were picking beans!"

Donna said, *"Joanna!"* But her eyes were sparkling, and Stephen laughed till his own eyes ran water.

'That's the spirit, Jo! You're a real Bennett!" he applauded her. "You can stay home and have your baby. Thank God for the telephone and the Coast Guard, if we need them."

Now, lying in bed, she heard faintly the voices in the kitchen, someone bringing in a pail of water, Mark dumping a load of wood in the box, Winnie asking to go out. All sounds mingled with the sound of the Island outside into a harmonious whole. Her mind drifted toward sleep, and on the very brink of it she thought of Alec, as she always did when she was alone in the dark. Perhaps she should still be crying for him, but she couldn't cry. If he knew — and he must know — he would be the first one to be glad she had reached this serenity. Alec hated tears and long faces. Against the darkness she could see him, long mouth twitching with suppressed laughter, eyes crinkling at the corners, alight with tiny sparkles, eyebrow tilted.

Joanna, honey, if you turn out to be one of those mothers who howls while she rocks the cradle, and drips tears all over my child's face, I'll never forgive you.

That was how he'd say it. She could hear his voice, with laughter running warmly under it.

"Darling," she said softly in the darkness. "I promise. Maybe I'll cry when it's born, because I'll never see you holding it in your arms. But I promise I won't howl over the cradle."

She went to sleep then, and dreamed she was climbing up the slope from Spanish Cove on Pirate Island, up toward the blue sky and the sparrows and the wheeling gulls. She could feel the sun hot on her face, and she knew that when she reached the top, she'd look down and see Alec coming up after her.

*   *   *

While Joanna dreamed, Nils was walking home, briskly in the cold night air. The Island slept under the distant, frosty twinkle overhead. Nils liked to sleep, and to sleep late on winter mornings, as well as anybody. But the Island, lying around him under the stars, had chosen him for its agent, and his sleeping hours would be short until his job was done.

He was almost home before he remembered that he'd left his dinner box out aboard his boat. Kristi always made something special for his lunch, and put it where he could find it, and he liked to take some coffee along on those long days on the water. There was nothing for it but to go out aboard and get the box.

He walked back to the beach, untied his punt, and rowed out across the harbor. The wind was around to the northeast, and the water was kicking up outside: he could see the white surge of it in the starlight. The long swells raced by the harbor mouth and piled up on the rocks with a sound like thunder.

The harbor was placid enough. He climbed aboard his boat, gave the skiff's painter a twist around the winch head of the hauling gear, and went down into the cuddy. He reached for the flashlight he kept aboard the boat, and found the dinner box just where he'd left it, beside the stove. He found something else, too—his charts, strewn across a locker, some of them half-unrolled. They marred the tidiness of his cabin, and he sat down to roll them up again and put them away. David and Stevie had been aboard in the afternoon— they'd probably had the charts out, and left them like that when Owen yelled at them to shake a leg if they wanted to go to Brigport with him.

It was only when Dave was in a hurry that he'd leave stuff around like that, especially aboard Nils' boat. The cuddy was warm and snug, a man could live in it if he had to. Nils kept it scrubbed up, its white paint fresh, and everything stowed in its place. His papers were framed under glass to keep them clean.

He laid an unrolled chart across his knees and studied it by flashlight, following his penciled course to Cash's, the course he had marked in with Owen and Alec leaning over his shoulders.

The water slapped and chuckled under the smoothly flaring sides, and sometimes the boat pulled a little at her mooring, like an impatient colt, but not very often. A muffled sound startled him into instant, questioning alertness. He switched off his light, and listened. Somebody was out rowing around, shipping oars close to the bow of his boat.

There was another noise, a jarring bump. A skiff under the bow would bump like that against the stem iron . . . if somebody was fooling around with the mooring.

Nils picked up his flashlight, moved lightly as a cat toward the slide, and pushed it back. In almost the same instant he was out through the hatchway, and had flashed the light across the low cabin roof at the bow beyond.

It caught and glittered on the broad, long blade of a bait knife; and Simon Bird looked back at him. If it hadn't been for the gleam of his red hair, this sharp and startled white face with the light reflected like fire in its eyes might have belonged to a desperate, half-crazed stranger who was trying to cut Nils' boat loose from her mooring.

Nils said quietly, "We'll talk about this when we get ashore, Simon." Simon dropped from sight, and Nils heard the bait knife clatter in the bottom of the punt, and the rattle of oarlocks. He leaned over the side and kept his light on the punt as it skimmed shorewards. When it had disappeared beyond Stephen Bennett's boat, and he was satisfied that Simon was going to the beach, Nils ran forward to examine the mooring hawser. It was hardly damaged, the knife had only begun to go through the sturdy seizing of potwarp and burlap. But there was enough to prove someone had been at it.

Nils knelt on the bow, holding the light on the hawser, ignoring the wind that whipped across the harbor and would have taken his boat out past the point in no time at all, if he hadn't been there.

Nils was mad. He hastened across the cockpit, flashing his light upon the winch head and discovered his punt had gone adrift. The turn of the rope around the winch head hadn't been enough, the way the tide was pulling, and by now the skiff was probably far outside the harbor, dancing on her merry way.

He started up the engine and ran straight for Pete Grant's wharf. When he had walked up through the shed, his footsteps echoing in the empty darkness, he turned into the path that led around the shore to the beach. He didn't run, but he walked like a man with business to attend to. He stopped sometimes to listen, but there wasn't a sound. Not even the faintest suggestion of a beach rock turning under a boot.

He walked back again, and stopped between his father's fish house and the Binnacle. Simon was not there. And there was no way to find him in this bitter-cold dark.

Nils walked up toward his grandfather's spruce windbreak. When he stopped to look across the field toward the Birds', he saw a moving light through the kitchen windows. It was only for an instant, but it was enough. Someone was walking around the Birds' kitchen with a flashlight. Nils went past the well, with his long even stride, crossed the lane, and turned into the Birds' path. There was no faintest gleam of light showing now, and the house seemed to sleep in the starlight. But there *had* been a light there.

The back door was unlocked, and Nils walked in. The darkness was warm, there was a coal fire in the stove, and he sniffed coffee in the air, as if somebody—Simon—had just had a quick drink. Nils scratched a match and lit the lamp over the sink; then he lifted a heavy fist and knocked hard on the cupboard doors.

"Ahoy the house!" he shouted. "Get down here, George! And be quick about it!"

"For Christ's sake!"

He turned quickly and saw Ash standing in the doorway of a room off the kitchen, staring at him with red-rimmed eyes. Ash, scrawny in his undershirt and pants, his suspenders hanging, his hair on end, was even less attractive than usual. "What the hell do you want, rammin' around in this house like you owned it?" he demanded.

"I want Simon. Where is he?"

"Simon?" Ash blinked, and looked at the line of jackets and coats and caps behind the door. "Ain't he home yet? No, by Jesus, he ain't, and his heavy jacket's gone, too." He scowled at Nils, and then looked bewildered. "It was here when I went to bed—he must've been in since. What do you want him for, anyway?"

"If you're lying, I'll wring your stringy neck, Ash," said Nils coldly, and turned around to confront a belligerent and even more unbeautiful George, with his long winter underwear wrinkled around his legs and his eyes bleary with sleep above his black-stubbled cheeks and chin. He stared at Nils. Then he said anxiously, "What is it? What do you want?"

"Simon." Nils looked him up and down. "Ash here says he's out somewhere."

"Why, I—" George looked at the jackets too. "He must be. What do you want him for? It's 'most two o'clock."

"I'll wait for him," said Nils. "He won't stay out for long. Too damn cold, even if he did hop in for a swig out of the coffee pot and his thick jacket."

"I never heard him!" said Ash defensively.

George came all the way downstairs and huddled over the stove like a disconsolate rooster shut out in the rain. "What's he done, that's what I want to know. Ain't I got a right to know?" he said plaintively.

Nils leaned against the dresser, his arms folded, and looked at George with cold blue eyes. "My business is with Simon and nobody else."

"Oh, Jesus." George shook his head, and almost wrung his hands. "I give up. I can't do nothin' with that boy, Nils. Nothin'. He's like a wild hawk. Always has been. He's breakin' his mother's heart, that one."

"I don't think you and the other one there ever did much to keep him from breaking it," Nils remarked. He took out his cigarettes. "I'll give him one hour to get in here. You've heard of smoking people out, haven't ye? Well, we'll freeze him in."

"What is it, George? *George!*" Mrs. Bird was a frightened voice at the head of the stairs.

"You better go back to bed, Flora," said George heavily. But his wife came down, a confused, withered little woman in a full flannel nightdress like the kind Nils' grandmother wore. Simon had got his red hair from her, but certainly not his brass. She looked at Nils as if he were the devil in person.

"What's the matter?" she whispered faintly.

"I just want to talk to Simon, Mrs. Bird," said Nils and his voice was gentle. His grandmother had told him what a nice girl Flora Arey had been, too nice to throw herself away on George Bird. "You better go back to bed, like George says. It's nothing for you to get fussed up about."

But she sat down weakly in a rocking chair and started twisting a handkerchief in her fingers. Ash yawned loudly and went back to bed. George still hovered over the stove, and Nils watched them all with his unclouded, sea-blue gaze, his arms folded across his chest, and the lamplight yellow on his hair.

The clock on the table ticked very loudly in the stillness of the room. George's breathing was wheezy; his wife didn't make a sound, but she looked at Nils with scared eyes, and kept on twisting the handkerchief. The hour crept by, and his rage burned deeper and deeper.

Suddenly, in the quiet, they heard an engine in the harbor. They all three stared at each other. Then Nils turned and went out. Simon must have hung around in the cold and the dark, up in the woods behind the house or even as close as the shop, waiting for Nils to go. Then he got tired of waiting. Nils walked down to Pete Grant's wharf to be sure his own boat was all right.

She was safe and fast; he inspected the lines carefully with his flashlight, and then stood on the car a long time, listening to the fading sound of Simon's engine through the wash and roar of surf on the harbor ledges.

When he couldn't hear the engine any more, he went back up the wharf and walked around the shore. If he had been mad before, he was twice as mad now. His anger was a quiet and self-contained thing; it could contain itself for a long time, until Simon Bird came back into his reach again.

In the east there was a faint lightening in the sky; it was after four. No sense to go to bed now. Nils went into the fish house, lit a lantern, built a fire in the stove, and began stripping the broken laths from a trap battered by the last storm. He worked steadily, his face stern and absorbed, until the lantern light grew pale and sickly against the first ruddy fires of sunrise. Then he went up to Stephen's house.

50

THIS DAY THAT NILS HAD WATCHED grow from the darkness was full of sunshine and wind; wind that whipped the sea into a glittering blue-green wilderness of mountains and deep shining valleys.

It was too rough to haul. So almost every man on Bennett's was in the store, waiting for the mailboat, when Simon Bird called up from Brigport. No one but Nils and the Bennetts knew about the events of the night before. But the fact that Simon's boat was gone from its mooring, and that George was cleaning up his fish house in a very agitated manner, and jumped whenever he was spoken to— this was enough to drop an interested silence over the conversations around the stove and candy counter when Pete turned away from the telephone and barked, "Ash, it's that brother of yourn!"

Ash, somewhat pale and uneasy, took the receiver and said nervously, "Hello . . ." The rest of his conversation was flat and monosyllabic. The listeners learned absolutely nothing. Ash hung up, rang off, and walked out of the store, as if he would like to hurry but didn't quite dare.

Nils and Owen walked out behind him. They caught up with him in the path, one on each side of him. Owen rested a heavy hand on his shoulder and said companionably, "Hello, young Ash!" Nils said, "Hi, bub. Where's Simon?"

Ash's voice came out in a squeak. "He won't be back— he'll never be back in this godawful hole! He's sold his boat to Tom Robey, and Tom's runnin' him ashore in her right away—prob'ly they're gone already!" He glared at the two taller men like a bantam rooster. "And I'm gettin' to hell off as soon as I can get my gear together."

"That's fine," said Owen jovially. Nils said nothing at all. They let him go, and watched him scoot along the path toward his father's shop.

"Well, you got gypped out of breaking Simon's neck, Nils," Owen said. "We should've gone over there first thing this morning and tended to the red-headed bastard."

Nils shrugged. "So he's never coming back. Well, he wants to remember that." He looked over at Brigport, its fields tawny in the brilliant sunshine, its shores white with surf. "If he ever comes back, I'll be waiting for him."

George and Mrs. George and young Ash moved away on the next boat day. Everybody was very polite to them, and bought up their traps at fairly good prices, considering the fact that the Bird strings seemed to have been built up mostly from other men's property.

A week after they had gone, Nate Bennett wrote to his brother Stephen to tell him he'd seen George in town, and had made him an offer for the house and shore privilege, and George had been almost too ready to sell.

"Never want to go back to that place," he'd muttered. "They'd just as lief cut your throat as not."

No one seemed to know anything about Simon or his whereabouts. But it wasn't long before Joanna had her last contact with him—a strangely roundabout contact. There was a letter from a Boston lawyer. Simon wanted payment on the house, right away.

He was paid, even though it was a bad winter. The Bennetts dug deep into their pockets, and Stephen finished up a bank account that had been already sadly depleted by loans to Marcus and Forest, and several others, and his own heavy expenses for keeping his gear in repair.

"You shouldn't be paying this," Joanna told her father bluntly. "Let him have the house."

"It's worth the money to know the Birds won't have a foothold on the Island—they won't have anything to come back to," he said.

The day the receipt came, he took it out of his pocket at the dinner table and held it up. "Do you know what this means?" he asked the family, his dark face somber. "This means that the Birds have left the Island for good. How does that sound, after all the chewing I've listened to in this kitchen?"

Stevie grinned broadly. "Sounds pretty swell to me!"

"We never got a chance to mess 'em up," gloomed Owen. "I'd like to have given Simon a good send-off, but he slipped right out from under our hands. If we'd gone after 'em way back in the beginning, they'd have been gone a long time ago."

"So you're going to growl because you didn't get a chance to paste somebody," said Philip. "Instead of being glad they're gone, and for once you can rest easy, without having to go out and sit on your traps like a hen on eggs."

"Oh, I'm glad enough. We made George squirm a little, too. And maybe I'll meet Simon ashore sometime."

The talk went on, over and around Joanna, and she thought, they're gone, but it doesn't seem real. Gone as easily as that. The slip of paper by Stephen's plate was sign and symbol of something she had thought about ever since she was fifteen years old. She tried to fit it into her brain. The Island without the Birds; the Island without Simon. She would never have to meet him again. She tried to imagine it, remembering those wordless passings in the lane, the time by the rain barrel outside the store—oh, the countless times when her sick rage had come over her just at sight of him. And she would never have to hear his voice again, perhaps she would even forget the echoes of his soft, insolent words on that very last time, when he told her the house wasn't hers.

Now, eating dinner in the kitchen, bright with noon sunshine and warm with the wood fire crackling in the stove, her parents and brothers talking around her in pleasant voices, she could almost make Simon Bird seem a dream. And did Alec know, wherever he was?

Sunshine struck red lights from black crests of hair, slanted across rich, healthy brown skin, glinted in restless black eyes or in clear blue-gray. She thought, I should be happy now—as happy as I ever could be. I've got what I wanted. Why don't I feel as if everything was all right for us now?

She didn't know the answer to anything. The Birds were gone, and they wouldn't rob Nils, or Marcus, or Nathan, or anybody else, ever again. Men could leave their fishhouse doors unlocked. But how long would there be men on Bennett's Island to leave doors unlocked, and set traps in the calm knowledge they wouldn't be touched?

The kitchen was flooded with sunshine, but it was a strange sunshine; there was no brightness in it.

As if she had been patiently and considerately waiting for the Birds to remove themselves and for the Island to settle down into its mid-winter hush, Joanna's baby was born the day after the receipt came. Joanna was sleeping in the ell chamber now, and she awoke that morning with the certainty that this was the day. She felt very tranquil. She lay in bed and looked out at the snow falling quietly in the windless dawn, dropping its light veil over the face of the meadow, rimming the dove-colored serenity of Goose Cove with white, falling faster and faster between Joanna's windows and the black wall of spruces across the meadow. It seemed to her there was no sound anywhere. No single gull, no surf, no wind.

Ellen Douglass was born when the snowy day was slipping into a snowy dusk. She came with no long and annoying delays, and with a minimum of trouble for all concerned. Afterwards Joanna's chief sensation was surprise. It hadn't hurt half as much as she'd expected, after listening all her life to Aunt Mary's vivid accounts of her own experiences, and knowing without being told how her mother had suffered when the last two boys were born.

Before she fell asleep she spoke of it drowsily to her mother. Eric Sorensen's wife and Stella Grant, who'd been a nurse once, were out of the room, and Donna stood by the bed holding the baby in her arms.

"Of course she didn't give you any trouble." Donna looked down at the little red face in the blankets and a pair of intensely blue eyes stared unwinkingly back at her. "She'll never give you any trouble. She's a good girl, she is," Donna said, and carried her newest granddaughter out of her room.

Joanna smiled as she slipped gratefuly into sleep. Her lips shaped the words she was too tired to say out loud. "A little blonde girl named for your mother, Alec. How you'd love her!"

No baby that had been born on the Island in the past five years aroused such interest, unless it was Susie Yetton's last one. Everybody had gone to visit Susie, and compared notes afterward on whether or not the baby looked like Johnny. At three it was the image of Marcus, so at last they'd given up speculating. But Joanna's baby — Alec's baby — was something different. There was not a woman on the Island who didn't bring a gift. They told Joanna she looked wonderful, and then they looked at Ellen, placidly asleep in her basket, and wiped their eyes.

Joanna was touched by their feeling for her; she felt that she loved them all, even the bedraggled Susie, who, with her oldest girl Annie, had crocheted a little afghan. Grandma Sorensen, very feeble now after her shock, had made some little shoes and sent them up by Kristi. In spite of the winter weather, Mateel came up often through the woods from the Eastern End.

As far as the family was concerned, Ellen was its jewel. They weren't chary, like most men, of holding a tiny baby; before she was out of bed Joanna was used to the sight of her brothers carrying her daughter, looking bigger and blacker than ever because the baby was so little and fair. Stephen called her a humming star and said none of his own children had ever been so good. They came in from hauling, scrubbed up, peeked to see if she was awake, and had her up in their arms in her nest of blankets while Donna's back was turned.

It was hard for Joanna to stay quietly in bed for two weeks; she awoke each morning full of a vitality that flushed her skin with color and glowed in her voice. Now she was slender and supple again. Now, if she wanted to, she could run and bend and twist. And Ellen was such a sweet baby for her and Alec to have made between them, with her unsurprised blue gaze and her fluff of fair hair, and the deep dimple in her chin. Would the day never come when she could get up?

It came. Out in the kitchen, feeling beautifully flat in her taken-in dress, her shining dark hair caught back with a red ribbon, Joanna lifted her baby from the basket and carried her to the seaward windows. "Here comes Grandpa," she said, "back from hauling. I'll bet he's thinking what a funny little mite you are.' She smiled at the idea of calling her father "Grandpa," but in a year or so that's what Ellen would be calling him. Little Charles said it already.

Then, without warning, the old sense of loss and desolation flooded over her in a great bitter wave. Little Charles could look out and say with wild joy, "Daddy's coming, Daddy's coming!" But Ellen would never say it; Joanna would never hold the small body up against her shoulder and point, and say, "See Daddy out there? He's coming home to see his girl."

Her eyes watched the eternal tossing of the water outside, the everlasting circling of the gulls, but they were seeing something else; Ellen, sunshine tangled in her yellow hair, running down to the gate, and Alec swinging up the lane. Light and shadow fell across his white shirt, his cap was pushed back on his head, he was whistling. And then he dropped to his heels by the gate, at just the right level for a small girl to fling her arms around his neck and hug with all the warm, worshiping intensity her little body could hold.

Alec hugged her too, and came up the path with her perched on his shoulder, one small tanned hand gripped tightly in his hair.

Joanna turned away from the window and went to sit down in a rocking chair near the stove, the baby still in her arms. She leaned her head back and shut her eyes.

"What's the matter, Jo?" said Kristi anxiously, turning from the dresser.

Joanna smiled at her. "Just tired, that's all. I'll rest."

Kristi didn't stay long after Joanna was up. She went home again, to keep house for her grandmother and work on her things for her chest. Peter had given it to her for Christmas; he had made it lovingly with his own hands, and it was truly a beautiful piece of craftsmanship. Perhaps this proof that Peter could work with tools as well as any old-country boy softened Gunnar; at least he'd stopped his sarcastic objections to the marriage.

On a windless day in early February, when the men had all gone out to haul, Donna walked down to the harbor to spend the afternoon with Eric's wife, and Joanna stayed home with the baby. Alone here in the kitchen, with Ellen asleep in her basket, she ironed minute dresses and gertrudes, and was surprised at her own quiet content. There had been a tortured period when she'd never expected to feel like this again . . . if indeed she'd ever felt like this. Peace after pain—the heart's pain and the body's pain both—had a different texture. It must be always tinged with sadness, but it is overlaid with a deep thankfulness that the edge of grief had been blunted a little, at last.

She caught herself humming as she worked. Looking down toward the harbor, she saw the village around the shore, its windows silver in the sun; the harbor was silver too—liquid, living silver, never quiet, but forever flashing.

Someone was coming through the gate. She narrowed her eyes

against the glare, wondering which of the men was back from hauling so early. It was not until he was almost up to the house that she
saw it was Nils.

He came in quietly, as he always did. "Hi, Jo."

"Hello, Nils. How's everything?"

He laid his cap down on the dresser and walked across to Ellen's
basket. "I suppose you mean lobsters when you say how's everything.
Well, they're less and less." He leaned over the basket and said in
interested surprise, "Hey, she's awake! Hi, Ellen. Is she old enough
to smile yet? She just did."

"Gas," said Joanna briskly.

"I don't believe it. I'll bet she knows me." He put down his forefinger, gently prying open an infinitesimal pink fist, and the minute
fingers closed around his big one, and clung.

"Look at that," said Nils in a hushed voice. As Joanna leaned
over the basket with him, he looked at her with eyes that suddenly
deepened in color; his face was intensely serious. She thought of the
way his face had matured and hardened, the bones showing cleanly
and strongly through the flesh, the mouth composed and still, and
strong in its very stillness. But that expression on his face—it struck
an echo deep in memory. She couldn't quite catch it.

Nils said abruptly, "Joanna, what are you going to do?"

"What do you mean?"

"Are you staying here, or planning on a job?"

"And leave the Island?" She stared at him. She hadn't thought
of a job, and now it was a new problem with which she had come
face to face. How could she expect her father to feed and clothe her
and Ellen, to pay for Ellen's schooling as he'd paid for hers? He wanted
to, but it wasn't his responsibility, this child lying there with Nils'
forefinger in her fist, looking up at them with her calm blue eyes.
Yet—leave the Island? She hadn't counted on that.

"I don't know," she said slowly. "Nils, I don't know. My mother
needs me here right now, but the boys will be marrying and having
their own homes, and there'll be less and less for me to do."

"That's what I wanted to talk to you about." Gently he freed
his finger from the baby's clasp, and straightened up. "Jo, I'm no good
at talking, but maybe I can get this over to you. What I want to
know is—when things get straightened around—if you'd think about

marrying me." His eyes held hers as he talked. "I know this is no time to talk to you about it, but I've got to tell you now, because of the way things are."

She said slowly, "Nils, why do you want to marry me? Are you still in love with me?"

It was queer, asking him that. On the Island people didn't talk much about love. But he was answering her, directly. "I'm still in love with you. And if you ever married me, I'd want you to make it the kind of a marriage you wanted it to be. I mean—" For the first time he hesitated, a slight flush ran up under his skin. "I know there'd never be anybody else for you like Alec. That you'd think of, that way. You wouldn't ever have to worry." The flush deepened, and his cool straightforward voice was suddenly husky.

"But Jo, if you'd let me look out for you and Ellen— well, that's all I want. There wouldn't be any strings. And Ellen would have everything you wanted her to have."

Joanna looked into his eyes and they looked steadily back at her. She knew, beyond a shadow of a doubt, that he meant what he said; that he'd be willing to take her in a sterile marriage that wasn't marriage at all, and be grateful to give her child and Alec's everything she wanted her to have. Those were his words, and they were true. She felt humble, suddenly.

"Listen, Nils, you deserve a whole lot more than what you'd be willing to expect from me! You ought to have somebody who—well, for her there'd never be another man like you, no matter what happened. You said it was that way for Alec, and it ought to be that way for you, too."

Nils' mouth twisted in a little grin. "What if I'm one of those one-woman guys? 'Twould be kind of a nuisance, being married to a woman who was crazy about me, and I didn't care much about her."

"Nils, do you honestly think you could stand it any better, being married to a woman you're in love with, and who isn't crazy about you the way she should be?" Joanna shook her head. "Nils, I can't ever marry you. It's the way you said—there'll never be another Alec for me, and if I couldn't bring a man anything more than just being friends, I wouldn't want to marry him."

"Maybe in two or three years you'll feel different—"

"No. You think it's hard for me just to *talk* about it now. But it won't be any different then, Nils. She's Alec's child and mine, and I'm a little too proud to ask another man to feed and clothe her when I can't give him the love he should have."

Nils listened, politely and impassively; it seemed to her that she must make him understand. "Nils, don't you *see?* You're not a one-woman man—no man is, unless he makes himself that way. You haven't been around with girls enough. You've kept faithful to me, but I didn't want your faithfulness! I was in love with somebody else. You've got to open your eyes and look around, and find a girl who deserves a man like you. And you'll love her, and she'll love you, and you'll have children of your own." She stopped her eager flood of words abruptly, and added in a quieter voice, "I'm glad to think you'd want to be good to Ellen. So many men don't care much for a step-child."

Nils picked up his cap from the dresser. "I guess I'd better go. I just wanted to tell you what I was thinking, Jo. I thought in a couple of years we'd both be pretty lonesome sometimes—this Island can be damn lonesome—and where we'd always got along so well—" He stopped suddenly and his face broke into the old lines of youth and laughter, as if he were trying somehow to cheer her up. "You going to cry, Jo? What is there to cry about?"

"I'm not going to cry. I was just thinking about you and Ellen."

He stopped at the door, his hand on the knob, and looked back at her. "I love that little mite," he said in a level voice, "because she looks the way I always thought ours would look—yours and mine. so long, Jo."

51

JOANNA WAS STANDING ON the front doorstep shaking rag rugs briskly into the wind, and wondering if it was really spring in the air, or only the way the February thaw always smelled, when she saw Nils coming from the alder swamp that divided the Bennett meadow from Gunnar's land. He walked swiftly in his larrigans through the marshy space where the cranberries ripened in October; his faded shirt was a soft spot of color against the sodden meadow and the dark woods.

It had been two weeks ago, the afternoon in the kitchen, and Nils had been his quiet and natural self ever since. But Joanna, watching him come, felt a twinge of pity and guilt. No, the pity was wrong: Nils didn't need pity. You felt pity only for the weak, and Nils was anything but weak. Guilt? That was wrong, too. Foolish to feel guilt. But it wasn't wrong or foolish to respect him, to realize what a rare privilege it was to know a man like Nils.

She waited now until he came, and they went into the house together. It was then that Nils told her father and mother that he was leaving the Island. David was to have his boat. He hadn't decided what he would do, but he'd find something very soon. Work on a tanker or a freighter, maybe; he'd see some of those places he'd heard his grandfather tell about, from his days at sea.

If it was a shock to Stephen and Donna, it was more than that for Joanna. She sat rigidly still, her coffee untouched, and looked at him as if he were a stranger. Nils, leaving the Island. Nils, of all people. His roots here were as deep as hers — how could he bear to pull them up in this cold, matter-of-fact way, to leave his boat, to walk out?

It's not because of me, she thought. I'm not that important. Nils always knew how to put first things first. It's because he's lost faith in the Island, she thought. But I never thought he'd lose faith in it.

She watched him unbelievingly, and once he looked directly at her; his blue eyes stayed on hers for a moment, and she saw there no answer at all to her unbelief.

So Nils left Bennett's Island.

In March his uncle, Eric Sorensen, lost most of his traps in a storm, and couldn't replace them without going heavily into debt. He was in debt already, and it weighed on his tidy Scandinavian soul. There was only one thing to do; move to the mainland where a man conld haul his traps all winter long, even while Bennett's was lashed by gales. The traps for inshore fishing didn't cost nearly so much as the big deep-sea pots with their fifty and sixty fathom warps. There was some talk of lifting the Closed Season, and if he went lobstering all summer, he'd do it in some kind of comfort, by God! A man deserved a little peace of mind once in a while, and lobsters didn't pay enough now to make life on Bennett's worthwhile.

That was Eric's notion, and it was echoed around the shore. Eric was known as a man of sound ideas. If he didn't think lobsters would ever go up again in price, it was worth considering. Eric and Mrs. Eric and Thea—the latter radiant at the thought of working a new territory—left before the middle of March, and Eric's son-in-law, Forest Merrill, and his family, followed in a week. Forest still had plenty of traps, and he and Eric would work together till Eric's new string was built and set.

Two more empty houses. The Areys wrote that they wouldn't be back this spring. Another empty house . . .

Joanna walked down past her house and Alec's, past the clubhouse that had been used so little this past winter, past Jud Gray's house and George Bird's—all empty.

She looked across at Eric Sorensen's blank windows, and the Areys' neat, shuttered place. They'd miss Mrs. Arey's garden this year; she had wonderful luck with her gladiolas and larkspur. Across the harbor, Forest Merrill's house was closed up.

But the empty moorings were even more lonesome than the houses that would be locked against the Island spring.

There were always definite signs of spring on the Island. The robins came, and the bluebirds stopped for a while. Gunnar Sorensen always appeared on the scene with a resurgence of youth in his apple cheeks and twinkling eyes. He visited all the fish houses, whose doors hung hospitably open, and made sardonic little comments in his most agreeable voice, smiling all the while; when he had made the rounds and thoroughly ruffled everybody's temper, he went home to his coffee, smiled benignly at his wife, and said this spring he felt younger than ever.

And this spring Mark and Stevie left the Island. Joanna had hoped in vain that Mark would forget his lobster business. But he presented to his father a comprehensive plan, built on sound common sense. Stephen had to admit that. He agreed that if the spring crawl were good, they'd be able to pay for a second-hand truck. Yes, there was no reason why David and Pierre couldn't supply them with lobsters to peddle, and when they began to see a profit they could buy from Pete Grant, too—they'd already talked to Pete about it, Mark informed his father.

Mark was champing at the bit, and there was no way to hold him. He was twenty-one, and he'd saved enough money to make a good payment on a truck, and rent some sort of shack on one of the big wharves for his headquarters. Stevie wasn't twenty yet, and they could have kept him home. But the family had a good opinion of Stevie's level-headedness; he would act like a sea-anchor for Mark.

Hard as it was to see the two youngest Bennett boys leave the Island, Stephen wouldn't make one objection. In a grim, tight-lipped way he was proud of their initiative. But Joanna, feeling like a traitor to the brilliant ambition that burned in the Little Boys' black eyes, hoped secretly that the business would fail. Then they'd come home, satisfied to be Islanders again.

The house was oddly silent after they had gone. Donna said cheerfully, "It's like the days when they were in high school, only better—they can come across the bay whenever they want to." But they were much too busy to come across the bay.

The Fosters still lived in the Binnacle, going their quiet way. Ned did his work, moving about the beach like a shadow, speaking civilly in greeting but never joining the other men in their yarn sessions or their long post-mortems over defunct engines. Leah Foster was seen strolling about the Island on pleasant days when the ground wasn't too muddy or the wind too strong. She took a great interest in birds, and the older people on the Island considered her a very respectable little woman, neat as a pin. Odd, maybe — she didn't mix much, and she hadn't made any close friend among the other women — but she lived the way she wanted to, and wasn't it her own business?

Of the younger crew, what they knew about Leah Foster they kept to themselves. There was no sense in dragging things out in the open just to liven up the place, especially when they might be asked embarrassing questions. They hardly ever talked about her among themselves; it was only by accident that they ever found out who was the favorite of the minute. Sometimes they didn't even know if there was a favorite.

The state of the nation and the price of lobsters were of no concern to the Island itself, which burst into its usual froth of white blossoms and bird song. It happened like this every year, and each spring Joanna wondered if it had ever been so lovely. This year she thought: How could they go away and leave it, when they knew spring was coming?

But it was in this radiant May that two of Marcus Yetton's youngsters, wandering through the woods after school in search of trailing arbutus, found Leah Foster crumpled at the foot of a rocky slope in the darkest, deepest part, where the sun hardly ever struck, and the soil was damp and soft with its accumulation of dead spruce needles. There was an ugly bruise on her temple, where she'd struck against a rock.

Stephen Bennett, Charles and Philip, and the other men who came when the children told them, decided she'd been wandering through the woods following the hawks who lived in this dark sunless part, and tripped at the top of the slope. The expensive binoculars Ned had given her at Christmas lay on the ground beyond her outstretched hand.

Joanna was down in the meadow picking branches of wild pear when the men came out of the woods above Goose Cove, carrying Leah on a door. They had covered her with a blanket, but Joanna, standing motionless by the wild pear tree, saw a corner of the blanket slip just as they went by her, and she saw Leah's face, wearing a new pallor and the old, faint, ironically serene smile.

The men entered the short cut through the swamp, but Stephen went back to where Joanna stood. He had always been direct with her. "Leah's dead, Joanna. Go up and tell your mother, ask her to come down to the Binnacle. Stella Grant will come down, and between them they can take care of laying Leah out."

"Where's Ned?" Joanna asked him.

"Out to haul, but I think I heard him coming down the west side. I'll have to meet him at the beach." He sighed, and looked away from her, up at the high luminous sky with its little white clouds skipping airily across it. "The prettiest day we've had this year, and I've got to meet Ned with this."

"It's tough," Joanna said. She meant it was tough for Stephen. How tough it would be for Ned, she didn't know.

He'd been out hauling. She wondered if he'd taken a punt along. He usually did, in case he saw a trap washed up on a beach and thought it might be one of his. . . . Her father walked on through the alder swamp, and she went home, sniffing absently of her wild pear blossoms, and trying to make it seem true that Leah was dead. Death for Leah was a different thing from death for Alec.

She remembered, as if it were a hundred years ago, as if it were something seen through the wrong end of a telescope, the day she'd gone to call on Leah Foster. She had been so terrified at her own daring behind the cool insolence of her manner. But Leah had been terrified too — and Leah couldn't hide it. That nineteen-year-old Joanna had known a brief pity for the woman she faced.

But Leah was dead. Looking for birds in the woods, with the glasses her husband had given her. *He gives her everything,* the Island had said.

Joanna remembered something else; something that had happened just today. While she stood by the stove fixing Ellen's cereal at noon, she had looked down across Goose Cove and had seen Jeff Bennett going over the rocks to the woods. He had his hatchet in a sheath at his belt, and a coil of potwarp. Owen, looking out too, had said casually, "That boy's sure been cutting a hell of a lot of pot limbs this spring. He's forever legging it into the woods."

When Jeff came back again, an hour or so later, he'd stopped in for a drink of water. Jeff was always inclined to be morose, but today he'd been pleasant, and quick to laugh; he spoke to Ellen in her bassinet, scratched Winnie's ears, and sat down long enough to pass the time of day with Donna.

Joanna, going into the house now to tell her mother she must help lay Leah out, thought: A man might look like that if he'd been with a woman he was in love with.

She walked into the house and told her mother about Leah. When Donna had gone, she took Ellen into the kitchen and began to peel the potatoes for supper; there were fresh dandelion greens too, dug this morning. Owen would bring home a fish, if he found any on the trawl he'd set outside the harbor.

As she worked, her mind saw over and over again Leah's face when the blanket blew aside; and Ned, coming up from the shore like a gray shadow, tipping his hat politely when he spoke. And Hugo, lying in Johnny Fernandez' camp, telling her Leah was afraid of Ned.

Ned, a gray shadow. She wondered how many times, unseen in the other shadows of the fish houses across the path, he'd watched them go through the door of the Binnacle, Hugo, Owen, young Ash, Maurice . . . *Jeff*. Again and again she saw her cousin as he went up over the rocks into the woods beyond Goose Cove. She saw other things: Leah setting out for an afternoon's ramble in search of birds, her hair like silk, her dress starched, her shoes brushed and neat. Ned starting out to haul, and always taking his punt along . . . in case he had to row ashore for anything. What if he had rowed ashore this afternoon?

That part of the woods where the trailing arbutus grew was on the hillside above a tiny, sheltered cove far down toward the Western End. From a boat, hauling close to the shore, you might glimpse a light dress moving up the slope, you might row ashore — if you were Ned — to go up that slope like the gray shadow that you were, and hear voices beyond a granite outcropping, and wait patiently till you knew Leah was alone —

Joanna awoke with a shock from her speculation, as Ellen dropped her rattle on the floor. She finished fixing the vegetables and put them on to cook, vastly disgusted with herself. Someone on the Island had died, and she must imagine murder. The very word chilled her, and she knew she must not think of it again, lest it gain too much hold on her mind. Leah was dead, *by accident,* and her father must be the one to tell Ned. They would have to go through another funeral, and it was less than a year ago that she had stood in the cemetery and watched the apple blossoms drop down on Alec's grave.

Philip and Owen came in soon, with the promised fish. They weren't talkative, and neither was Joanna. When Stephen and Donna came home, supper was ready, but it was a silent meal. Donna's eyes were set in shadows, she looked white and tired. The lines in Stephen's dark face were carved deeply tonight, and the whiteness of his temples stood out. He made only one remark about the Fosters.

"Ned took it like a soldier," he said, and that was all.

52

THE FUNERAL WAS SIMPLE and moving; the minister, who had come from Leah's town, spoke tenderly of Ned's bereavement, of the Island's loss. Joanna was thankful that the apple blossoms were still buds, so that no petals could drift down.

The next day Ned went out to haul. He didn't take his punt this time.

A week later Jeff left the Island. He said he'd heard of some good jobs down Connecticut way, and he'd like to see a little of the country.

Summer came in with a June of heavy, clinging fogs that lay over the bay for ten days at a time without lifting. The gardens flourished, but the men couldn't get out to haul. It didn't make much difference, Owen growled, slouched morosely by the stove reading Western story magazines; no lobsters out there anyway.

On the mainland, Mark and Stevie were making enough to pay for their meals, and their room on Wharf Street — a location that distressed Donna. The Closed Season had been lifted, so they expected to sell lobsters all summer long. David and Pierre worked to supply them, going together in the boat that had been Nils'. She was a big boat, and expensive to run; when you saw the boys going out in their peapods on a calm bright morning, you knew they didn't have enough money to buy gas.

It was in that wet June that Kristi went ashore to marry Peter Gray. Karl hired a Brigport girl to help his mother around the house. She was a lusty, strapping girl with a carefree manner, and Owen and Hugo, after eight months of being on their good behavior with the schoolteacher, found a new interest to fill the long summer evenings.

Lifting the Closed Season didn't make any material difference. It certainly didn't keep the lobsters from their usual summer preoccupation with shedding and breeding. To save gas, it was better to go hauling only two or three times a week. The rest of the time, most of the men went trawling or handlining. But fish weren't bringing in a high price either, unless a man were lucky enough to get a big halibut once in a while.

A curious apathy lay in the air. In other summers, when the men loafed around the shore or in the fish houses, they had talked of plans for the fall; how many more traps they'd set out in September, the new engine they wanted to put in, how they thought they'd try setting their pots to the south'ard or the west'ard this winter. They could sit in the sun and smoke, and live without haste, secure in the knowledge they'd earned the right to take life easily.

Now if they talked about the fall, they left words in midair and looked out across the sunlit bay at the mainland, and then began to talk about something else. Joanna, hearing them, thought it was as if they had their fingers crossed; as if they weren't sure of anything any more.

So the summer idled by, with its long bright afternoons and its nights thick with stars or washed with moonlight. The mailboat still came three days a week. But she didn't bring as much freight to Pete Grant as she used to. He ordered only the barest necessities. There were times when there was no soda pop, and — catastrophe indeed — no ice cream. There was no profit in it, he said. The candy counter was bare at times, and you couldn't always get the kind of tobacco or cigarettes you smoked.

When Joanna was a thin brown ten-year-old in Owen's old overalls, it had been one of her chief delights to go to the store for her father, and bring back a can of copper marine paint or a pound of threepenny nails. In those days Pete's back shop had been a paradise smelling deliciously of the green twine ranged in neat pyramids, the glistening oilskins the color of daffodils, shiny black rubber boots hung from the ceiling; there were the boxes of shiny new nails she wanted to sift through her fingers, the brightly polished tools, the glass toggles like big green bubbles, the cans of paint along the shelves, and in the corners the coils of new rope that smelled so good to a short freckled nose.

Now, more than often, there weren't any threepenny nails, or a suit of oilclothes in the right size, or even twine of the special thickness a man asked for. The back shop was bare in these days, when one remembered the riches it used to hold.

It struck a certain homesick sadness into Joanna's heart as she stood by the candy counter one rainy morning, and looked through the doorway into the back shop. Nothing else could show so vividly how the Island had changed. Charles, standing beside her in his dripping oilclothes, waiting for his mail, said curiously, "What are you staring at? You look as if you'd lost your last friend."

She nodded toward the back room. "Remember how it used to be?"

"Pete's having it tough like the rest of us," Charles said.

It was almost time for the *Aurora B.* to blow outside the point, and the store was crowded with wet oilskins and sou'westers. Philip left the group around the stove and came over to Charles and Joanna, lifting an eyebrow toward Owen, who was laughing with Sigurd. "Nothing bothers him, anyway."

"As long as there's a woman to chase, and he makes enough to buy his liquor with," said Joanna. "I wonder if he'll ever marry."

"God help the woman," said Philip piously. "I used to say that about Charles' wife, but he's turned out pretty good. Beats her where it won't show, anyway."

"Looks as if I'll starve her to death next winter if things don't pick up," muttered Charles.

Nathan Parr was at the counter, looking very small and wizened in comparison with Pete, who loomed above him and said, "Well, chummy, what'll ye have?"

"Guess I'll have me a ball of marlin, before the boat gets here and you start rammin' around like a man of affairs." Nathan's chuckle was wheezier than ever. "Got to knit up some heads — almost think the damn lobsters been eatin' the heads, 'stead of the bait."

"They don't like pollack, do they, Nathan?" Philip said.

"Nope! Damn things want beefsteak, I guess." Nathan's eyes watered at his own wit. He hitched up his sagging overalls. "A plug of Black B.L., if ye got any on hand, Pete. And I'll lug home a bunch of them spruce laths you got layin' around out there in the shed."

He tucked the tobacco in his pocket and picked up the marlin. As he started toward the door, Pete cleared his throat. "Forgettin' somethin', chummy?"

"Nope, Pete. Got all I need, thanks."

Pete cleared his throat again. He seemed oddly embarrassed. "You intendin' to pay somethin' on account, Nate?"

There was a sharp hush in the store. Over by the post office, Sigurd and Owen became absorbed in reading the government notices; those nearest the canned stuff were engrossed in the labels. The rest looked everywhere but at each other, and no one said anything at all. Nathan, at the door, turned slowly and went back to the counter, a stunned astonishment on his weatherworn old face.

"I don't reckon I can pay anything right now, Pete. You know how it is with me. Soon's I get these pots fixed up an' overboard, though —" His voice faded, but his arm tightened on the marlin.

"Sorry, chummy." Pete looked at a point over Nathan's tattered sou'wester. "But I got a new rule in this establishment. Had to make it in self-defense. No more credit."

Joanna felt the shock that ran through the store; it vibrated in herself. *No more credit.* Why, over half the people left on the Island depended on Pete Grant to live, paying him a little when they could. She saw Marcus Yetton's face grow bleak, and scared under its bleakness. His eyes shifted toward the little boy Julian. There were six more besides Julian.

Nathan put the marlin on the counter with trembling hands

and took out the tobacco. He turned and walked out of the store, lurching slightly with a new unsteadiness.

Someone let out a long breath, and Pete said angrily, "You don't think I want to do this, do ye? But I got to. Christ Almighty, you ought to see my books! I ain't gettin' one goddam cent more out of this store than you fellas are gettin' from your traps. Prob'ly I get less. You keep chargin' stuff, even when you got nothin' comin' in. *Me—*" Pete stalked furiously into the post office, "me, I have to keep on orderin', and every goddam mail day I get enough bills to paper this whole store!"

"We pay when we got the money to pay with," said Maurice.

"Sure—when you don't send off for a quart, first. And it might int'rest you to know that the marlin people don't intend to send me any more twine till I pay somethin' on account. So it looks like you fellas'll have to give, if you want to knit any more heads."

"Who's to blame if the lobsters don't crawl and we don't get enough for 'em anyway to pay for the gas?" demanded Owen.

"I ain't blamin' anybody. And I can't very well pay you guys twenty cents a pound when I don't get more'n fifteen." Pete loomed large in the post office window, his face dark red. "Listen, I ain't gettin' any fun out of stoppin' credit. But I got to. Talk about keepin' your head above water—I barely got my nose out. I can't do it, chummy! That's all there is to it!"

The *Aurora B.* whistled outside the point. The mail had come.

Joanna and her three brothers walked home together after the mail had been given out. The east wind blew a cold rain against their faces and made conversation difficult. At the anchor they stopped and left a few things on Nathan's doorstep—the laths, the twine, and the tobacco. Nathan came out before they got away.

"What's all this?" There was water in his faded eyes. "Look, I ain't allowin' nobody to give me nothin'."

"Nobody's giving you anything, you old coot," Philip told him. "It's just a loan. You can pay us when you come out a little ahead."

They went off through the drenched grass to the road before he could say anything else. Joanna looked back and saw him standing there, the red bandanna in his hand a brilliant splotch of color against the grayness of the shack and the day. He wiped his eyes, and Joanna didn't look back again.

The marsh was bright green with summer now, spattered with blue flag that stood tall and vivid in the rain. The wind drove in from Schoolhouse Cove, and the Bennetts bent their heads against it.

"Pete didn't have to come out like that, with the store full of people," Joanna said furiously. "Who does he think he is?"

"I can see Pete's viewpoint." Philip was always moderate. "There's some men on this Island haven't paid him anything since the flood. I suppose he figured he'd get them all told at once."

"Well, when Pete comes right out flatfooted and says no more credit, you can see how lobstering's gone to hell," said Charles. "If Pete holds out another year, it'll be something for the record."

"Listen, they can't go any lower." Owen laughed at them. "You're a bunch of damned crape-hangers. The tide goes out just so far and then it comes in again. Cripes, we'll all be rich again a year from now!"

Charles tilted a skeptical eyebrow. "You think you're rich as long as you can tumble some little bitch like that hired girl of Sorensens', and get drunk once a week. That's all you want."

"Yeah?" Owen stood still in the road and tapped Charles hard on the chest. "I can remember when you were pretty good at getting drunk. And at that tumbling business too."

"I'm not saying I wasn't. But that's gone by now — I've got a wife and kids to look after, and I don't intend to have one of those Marcus Yetton rigs. A year from now we'll all be rich — *hell!* We'll be living from hand to mouth, you mean." Charles removed Owen's hand from his chest. "Well, I don't plan to live like that. I'm getting out while I've still got something to take with me."

"Are you fellas going to stand down here in the rain and eye each other like a couple of tomcats?" asked Philip. "Come on. Where do you plan to go, Charles?"

"Seining somewhere to the west'ard. Want to go with me?"

Joanna squeezed in between Philip and Charles and linked arms with them. She looked long and hard at Charles' stubborn dark face. "Charles, you wouldn't *really* go away."

"Why not? My God, Jo, what is there for me to stay for? I can find a nice place ashore somewhere between here and Portland, pick up a good boat, and make some money. There's plenty of it in seining, too."

"Do you hate the Island that much?"

"What is this, Jo? Witness stand?" He grinned down at her. "Hell, I don't hate the Island. It's home, isn't it? I'd never leave it if I didn't know I could make a better living for Mateel and the kids elsewhere. The Island's dead, Jo. It was all right for Grandpa and Father and all the other old-timers, but things have changed. The waters around here are fished out."

"I still say you're wrong," Owen said stubbornly, and Joanna felt her heart warm to him. Philip, on her other side, said, "I'm willing to give the Island a chance. Maybe you're right, Cap'n Charles. But it's damned expensive to start in anywhere else, when you're just as likely to come trailing home without a dime in your dungarees. Come on up and have some coffee before you start trekking for the Eastern End."

At the house they told Stephen and Donna about Pete's credit troubles. But nothing was said about Charles' plans.

Nothing was said of those plans for a week. Charles went ashore on the *Aurora B.* to see a doctor about his hand—a quarrelsome lobster had pinched his finger and started a minor case of blood-poisoning. He didn't come back on the next boat, but Mateel had a letter from him. She brought it up to the house and showed it to the family. His hand was fine, and Mark and Stevie were fine, too; they were getting enough to eat out of their business, anyway. And he'd be back on the next boat for sure.

The evening of the day he came back, he and Mateel walked up from the Eastern End to spend a few hours. He told his father and the other boys that night what had held him on the mainland. He had gone along the coast toward Portland, on the track of a good boat he'd heard about—a big one, bigger than the *Gypsy,* big enough to hold a crew of five men and go seining for herring, mackerel, and pollack. He was all set to go; there was nothing to hold him back except that the present owner wanted cash, and he didn't have enough laid by to pay for it all in one crack.

He talked fast and with enthusiasm, but there was a nervous edge to his voice. His eyes met his father's again and again; still Stephen listened in polite but unreadable silence. At last Charles leaned back in his chair and let out a long breath.

"It's not as if I wanted to go," he said simply. "But I've got to.

If it was myself alone, like Phil or Owen, I wouldn't be scared to stick it out."

It seemed odd to Joanna to hear Charles admit he was scared, but she knew it wasn't for himself, it was for the slight girl whose eyes never left his face, it was for the small boy and girl asleep down at the Eastern End. She almost felt the way Charles relaxed when Stephen nodded and said, "I know. You have to do what you think is best. How much more do you need for the boat?"

"I've got somebody to buy the *Gypsy,* and they'll give me a good price for her — bare boat. Her engine's got enough power for the other boat, if I get her." He looked across at Philip. "Phil, how about you? You've got something in the old sock, and I've got to clinch the sale in a week. Come in with me on it, and she'll be half yours."

Philip's blue-gray look met his dark one quietly. "I wasn't thinking about leaving, Cap'n Charles. And I *was* thinking about a new engine for my own boat."

"Look, inside of two months you'll have back everything you put into the seiner, with interest. And I'll buy your share off you and you can come back and buy all the new engines you want."

Charles was on the edge of desperation, though he tried to keep his voice light. Being a family man had changed him from the reckless boy he had been, the one who'd walked with a touch of swagger. The old arrogance was there, but it had been tempered. Charles knew now what it was to think about food and clothing for others beside Charles.

Philip smoked in silence. Owen said roughly, "If I had anything I'd let you take it. But I still think it's a lot of foolishness. The Island's got plenty of life yet."

"You mean Karl's hired girl's got plenty of life yet. If it wasn't for her, you'd be out of here in a minute. How about it, Phil? If you don't come in with me on it, I'm licked."

Charles and Philip, the two eldest. In all Joanna's memories, neither of them had ever let the other down. She knew now, without a doubt, that Philip must give in, even if he hated and dreaded it. Stevie had gone away with Mark, because Mark counted on it. So would Philip go in with Charles.

Before summer was over, Charles had moved his family away. Philip went with them. Donna cried a little when he said good-bye, in the kitchen, but he kept his arm around her shoulders, smiled down into her eyes, and said he'd be back before the winter was out.

Owen stubbornly refused to go with them and be one of the crew. In the end it was Hugo who went. Nathan and Mary Bennett came out for a few weeks, to clean up the house and sell the cows to a Brigport man; the first of September they locked up the white house and the barn, where the golden cow on the weathervane was bright against the autumn blue, and went back to the mainland.

Others left, too. Old Anna Sorensen was ailing, but she refused to be sent ashore to live with Eric, whose wife she'd never liked. In the end, Karl decided to move his parents to Port George, a place that was small enough so that they wouldn't miss the Island too much; yet there was a better chance there. He told Stephen about it.

"They think we're rich out here," he said. "When I told 'em I came from Bennett's, they said, 'What in the devil do you want to come here for? Out there you can make money!' Karl's mouth twisted ironically. "I said 'Sure, when there's lobsters to catch. But there ain't any, and our boats have to be bigger and our traps heavier, out on Bennett's.' Well, they says, 'You can fish all winter because it ain't ice-locked out there.' 'Sure,' I told 'em, 'but supposing the wind blows all the time? Can't haul in a living gale of wind, even when your pots are full. What's the use of sitting around on your backside all winter, waiting for the wind to stop blowing?' "

Karl was not usually so eloquent. He ran his hand wearily through his thick fair hair, so like Nils'. "Oh, hell, Stephen, I don't *want* to go. I've left the Island before—just for a few days—and been homesick every time I looked out on a good day and saw it out here. But I'm like all the others. I can't see any other way."

"Sure, I know," said Stephen, and for a moment his hand stayed on the stalwart shoulder of the man who had been his chum since their childhood together on the Island.

One afternoon before the Sorensens left, Joanna went down into the lower part of the meadow, near Gunnar's alder swamp, to pick blackberries. She took Ellen with her, and put her on a blanket where the grass grew short and thick. Ellen was a tall baby at eight months, with a cap of silky yellow hair and eyes like Donna's and Philip's; grave luminous eyes that looked at you long and consideringly, and then, disarmingly, crinkled into broad laughter. Sometimes Joanna wished her baby's eyes were like Alec's, but already there was a sweetness in Ellen's smile that spoke of him.

Now she played on the blanket, her legs tanned a soft biscuity gold where her blue creepers ended, and made cheerful noises to herself and Winnie. Joanna picked blackberries shiny as lacquer, feeling the September sun soaking warmly through the back of her dress, turning sometimes to look at the baby and the old tawny-coated dog lying at the edge of the blanket.

She was startled when Gunnar came out from the alder swamp, but only for an instant. "Come back here and be quiet, Winnie," she ordered the dog. Then with the old, cool politeness, "Hello, Mr. Sorensen."

"Hello, Yo." He blinked at her in the brilliant sunshine, and came slowly toward her and the baby. "Ha, young lady, how are you?" he said to Ellen in his deceptively mild old voice. Ellen gurgled. He stood there silently for a few moments, watching Joanna pick berries, and she wondered if he were going to tell her those were his bushes.

"Yo," he said unexpectedly. "What you t'ink of dem all going, huh? You going too?"

"*No!*" she answered sharply. "No, I'm not going."

"Your fadder won't go, will he?" Gunnar shook his head, still hardly touched with gray. "I used to t'ink Stephen, he vass the softest. But he's more like the old man than the udder one—Nate. Stephen gets his teeth in and holds on." He came closer to Joanna and looked searchingly into her face. "You still miss your man, Yo?"

She felt herself stiffen, her face went blank. "Yes, I do." And what business is it of yours? she thought. She was almost liking him when he spoke of her father, but now the old antagonism came back.

Gunnar sighed and shook his head. "It is too bad to miss someone. I miss dat boy Nils. Sometimes I wanted to beat him, but I miss him yust the same."

"Where is he now?"

"Karl, he got a card from Rio de Yaniero last week." Gunnar sniffed. "A beautiful place. I'm glad the boy can see it. But the women—" His grin split his cheeks, and for a fraction of a moment Joanna realized what a dashing young seaman he must have been. "They are very dark. Bad business, too. But Nils has sense."

"You never used to think so, Mr. Sorensen."

"Ya, I thought he vass stupid . . . dumb. But now I know different. He vanted to marry you, didn't he?"

She was too startled to be angry at his inquisitiveness. Besides, there was a sadness in his voice, and she felt something like pity for him, because he was so old, and it was too late to make up for the way he had lived. "Yes, he wanted to marry me," she answered him. "I was proud that he thought so much of me. Nils is a fine man, Mr. Sorensen."

"If he had married you, I would have been glad." Gunnar's narrowed old eyes were very blue, watching her. "You are a good woman, Yo. You are a good vife to your husband, and now you are a good vidow. Nils is right about you all the time, and I am wrong."

He lifted his hands and dropped them again, sniffed and sighed. Ellen had crept off her blanket, and Joanna caught her up to put her down in the middle again. Gunnar watched them for a moment, then turned back to the cool, sun-spattered dusk of the alder swamp.

On an impulse Joanna ran along the path behind him. As the old man turned toward her in surprise she said with the warm, winning sincerity of the Bennetts, "You're going away from here pretty soon, Mr. Sorensen. Shake hands before you go."

He looked down unbelievingly at the girl's brown hand, its fingertips stained purple with berry juice, then up into the dark eyes smiling at him through the thick Bennett lashes. "Shake?" said Joanna.

Without a word he took her hand into his rough-skinned one, and gripped it hard. Then he turned around and walked toward the alder swamp.

The day when the Sorensens were going to leave—Gunnar and Anna, Karl and David and Sigurd—Gunnar didn't wake up. He was dead when the girl went up to call him. It was his last and most irrevocable protest against leaving Bennett's Island.

As always, he had had his way. When the others left, Gunnar alone stayed behind. As autumn deepened into winter, and Joanna wandered alone through the Western End woods and the shaggy orchard, and the cemetery, she always looked from Alec's grave toward the small, neat stone that said *Father* on it, and was glad she had run after Gunnar in the meadow that day, and put out her hand.

53

THIS WINTER GAVE NO INDICATION of being worse than last year; it didn't sweep down on the Island with a howling gale or a premature cold snap. But in November lobsters dropped down to twelve cents again. To a community which had once considered fifty cents a fair price, and which never, in its worst imaginings, had known lobsters to go below thirty cents, the last few years had been bad enough. They'd touched twelve cents then, but here it was again, and winter coming on — it was almost too much to endure.

On the premise that if they must starve to death they preferred to do it in some sort of comfort, Johnny Fernandez and Nathan Parr sold their gear to Stephen Bennett and Jake Trudeau, and went ashore.

To Joanna, walking alone in the late November afternoons, the place was like a ghost town. In the harbor Marcus Yetton's shabby boat, Stephen's *Donna*, Owen's *White Lady*, and Ned Foster's boat rode their moorings. Very soon now the Trudeaus wonld bring their boats up from the Eastern End and moor them in the harbor for the winter. Then there'd be seven boats to look lonely where there had once been twenty or more. *The Basket* was on the bank.

Sometimes she saw someone moving around the beach or the fish houses, but more often the thin swirl of smoke from a chimney was the only sign of life. On boat days there was activity, but Link Hall was complaining about the small amount of mail and freight he carried for Bennett's. The Island knew that Link would be perfectly happy if he could get out of running to Bennett's this winter, and only come as far as Brigport.

The loneliness of the village, with its boarded-up houses, was

oppressive to them all. And sometimes the Bennett house seemed intolerably silent without the boys. True, Owen was still there, but he
wasn't home much; he went across to Brigport late in the afternoon
about four days a week, and if the weather breezed up, he didn't bother
to come home till the next day. No, it was Philip Joanna missed,
with his easy quiet presence, and the Little Boys.

There was no hope of Mark and Stevie coming home now.
They'd given up their lobster business to go as crew on Charles' boat,
along with Hugo and Philip.

"At least," Donna said often, her eyes pensive, "they're all together, even if they're not here."

Charles and Philip were doing well. Charles, in particular, wrote
glowing letters home. He wanted his parents and Joanna and the
baby to come to the mainland, for the winter anyway; he knew the
rotten price of lobsters, why did they try to stick it out? He could
get them a nice little place near him. He'd never known he'd like
a town so much, being an Islander born and bred, but this place
was different. There was a sardine cannery right there, ready to buy
his herring; and Joanna could work there for good pay, if she wanted
to.

So on, and so forth. Stephen smiled, and said it was fine they
were doing well. He was proud of them. But his place was here on
the Island.

Joanna, hearing him say it, was fiercely glad. Though sometimes the emptiness of the village frightened her, more often she knew
a sort of exultation as she walked through it. We'll show them what
we're made of, she thought. Just a handful of us, but we can stick
it out, and when the others come limping back, they'll see for themselves. They think the Island's let them down. But they're the ones
who've let the Island down.

There was still school on Bennett's Island, though Marcus Yetton's middle five were the only pupils. Miss Adams hadn't come back
this year, and the new teacher was a middle-aged lady who boarded
with the Grants, and spent most of the school session trying to break
the young Yettons of swearing and—Julian in particular—of smoking.

Joanna, walking home from the store once in a January dusk,
thought about the school. Her father must try to get some families
with children to move out to the Island by spring, else by next fall

there wouldn't be enough children to keep up the school. And once they lost the school, it would be hard to get it started again. She pictured Ellen, starting the first grade; brief yellow pigtails, a starched blue gingham dress . . .

Out on the harbor ledges the surf gleamed through the darkening day, and the wind sharpened. Lights burned in Marcus Yetton's house — the only lights on that side of the harbor now. She had a warm feeling toward Marcus; there was more to him than she'd thought, when he would stick like this. Maybe it was just weakness, because he'd leaned on her father so long he was afraid to strike out for himself. But all Stephen could let him have now was a rent-free place for his bait butt and his small gear, at the far end of the boat shop. So it could be loyalty that made Marcus stay; loyalty to Stephen or to the Island, it was the same.

She was passing the old wharf now, and the boat shop loomed in the dusk. It was in the shop that she had said good-bye to Alec for the last time, in the red glow of sunset; she had knelt beside him, and had looked up to see the Coast Guard men coming past Jud Gray's half-built boat. It seemed to her that she remembered with a vividness that grew with time. Yet in June it would be two years since Alec died.

There was someone moving in the dusk down at the far end of the wharf, amid the usual clutter of hogsheads and traps, and she caught the tiny red glow of a cigarette. She left the path and went toward the glow. It could be her father, just starting home — he worked on his traps at the harbor now, instead of at home, in the barn.

But it wasn't Stephen Bennett who dodged out of sight among the hogsheads at her approach. She smiled and went after the fleet shadow, to corner it when there was nowhere for it to go but over the edge of the wharf into the water. It was Julian Yetton. He had got rid of his cigarette before she caught him.

"My golly, I thought you was Miss Martin!" he said with breathless relief. He was a scrawny and undersized twelve. Miss Martin had the right idea about stopping his smoking, but the wrong approach, Joanna thought.

"If you're that scared of her," she said frankly, "I shouldn't think you'd take any chances about smoking."

"My father sent me over here for some twine. I thought —" He peered at her through the grayness and said belligerently, "You gonna tell?"

"I've got more to do than carry tales," said Joanna. "I'm in a hurry right now. But I'm not going to leave you here." She steered him before her, a firm hand on his bony shoulder. "You get your twine and skip home."

"You smoked when you was a kid!" He tried to twist free. "My pop told me—"

"Yes, but I stopped. See how weak you are? You can't get away. Soon as I found out how little and skinny I'd be if I kept it up, I stopped. And that's what the matter is with you."

"Honest?" He squirmed around to peer at her again.

"Honest. How do you think you'll ever get to be as big as—" Not Marcus, because Marcus was undersized too. "As big as Owen? You want to be big like him, don't you, and sling traps around as if they were chips?"

Julian said with bravado, "Cripes almighty, smokin' a couple weasly cigarettes don't make all that difference!"

Joanna shrugged. "If you know so much about it, just wait and see. Anyway, I'm not preaching. I'm just telling you what'll happen." They reached the path and she released him. He walked with her, unwillingly, as far as the anchor.

"G'night," he said gruffly.

"Good night, Julian." Her voice was pleasant and casual. "And listen, do your smoking away from the shop from now on. If I catch you again, with all that dry wood and shavings around, I'll pound you myself—in person. Catch on?"

"Yep," said Julian breathlessly, and she heard him running along the boardwalk toward the safe lights of home.

She walked up through the marsh, the frozen ground ringing under her feet. The wind blew through the darkness, an unseen presence that stayed always with the Island. It was heavy with salt, and stinging with cold, but she loved it.

The lights of the house looked down at her, warm yellow and unwavering, and they kindled an answering warmth in her heart. As long as there was one gallant handful to stiver out the winter on the Island, as long as the lights still burned at dusk from the big house at the top of the meadow, the Island was all right.

*   *   *

There was a bad storm in March. For a week the wind blew like all the furies of hell, screaming, whistling, lashing the sea into chaos around the Island, crashing against the houses with a demon strength that made the sturdiest timbers shake. It blew trees down here and there; it wasn't safe to walk in the woods, for there was always a treacherous creaking and swaying far up among the tallest spruces. It blew out windows in some of the empty houses. Stephen, Marcus, and Owen went around the village with nails, laths, and glasscloth, and covered the windows that needed protection.

The gale came from the northeast, so the harbor was safe. But down at the Eastern End the most dilapidated fish house collapsed.

"Make good fire wood," Jake said, and shrugged.

At last the storm blew itself out, but it was almost two weeks before the water subsided. The sun shone, and the sky was deceptively blue, the gulls thought it was spring at last and were noisy in the mornings; but far below them the sea tossed and moaned, day in and day out. The sound of it was always there, you grew used to talking through the muted thunder that increased as you neared the shore. In some places the surf was incredibly beautiful. Everybody went out to watch it, the children squealing and capering in reach of the glittering spray, the men's eyes and mouths set in a sort of desperate resignation.

"Almost seems as if somethin' was against us stayin' here," Marcus Yetton said. "We'll be lucky if we got more'n two or three pots left."

For some, it wasn't so bad. In spite of Marcus' worrying, he wasn't harmed as much as Owen, who came in with the *White Lady* loaded with smashed traps, dumped them ashore in a black silence nobody cared to break, and went out for another load. Some were lost altogether. When the men got together in Pete's store and compared notes, it was Owen who had lost the most, with Stephen a close second. Their favorite winter grounds, the shoal called "The Ripper," had betrayed them.

Stephen began at once to rebuild. He was patient, for patience is of the essence for a good lobsterman, and he had rebuilt many times in his life on the Island. He told Donna and Joanna briefly how many pots he had lost, how long it would take him to straighten out, and that was the end of it. If he worried deeply behind those steady dark eyes, if he was discouraged or even afraid, no one would guess it—except possibly Donna.

Owen piled his broken traps beside the boat shop on the old wharf, and apparently went for a walk. He didn't come home all day, and toward supper time, Donna began to grow anxious. She never fidgeted or worried aloud, but Joanna knew the signs. Her own idea was that Owen had gone somewhere on the Island to get over his ugly mood, and she would have left him to sulk—when he was hungry enough he'd come home, and in a decent temper. But the March wind was blowing up cold, and Donna's eyes went again and again to the window, as if she were watching for him to come through the gate.

Joanna fed Ellen and put her to bed, then went out to look for Owen. She discovered, when she took her coat from its hook, that the keys to Nate's place were gone; the ring usually hung on an empty hook by the coats. That simplified her search.

Schoolhouse Cove was dark blue and benignly calm as she walked around it, but the sea wall, no more than a long heap of tumbled boulders now, showed that the cove had been neither calm nor benign in the past few weeks. The brown fields turned a warm, tawny color in the late sunshine, a few little clouds showed edges of fiery gold. The windows of the big barn against the woods seemed afire, the weather vane glittered against the sky.

When she reached Nate's place she went past the house to the barn, and found what she was looking for—the key ring dangling carelessly from a small door next to one of the big sliding ones. And in the hayloft, in last summer's hay, Owen was asleep.

She stood there for a moment watching him in the yellow light that came dimly through a small, cobwebbed window near his head. He lay on his back, arms flung wide; there was hay in his thick black crest, he needed a shave, his breath came harshly, and the whole chill, dim atmosphere of the place smelled of whiskey.

Joanna was suddenly furious. "You beauty," she said aloud, and kicked the nearest foot. Apparently he didn't feel it through his rubber boots, so she kicked again. He came awake then, with a choking start, and stared at her through dulled black eyes.

"What do you want?" he said thickly.

"Get up and go home," said Joanna. "Mother's worried about

you. If it was me, I'd let you stay out here and make a fool of your-self." She wrinkled her nose in disgust. "The answer to a maiden's prayer. God's gift to the women. Roll out of that hay and get moving."

He came up on one elbow, groping around in the hay. He couldn't find what he was looking for, and dropped back again with a groan, his eyes closed.

"Got a headache, haven't you?" said Joanna with relish. "Feel mean, don't you? Well I'm glad. It's no more than you deserve. What if you did lose some traps? Is that anything for a grown man to run away and sulk over?"

Her foot clinked against the bottle, and she handed it to him, her mouth twisting as she watched him drink. He took a long breath and opened his eyes again; color came back into his face. He looked at Joanna with the beginning of his old smile.

"Teaming me around, are you? Well, who in hell do you think you are?"

"Who do I have to be, to tell you what I think of you? You're no help to the Island, I can tell you that much. Father's got seven traps fixed over already, while you've been lying up here like some filthy old derelict."

"Oh, shut up and leave me alone." Owen turned over on his side, and Joanna kicked his boot again.

"I will *not* leave you alone," she said between her teeth. "You're going to get out of here and go home. Maybe the wind'll blow some of that bar-room smell off you."

A hand like steel closed around her ankle, caught her off bal-ance, and jerked; with a gasp, she found herself tumbling headfirst over Owen and landing beside him in the hay. "That'll learn you," he said. "Seems to me you ought to know by now it's no time to start talking a man to death when he wakes up with a hangover."

"I'll talk whenever I feel like it," she said furiously. "You ought to have somebody telling you just what you are, Owen Bennett. Sure, I know the women across at Brigport practically fall on their faces with joy when they see you coming, but I'm not one of them. I'm your sister, and I know just what kind of a guy you are." It seemed suddenly as if she had saved up all these things for a long time, and there was no holding them back. "I thought it was pretty good when you said you wouldn't leave the Island. I thought you were going to help Father and the rest of us to keep the place going. But I know now it was just damned shiftlessness. You thought you could rot in peace and quiet if you stayed here. I used to think you were a worker like the rest of the Bennetts, because you made money once, but I know better now. Anybody could make money in those days. But you have to have *guts* to keep going now, and you haven't got enough. You lose some traps and you get mad, and go off in a hayloft, and kill a quart of whiskey—"

She picked up the bottle. "I've a good mind to break this over your head! Father's working his head off to keep the Island going, and here you are. Liquor and women, and you get worse every year. Oh, I wish—" Her words caught in her throat. She stared at him with widening eyes as if she had never seen him before, and got to her feet. As she reached the hayloft stairs, she heard him call after her, but she didn't answer.

She walked home swiftly, the wind blowing against her face and cooling it. The sun had gone down, and she saw one star in the clear, pale, western sky. Yes, the wind was cool against her face, but it didn't cool the thoughts that burned and twisted inside her head.

I wish, she had been going to say to Owen, *I wish it had been you who drowned that night, instead of Alec. I wish you were dead now, and he was alive. In spite of everything—gambling and all—he was a better man than you could ever be.*

And it was true. It was so true that she could have wept, here on the road. Alec would be here now to hold her in his arms—it seemed an eternity since that last kiss he had given her; he would know his child and she would know her father. And Alec would have been, in spite of everything, a better son to Stephen than Owen had ever been.

Owen came along the road behind her, whistling to her to stop, but she pretended she didn't hear him. Walking thus, they came to the house.

54

IT WAS ALMOST TIME for the spring season again, and as always, there was a resurgence of hope and energy. The freshness in the air, the mild days when the song sparrows sang beguilingly from the wild pear bushes and the ice melted in the wells, the tiny spears of green grass coming up in the sheltered spaces — it was enough to lighten a man's heart as well as his step.

The new strings put overboard this April would be considerably smaller than they used to be: a big string was expensive, and they must do the best they could with a few pots, and if the lobsters crawled into them — well, it meant more pots. Stephen worked long and hard getting his traps ready; he tended with a mother's care the ones the storm hadn't touched, and was ready to start the spring season without any bills for gear on his conscience.

This was encouraging to Marcus and Jake and the others, whose belief in Stephen amounted almost to a tradition. No matter what the others said when they left the place; as long as Stephen Bennett stayed and went lobstering, there was still a chance for the business. And they'd stay, too.

Maurice went to join the crew of the dragger the Robey boys had bought. With his going, Owen was the only young man left. Joanna had been short with him ever since the day in the hayloft, but she noticed with some satisfaction he had cut down on his drinking and didn't go to Brigport so much. He still moved through the days with an air of intense boredom, and Donna reminded him occasionally that he needed a shave. But at the same time, he worked on his traps. Going back and forth between the store and the house, Joanna saw him there on the old wharf, working in the sunshine and whistling. He didn't seem to drive nails with any great hurry, she noticed, and more than once she saw him lounging against the shed wall, out of the wind, smoking while he watched the gulls or the water on the beach.

If he saw her looking at him, he waved and whistled, and she could catch the white gleam of his grin in his brown face. He had been very agreeable around the house ever since the day in the hayloft; it was almost as if he were trying to win Joanna back to the old comradeship.

A little less charm and a little more work would make me think more of you, brother, Joanna thought.

Stephen came in one day from a long morning at the shore, to find Owen already home, where he had been since ten o'clock. Stephen had been up since daylight, and he moved a little slowly as he hung up his jacket and took off his rubber boots.

"Working hard?" he asked pleasantly. Owen, trotting Ellen on his knee, grinned back at him.

"Yep! How d'you like my new girl?"

Stephen touched Ellen's silky head with his calloused fingers and sat down as if he were tired. "At the rate you're patching pots, the spring crawl will be done before you get them overboard."

"I'm in no hurry," said Owen, and Joanna, setting the table, paused to look at him.

Stephen said carefully, "Did I hear you say you're in no hurry?"

"You did," said Owen. He put Ellen in her high chair and went to stand by the stove, one foot on the hearth. His voice came slowly and easily, as unhurried as he was.

"I'm about fed up with lobstering. Seems to me I can't drive myself to put another trap out. I'm young and healthy — what am I doing, creeping along from day to day, making a dollar here and losing it there? There's more to life than that."

"I don't see that you've been driving youself overhard." Stephen appraised his third son from head to foot.

"I'm goddam tired of it, Father," Owen said. He was smiling, as if he liked talking about it. "Ever get tired? No, I guess you never did, else you wouldn't have hung on to it this long, but I'm a different breed of cats. When that northeaster came along, and I got a look at my pots, I knew I was through."

"Through with lobstering—or with the Island?"

"With both of 'em. With the whole shootin' match. I'm clearing out of this, Father. You'll be better off without me, anyway. I'm no help to the Island, nor a credit to the family."

"Don't talk like that, Owen," Donna spoke up. "Please don't."

"Mother, you know it as well as I do." He went to her and put his big arm around her shoulders. "Ever since I could walk you've been worrying about me, a hell of a lot more than you worried about the others. Well, it was a waste of time. I'm the sport of the litter, and it's time you and Father admitted it."

Stephen stood up. His face wore the iron-dark look that Joanna knew of old, and his words came level and hard. "Owen, maybe you've helled around and given us a lot to think about, but I never thought I'd raised up a fool. So don't talk like one. You're a born lobsterman—I knew that when you put out your first fifteen pots. Right now you're becalmed. I've felt like that, son, many a time. Your mother can tell you that."

Stephen's warm smile touched his eyes, as he put his hand on Owen's shoulder. "Go up and stay with your brothers awhile—ship out with them, go seining, and come back when you're ready."

Owen said slowly and distinctly, "I'm tired of the sea and all that goes with it, whether it's lobster pots or seines or the Island. I'm fed up, Father. I've been wondering for a hell of a long time what was ailin' me, and now I know."

Tired of the Island. When Joanna shut her eyes she saw those words burning against her lids. She opened them again and looked full at Owen, and felt it rising in her—the scornful anger she'd felt so many times, when she looked at Owen. But she'd never felt exactly like this before, because she had never heard, or dreamed she would hear, those words from a Bennett's mouth.

Donna said quietly, "What are you going to do?"

"I don't know, Mother. Just get out of here as quick as I can. I aim to see a little of the country before I'm too old. If I don't go now I'll never go, and I'll end up like Nathan Parr or Johnny Fernandez."

"Just go without shaving a few more days and you'll look like them now," said Joanna. She turned and walked out of the room.

*　　*　　*

Stephen bought Owen's traps and Marcus Yetton bought his punt, Ned Foster bought a few things and so did Jake. Owen left the *White Lady* on the mooring, and wrote out a paper empowering Stephen to sell her if the chance arose. He was very cocksure about the whole business, as if the feeling of the money in his pocket had set him on top of the world again. Joanna, remembering how he had dreamed for so long of the *White Lady* before he built her, and how he had lived in alternate torment and exaltation while he was building her, wondered how he could give her up so easily. Boats weren't like the automobiles people owned on the mainland; boats had hearts and souls, and if you built your own boat, your own heart and soul went into it.

But it was as if he could hardly wait to go. In fact, he was ready a week after he had talked to them in the kitchen. On the last morning he was his old charming self, making Donna laugh in spite of herself, making Stephen's mouth twitch and his eyes crinkle. Joanna herself felt a sudden rush of affection for him. It was impossible to stay mad with Owen when he was so merry and so superbly sure of himself. No wonder those Brigport women were crazy about him. There'd be tears over there today when the mailboat had gone.

The world lay before Owen — the whole, great, wide, enchanting, lusty world, and it was his. He was going out to it with money in his pockets, his big handsome body, his young and vibrant health. They might have known the Island would some day be too small to hold him.

There was only once that his face shadowed. It wasn't when he lifted Donna off her feet and kissed her good-bye, or when he rumpled Joanna's hair and kissed her too, or shook hands with his father. It was when he lifted Ellen from her high chair and she put her small hands on his brown cheeks and touched her brief nose to his — a trick he had taught her.

"Don't grow up too fast," he said to her, and put her back in her chair. A few minutes later he had gone; he didn't look back when Ellen called to him, and waved her hand in vain.

55

In June, Pete Grant closed up his store. He had kept the store and bought fish and lobsters on the Island since long before Joanna was born; she couldn't remember a time in her life when he wasn't there. When he gave up, it was somehow shocking.

Stephen went his calm way, working hard from early morning till dark. When she talked bitterly about Pete Grant, Stephen hushed her.

"Pete's been a good friend to us all out here—the best friend some of us ever had. He's stivered it out as long as he could, but you can't expect him to try to live on the few cents' worth of trade he gets here. He thinks the place is going under, and he'll get out while he's got a little something to take with him."

"Abandoning ship," said Joanna. "It'll be a surprise to all of them when they find out the ship isn't sinking, after all."

"No, I don't think it's sinking." Stephen looked out across the broad blue waters, placid under the June sun. "It's about time the lobsters hit us again. I wouldn't be surprised if there was a big difference, come fall."

It was something to think about during the summer that followed. There had never been such a quiet summer on Bennett's Island in all Joanna's memories, nor for the others, except for her father, who had been a child here when his family first owned the Island.

Now they went back to that old way of doing things. They took their lobsters to Brigport to sell, bought their supplies there, and collected their mail. This life had a strange serenity unbroken from day to day. Now that the *Aurora B.* didn't come any more, and Pete wasn't there to buy lobsters, his wharf was seldom used. The old wharf was the center of activity — such activity as there was, with only Stephen, Marcus, and Ned Foster to bring their boats in, and Jake Trudeau coming up sometimes from the Eastern End.

Joanna walked to the shore daily with Ellen, who trotted along ahead of her on sturdy brown legs, with occasional side trips into the marsh to pick blue flag or morning glories. When they reached the water Joanna sat on an old dory in the sun to wait for Stephen to finish his morning's work on his traps, or to come ashore from the mooring. Ellen threw stones into the water, watched the gulls squabble over a dead fish, or gravitated like a needle toward a magnet to where the Yetton children played in and out of the water and over the rocks.

Sitting there in the sun-drenched silence, a faint breeze stirring her hair, and no sound but the gulls and the children's voices, Joanna thought of the time when the beach was deserted only at noon, when everybody had gone home for dinner; and even then there was always somebody coming in late, rowing ashore to haul up his punt and tie it with the others. Maybe he'd be carrying a fish, or a bucket of forbidden short lobsters, and he'd look around cautiously to be sure a Bennett wasn't about to step out from behind a fish house . . . Joanna smiled at the memory.

It hadn't been such a long time ago, at that. It hadn't been so long ago that she couldn't look up without seeing Charles, or Philip, or Hugo, or the Little Boys. The thought made her sigh a little, but not deeply. She was still young enough to see this hushed and dreamy summer as the neap tide, a pause, a moment of silence. In a little while — perhaps sooner than she thought — the moment would break, the world would move again, and the flood tides would come.

If she turned her head she could see her father's pots stacked in long rows against the walls of the boat shop, Marcus' pots beyond them. Her father had only a few traps out this summer; he hadn't approved of lifting the Closed Season, he wouldn't have lobstered during July and August if he hadn't been driven to it. But when the fall came he would have two hundred and fifty traps to put overboard.

Joanna looked at the long ranks upon the wharf, all ready to be set; ballasted with flat rocks, the warp coiled neatly inside and the freshly painted buoy, black and white, set on the coils. Those traps represented the future for Stephen and Donna Bennett, for

Joanna and Ellen, for the Island. He had added Owen's string to his own, patching with infinite pains. He had put almost all that was left in his money box into new laths and rope and nails. Joanna had knit up the new heads, and she was still making bait bags whenever she sat down for a moment with nothing to do.

Yes, there was going to be a difference this fall. And those who'd stayed with the captain would be riding the crest of the wave. The others — Joanna shrugged. They'd come flocking back, the boys and all. They might keep up their seining — the Robey boys still lived at Brigport, and they did all right. Of course there was a sardine cannery over there where Charles and the others were. But Joanna was willing to bet that if the lobsters struck Bennett's again, and the price went up to normal and above, there was nothing that could keep her brothers away from the Island. They might be getting rich on herring, but they still belonged to the Island, wherever they were. Owen, too, in spite of what he'd said — that he was tired of the sea and the Island both.

He'll be back, Joanna said, and at the thought of having them all home again, and the boats back in the harbor, the punts and dories on the beach, the hammers going in the fish houses — there was no scorn left in her, only a steady warmth spreading outwards from her heart.

Stephen sat back in his chair after supper one night, lifted Ellen to his knees, and said casually, "Guess I'll set another load of pots tomorrow. Want to go with me, Joanna?"

"Are the lobsters starting to come?" she demanded. *"Thick?"*

"Well, no, I don't know about the thick part." Stephen's eyes smiled at her eagerness. "I know they're about done shedding and they're poking their heads out to see how the wind is. About the time I get the whole two hundred and fifty set, I'll be able to tell you how they'll be. Did you say you were going with me?"

"You bet I am," said Joanna emphatically. "I'll get my dungarees out tonight. I haven't had them on for a hundred years." She looked down at the table, her lashes hiding her eyes, and felt a swift running flash of pain. The last time she'd worn her dungarees had been down on Pirate Island, when she and Alec had speared flounders for bait. Except for Ellen across the table there, her head a soft glow of gold against Stephen's darkness as she rummaged through his shirt pockets, that day on Pirate Island was a dream, a story she had once heard.

"You'll have to be up at daylight then," her father was saying. "Maybe I'll get to set two boatloads tomorrow."

"I used to think," said Donna, "it was a shame that Joanna wasn't a boy—she'd have made a good fisherman. But we wouldn't have had Ellen, then. Stephen, don't let her drink out of your cup! You're getting as bad as the Yettons."

There's nothing in the cup," said Stephen, but he took it away from Ellen and gave her a cookie instead. "Speaking of the Yettons—young Julian's a bright kid, if he is a mite on the scrawny side. Wants to put some pots out—I told Marcus the boy could use that peapod of Owen's."

"You going to give him the pots too?" Joanna fixed him with a stern eye, and Stephen laughed.

"You're a hard one. Don't you believe I ought to lend the boy a hand, if he's willing to work?"

"I give up," said Joanna. "You're hopeless. Now you'll be supporting Julian and his descendants for the next twenty years."

Winnie let out a salvo of barks that all but shook the stove as she crawled out from beneath it. Ellen wriggled down from Stephen's lap and reached the door before the old dog did, trying to turn the knob. She looked back at her mother and her grandparents with a sparkling blue gaze. "Owen?" she said. "Owen?"

"Not Owen tonight, honey," Stephen said. He got up and went to the door, calling out, "Hold your horses there, don't knock the house in!" He went through the entry, Winnie crowding past him and Ellen at his heels, and Joanna and Donna began to clear the table.

"Speak of the devil," Stephen said good-naturedly. "Hello, Julian. Out of breath, aren't you, son? Come in."

Joanna, standing by the table with the coffee pot in her hand, saw a gasping and greenish-pale Julian stumble into the kitchen. Stephen, following him, said in a leisurely voice, "Come up to see me about those traps, did you?"

Then he saw what Joanna and her mother saw—the pure terror that stared at him from the boy's eyes. He caught Julian by both thin shoulders.

"What is it, boy? What's happened down at the house? Somebody hurt? Speak up!"

Julian spoke up. One word—the one word that had been the unspoken fear of the Island since the first man had come to live on it.

"Fire!"

He dropped into a chair and began to cry. Stephen pulled his jacket from the hook. "Is it your house?"

"It's the boat shop," the boy choked. "The traps—it's all afire!" The last word was a desperate wail, and Stephen was gone on the run the instant it was spoken. Joanna and Donna looked at each other across the room. Donna had gone white as her apron, and Joanna knew by her own sudden coldness that the blood had left her face too. She set down the coffee pot with a clatter.

"Mother, all those traps, and they're dry as tinder!" She reached for her trench coat. "I'm going down there. I can do *something!"*

"There aren't enough people left on the Island to stop a fire." Donna moved to the window facing the harbor. "Look."

Joanna saw the flames then, burst against the night, beyond the dark mass of trees at the foot of the meadow. It seemed as if the whole sky was aflame; she had never seen anything that filled her with such sheer, devastating panic. But she said quite steadily, "They'll see it from Brigport and come over. And I think the wind's right to blow it toward the harbor."

She went out, and started for the harbor on the run. She was right about the wind—it would blow the fire away from the land. But the traps—two hundred and fifty, with buoys and warps, as well as Marcus' handful. Sickened, her mind turned from the thought and fastened on the wild hope that the fire wasn't as bad as it looked. Maybe it wasn't so much out of hand that three men couldn't control it.

But when she was halfway through the marsh and had a full view of the old wharf, she knew it was foolish to hope. She had heard of a raging inferno, and now she knew what it was. The whole beach, the marsh, the houses across the harbor, were illumined by the glare, and she could feel the heat and hear the deadly hiss and crackle. *The traps,* she thought, and found herself crying furious, bitter tears.

There wasn't much for the men to do but let the fire burn itself out. A boatload came over from Brigport, ready to help in the fight, but they could only stand around with the others and wait, or work around the edges with brooms and buckets, dragging out a trap when they could. The tide was high, washing up the beach, and they threw the traps overboard. But they could salvage only a few, and some of those were mere black skeletons. The shed crashed in at last, with a roar, a burst of flame and smoke, a shower of sparks against the night sky.

Joanna went to stand beside her father, who might have been a figure of stone as he stood watching the end. In the red flickering light his face had never looked so strong or so austere. There was something in it that kept her from speaking to him. Besides, the heaviness of her own despair weighed her tongue. She had stopped crying, and watched the dying fire with eyes as stony as Stephen's.

At last someone said, "I guess it's about done, boys," and there was darkness and a chill and the sound of the sea again, where there had been streaming flames and heat and the roar and crackle of fire. Joanna heard men talking all about her—mostly the Brigport men. A woman was sobbing hysterically. That was Susie Yetton, with the youngest child in her arms and two others hanging to her skirts and wailing after her. Marcus was with her.

Stephen walked away from Joanna, and she heard him after a minute, talking in his own pleasant, level tones. "Well, Marcus, we've been in the same boat all along, and we're still in it."

"My God, what are we going to do now?" Marcus' voice trembled and broke. "Stephen, what'll I *do*? Every last one of my pots gone, an' no money, an' there's Susie an' the kids—"

"Every last one of my pots is gone, too, Marcus. And no money. I know what it means as well as you do. But—" He paused, and Joanna knew, as if she were seeing it, that his hand had gone out in the familiar reassuring gesture she had seen so many times, the hand on Marcus' shoulder, gripping hard as if he would pour his own courage and strength through his fingertips into the younger man. "Don't worry, Marcus," he said quietly, and then came back to Joanna.

"Joanna, you run along home and make up a big pot of coffee. We need it."

"Yes, Father," she said, and turned toward home. She couldn't run, going back. She couldn't cry. She felt dreadfully weary, as if it were an intolerable effort merely to walk. She wished she could go back to Stephen and put her arms around him; for she was of his blood and bones, and though he had spoken to Marcus as he did, she knew that this night had brought his courage and strength to an end. He had kept his faith through everything. But this was something a man couldn't fight against. This was something to break a man's heart.

When she came into the kitchen Donna sat by the stove rocking Ellen; Julian still sat huddled by the table, he looked up at her with a swollen, tear-grimed face.

"They couldn't save the traps," she said quietly, and the boy broke into fresh sobs. Joanna looked down at his racked shoulders and knew with a curious lack of emotion that Julian had been smoking in the shed. But it was no use to say anything about it. It wouldn't bring back the traps. Maybe Marcus would thrash the boy, but that wouldn't bring them back, either. And Julian was suffering now, he would suffer for a long time. Probably he'd never want to smoke again, she thought with wry humor.

Without a word between them, the two women began to make coffee and set out cups. After a moment the boy Julian slipped quietly through the back door, into the windy dark. In a little while the men came.

56

STEPHEN BENNETT WAS THE LAST TO LEAVE the Island. The Trudeaus and Ned Foster rented camps at Brigport; the Yettons went to the mainland, to Port George. Stephen knew a man there who owned a small cannery and a fleet of sardine boats. He hired Marcus—in return, Joanna thought, for something Stephen had probably done for him in the past. But it was not very often Stephen looked for return. When his traps were gone, and there was nothing—nothing but the Island—he tightened his jaw, lifted his indomitable black head, and said, "We don't need help. We'll get through this somehow."

But they had to leave the Island. If he were a young man, and unmarried, he said, he could fight it out and build up again from the very beginning. But no matter what good soldiers his women-folk were, he couldn't make them face it—they had gone through enough with him already. They would go where the boys were, there'd be some sort of work he could get.

That was all he said, and then they had to begin the new—and heartbreaking—business of closing up the house.

It seemed as if the Island had never been so beautiful. Every scent on the wind, every daybreak and nightfall, every changing tint in the sky and wheeling flight of gulls, even the hoarse chatter of the crows and a song sparrow calling at dawn—everything that Joanna had known all her life, that was as familiar to her as breathing, stabbed her a hundred times a day. She lay awake at night looking at the familiar pattern of stars beyond her window, listening to the surf whose sound was as close to her as her mother's voice, and she knew all over again the heavy and hopeless grief that stayed with her for so long after Alec died.

To pass a window was to see loveliness that burned and ached; but the young woman Joanna wasn't so lost in her own unhappiness that she didn't know what went on behind her mother's serene blue-gray eyes and her father's steady dark ones. All three of them smiled more than usual in those days. They kept their voices light, and talked with determination about the pleasures and advantages of the new life ahead of them.

"We'll all be together again," Donna said over and over, and then her voice would falter—almost imperceptibly—and she would have an errand in the other part of the house. And Joanna knew that her mother knew the truth; they would never really be together again.

Before Ned and the Trudeaus left, they helped Stephen haul the *Donna* up on the beach, into the marsh. With the *White Lady* beside her, she was safely and snugly cradled against the force of winter storms and flood tides. Joanna stood by, watching with that bleak tightness around her heart that had been there ever since the traps burned. It was midafternoon in October and the sun was bright and warm, the sea was peacock-colored between the islands, the gay little clouds of autumn scudded merrily across the sky.

The *Donna* had been newly painted for the fall season; her white paint dazzled, there against the green and rust and fawn of the marsh. When she was settled and fast, and the other men went down to the beach to bring up a dory, Stephen stood looking at his boat. Then he laid his hand on the glistening flare of the bow.

"You won't be on the bank for long, old lady. We'll be back."

Joanna walked home quickly then, her eyes burning.

The Island lay long and dark under the threatening sky that last day. Long and dark and alone . . . and betrayed, Joanna thought, standing in the stern of the mailboat and looking back for as long as she could. Her mother had taken Ellen down into the cabin. Stephen was in the pilot house with Link Hall; they wouldn't look back. But Joanna must look. The wind was edged with winter, the sea whipped up into a gunmetal chop, and the gulls rode high above the mailboat, crying and crying.

Yes, Joanna must look, and as the dark sea widened between the *Aurora B.*'s creaming wake and the creaming surf on the Island's shores, the forsaken Island, where nothing lived now but the little wild things, she knew she must feel like a homeless soul forevermore.

57

OUTSIDE THE EMPTY HOUSE a breeze stirred the untended rose bush and a long trailing branch tapped faintly on the window pane. The woman looked toward the sound. Beyond the slender bough, beyond the sea of ripening grass sloping down to the weather-silvered gate, the marsh stretched lush and green to the harbor and the camps on the beach. They were little and huddled and old.

Her footsteps echoed in the listening silence of the bare room. For a fantastic moment, as she reached the window, it seemed to her there had always been this silence, that it lay over the whole world — at least this world that lay beyond the glass.

The houses on the other side of the harbor, their paint scaling away in the unshadowed sunlight of noon — they too held this hushed and echoing stillness. If even a gull had lighted on a roof as the woman watched, it would have been life; but at the instant there was not a gull in sight, and from the locked quiet of the room where she stood, the whole scene had the timeless unreality of a toy village inside a round glass paperweight. And somehow she had been caught there, inside the glass.

The men who had come ashore down there, the children who had run back and forth between those houses, paddling in the tide-water pools, their voices mingling with the sound of engines and the dogs' barking and the cries of gulls, the women who had stood in those doorways and looked out to see if their men were on the mooring yet, the people who had laughed and quarreled and laughed again in this room behind her — they had never known or even dreamed that the grass would grow so high, or that some day they would all be gone and this silence would have come down over the Island. They would have laughed, if any one could have told them about it.

Yet it had been coming for a long time before they knew. The woman leaned her forehead against the glass and wondered if there had been one of them who knew the signs for what they were. No matter now. It was long past.

She wished with a weary passion that she hadn't come. How long would it be before the dragger came back? It didn't seem as if she could endure this much longer. She opened the front door, and at once the breath of the Island blew against her face, intolerably fragrant with the mingling of bayleaf, and clover, ripe grass, the first strawberries that always reddened so early just below the house. It was a breath that had blown eternally through her childhood and her growing up; now it brought a new force of memories to clamor at her brain. She had an impulse to clap her hands over her ears, as if she could shut them out.

But at least there was other sound out here, it wasn't like the house. She sat down on the stone doorstep, the white rose bush trailing above her. On the other side of the house was the sea, but some unknown instinct kept her from going toward it. It was as if some worse loneliness would appall her at the sight of that vast, twinkling blueness.

She didn't know how long she sat there. At last she stood up and stretched her cramped arms. She stepped out of the cool shadow into the sunshine, and it was kind to her lifted face. She felt tired, as if she had come a very long way, and nothing mattered now but rest.

It would be a long time before the dragger came back. She supposed she must eat; she'd take her lunch down into Goose Cove and eat it, and perhaps she could see the boat far out on the horizon.

She walked toward the corner of the house, and came out into the flood of sunshine again, and there was the sea before her, the ledges serene and yellow in the light with a little edge of white tumbling easily around them, the towers of the Rock gleaming on the horizon. The thick dark woods of the Western End marched from the shore to the sky. The sea moved lazily into the little coves, as lazily as the gulls rested on the glistening water, their white breasts reflected below them.

The Cove itself brimmed with a high tide that washed quietly at the base of the rocks whose reflections were a tawny shimmer across the blue. She started to walk down to the beach, walking among lichened boulders with wild roses blooming pinkly against them.

And then she saw the traps on the beach. She stood still, her mouth drying, her heartbeat seeming to shake her body. Traps on the beach, new traps, of yellow laths that gleamed in the sun. A peapod pulled up above the water's edge.

A man was sitting on his heels with his back to the sun, Painting a buoy. It was yellow, and he was painting a black stripe around it with painstaking care. She looked down at the squatting figure in dungarees and blue shirt and peaked white cap, every detail fantastically sharp in the brilliant air, and the colors of the buoy seemed to be printed indelibly on her brain. *Black and yellow, a stripe around the middle.* A brush wielded carefully by hard and square-tipped fingers.

How many times had she watched a brush in those fingers, making a black stripe around a yellow buoy? She hardly breathed as she walked down over the slope. The grass muffled her feet. She reached the pebbles and went across them, and they moved under her shoes; in the noontime hush the sound was very loud. But even before the man turned his head and saw her, she knew it was Nils.

It seemed like a long time that they stood looking at each other, not speaking. Then she said, "Hello, Nils," and put out her hand. His own closed around it, and he smiled for the first time, a smile that began in his deepset blue eyes and finally reached his mouth.

"Hi, Jo."

"It's been a long time, Nils."

"Six years." He added surprisingly, "Ellen must go to school now." "First grade," Joanna said. Sensation began to creep back into the numbness of surprise and shock, her voice gathered color. "Nils, where did you go when you left the Island? And how long have you been back here?"

"I've been everywhere, just about, Jo. And I came back in April, back to Grampa Gunnar's place." His smile deepened. "Couldn't miss the spring crawl. I've been doing well, too, hauling from a double-ender. The cove here's a mite smaller than the harbor—lots less lonesome for one little peapod, anyway."

Joanna said with a suddenly shaky laugh, "I don't know what to say—I—"

"Don't say anything. Sit down." With those few words she knew Nils was exactly the same. He'd grown older, and he'd been around the world. But he was still Nils. She realized with a great upsurge of gladness that he hadn't lost faith in the Island. It had called him back, and he had come to it.

Sitting there on a warm rock in the sun, watching him as he went back to his painting, she had a curious delight in imagining how he had lived here alone since April, working the way he had always worked, at the same steady pace from daylight to dark.

"Nils, are they really crawling?" she asked him suddenly, and he nodded.

"They've been crawling for me, anyway."

They were quiet until he had finished the buoy, and then he came and sat down beside her, taking out his cigarettes. "I'm sorry about your father," he said at last. "I didn't find out till I landed in Port George last March—my father told me."

Joanna could talk about it to Nils, as she had always been able to talk to him. She had never talked to anyone else about Stephen. "It was queer — we were always worried about Mother's health and never thought about him. He seemed so young and strong, even when his hair began to get a little gray at the temples. But it was as if losing the traps in the fire broke his heart — that, and leaving the Island. As if he couldn't live anywhere else. He died before we'd been gone a year."

She looked back at the house above them, against the sky. "It was real enough over there on the mainland, but out here it's just as if the mainland didn't exist, and we never went to it — as if it was all a dream, and he'll come down over the slope in a minute."

Nils watched her steadily. "I know. But what about you? What did you do over there?"

"I went to work. We live with Charles and Mateel — Mother and Ellen and I." She looked down at her firm, strong hands. "I've cut the heads off more herring than I ever knew existed, Nils."

"Sardine factory, huh? Like it?"

"There were the boats coming in all the time, and the harbor. It was the sea, after a fashion. Only it was pure hell for a while." She could talk to Nils about that, too. No one else had ever known, or even guessed. She had been a good actress. "I felt like a wild gull shut in a cage. Then I got so I could stop thinking about it, but sometimes a little thing would bring it all back again."

"What brought you out here?"

"That was one of the little things, Nils. I'd been almost contented for a long time — I've made friends over there, and Ellen's in school, and she's such a funny little mite, Nils — and then, yesterday, I was going home from work and two men came around a corner in the dusk, talking, and I heard just one word . . . *Bennett's.*"

"I saw it on a chart," said Nils briefly. "It rose right up and hit me in the face . . . same thing, I guess. What then?"

"They were going out by here in their dragger today. I knew them, because the boys know them. So I spoke to them — I guess they thought I was crazy — and today, instead of going to work, I ran away."

Nils turned his head and looked long and hard at her. "Jo, are you glad you ran away?"

"*Glad!*" For a panicky instant she thought she was going to cry. After all these years of a lifted chin and a steady mouth, she was feeling weak and trembly and undone. She had a dreadful suspicion that if she spoke her voice would wobble and the tears would well out like a spring. She said, very carefully, "Nils, what made me run away? Why didn't I just stay over there and figure that it was best not to come back here and make myself miserable?"

"You had to run away because it was stronger than you were, Jo," Nils answered her. "And maybe there was something in you that knew the Island wasn't alone any more. Jo, it'll never be alone as long as it's above water. When I went away, I knew I'd be back, sometime. And there'll be others coming here, too — maybe not the same ones, but there'll always be people here."

He paused, his brows drawn in thought as he watched the shimmer of high tide in the cove. "Jo, the people who came out here and settled when there wasn't anything here — your grandfather and mine and the other old-timers — they were like the folks who settled this country. They wanted to make something big out of it, so they put everything they had into it. That was why the Island meant so much to them. That was why my grandfather couldn't leave it, and that was why your father couldn't live away from it. The others, they came afterward when they began to hear about the Island. They came for what they could get, they took it, they didn't give anything back, and then they walked out on it."

She listened, her breathing light and quick. Why hadn't she thought of it before? Nils could be right about it. Wasn't he always right? He went on talking in the slow, quiet voice she'd always known.

"Jo, I used to think about the Island in the damndest places. Calcutta, Liverpool, Rio. In the hot countries it was like a vision, you'd call it — always in my head. The wind and the woods, the sound of the water on the rocks, and the feel of a gaff grabbing a toggle. Then I came back, and it was just the way I remembered it, without the people, of course. So then I did a different kind of thinking. And when I saw you coming across the beach today, I knew my thinking'd been right."

He stopped and watched his cigarette as he knocked the ashes from it. "Maybe I've been wrong all this time, Jo. It's for you to tell me. But I've been wondering if maybe out of all the folks who've belonged to the Island there were any special ones who were supposed to lead the way. Building up again, starting from scratch the way your grandfather did. And it seemed to me that if I was right, they'd show up out here — be the first ones to come back. Well, here I am. And here you are."

Their eyes held for a long moment before he went on, in his unhurried way. "Jo, when I talked to you the last time, I never said I wouldn't ask you again. Maybe we both thought we wouldn't be talking together again. But the way it looks to me now, it's like it'd all been planned out without us knowing about it." His smile flickered up warmly. "A man gets to thinking a lot of strange stuff when he's alone with just the wind for company . . . Joanna, what kind of a life do you think we could have together out here, helping the Island start all over again?"

She sat there without moving or speaking, looking at him and the unflinching steadiness of his gaze, the calm and kindly purpose in his face. No, she couldn't deny it, no matter how she tried; Nils and herself together could do great things for the Island, they could do even more than Stephen and Donna had done, they could bring life to Stephen's dreams.

She looked out at the sea, her hands lax in her lap, and Nils said, "Ellen would be here, too. Joanna, everything I said that other time about making it the kind of a marriage you wanted it to be — that still goes. But we'd make a good partnership out of it. We've a mighty lot of work to do, and the best way we can do it is together."

"Together," she repeated. Together after all these years. Maybe Nils was right and it was meant to be like this. Maybe you had to go through just so much, and then you reached the place where you were supposed to be. "The longest way round is the shortest way home," Stephen used to say.

She looked up at the trees marching over the slope to the cemetery in the woods. It was seven years that Alec had been dead. When she had felt him slipping away from her, retreating farther and farther into memory out of reality, she had tried desperately to keep him close, but there was no holding him. When she found herself telling Ellen some funny thing Alec had said or done, and laughing wholeheartedly with the child, she knew it should be like this. You must live for the living, and not for the dead. Was it wrong to remember Alec with a smile because she had known and loved him, instead of with pain because she had lost him?

She thought of all this as she sat on the rock with Nils beside her; she thought of all the times in the years gone by when she had wondered about Nils, if he were alive or dead, if he ever thought about the Island, if he ever thought about her. And she thought of the great and almost suffocating gladness that had welled up in her when she realized that it was no stranger on the beach, but Nils.

It wasn't hard to tell him. After all, they had never needed many words, herself and Nils. She said in the clear, confident voice of the young Joanna Bennett, "Nils, will you go back with me on the dragger tonight, and see the family? And Ellen?"

There was a question in the way he glanced at her, without speaking, and she answered it swiftly and directly.

"We'll make it a good partnership, Nils. The way you said we could. And we'll make it the kind of marriage we both want."

He didn't touch her. But the look in his eyes was a real caress, as if he'd taken her in his arms and kissed her. Then he went back across the beach to his paint and his buoys.

Joanna took off her jacket and rolled back her blouse sleeves. "Nils," she called to him, "I'm going back up in the meadow and get my lunch box—there's plenty for both of us. Be right back!"

She ran across the beach stones and up among the granite boulders where the wild roses were. Quite suddenly she stopped. She felt tranquillity flooding through her, a great high tide of content, a noontide richness of peace. She stood without moving, and let it take possession of her.

About the Author

Elisabeth Ogilvie lives for the better part of each year on Gay's Island, Maine. There she enjoys long walks among the rocks and woods of the island, reveling in air and space and sky. The remainder of the year is spent across Pleasant Point Gut, at her nearby mainland home, where plumbing, a telephone, and other amenities await. Her interests include the Nature Conservancy, Foster Parents Plan, reading ("a necessity of life!"), and music of just about any kind.

Miss Ogilvie's latest book is a historical romance, the second of a planned trilogy. Despite some thirty-six books for children and adults produced over the past forty years, though, the author is still caught up in the spell woven by Bennett's Island and its inhabitants and is presently at work on a fifth installment (the fourth, An Answer in the Tide, *was published in 1978) in the continuing story of Joanna Bennett.*

To order the other two volumes of Elisabeth Ogilvie's Tide trilogy, or any of our other fine New England books, write for our free catalog.

Down East Books
P.O. Box 679
Camden, Maine 04843